— AN ANGELA HARDWICKE SCI-FI MYSTERY —

BLUNT FORCE RISING

RUSS COLCHAMIRO

CRAZY 8 PRESS

PART I:
THE DEATH CODE

The only way organics would accept android citizenship is if they were openly marked *as* androids. Too many organics, or enough with the loudest voices, contended that an unmarked android was an act of sedition—condoning, if not encouraging them, to operate in secret. As if they belong to some kind of cult.

If androids want the freedom and privilege of citizenship, they said, we want to know who and where they are. No hiding in plain sight.

I've always found that argument detestable. It not only humiliates androids but belittles us all. You're either a citizen, or you're not. Marking androids only fuels mistrust and serves to undermine their sense of self-worth.

If they're marked, the theory goes, there must be a justifiable reason for it. And of course that reason couldn't possibly be an egregious act of bigotry and hatred. Because that would mean organics are the real monsters, not androids.

And that couldn't be possible. Right?

CHAPTER 1

As a private detective—essentially, a spy for hire—I get called to work the kinds of cases you might expect. Missing persons, kidnapping, homicide, blackmail, burglary, forgery, arson. I've also done more than my share of infidelity investigations, but I don't take those anymore. With social media apps and police drones spying on everyone 24/7, and various snooping software available for a song, it's cheaper to do it on your own. Besides, it's scummy work.

Not sure what it says about me, but I prefer the *other* cases.

You know the ones I mean.

Give me a runaway shapeshifter, galaxy hopper, memory thief, or miles-long helix of the Universe's DNA any day of the week and twice on Sundays. Over the years I've also been hired to reposition Haley's Comet, track down a madman from Earth, retrieve a missing shard of a teenager's soul, hunt a dimension-jumping serial rapist, and several other dubious cases I can't mention, for reasons I can't mention.

Those cases.

The cases here in E-Town—the core city in Eternity, the cosmic realm responsible for the design, construction, and maintenance of the physical Universe—that separate private detectives from *Private Detectives*.

The kinds of cases only me and a handful of other PIs will take. The kinds of cases that should motivate any rational person to run as far and as fast as they can in the opposite direction. Because cases like those will—one hundred percent guaranteed—lead you into one nightmare or another.

So why do I take those cases? What am I trying to prove?

Who the fuck knows.

I'll leave that up to my shrink to figure out. As soon as I make time to go see one. For now, though, I'm dealing with other problems.

My seven-year-old son, Owen, is showing a gift for increasingly complicated interstellar construction and repairs, a pipe burst in my apartment, my dog walker just quit, and my protégé Eric Whistler is a huge pain in the ass.

Which is to say, he's my partner. That's a big thing with him. Being *partners*.

Whistler and I have been working together going on three years now. He first came to me as an overeager little beaver who had his eye on one specific prize—join Team Hardwicke. He was as green as a wheat-grass smoothie, but right off he displayed a real instinct for research. He listened. He learned. And most important, he was loyal.

A good-looking kid, he had a jovial, cocky confidence and charm that worked more often than it didn't. Until he discovered that without a rock-solid approach and legitimate investigative skills to back them up—and an ever-present respect for danger—confidence and charm only get you so far.

And in our line of work, get you all kinds of dead.

Short of firing him, I did virtually everything I could to chase him away, to motivate him to follow another career path. Any other path. But the kid never quits.

Yeah, he took my shit. A lot of it. Maybe too much. But he stood his ground. He hung in there. Until one day he dropped a truth-bomb on me. That he wasn't my intern or assistant any longer. He was, as much as I couldn't quite accept it, a licensed private investigator, and it was time I treated him like one.

Only that wasn't enough. He was so relentlessly dedicated to becoming my partner—and a damn good one—that he wore me down. He got me, of all people, to care about him.

I mean… what's that about?

Which led to a truth-bomb of my own. He was right. I did push him away. Not because of him. Because of me. The only way I knew how to be the Angela Hardwicke I'd always been, and thought I'd always be, was to fly solo.

Sure, I called in help when I needed it, but that was always case by case. Then Whistler came along, and without even realizing it, he challenged me to change. To grow. To mature.

Holy crap, I hated him for that.

I was already adjusting to my life as a single mother, another twist I never saw coming. Talk about change. Don't even get me started with the diapers.

And then Whistler goes and makes me care about him, too.

I may only be thirty-four, but I've been down enough dark alleys and been caught in enough folds of time, space, and dimension that I developed calluses from toe to soul. When it came to case work, I'd gotten to the point where I felt I could handle just about anything, as long as it happened to *me*. I knew the risks and was willing to face them.

But if anything awful happened to *Whistler* on my watch, I don't think I'd ever be okay again. Not really.

Which left me—left us—between worlds. And that never works.

The friction can't last. So Whistler told me, in no uncertain terms, that I needed to get my head out of my ass if we were going to continue working together. Either we'd be partners for real, or I'd need to cut him loose.

As I stand here now at the Scherzeron Cruise Port, staring up at the *Triumph*, surrounded by angry protestors beneath the noon sun, I'm asking myself why I didn't cut him loose.

"Will you look at that," he says, fawning over the galaxy cruiser we'll be occupying for the next few days. "Will you look. At. That."

Okay, I've accepted him as my partner. In the field.

But I'm still running a business. I cover all expenses and pay all the bills, including his salary. So I told him, in no uncertain terms, that if he wants to make more money, if he wants, someday, to have at least a small voice in the financial decisions that impact the business, then he needs to sign clients. He needs to bring in revenue. Like I do.

Life ain't cheap and it ain't getting cheaper. So you know what the little sonuvabitch did?

He landed a client. And not just any client. A whale. One of the whaliest, whale-type whales in an ocean full of whales.

But that's Whistler for you. Push him to step up, whether I really want him to or not, and he does. Yet there's always a wrinkle.

"Ther'eda Ranadyne," he says as we approach the newly renovated Scherzeron Terminal. "Now *that's* a client."

Ther'eda Ranadyne founded, owns, and operates Ranadyne Cybernetics, a leader in the development of Artificial Intelligence, and the sole manufacturer of androids.

It's not the kind of gig I usually take, but she hired us to provide additional security on the *Triumph*, the venue for the annual Cybernetics, AI, Biotech, and Robotics Conference. Ranadyne Cybernetics is the lead sponsor. Ther'eda Ranadyne is the event chair.

The conference will have the usual set-up for these kind of events, lots of info panels, breakout sessions, and expert discussions, as well as dinners, parties, special entertainment, and other late-night shenanigans.

I hate to admit it, but even though I complain about how annoying and lame most of these industry events can be, I usually wind up going to the annual PI convention anyway. I can't help myself.

Our view is blocked by the terminal in front of us, but beyond it we can make out the top half of three galaxy cruisers—essentially luxury ocean liners, except designed for space.

Whistler tugs on the lapels of his brown leather jacket. A strange breeze rolls in, the last wisps of a brutally cold winter mixed with the early warmth of spring. "Not a bad get," he says, "if I do say so myself."

"Unless you have more girlfriends with access to new clients," I say, keeping an eye out for snipers and suicide bombers, "let's call this one a *nice* win and see how it goes."

Whistler tilts his head at Selene Garin, his latest strawberry blonde girlfriend, and flashes his big brown eyes at her. She approaches us like an Olympic athlete, her motions controlled but graceful, excellent posture.

At twenty-five Whistler's still carries himself with a cocky mojo, sorta winky/flirty, but underneath he's a sweet guy, a romantic. He chuckles at me a bit too confidently. "Nice? Oh, please. One of these days you're gonna realize, when you fly with me, you fly first class."

"On this trip you do." Selene kisses his light brown cheek, then rubs off most of the red lipstick left behind. Marking her turf. "Ms. Ranadyne is generous that way."

Selene recommended us for the job. She's Ther'eda Ranadyne's Executive Assistant at Ranadyne Cybernetics, a role that brings its own heat.

Selene is also an android.

Though enacted less than ten years ago, androids have full rights and protections under the law. On paper. But that doesn't mean everyone in E-Town accepts androids as legitimate citizens. Even fewer tolerate android/organic relationships.

Diligent as ever, Selene advises us as the crowd begins to grow around the terminal. She has the mandatory J-scar under her right eye.

"I don't mean to rush you, Ms. Hardwicke. I doubt we're in any danger. But with the death threats against Ms. Ranadyne, it's probably best if we go aboard."

Approaching us now, Ther'eda Ranadyne is a handsome woman, mid-forties, with wire-rimmed glasses. Her eyes dart back and forth, surveying the cruise port, as if she's running multiple scenarios in the back of her mind and considering the hypothetical results, comparing and contrasting the value of each, and how, or if, she might best utilize any conclusions she gleans from them.

Flanked by two security guards dressed in matching gray suits and white dress shirts, she extends her arm, and shakes my hand. Firm grip.

"Wise counsel," Ther'eda says. "This is my personal security team. He's Kowalcyzk. She's Nenn. They'll be with me throughout."

Built like an armored car capable of inflicting and absorbing pure brute force, Kowalcyzk is wide-shouldered and bald, with a graying beard pulled into a point. Nenn, meanwhile, is short and slight like an underdeveloped tween. But by the way she carries herself, she strikes me as a surgically tactical killer, quick and lethal, unwilling to waste even a single thought or motion.

I've never seen this much security at the cruise port before. There's the standard infrared and x-ray machines, retinal I.D. scanners, intercept towers, and armed guards. In addition to the cruise port's fleet, I've spotted several Ranadyne security drones and bomb-sniffing dogs.

Kept at a distance behind concrete barriers and patrolled by a combination of E-Town PD and port security, protestors shout at the arriving passengers.

The pro-android crowd hold up their signs including *ANDROID LIVES MATTER, STOP ANDROID HATE,* and *NO ONE SHOULD KNOW THEIR FATE.* The anti-android sentiment is equally enthusiastic: *ANDROIDS ARE AN ABOMINATION, NO ONE LIVES FOREVER,* and *REPLACE THER'EDA RANADYNE BEFORE SHE REPLACES US!*

"Watch it!" someone shouts. A clear liquor bottle with a flaming gray rag stuffed into the spout arches over us. It shatters on the asphalt about twenty feet away. Glass shards pop. Flames erupt. Shocked but probably not surprised, the crowds scream, hunching and ducking for safety.

The larger of her two private security guards, Kowalczyk shoves Ther'eda behind him, using his hulking size as a shield.

A tiny raven-haired woman with a bob haircut and pointy jaw, Nenn lasers in on the crowd. Behind dark sunglasses she reverse-engineers the flaming bottle's flight path. With a raised chin, she follows the trajectory from the impact site, back though the air, and to the launch site. She isolates the coordinates.

Likely assuming the assailant has fallen back into the crowd to voyeuristically watch the resulting chaos or has slinked away to avoid capture, Nenn scans for the attacker.

With impressive quickness, she jack-rabbits through a line of frazzled passengers waiting to check their luggage curbside or enter the glass-walled terminal. Nenn hops over a barrier and slides feet-first into the legs of a gangly young punk. With a single punch to the jaw, she knocks him unconscious.

Nenn drags his limp body by the collar and, without a word, drops him in front of three uniformed police officers who were not as fast on the draw.

That's the other consideration that comes with landing a

whale. They pay very large fees. One, because they can. Two, because they have a problem not easily resolved. Three, because you're more expendable than they are. If it means you taking a bullet so they don't have to, they consider that to be very much *your problem.*

Whistler keeps Selene close to him. Her left pinky twitches. I didn't realize androids can process stress that way.

With the chaos subdued beneath the midday sunshine, Ther'eda raises her black, pencil-thin eyebrows beneath her styled, platinum blonde hair. Seemingly unfazed, she heads toward the terminal. "I hope you enjoy the circus, Hardwicke. It should be quite the weekend."

CHAPTER 2

There's something fundamentally exotic about hotels. Especially five-star hotels. Now, take that hotel, tip it on its side, and launch it into space—you've got yourself a galaxy cruiser. We should be departing within the hour.

"Mache!" Whistler shouts giddily from his stateroom, 1161. "Look at this bed. It's huge. And a gift basket. It's got cookies, dice, champagne. And chocolate-covered strawberries. Sweet."

To establish boundaries, I made Whistler call me Ms. Hardwicke the first few months he was under my charge. But eventually he started calling me Ms. H, which devolved to Mizzache and then, finally, Mache. As far as nicknames go, I've had better. I've definitely had worse.

"Yes, it's all very fancy. But that's not why we're here."

Whistler trundles out of the compact, marble-lined bathroom with more goodies in hand. "Shower caps and little shampoo bottles with the *Triumph* logo!" He drops his stash on the impeccably made bed with luxurious linens, then slides open the glass door leading to a bubble-domed balcony. "I'm loving this gig!"

I let him have his moment. It'll get old, and fast, but I remember my first galaxy cruise. In our line of work, I tell him to appreciate the little moments whenever they come, because they don't come often. I shouldn't begrudge him when he does.

"Take a half hour to get settled. Then we meet with Ther'eda."

"I was gonna meet Selene." He says it in a way that suggests he's not asking permission, but not so defiant as to instigate an argument. Whistler's been with Selene nearly six months. He says they might move in together, but I'm not sure how much I believe that one. Young love's a helluva thing. It can blind you to what's obvious to everyone else.

Still recovering from our time on Arcasia—a brutal case, even for me—Whistler wants everyone to know he couldn't give a damn what they think about androids. But I suspect he may have pursued Selene, at least in part, to antagonize social convention. To prove he can't be pushed around or told what to do. Not by anyone—including me. Especially me.

"And I was gonna start caring about your love life. Guess we were both wrong. Get your shit together. I'll see you in thirty."

My stateroom, 7414, is four decks down and on the other side of the *Triumph*, per my request. We'll cover more ground that way. And let's face it, we need distance from each other.

The hallways are a mix of custard-colored paint and tiles, gold trim, polished oak panels, taupe carpeting, and silver-plated dome lighting.

At the hallway's midpoint I come to the wide, spiral staircase leading up and down. As is the case on every deck I've seen, next to the staircase are two straight-backed chairs flanking a thin table with a vase of fresh flowers. Above it is an original piece of loudly-colored abstract art—a different one on every deck and at various points throughout the *Triumph*.

Ther'eda will be giving a speech later at the Parallax Grille. Whistler and I will need to review the security protocols and walk the space.

Ther'eda hired us as backup. But that's not the only reason. If Kowalczyk and Nenn aren't enough personal security, Ther'eda's in more danger than she's acknowledging.

When I come to Deck Six, about to turn down the staircase to Five, I catch a glimpse out of the corner of my eye. A face I know is reflected in the mirror.

"Nini?"

Her skin black as night, a striking contrast to my modest white complexion, Nini's a tiny thing, barely four foot ten, but she's as tough as they come. After a dozen years as an ER nurse at E-Town General, she's seen it all. Outside the hospital, though, Nini's glam all the way. Even her casual wear is foxy cool, with open-toed sandals, designer jeans, and a red blouse.

"Angela?" With a rolling suitcase in her grip, she side-kisses my cheek. "What are *you* doing here?"

"Working. What about you?"

"Same."

"Uh… explain, please."

"I'm here for the conference. I'm up for Nurse Manager when Joycelyn retires. We're getting more androids in the ER. I need to brush up on my android physiology. I don't love the classroom, but…"

"You love cruises."

Nini smirks. "You bet yer sweet ass I do."

"The hospital's paying? Doesn't sound like them."

"Well… not exactly."

"Oh, there you are!" bellows another voice I know well. "Where'd you go?"

A massive woman, Dolores does muscle work for me now and then. Because of her day job as a baggage handler who works at this very cruise port, she also has a network of eyes and spies, including delivery drivers, mechanics, engineers, and dockworkers who are constantly on the move from one end of the realm to the other.

"Hey, D." I barely pretend to hold back a smile. "How did *this* happen?"

About as opposite as two people can get, Nini and Dolores have been best friends since before I met either one of them. But they bicker. All. The. Time.

"You know Dolores isn't just about hauling luggage," Dolores says, referring to herself in the third person. I don't know why she does it. When it comes to Dolores, I find it's best not to ask. "She loves her some cruise ship buffet. And profit. Lots of opportunity on this bad boy."

Dolores is also a private investor. Food trucks, real estate, artwork, tech, billboards, vitamin water. Whatever she thinks will pay off. She typically keeps her investments smaller, more manageable, preferring to fly under the radar. I resisted for years, but she finally got me to go in with her on a deal. I didn't have much to invest—between childcare costs and Whistler's salary I'm barely breaking even these days—so I'm a very limited and silent partner in an 18-unit apartment building in Tim's River.

The barely-there investment, which consisted of pretty much every last credit I had, will take about eight years before it becomes profitable at its current rate of return.

Listen to me. Rate of return. Who the hell am I?

But I'm willing to scrape along until then because it isn't for me. It's for Owen. I need to make sure he's taken care of, that *I'm* taking care of him.

Yet knowing Dolores the way I do, I have to ask: "You invest in androids?"

"Oh, fuck no! You know I hate those freaks. Fake fuckin people with fake fuckin lives. All filled with wires, and com-puter chips, and"—she gestures to her groin—"synthetic junk." She shudders. "Yuck."

"Dolores!" Nini groans. "Can you not? There're people here."

"Oh, sor-ree, Ms. Sensitivity. Since when do you care what people think?"

I've seen Nini stay as frosty as a harsh winter breeze when the ER is slammed. But on her off time, Dolores gets under her skin. "I always care! You're so embarrassing!"

Twice Nini's size, Dolores grimaces. "Then why did you come with me?"

"Why did *you?*"

"Alright, ladies. I'm here, you're here. We're all here. It's a big ship with lots to do. I'm gonna check out my stateroom, then take care of some business. I'll catch up with you later. Try not to kill each other before dinner."

I head down the staircase when they respond in unison, "No promises!"

Immediately after I took this gig, Whistler and I studied the cruiser's schematics. Security globes are lined along the ceiling every fifty feet. Not a bad ratio, but it still leaves more blind spots than I'd prefer. The *Triumph* also employs 22 secu-rity staffers, most of whom have at least some law enforcement, military, or private security experience.

Despite the security staff, however, they are not the police. Their mandate is to intervene in any obvious attempts of physi-cal or sexual assault of the passengers or crew, sabotage of the vessel, or theft, and to preserve any evidence or crime scenes until the cruiser can return to port.

Because in-flight cruisers are not based within E-Town borders, they do not technically fall under ETPD jurisdiction. The crew also doesn't have the resources to thoroughly investigate an entire cruise ship, or the legal authority to place anyone under arrest. If a serious crime is committed, however, the Captain has discretion whether to continue the cruise or immediately return to port and turn the offender over to the police.

So imagine my surprise when I enter the Parallax Grille, one of eleven restaurants on the *Triumph*, only to find Ther'eda, Selene, Kowalczyk, and Nenn having a security chat, with a certain someone, without me.

"It's almost like you didn't know I was coming," I say.

The waitstaff sets up cocktail tables and stools for tonight's party. The restaurant is laid out with cranberry leather chairs, beige leather booths, tulip-shaped lighting, a flowing water wall, and dark beige carpeting.

With the air conditioning on full blast, it's so cold in here my knuckles are frozen. The room will warm up once more passengers enter.

"Hardwicke, yes, my apologies," Ther'eda says. "There's a lot to review and Lieutenant Tarrish needed a minute. He's with the Intergalactic Crime Division."

"You don't say." I give a slight nod. "T."

"Hardwicke," Tarrish says.

Tall, Black, and lithe, Lionel Tarrish shakes his head. His close-cropped salt-and-pepper beard looks old and worn.

I don't like that he's here. Tarrish is not quite a friend, although he's not *not* a friend. He's my mentor. Ish. But what really fries my ovaries is that I didn't know about it. I'm not sure if he knew I was working this cruise or if he just found out. Either way, his presence means some serious shit is about to go down. Or he thinks it might. And I don't know why.

"I've done a manual sweep of the ship," I interject, my attempt to reclaim some authority. I don't have any, but just like Selene did with Whistler, sometimes you have to mark your turf. If you don't, somebody else will. "I'd like to get a closer look at the security feeds. Want to know where we have eyes, and where we don't."

A fit Black man approaches assuredly. An overhead light glimmers on his bald brown head. His uniform is pressed and neat, navy blue trousers and white dress shirt. Three triangular stripes are emblazoned on his upper right sleeve.

"We can take care of that," he says with a deep voice. "Sorry I'm late. I'm Captain Barry B. Dobbs. I had a crew meeting."

He also has a J-scar under his right eye.

"Thank you," Ther'eda says. "We may or may not have a situation. But I wanted you to be aware—" She pauses, gestures her head toward the nearby waitstaff. "Can we go somewhere private?"

Dobbs leads us through a side entrance and into a small executive suite, windowless, with an oval conference table and chairs. Kowalczyk and Nenn secure the door behind us, then take their places on either side of the door to keep anyone from entering. Or leaving.

"Sit," Ther'eda says. "Do you know about the—?"

There's a thud on the other side of the door. Kowalczyk and Nenn immediately square up, Kowalczyk slipping on brass knuckles with metal spikes, Nenn with a short baton. Though she wears no other jewelry, a silver bracelet dangles from her wrist. I still have my retractable taser and sheathed boot knife. But no one, not even staff security, is permitted to carry firearms on board a cruise ship.

Tarrish, Dobbs, and I hop to our feet. The door rattles.

"Mache. It's me. Let me in."

I sigh. "It's Whistler. It's okay."

Kowalczyk takes two steps back so he's directly in front of the door. Nenn stands to the side, in stealth mode. They don't take chances.

Selene raises her hands and nods at the private security, signaling them to let him in.

"Oh, hey," Whistler says, seeing Selene. "What are you guys talking abou—?"

Kowalczyk sticks his spiked fist in Whistler's face. Cold steel against hot flesh. "Hands," he says.

My fear of bringing Whistler deeper into my world only served to undercut him in all the worst ways. I handled it badly. He wanted so desperately to prove he could deal with any case I could throw at him, and when he couldn't, it scared me down to my bone marrow.

Don't get me wrong. Fear is good. It helps keep you alive. But only if you know what to do with it.

"Mache. What the fuck? Tell him—"

Nenn sidles up from the other side, sticks her baton in Whistler's ribs.

"Hands," Kowalczyk repeats.

"Okay, okay. Take it easy." Whistler slowly raises his hands. "Nobody needs to get their face bashed in. Especially me."

Nenn pats him down. She removes Whistler's retractable taser and I.D. She eyes his P.I. license suspiciously, studies his face, checks his I.D. again. After what seems like an excessively long consideration, Nenn gives Kowalczyk a slight nod.

Kowalczyk lowers his spiked fist. "He's good."

Nenn slaps Whistler's wallet against his chest.

"I apologize," Ther'eda says. "Don't take it personally."

Whistler does his best to maintain composure. "Why would I?"

"You've flashed your muscle," I say to Ther'eda, "threatened my partner, called a secret meeting, and brought in the ICD. What's up?"

The small contingent of players look to me, to each other, and then, finally, to Ther'eda.

She removes her glasses, pinches a black cloth, and rubs away fingerprint smudges, dust particles, and facial grease from the lenses. She puts them back on and regards us.

"What you do you know about the Death Code?"

CHAPTER 3

Unlike Dolores, I have no issue with androids. I like androids. They remind me that it doesn't matter if you're purely organic, an artificial being, or fusion of both. Yeah, I have a son I love and a few close friends. But mostly... people suck. Where you come from or what species or gender you associate with is meaningless to me when it comes to the suck factor. I'm agnostic in that regard.

"Androids have a Death Code?" This is a new one to me. "What does that mean?"

Ther'eda gestures to Kowalczyk and Nenn. They confirm the door is locked, then run a mechanical wand around the room, checking for bugs, cameras, microphones, or other recording devices. Nenn offers a slight head nod.

"All clear," Kowalczyk says.

"I'm sorry for not looping you in sooner," Ther'eda says, taking her seat at the head of the table, facing the door. We fill in on either side, Selene to her immediate right, flanked by me and then Whistler. Tarrish sits opposite us. "I was hoping to avoid the whole business."

Whistler jumps in ahead of me, and for once I don't care. "What business?"

Ther'eda is a closed-jaw talker, which pulls her lips taut. Her mouth hardly opens, as if taking out her frustration on her teeth.

"As I believe you know, the previous generation androids, the Lansing model, have a maximum lifespan of twenty-five years."

"I am," Whistler replies.

"While a huge advancement, Lansing lifespans are primarily due to our proprietary fuel cells. Even though they can actually—"

"Recharge their batteries?" Whistler interrupts.

"That's a crude description," Ther'eda says as Selene squirms uncomfortably. "But yes." Even with a daily recharge, she explains, fuel cells have a limited lifespan. To interface with an android's synthetic physiology, the fuel cells are powered by a combination of rare minerals and complex microcircuitry. "They're difficult to produce and incredibly expensive."

"I often wonder about that," I say. "How do you stay profitable?"

"On the androids, we don't. Not yet. But between our divisions in A.I. computing and synthetic organ production, and several patents we own and more on the way, we're well funded. That said, despite what the masses think, net *value* on paper rarely matches credits on hand. I had to invest all of my own money during startup. The rest came from private investors and tax incentives. E-Town subsidizes a portion of my investment. If I'm even a single day late on a single payment, lawsuits and injunctions get filed. Most of my money is tied up in the business. I am, as the saying goes, credit poor."

"So what's that got to do with a Death Code?"

She's stalling. She's waiting to see how I respond. It's clear she doesn't want me to know the whole story, but now feels she has no other choice. And resents me for it.

"Our engineers developed a next generation fuel cell. It lasts fifty years."

"The Jericho model," Whistler says and pats Selene's hand, letting it linger there just a little too long. That gesture elicits uncomfortable stares. Selene, being the professional she is, gently retracts her hand.

"Fifty years," I say. "Impressive."

"Double the pleasure," Whistler says, "double the pain."

Ther'eda raises an eyebrow.

"I thought you were upgrading the Lansing models with Jericho fuel cells. Giving them extra years."

"We are," she says. "Our Captain here is one of them. But it's a complicated process with a sixty percent success rate. There are compatibility issues we haven't been able to account for."

"Sixty-two point four seven percent," Selene says.

"Right again, Selene. As always."

"When the procedure fails," Whistler asks, "what happens?"

Ther'eda is slow to answer. "Other than a few anomalies… they're no worse for wear."

Whistler's suspicious look mirrors my thoughts. "For Lansing models who won't take the risk," he asks, "or when the procedure fails, how do they feel about it? Are they jealous, or resentful? To live half as long?"

I've wondered the same thing.

"Some are, yes." Perhaps an unconscious response, Ther'eda's gaze darts to Selene, and then, rather than Whistler, over to me. "I suppose there's no getting around it. Most are excited that next-gen androids will have opportunities they don't. They're advancing the cause."

Even artificial life forms seem to have an inherent drive to perpetuate their species. So I ask, "How many Lansing models are still active?"

"About two thousand, give or take."

"One thousand eight hundred and twelve," Selene specifies.

"Unless they've aged out," Whistler says, "still time left on the warranty."

This isn't like him, being so cavalier during a meeting this important. He's had trouble in the past, letting his excitement and nervous energy overtake his common sense. But here, now, it's something else. I don't know if he's trying to impress his girlfriend or what, but he's edging against the line we don't cross. I need to talk to him about that.

"I think what he's trying to say," I interpret, "is that, since you've discontinued future production on the Lansing line, they're a dying breed. Their extinction is inevitable."

The room goes quiet. There's a palpable tension. I let it linger until someone breaks.

Ther'eda does, with a restrained edge to her voice. "I don't care for that word. *Extinction* implies we've overtly acted against them, which is absurd."

She says Jericho models will be the new standard for the foreseeable future. Developing a fuel cell lasting longer than fifty years is, at the moment, beyond their reach. "The raw materials simply aren't available."

Scrolling through his phone, as if he's expecting something imminently, Tarrish looks up. "And exceeding fifty years is against the law. A cease-and-desist order would go into immediate effect, with a special servicer taking over the firm and all of its financials."

"Yes," Ther'eda says, the edge in her voice as sharp as a tungsten needle. "Regulation is a significant hurdle." She emphasizes *regulation* and *significant* as if those words are meant to slice Tarrish's throat.

"Guardrail," he retorts.

Ther'eda tosses a look at Tarrish that could stop a planet from forming.

"So..." Whistler stands up, claps his hands once, and rubs them together. "Why don't we talk about something a bit more fun." He winks playfully. "What's up with that Death Code, huh?"

There are a few heavy beats, followed by some soft chuckles, lightening the mood.

Nice recovery. Maybe I misread him.

Ther'eda quickly shifts her gaze to Selene then back to me. I need to get to the bottom of whatever's going on between them. It'll have to wait.

"Organics... humans...," Ther'eda says. "We are subject to physical fragility and a vast array of partially or entirely incurable or untreatable genetic and biochemical anomalies. They render each individual's lifespan random and unpredictable." She pauses, assessing whether we're following her line of thought. "But with androids, outside of accident or rare malfunction, their lifespans are entirely predictable."

"Knowably finite," I say.

"Correct."

I've seen it myself. Those limited lifespans and their awareness of it deny androids the delusion so many organics cling to. That through medical advancement, meditation, drugs, sex, fame, money, or simply because they're who they are—they can cheat death.

And because androids don't suffer those particular

delusions—at least not that I've ever witnessed—they seem to appreciate their experience as sentient beings far more than the rest of us. Which is ironic, given that androids are generally treated so poorly, regardless of their rights under the law.

"Captain," I say. "Any thoughts on this?"

He eyes me, careful to maintain his sense of order. "My sole focus is on the flight, and the safety of the passengers and my crew."

"Fair enough." I'm sure he has more to say, but knows this isn't the time or place to get involved. Then I shift. "Selene? What about you?"

She sits with perfect posture. Her back is straight, chin out, eyes forward, like a string attached to the top of her head is being pulled gently up toward the ceiling.

"There are three kinds of androids," Tarrish interrupts. "Those who go along to get along, suffering any and all indignities to survive in a realm that subjugates them. Others fight socially and politically, to finally be seen, and treated, as actual equals. You've seen the signs, heard the chants. *This is our home. We're not leaving. Deal with it.* That kind of thing. Some are more savvy, some are more militant."

"Whoa," Whistler says, trying, I think, to defuse this renewed tension and defending his girlfriend. Although she doesn't strike me as someone who needs defending. Especially by an organic. She's quite capable of defending herself. "Let's bring it down a notch."

"T," I say. "What's the third one?"

Everyone is waiting. Even Kowalczyk and Nenn, who haven't shifted a muscle since they locked down the room, betray glints of curiosity.

Tarrish leans forward, looming over the table. "The ones who say, 'I'm tired of organics determining how, if, and for how long we can exist. You will never be our masters again.' The Captain and I already have an understanding, so the question I have for Selene, and one I'm sure is now on all your minds is... which one are you?"

I've known Tarrish nearly 15 years. He's not exactly the touchy-feely type, but this is the first time I've thought he was totally out of line, particularly with someone who's never done him wrong. He's also never demonstrated a hint of android prejudice. Then again, he's never shown them extra consideration.

What he *does* have is a history of antagonizing Whistler. I don't know if that's happening here, but Whistler sure seems to think so. My partner lunges across the table to attack him. Nenn rushes to Ther'eda's side while Kowalczyk, with his hulking forearm, grabs Whistler from behind, putting him in a choke hold. Whistler's face is turning bright red as he struggles to breathe, pawing ineffectually at Kowalczyk's grip.

I make a move to intervene, but Whistler gets things under control himself. Recalling his Arberian martial arts training, he reaches behind him with more precision, digs his fingers into Kowalczyk's forearm, and plies it away from his throat. Whistler dips his neck, then spins his shoulders, freeing himself, knocking his chair over in the process.

"Enough!" Ther'eda barks. "This is why I kept the circle small. You're at each other's throats already. This ship is scheduled to depart in..." She looks to Dobbs.

He checks his watch, but only to placate we organics, help us feel more comfortable. As an android, he has an internal clock—and we don't. "Two hours and nineteen minutes."

"I've discussed it with the Captain and Lieutenant Tarrish, but we have an actual emergency to deal with before that happens."

"I'm negotiating with the Scherzeron Tower to see if we can delay another hour," Tarrish says. "But even if that happens, that's as much time as we'll get."

"Thank you, Lieutenant. So please everyone, I shouldn't need to say this, but I'm saying it regardless so there's no confusion or misunderstandings. What you hear in this room stays in this room. You are not to discuss it with anyone. If you hear chatter throughout the conference... engage appropriately, if warranted, but do *not* initiate. Not a single word. Understood?"

It takes a minute for everyone to settle down, scowls decelerating to frustrated glances, and finally to nods indicating at least a temporary truce, which, in this case, is about as good as we're going to get.

"Here," Kowalczyk says, slapping Whistler's phone against his chest. It had fallen to the floor.

Whistler snatches it from him, then rubs his sore neck. He hasn't mentioned them lately, but I think he's still having nightmares. "Do that again and we step outside."

Kowalczyk grins with delight. "And toss you off the side."

I give Tarrish a disappointed stink-eye, then return to my seat. The others do the same.

Kowalczyk and Nenn are back at their sentry posts guarding the door. I shift my gaze to Whistler. Calmer than he was, he moves his seat to the other side of me, putting himself between me and Selene, with a direct sightline to Kowalczyk. Whistler's not turning his back on him again. I put my gaze back on Ther'eda at the head of the table.

"Tonight," she says, "after the entertainment, we'll present the Software Engineer of the Year Award to Warren Buckley."

I look to Whistler, who shrugs. "Who's Warren Buckley?"

"He was a coder on our team. But he resigned about a year-and-a-half ago."

"Twenty-three months, eleven days," Selene clarifies. "He said he was burned out and needed a change. After that he went freelance, developing his own projects. Candidly, we forgot about him."

"And that's important because…?"

Ther'eda interjects. "As I'm sure you can imagine, artificial life forms… in this case"—she offers a slight hand gesture to Dobbs, then Selene—"in their case, androids have complex internal systems. The source code that powers and regulates an android's cranial CPU, synthetic organs, and nervous system is incredibly sophisticated. It's far too complex for a single coder. Smaller, dedicated teams work on specific segments of the source code. It also motivates them to step up their game. The stigma of being the weak link in the chain is both cruel and unforgiving. Buckley was assigned to synthetic organ stabilization."

I'm looking for the connection. "And you think he… what? Created the Death Code?"

The room is silent. All eyes on Ther'eda. "As Selene said,

Buckley is an excellent coder. But his ex-partner, Davi Nolasco, is brilliant. And like many coders at his level, his talent is only surpassed by his arrogance. He insists that his work is perpetually beyond scrutiny or reproach. That *we* should be answering to *him*."

Whistler looks perplexed. He's not the only one. "So this guy? Nolasco? *He* created the Death Code?"

"Yes," Ther'eda says. "Without my knowledge. In violation of his contract and company policy, he also found a way to circumvent our security protocols—already magnitudes beyond industry standards—and *implement* that Death Code into the entire Jericho line. It's buried so deep within the source code it took months before we realized it was there. Since then I've had dedicated teams working on it around the clock, but they're nowhere close to finding a method to extract, alter, or neutralize the Death Code. That sonuva... Nolasco infused a poison pill. If we tamper with the Death Code in any way... alter just a line of code, even a single keystroke... the *entire source code* eats itself. The individual android would, in layman's terms, self-destruct.

"And since androids are naturalized citizens, there's no legal remedy to round them up and take them offline, even for their own protection. Which I wouldn't want to do anyway, even if I could. Take them offline, that is. There are thirty-two hundred active Jericho androids and another nine hundred ready for activation."

"Three thousand four hundred seventy-seven, including myself, are E-Town citizens," Selene corrects. "Nine hundred forty-seven are scheduled for activation."

My head is spinning. I have many questions. "Where is he now? Nolasco?

"Unfortunately," Ther'eda says, "we don't know. His contract expired about six months ago. He'd been approached by several outside firms. To remain with us, he demanded massive equity, which, of course, I would never give. I responded with what I considered to be a generous compensation package, far and above the industry norm, even for elite coders. His ego was so inflated by then that he took offense, regardless, and declined the offer. He took a sabbatical so the industry could chase him."

"He dropped off the map," Tarrish says. "Almost six months to the day. I'm guessing he'll turn up eventually, or if we look hard enough we'll find him."

"So Nolasco leaves," I ask, "then soon after, you discover the Death Code?"

Ther'eda nods. "Yes."

This is starting to make more sense. "I get why you didn't make this public. But I still don't understand. This Death Code does *what*... exactly?"

Ther'eda's frustration appears to be mounting. "That's the other problem. Often... it does nothing whatsoever."

Whistler's face scrunches in bewilderment. "What does *that* mean?"

He's right. There's a lot to unpack from that tightly coiled evasion.

"The Death Code initiates randomly," Ther'eda says, "with no predictive models of when it will occur, if ever. It could initiate ten minutes, three months, or nine years after the individual Jericho android is activated, or six seconds before the fuel cell goes into permanent degeneration. Or any time in between. Or never. There is no known method for predetermining the activation point."

I probe further. "But when it happens... *what* happens? Because of the Death Code, the android just... drops dead?"

Ther'eda chuckles angrily. "Not exactly."

"If that's not it, *exactly*," Whistler says, staring at Selene with concern behind his eyes, then back at Ther'eda, "then what *is* it, exactly?"

She explains that in a Jericho android, with a fifty-year lifespan, the fuel cell will initiate a one-year wind-down at precisely the forty-ninth year and one second.

"After living in prime physical and cognitive condition, the android will experience the deoptimization algorithm."

"The deoptiwhatnow?" Whistler says.

"Deoptimization," Selene says. "The effective equivalent of what you would call a rapid aging process."

"Correct," Ther'eda says. "Once deoptimization initiates, to varying degrees the impacted android experiences organ failure.

Motor function and cognitive reasoning becomes impaired. Strength and stamina deteriorate. The purpose of a year-long wind-down is to give these sentient, albeit synthetic individuals a more… organic-like process to experience the end of their life. To more humanely—humanly—approach death. A chance, as they say, to get their affairs in order and say their goodbyes."

Whistler scrunches his brow. "So a wind-down instead of an off switch?"

"Yes," Ther'eda says. "That's a fair description."

"And the Death Code," he continues, "without warning, randomly initiates the final, one-year wind-down. Like early, forced retirement."

All eyes are back on Ther'eda.

"That's exactly what happens. And once that wind-down starts, there's no way to stop it."

CHAPTER 4

Death Code? I'll give you a Death Code.

Fucking Whistler. I could strangle him.

That's what I get for letting him run with a new client. I know it's petty, jealous, and immature, but part of me wanted him to crash and burn on this one. It took me almost six years, on my own, as a young woman, starting a practice from scratch, taking every case I could while I was still figuring myself out, to land a client this big. And he does it within months of me giving him the green light to chase new business?

Fuck that guy.

Really, though, fuck me. I'm in it now and there's no turning back.

We worked a case last year that pushed us both to the brink. A middle-aged widow hired us to reclaim the real estate empire she was set to inherit from her late husband, until her step kids stole it from her. The case ended up taking us off-realm, to planet called Arcasia.

It didn't go well for either of us. That's why Whistler's been having the nightmares, reliving the horror's we endured there. He saw three teens get executed at point-blank range, and in his worst moment, he beat a man to death with his fists, the first time he killed anyone.

I don't care who you are, that's a transformative event you can't push aside. Even in the heat of battle, taking a life changes you, alters you at a psycho-spiritual if not a molecular level. And rarely for the better.

I've encouraged him to go for grief counseling, which he's ignored, and I've tried to talk to him about what he did and how it's affected him. But anytime I bring it up he changes the subject, snaps at me, or disappears for hours on end. I don't know how to help him. I'm still struggling to help myself.

I'm not sure I've handled my own trauma all that well, but at least I'm doing something, even if my efforts are inconsistent and misdirected.

Long before that case, I almost drowned, caught in an ocean riptide. I've been terrified of the water ever since. But if I want my son to grow into an adult who's willing to face his fears and do his best to overcome them, me being a big ole scaredy cat about the water doesn't exactly advance that cause.

Plus, Whistler called me a wuss. So like I said, fuck him. And it distracts me from what I know I should deal with.

Up on Deck 14, the *Triumph*'s indoor swimming pool is pretty damn nice as far as natatoriums go. Clear water ripples against blue/gray tiles. It's a tiered pool, with subdued lighting, flowing water walls beyond each short side of the pool, and mammoth palm trees, one on each long side, with several deck chairs and mini tables.

Above is a double-height glassed-in ceiling with diamond-shaped panes, allowing for an incredible view of the galaxy.

I'm so wound up I can't concentrate on the job, so I focus on my form. One overhand stroke after the other, back arched at surface level, head-turn and breath every fourth stroke, like my swimming instructor taught me. Shanequa's got a wicked sense of humor. She's also an android. *Swimming good*, she likes to say, *drowning bad*.

So now I'm wondering, when will Shanequa's Death Code kick in? Today? Or ever? I have no idea. Neither does she. Neither does anyone, apparently.

"You're not kicking your legs enough," Selene says to me.

At the end of the swimming lane, I hug the edge of the pool, peel back the goggles tight around my eyes and head. They pinch the hair behind my right ear.

"Thought I was," I say, breathing heavily. I still run four miles a couple of times a week and continue my Arberian Martial Arts training with Master Neering, so I'm in pretty good shape. But swimming is an all-over exertion. Good for the back and hips.

In her skirt, blouse, and open-toed dress shoes, Selene

daintily goes into a half-squat, her exquisitely manicured toe-
nails, buffed blueberry polish with a lacquer, now at my eye
level. She hands me a towel as I exit the water.

I always hate this part. That cooler air, mixed with chlorine
and sweat, hitting my skin after my body is warmed up. It's like
washing yourself with a dirty bar rag. Gives me the heebee-
jeebies. My entire body shudders spasmodically. I dry off, then
toss the towel on a poolside deck chair in a row of chairs lined
side-by-side.

"Your right leg is strong," she says, "but your left is lagging."

Though I shouldn't be, I'm self-conscious in my one-piece.
Some of my scars are visible to Selene, who is, by any measure,
a beautiful woman.

"My instructor told me to grab the edge of the pool, facing
backwards, stretch out and do three sets of ten leg kicks. To
strengthen the left leg."

"Good advice. Did you?"

I expel an exercise-induced sigh of exhaustion. "Not yet."

"Give it time. You'll get there."

"Maybe. But this is my only time off for the rest of the night.
What's up?"

"To be candid...," she begins, the fading daylight visible
through the glassed-in ceiling.

"Why would you be otherwise?"

She ignores the poke. "You seemed a bit... annoyed."

"When I was told about the Death Code? I wasn't annoyed.
I was upset. And more often than not, whether I should or I
shouldn't... when I'm upset, I drink. But it's a work night. So I
exercise."

"A better choice."

Or I have sex, but she doesn't need to know that. I'm in no
mood to be lectured on how I manage my emotions. I used to
do far worse to myself.

"Look, Selene. I'm used to clients holding back, but that was
a big one. Even at the rate you're paying, I almost fired you as a
client. I can't do my job if you don't tell me what the job actually is. You and Whistler ran a game on me. I don't like being
played."

She half smiles, half squints. "Who does?"

That gets a chuckle out of me.

"Don't be mad at Eric. He didn't know. He was thorough in his due diligence. According to him, you set a very high bar. I wanted to tell you, to tell him, about the full scope of why we hired you for the event. But Ms. Ranadyne has her own way of doing things."

"Speaking of my soon-to-be-*ex*-partner... where is he?" I'm venting. Probably shouldn't talk shit about Whistler behind his back. And certainly not to her, the client/girlfriend. But he's not here where I can rip him a new one in person.

"He's embarrassed for himself," she says, "and embarrassed for embarrassing you. So he's doing another sweep, floor by floor, in case Davi shows up."

"I still don't get that one," I say and slip into my flip-flops. "If Nolasco did what you say, creating the Death Code, shouldn't the police pick him up? Or you could sue him for corporate espionage, sabotage, or theft of intellectual property."

I hear rubber soles squeak on the tiles. I know that gait anywhere.

"Ther'eda only called me a few weeks ago, under restrictive NDAs," Tarrish says. "I took her seriously because of who she is."

"And Jericho androids are going missing," Selene says.

That's a new one. "They're what?"

Tarrish hates being interrupted. And having someone offer details he isn't ready to share.

"Yes," he confirms, holding back his ire. "We've had a few more missing android reports than normal. And when we looked into Nolasco, he'd disappeared, too. I don't know if he skipped town, was kidnapped, or if he's lying face-down in a swimming pool somewhere. But for now, I've got no obvious leads to follow."

"Why didn't you tell me about the missing androids?" I say. "Or that you'd been on this for weeks?"

"Why would I? I don't answer to you. You always seem to forget that."

He's right. He doesn't answer to me. So I push back. "I wasn't talking to you." But I *was* talking to him, posturing in front of Selene, a sad attempt to save face. Even after all these years, having proved myself, *to* myself, that I can do this job as well as anyone and better than most, I still crave Tarrish's approval. I want him to think highly of me. I want him to be impressed. Right now I'm sure I look pretty far from impressive to him. Which mortifies me. What he thinks about me shouldn't matter this much, but it does.

I try not to show it, but I cringe inside. I wonder if this is how Whistler thinks about me.

I run my hands through my wet hair and slip on my pool robe, a gift from Nini. A thought had occurred to me earlier, but I lost track of it until now.

"After Nolasco left," I say to Selene, "and you realized what he'd done... why didn't you hire a PI to track him down?"

Selene looks to Tarrish, down at the water, then back to me. "We did. Jack Belle."

I chortle.

"You know him?"

"I know him."

"Is he good?"

"A little late for *that* question."

She does her best to contain an eyeroll, but it's there. "Belle had a lead on Davi Nolasco in the Tahc Sho Islands, but said the trail went cold. He said he could keep looking, but it would take more time and money. Time we didn't have. So we went another way."

"Jack's a solid investigator," I say. "But he's... easily distracted. You should've called me first."

"We considered it. But we were..."

Gotcha.

"Conflicted about Whistler. Because you two..."

Selene freezes, caught in a truth-trap.

All three of us are reflected in the gently lapping water, our shapes and faces distorted by the tiny, sloshing ripples. Which gives me a thought.

"What about Buckley? Did he quit because of the Death Code? Or help create it?"

"We considered it, yes, but there's no evidence to suggest

Warren had a hand in it. All lines of code have a programmer's tag. Anything related to the Death Code was time-stamped sixteen months after he left. Nevertheless, we analyzed all materials Warren personally worked on or reviewed, his entire workstation, and all his backup files. We couldn't find anything, not a single notation, suggesting foreknowledge of the Death Code."

"That's a good start. Did you ask him directly?"

"Of course. Discreetly. Either he's a remarkable liar or he actually doesn't know. It's also important we don't push him too hard just yet or accuse him of something he didn't do. We're trying to contain the problem before it becomes a PR nightmare."

"Sounds like you're almost there."

"We almost are."

I'm trying to get a read on her. It's tougher with androids, because they have fewer tells than organics, but they do have them. So I focus on the J-scar under her right eye. Androids may have rights under the law, but they're the only citizens physically branded, under penalty of deactivation, if they're not. And people wonder why there's tension. There's my in. I keep my next question vague. Let's see where it leads.

"You never said... how do *you* feel about the Death Code?"

Selene gazes down at the pool, then turns to me so we're now looking at each other.

"Is it better to have advanced knowledge regarding the date of my devolution? Would I be better served? Or is ignorance bliss? There are many androids who feel cheated. They feel manipulated by the Death Code, even if it hasn't impacted them yet. If it ever does."

"Are you one of them?"

Leaning slightly forward, her body language tells me she's aching to retort. She hesitates before answering. "No."

"That's surprising." Because it's bullshit.

"Why? Are organics of greater value because they were born rather than created? Am I of lesser value than you? Are you of greater value than me?"

"I never said that."

"I didn't either," she says. "But some people do."

"So what's your take, then? If we're all citizens, we're all the same?"

"Organics. Androids. Aren't those semantics?"

"Are they?"

"In whichever context you choose to view us, androids are sentient beings. The origin of my existence doesn't faze me. Nor do I dwell on it. And while I understand the rationale of those who refute the organics-to-androids equivalency, I don't share it. Obviously, organics and androids are physiologically different... under the hood."

I smile. "Of course."

"My existence," she continues, "is the result of intentionality. I was not an *accident*, as organics are known to say about unintended pregnancies. I was *created*. Planned. Afforded the opportunity to experience life, albeit in a way that's unique to androids. I have spent enough time interacting with organics, including Eric, to have concluded that very few seem happy, and for those who are, happiness is fleeting. I'm no different. But I don't judge the quality of my existence on how I may be feeling at the moment. My fuel cells will last fifty years. Which means I have forty-three years, seven months, nine hours and"—she seems to access her internal clock—"twenty-one seconds before my one-year devolution."

Androids aren't born, they're brought online, activated as full-grown adults. They spend one year at the Ranadyne facilities, undergoing diagnostics and being properly socialized. As part of the subsidy program afforded to Ther'eda by the City, androids are then legally mandated to spend four years in service of E-Town—full-time community service—paying off their debt, essentially, buying their freedom, in exchange for room, board, and a microscopic stipend.

After those years of service, they are granted status as full-fledged citizens who are free to live as they see fit, until their wind-down begins at the beginning of their 49th year, assuming they make it that far.

"I'm not certain knowing this specific timeline motivates me any more or less than if I only *suspected* I would last this long," she says, "so it's not something I lose sleep over."

"What *do* you lose sleep over?"

For just a second, it looks like she wants to tell me something real, but catches herself. "I prefer to focus on contributing the most I'm able, while I'm able, before my devolution. Perhaps by then, organics and androids will find a place of equilibrium."

Selene continues to impress. Not only is she a woman, she's an android, working in a cutting-edge field with one of the pioneers in the industry, and in a relationship with an organic. Anything and everything she says and does is scrutinized somewhere, by someone, every second of her life. She claims to be unaffected. But I suspect there's more than meets her synthetic eye.

I scan this natatorium, just a fancy word for an indoor pool room and consider why we're on this fancy galaxy cruiser to begin with. I nod to myself, smiling with a sense of relief. "Buckley's bait, isn't he? You're trying to draw out Nolasco."

Selene confirms that Nolasco and Buckley were an excellent team before they became bitter rivals, each fighting to be recognized over the other. Buckley had even filed complaints against Nolasco for harassment—messing with his desk, raising and lowering the lab temperature at random, stealing his lunch from the fridge, that kind of infantile hazing—but the complaints came across as childish nonsense, so he retracted them. Finally, he quit.

"Davi has to dominate every room he's in," Selene says. "And Warren doesn't like to argue. Which only enraged Davi. He thinks everyone's out to steal his tech because, in his mind, it's worth stealing. It often is."

"Giving Warren Buckley the award. That's your way of provoking Davi Nolasco."

"Especially this award, in front of the best coders, innovators, and investors. We reached out to Davi through every channel, and advertised the event far and wide. We offered the award to him first."

"But if Nolasco's in this much trouble, why would he show up?" I ask. "That makes no sense."

"Because he doesn't *know* he's in trouble," Selene answers. "We know there have been rumors circulating about the existence of a Death Code, but we've said nothing publicly."

I see what they're up to. Clever.

"It's like a serial killer who shows up at his own crime scenes," I say. "He gets his rocks off by blending into the crowd, under everybody's noses. You think Nolasco can't resist being in the lion's den, rubbing it in your face without you knowing it. And with Buckley getting an award Nolasco thinks is *his*... that'll seal the deal."

Selene nods. "That's what we're hoping."

"And if he doesn't show?"

"Then as soon as we get back on-realm, we put you on the payroll for as long as it takes for you to find him. You and Lieutenant Tarrish can work out the details amongst yourselves about how or if you work together."

Tarrish gives me a microscopic but superior smile. We both know if he's going to investigate the Nolasco disappearance, he has legal authority over me, and more resources than I could ever hope for. Which means, as always, I'd have to work *around* him while working *with* him.

It takes a few minutes after I cool down, but my mind clears. This often happens after I exercise. "I'm no coder, and you'll have to forgive my ignorance, but how could Nolasco have inserted a Death Code without your knowledge?"

"It's a good point," Tarrish says. "I asked Ther'eda the same thing."

"What did she say?"

Tarrish checks his phone again. "What they all say. 'It's complicated.'"

"Candidly," Selene says, "it is."

I'm tired of this. "How about you *uncomplicate* it? Because I'm not working another minute on this case unless you give me more to go on. Whistler and I are out."

Selene's about to respond when an announcement comes through the ship-wide comms:

"Good afternoon, everyone. This is your Captain, Barry B Dobbs. I hope you're having a wonderful day and have gotten settled into your staterooms. I apologize for the delay, but we've been cleared for departure. We have clear skies ahead and will be getting underway in ninety

minutes. *On behalf of myself and the entire* Triumph *crew, let me welcome you aboard, and we look forward to serving you on what I'm sure will be a delightful trip amongst the stars. As a reminder, the conference begins with panels and speakers at 5 p.m., followed by cocktails, and then an exciting event at 9 p.m., when we'll be cruising past the* aurora risus, *which is a sight to see. Thanks again, and from myself and the entire crew, enjoy the* Triumph."

Tarrish smirks. "You were saying?"

CHAPTER 5

After a quick shower and change, I get a VidChat request. Owen. My baby boy. I accept it from my laptop.

"Mommy! I'm watching your flight path! We can see every ship that launches. We see everything!"

In many ways, Owen is just like his dad, Eddie "Patch" Azarante. As a Patch, Eddie is part of a specialized team of construction workers and engineers. They're summoned when the fabric of the Universe suffers a significant tear or other injury across time, space, or dimension, requiring a cosmic patch. Thus the name.

Patches are a rare breed. Children of the Universe. I have no idea how, when, or where the first Patches arrived, but their essence is beyond that of any standard citizen. Patches are part Eternitarian and part cosmological, in organic form. Eddie descends from a long line of Patches, and continuing that tradition, Owen is a Patch, too.

Eddie and I were never married, and though he was once the love of my life who altered my trajectory forever, our relationship is still loving, but purely platonic now.

These days Eddie teaches full-time at the Patch Institute. Ultimately, I decided it was best for Owen to also live at the Institute, where he can get the training and guidance he needs to help him become the best version of himself.

I still get Owen on weekends, and we VidChat almost every day. I may not be a typical mom. But Owen isn't a typical kid.

"Is it a nice cruise ship?"

"Yeah, pretty nice, buddy. Why? You wanna take a cruise?"

"Mah-mee! Nini's taking me on the dinosaur cruise, 'member?"

"*Just* kidding. I know. For your birthday!"

Owen smiles excitedly. Then his look turns nervously hopeful. "Is Darren gonna come?"

Darren. My kinda/sorta boyfriend. He was a drummer in a touring rock band, but ever since they broke up and he's been giving lessons and gigging locally, he's been wanting to get more serious. I might have to break it off. I've got enough relationship problems these days as it is. He's really connected with Owen, though, which complicates things.

"Maybe," I say. "We'll see."

"But Mah-mee. You promised."

Owen forgets to put his clothes in the hamper *every day*, but of course *this* he remembers. "We'll talk about it when I get back. Look, buddy. I gotta get going. I love—"

"What's wrong with Whistler, Mommy? Is he mad at me?"

"No, baby. Why do you ask?" Now I'm the one who's nervous.

Owen looks away, plays with a fidget cube. "He doesn't text me anymore."

It's true. Since Arcasia, Whistler hasn't been the same. It's been impossible not to notice. "No, baby. He's not mad at you. He's just... got a lot on his mind. He's trying to figure some stuff out. He isn't texting lots of people."

Owen looks up again. "Is he okay?"

Good question. I honestly don't know. "Yes, baby. He's okay. It's just that sometimes... when grownups take new jobs, and the jobs are harder than they thought they'd be, they..."

"Have quiet time?"

I love this kid. "Yes, exactly right. Whistler's having quiet time."

Owen thinks on it. "Okay! Thanks, Mom. Love ya!"

"I love you, too."

"Maahm. You didn't say it. The *special* way."

He's right. I didn't. "And I love *yoouuuuu*, baby. Kisses."

Owen puts his face up close, smooches the screen. "Mm-wah! Love ya!"

He then closes out the VidChat.

Out in the hallway on Deck Five, I activate the outerwear setting on my jacket to keep in line with the fashion of the event.

Easier to blend in. I go with the charcoal schoolboy blazer that extends just above my hips, with quarter rolled-up sleeves, and notch collar with felt undercollar.

A nifty upgrade from Bernice, my tech ninja I have on retainer. My standard utility jacket is arugula with various pockets, seams, and folds to stash my gear and an emergency aid kit. Bernice updated the jacket with an adaptable fabric.

I'm on my way to meet with the security chief down on Deck Two when I get into the elevator. Two passengers stand side-by-side in the middle of a conversation. Their name badges, dangling from lanyards around their necks, say *Alec* and *Regina*. I slip behind them, at the back of the car, their backs to me.

"I don't know," Alec says. "My wife died last year. Cervical cancer. She was only thirty-six. I've got three kids under the age of five, including twins. I was such a mess. I would've completely fallen apart if not for Jess. She's my live-in nanny. How was I going to work full-time and raise them by myself? She's a lifesaver."

"If that's what you need to do," Regina says dismissively when I realize I got on the wrong elevator. This one's going up. "But I wouldn't let an android anywhere near my kids. The whole lot of 'em should be put on trial. I'd love to be the judge on that one. The black robes and everything. Judge, jury, and executioner."

"Trial? For what?"

"For taking up space! For sucking up resources meant for *us*. You're one of *those*, aren't you? You think androids are some kind of marvel, some new life form"—and she says this next bit with all the snark she can muster—"*worthy of their place*. You're delusional. You know what they're really gonna do? They're gonna replace us. And unless we do something about it... something real... that's what's gonna happen. Soon. Lie to yourself if you want, but not to me. I know the truth."

There's no talking to someone like this. Alec tries anyway.

"I think you're being kinda harsh. Androids are like us. They're just trying to get by."

"Get by? They're blenders with fake organs. What the hell's a robot even need with a fake liver anyway?"

"Androids," he says. "Not robots."

"Like it matters."

"It does, actually. Robots are mechanical inventions with no ability to reason for themselves."

She ignores him. "They're even talking about splicing *our* organs with *theirs*! What kind of twisted shit is that? They're doing a panel on it! Like there's nothing more important to talk about. And now with the whole Death Code thing? What if they just start, you know, dying there right in front of you? Though how can you *die* if you're never really alive?"

"I don't think that's what the Death Code is," Alec says. "Even if it kicks in, which isn't all that common, they randomly get sick, like us, then it takes almost a year until—"

"How's a kid supposed to recover from a thing like that?" Regina's clearly uninterested in any point of view other than her own. "It'll mess them up for life. For *life*. Do you get that? A mechanical... whatever... just gasping and dying in front of them. It'll be imprinted on their little brains forever. And I don't care what the 'droid-lovers say. No amount of therapy will scrape that memory away. It's cruel to have androids as a part of your kids' life. No offense. Your kids, your rules. You do what you want. But to parent that way? That's fucked up."

I should get off at the next deck. Or punch her in the throat. I don't want any part of this woman—her vibe is a cup of cold piss on a hot day—but I can't help myself. I see Alec cringe at her every word.

From behind, I ask, "How many kids do you have?"

Surprised I intervened, Regina peeks over her shoulder. "Me? Uh, none. Zero. Not now, not ever. It's just me and my boyfriend. He's an ex-cop. He hates 'em, too."

"He hates kids?"

"*Pfft*. Androids. Kids aren't much better. Needy little fuckers."

"Then why are you here?"

Regina huffs, gives me a *who the fuck are you?* look, one implying I violated a sacred covenant that forbids me from challenging her rigidly myopic worldview. She eyes Alec derisively as the doors open to Deck Seven. "Good luck with your kids," she says as she exits into the hallway. "And your"—Regina makes air quotes with her fingers—"nanny." The doors close again.

"She's a real peach," I say to Alec.

"It doesn't bother me." It clearly does though. And why wouldn't it? Her disgust wasn't even about me, and yet I'm disgusted, having sadistically violent thoughts about her I usually reserve for, well, people like her. "I'm used to it," he continues. "Half the people I know think it's great I have a nandroid. The other half either don't care or are just like her. Tell you the truth, since my wife died, androids have been a whole lot nicer to me than anyone else. They don't pity me. They just help."

In my experience, androids aren't all that much different from us, although it pains me to say there's a tiny part of me that understands where people like Regina are coming from. A few years ago, nanobots were implanted in my shoulder to repair torn ligaments I suffered on a case. The procedure worked, but it wasn't without its side effects, and not something I'm eager to do again.

And yet after severe injuries of her own, my tech ninja Bernice is now part-synthetic, part-organic, with a hoverchair she controls by way of a chrome-plated implant fused to her right temple with a cybernetic interface, and attachable arms. I trust her with my life. If it came to it, I'd trust her to protect my son. I don't care if your wiring is organic, synthetic, or day-old cream cheese. You're either good people... or you're not.

"I'm sorry about your wife," I say. "That's gotta be hard."

"It is."

"For what it's worth, you sound like a pretty great dad."

The elevator stops on Deck 12, top level for staterooms. The doors open. "This is me," Alec says. "Thanks for that."

"No problem." The doors close again. But I do have other problems.

The elevator starts its trip back down, a few passengers getting on and off until, finally, I take it back down to Deck Two. Bottom of the ship. I was down here to see the security room earlier with Tarrish, Whistler, Kowalczyk, and Nenn, but I want a second look.

Turk Candelaria is the security chief. With a full head of

wavy gray hair and sinewy features, he's sitting behind the
desk, reviewing the surveillance screens giving him eyes on
every deck with various vantage points.

He scrolls from screen to screen—commissary, engine control room, stateroom decks, natatorium, SunDeck, MoonDeck,
Experience Theater, spa, sauna, gym, chiropractic and acupuncture salon, restaurants, disco, video game center, dream emer-
sion pods, giftshops, and other amenity spaces throughout the
Triumph.

"Hey, Turk. You seen this guy?" I show him Buckley's photo
on my phone. "Can you run facial recognition from here?"

He looks at me like I swallowed a porpoise. "Uh… no. We
don't have that kind of tech here. This is a cruise ship. Not
the ICD."

I chuckle at myself. "Yeah. Just figured I'd ask."

"Besides," he says, "your partner was down here before bust-
ing my balls about this guy. He tried slipping me some credits
to keep an eye out. I spent twenty-seven years on the Force. I
know how the business works. You gotta spread it around. But
you might want to tell him to slow his roll. As a professional
courtesy, I let it go."

That's all I need. Piss off the security chief. "First big client
he brought in. He's being extra diligent. I'll talk to him."

I don't want to overreact. Whistler might be doing exactly
what I said. Being overeager to course-correct his first big client. But slipping credits to the security chief is over the line.
Whistler knows better. He might be less okay than I thought.

"How long you been on this ship, Turk?"

"As security chief? About three years."

"You get a lotta trouble on these things?"

He laughs. "Nah. Not really. It's usually just sticking some
dumbshits in the drunk tank to cool off. With all the alcohol on
board and being so far off-realm, you'd think there'd be more
fights, but mostly it's just nuisance calls."

"What about burglary?"

"Some of that, too. It's unavoidable."

"Rape?"

He knows the drill. He has to be careful how he answers.

"It happens. You know it does. But we can only get involved if we know about it. Unfortunately, most rapes are never reported. You know that, too. Besides, we're not the police. We don't have the manpower or jurisdiction for that. We can't be everywhere at once. We do the best we can with the staff we have."

"You ever kick someone off?"

"Once or twice, yeah. If someone really gets outta line, we stick 'em in the brig. We hold 'em until we reach the nearest port, or get back on-realm."

"And what if someone gets ambitious, tries to hijack the ship?"

"Crazier shit's been known to happen."

"And if they try?"

"We've got a gun locker back here. I'll show ya."

To the side of the security desk are three large lockers with metal, cross-hatched doors. Inside are revolvers, shotguns, ammo, bulletproof vests, flares, mace, zip-ties, and batons. A respectable cache.

"You expecting a zombie apocalypse?"

He chortles. "Expecting? No. But if it happens, I'm not going down without a fight."

The tension is already mounting on the cruise, so I ask.

"The Captain's an android. That bother you?"

Turk looks at me oddly. "Why would it? Dobbs is a good guy, good Captain."

"It bothers some people."

Turk leans back in his chair, then forward. "I was a cop for a long time," he says. "And I admit, I was suspicious of them at first. Androids are stronger than us, have computers for brains, and can transfer data with the blink of an eye. Of course people were nervous. But their source code prevents them from accessing restricted data."

Ther'eda had already done this on her own, but by legal mandate she is required to infuse all androids with impenetrable data blockers. No matter how minor, any attempts to alter, tamper with, or circumvent those blockers could shut Ther'eda down, and possibly for good.

"So I gave androids a chance. From what I saw, they weren't better or worse than anyone else. Some were okay, some were assholes. Just like the rest of us. And if we're talking truth... organics can hack computer systems, too. Cybersecurity is one of the biggest industries on realm. But you know what? What if androids *do* get access? To personal banking records or healthcare systems? Or the power grid? What if they reprogram our systems without us even knowing? Under the right circumstances, could androids overthrow the realm? Could they enslave us? Could they become *our* masters? Or kill us all? I want to think they can't, and that they never will, but given how badly they've been mistreated since their inception, if the opportunity presented itself, could you blame them if they did?"

If anything, I'd say they have ample justification for it.

"I'm not saying they don't deserve to be citizens," Turk says. "I'm not saying they do, either. As long as they don't try to digitally overthrow throw the realm, I got no problems with them. But the reality is... I just don't know. Maybe it's the cop in me. Maybe I've seen too much. And maybe it's because I get paid to be suspicious and assume the worst about everyone and everything whether it's justified or not. But androids make me a little nervous." He checks his watch. "Then again, so does everyone else."

There's not much I can say to that. So I don't say anything.

"Anything else I can do for you? I got a briefing now."

"I'm good. But just in case, here's my number. Would you mind texting me if Buckley gets in trouble?"

"Why?" he says. "You expecting it?"

I give a squinty half-smile. "No. But if it happens, I'm not going down without a fight."

CHAPTER 6

It wasn't so long ago that androids weren't even a part of our lives in Eternity.

As the cosmic realm whose sole purpose is to serve the physical Universe—designing galaxies, building planets, reorganizing asteroid fields, stitching up critical tears in the fabric of space/time—the infrastructure and ecosystem changes for us down at street level, realm-wide, at the discretion of the Minders of the Universe.

As the story goes, Eternity went through an industrial phase eons ago. The Minders of the Universe—existential beings who created and oversee Existence and everything in it—figured automation would speed things up for us, allowing for greater efficiency in our ability to design, build, and maintain the Cosmos at their behest. But the environment in Eternity became so toxic as a result, the illness rates so high, the Minders scrapped it completely.

With a blink of their unfathomable eyes, the Minders supposedly replaced that model with a wintry habitat, positing that constant frigid conditions would keep everyone moving, just to stay warm. Can you imagine? Freezing my tits off year-round? No thanks.

Not sure how long that tundra lasted, but as the Minders do, they supposedly changed their minds once again, going in the opposite direction. They completely reinvented Eternity as a tropical paradise, positing that happy, relaxed, and well-rested workers would consistently give their all. Another misfire. Eternitarians spent too much time windsurfing, fornicating, and getting drunk on the beach.

So the Minders gave Eternity yet another new look and feel,

the one we have now, including the introduction of androids.

If there is an external threat against Ther'eda because of them, there's one surefire place to pick up loose intel. Which is why I make my way to the SunDeck.

Extending out on the port side of the *Triumph*, the two-level SunDeck sits beneath a transparent dome. The lower level, just below us, has a wading pool and three hot tubs, while this upper level is an enclosed garden with oversized, multi-colored, metallic sculptures, flower-shaped, the floor layered with real, finely trimmed grass, and smelling of a summer breeze.

We can't see it yet against the hazy afternoon sky, but soon we'll leave the realm's atmosphere and enter the vastness of space, arriving in the Priachi quadrant.

An announcement confirms:

"Good afternoon. This is Captain Barry B. Dobbs. I'd be out there with you myself for a light cocktail, but it's time to get this cruise underway. Thanks to our ship-wide gravity matrix, feel free to remain as you are. You won't feel a thing. Ha ha. On behalf of the entire crew, please enjoy the drinks, the view, and each other. The Triumph *has left the building."*

The passengers erupt into light applause. It's a cathartic moment acknowledging that any concerns the trip would get further delayed, or even canceled, are behind us.

And now we're off that realm. Whoop-dee fuckin do.

Even that's partly bullshit.

I'll never admit it openly, but I get caught up in the moment, watching E-town below us shrink from view. The various galaxy cruisers still awaiting to depart the Scherzeron Cruise Port. The Rubiyat Highway, the Chabaqua River. The Manuela Projects, the expanding city-wide Monorail, the rebuilt Downtown marina, and the cargo ships waiting to haul goods to and from galactic regions beyond the realm.

As we approach the clouds, they all continue to miniaturize, until we're far enough away that we can see the entire city now, the skyscrapers, residential towers, hosts of traditional and hover vehicles, hordes of people bustling this way and that.

E-Town seems so peaceful from up here. Even the swarms of

ever-watchful police drones whisking high above the streetscape look like harmless fireflies. Because even though I know how much filth and grime and hate and treachery flows through the city's arteries, all the drugs and gangsters, the corruption and violence, the Dream Pods and holoroom orgies, the hungry and homeless, the rich and even gluttonously wealthy—distance helps wash it all away from consciousness.

It's sad, and a little bit terrifying, how easily that happens. How the struggles and horrors of daily life seem to no longer exist by the virtue of ignoring them. Out of sight, out of mind.

Is this my penance? Surrounded by cocktail party chatter? At first it's all about the view and the *Triumph* and how great it is to get away from significant others and kids and traffic and the office and chores and bills, but in short order the chatter shifts to the inevitable shop talk.

Computer linguistics this, android synthesis that, ethical quandaries about the very nature and existence of androids. Debates about what caused a Monorail car full of passengers to pass out a few months ago, and again in Britton Square. And, of course, petty, cynical gossip about Ther'eda Ranadyne. That even with her stranglehold over the manufacture of androids in E-Town, this entire event is nothing more than a commercial for her outsized ego.

But it's not her ego I should be focused on. It's mine. I was a kick-ass PI working solo for nearly fifteen years, taking cases on-realm and off, then something happened to me. Well… some*one*. Speaking of which…

"Mache." Whistler hands me a beer. I take it. He leans his bottle in my direction.

I wait a beat, allowing my insides to uncoil. When I feel my chi opening back up, flowing a bit more freely, I clink my bottle against his.

"Got your shit together?" My snark is directed at him, but really, I'm talking to myself.

Whistler nods. "I'll live."

We both do casual spin moves, rotating 360 degrees to sur-veil the SunDeck. A wait staff is handing out hor d'oeuvres, including balsamic garlic shrimp, sushi rolls, sesame chicken strips, steak tartare with dill sauce, beetroot hummus on olive-oil flatbread, chickpea bruschetta with sundried tomatoes, and artichoke puffs.

"Nolasco's a no-show," Whistler says, getting us back to the case.

I don't even know if this really is a case. More like an assignment. Quasi-security detail and investigation. Ther'eda suspects, or maybe even knows, that Nolasco left a trail about the Death Code. Trail led to the *Triumph*. If anyone was working with Nolasco, or has a line on what to do about the Death Code, good chance they're somewhere on this vessel.

"I checked the front desk," Whistler says. "There's a reservation for Nolasco, arranged by Ther'eda. He hasn't checked in. I ran into Tarrish. Still no word."

"That doesn't mean there's nothing to learn about Nolasco. Or the Death Code. Let's work the room. And remember... don't bring it up. Let it come to us."

Passengers are milling about, some playing croquet and bocce on the far end of the lawn, while a level below, a water volleyball game is already at full tilt.

Surrounded by three large tulip sculptures, a gaggle of coders huddle around a cocktail table laid out with discarded plates of finger food. I forgot how young coders are, most in their 20s and 30s. Old enough to have developed legitimate technical skills but young and immature enough, even in an age of hyper PC, to have no qualms about acting like class A twat-waffles no matter who's listening.

"Dude," one of them harrumphs, sucking down a pint of a new microbrew that's been making the rounds. It tastes more like diabetic cat piss than beer. "Buckley's getting the award? Warren Fucking Buckley? Seriously?"

According to the badge dangling from the lanyard, his name is Ralph. The name is fitting.

"I know, right?" says Suraj, another coder. "Buckley. More like *fuckley*! Hay-oh!"

That earns him a bunch of dude-bro high-fives and beer chugs.

"Still," coder Aaron says, "he did impressive work with

Nolasco on synthetic organs. Too bad he didn't stick with it. Then again, I'm not sure I would've stayed either. You know Nolasco. He's a lot to take. Maybe that's why Buckley never got credit. Until now."

Wearing a maroon collared shirt, beige pants, and a brown leather belt, Aaron is far more professionally dressed, and behaved, than the other coders, who are wearing khaki or jeans shorts, t-shirts with various pop culture logos, and leather sandals.

"That was like *two years ago*," Ralph-waffle says, spilling beer on a middle-aged woman to his left. She grimaces, rolls her eyes. Ralph seems oblivious. "Might as well've been a *million* years ago. He can suck ass."

I consider inserting myself into this high-minded conversation when a young-looking woman, with a corona of curly brown hair and large, round glasses, beats me to it. "Warren has some amazing theories," she says, then coughs roughly into a closed fist. Nametag says *Chipper*. "Davi was difficult even on his best day."

The coders go still, eyeing Chipper awkwardly. They don't seem to know how to handle her. Coders with poor social skills. Particularly when it comes to women. Shocker.

"Say what you want about Warren Buckley..." Dressed in faded blue jeans, a white blouse buttoned up to the neck, and a tweed jacket, Chipper squints uncomfortably. She produces an inhaler from her right pocket, shakes it a few times, and takes two deep inhalations. She holds the medication in her lungs to help relax the muscles that have tightened around her airways, then exhales. "He's going to be a force in our industry. Warren may have left Ranadyne Cybernetics. That doesn't mean he's got nothing to offer."

Having said her piece, Chipper wanders into the crowd.

Whistler gives me a quick look, which I acknowledge. He blends into the party.

"Fuck that little scrub," Ralph mumbles. "She's a mechanical engineer. Doesn't know shit about coding. Just because she was on a college course rotation, for like ten minutes, with her stupid migraines, doesn't mean she—"

"Fuck that who now? She's a what? And why are migraines stupid? They're brutal, no?"

If these code-waffles actually have testicles, I just heard them shrivel up.

"She's, uh," Ralph stammers. "She..." He right-sizes. "You a coder?"

I chortle. "Me? No."

"Then what do *you* know about it?" The other code-waffles aren't sure what's happening here. But they can't look away.

"It's not what *I* know that matters. What's the deal with Nolasco and Buckley?"

Ralph looks to his fellow code-waffles, smirks at me. He thinks he has the upper hand.

"You don't know? Come on, guys. Let's bounce."

"Easy, there, bounce-house. Show me that big ole sexy brain of yours. Enlighten me."

Ralph offers a snide chuckle. "What's your deal?" He drops his gaze toward my chest, pretending to study my name badge. Subtle. "Hardwicke, huh? Says you're a consultant. What *kind* of consultant? Never heard of you."

"The kind that consults. Ther'eda Ranadyne asks my opinion. I tell her."

"*Oooh,*" he says mockingly, waving his hands for effect. "*Opinions.* About what? Or is that a big secret?" He's both loving and hating this. He's not sure where he stands.

"That's the thing about secrets," I say, drawing him out further. I can't quite tell yet if he knows anything of value, but he definitely knows something. And he's dying to say it in front of an audience. "If you tell someone, it's not a secret anymore."

So frustrated he's now nearly shaking, Ralph reaches for my badge, like he needs to hold it in his hand to verify its authenticity. And to prove he can exert power over me. Fondling my badge isn't the same as fondling my body, but that's what comes next if I don't teach him some manners.

"Ah-ah-ah." I smile and lean in close, as if to whisper playfully in his ear. Instead, I bend his left pinky back just enough to command his full attention, but not enough to make a scene. His knees buckle. "Was that as good for you as it was for me? Wanna start over?"

Grimacing, he nods wordlessly. I release his pinky, then step back.

Embarrassed, he massages it with his other hand.

The only adult among them, Aaron reengages. "Nolasco and Buckley wrote advanced code that improved synthetic organ function in androids by seven point one six three percent, which is substantial. There was talk about them being assigned to higher brain functionality. But then..."

"Buckley resigned," Suraj says meekly.

"I heard they had a falling-out," I say. "What happened?"

The coders gaze back and forth at each other.

Ralph flexes his sore pinky. "Let's just say," he says finally—there's more than a hint of stupid, smug glee on his stupid, smug face—"they dipped their pens in the same ink."

Mister subtle strikes again. Still, I make him work for it. He's earned a whole lot worse. "Separately? Or at the same time?"

Ralph sighs, annoyed. His unwarranted arrogance demands he be understood and praised at all times, and be the center of attention. "They were...," he starts aggressively. Seeing the uncomfortable reactions from his fellow code-waffles, he takes it down a notch. "They shopped in the same aisle."

"They broke up their work over a lover's quarrel? That's what you're saying?"

Ralph leans back on his heels, palms up, chin retracted, eyes wide open. "I'm not saying anything." He leads the other code-waffles away, then calls back over his shoulder. "But if you thought *that* was a secret, you don't know shit about secrets."

Oh, I hate that little fucker.

In need of instant reprieve, I wander aimlessly through the various conversations. About half the passengers say they're planning to attend at least one of the panels that will run concurrently during the 5 p.m. to 6 p.m. and 6 p.m. to 7 p.m. tracks. The rest are planning to nap, shower, have sex, chill on the various decks, or keep drinking until the big event tonight.

I want to reconnect with Ther'eda and Tarrish, find out if they've gotten word about Nolasco. And if they have, what the plan will be now that we're off-realm and won't be back until Sunday.

It doesn't take long, but suddenly I realize the sky above has faded from blue to gray, gray to white, and growing darker now, such that not just E-town but all of Eternity is nowhere to be found.

I think about heading out when I spot Chipper again near the edge of the SunDeck. She's staring out into the black of space as soft interior lights come on under the dome. In her brief encounter with the coders, she calmly defended Warren Buckley.

Don't know why neither Ther'eda nor Selene mentioned her. Oversight? Intentional? Or maybe there's nothing to tell.

I give my empty beer bottle to a waiter with a small serving tray, then move toward—

"Hardy!" Dolores nearly shoves passengers out of her way to get to me. Intimidated by her natural heft, most of them make room to avoid conflict. Wise move. "There you are."

"Hey, D. Look. I'm in the middle of—"

Dolores grabs me by the shoulder, twists me sideways. Sometimes I forget how strong she is.

"Will you look at that?"

I respond with the same voice I use when Owen wants me to watch the same video with him for the seventeenth time. In a row. "What am I looking at?"

"At her. At Nini."

"Where? I don't... oh, there she is. She's having a drink."

"No shit. But look who she's with."

"Yeah? So? Good-looking man. Well-dressed, dark skin. Nini's type all over. Very nice."

"No. Not nice. Look under the eye. J-scar." With her mammoth hand, Dolores shifts my proportionally tiny chin a few degrees to the left, like that's going to matter. "Not a man, Hardy. Android. It's like she does it to piss me off."

My sigh is heavy. I'm not in the mood for this. "Why, D? Why do you do this?"

"Do what? It's..." Realizing she's talking too loud, even for her and in a crowd like this, Dolores lowers her voice. "It's not right. I don't know what Nini sees in those mechanical freaks. She lets them, you know... *do* stuff to her. Naked stuff. And she does stuff to *them* and..."

With no time, energy, or desire to have this argument yet again with Dolores, I'm let off the hook with the flicker of the SunDeck's interior lights. A member of the concierge staff emerges, reminding everyone the conference panels will start in ten minutes on Decks Four and Five.

Saved by the bell.

Dolores peels off, which allows me to look for Chipper.

Unfortunately, she's gone.

CHAPTER 7

I'm not sure how focused the passengers are going to be, given that the individual conference rooms are positioned between the *Triumph* Casino, Quasar Bar, Tapas Café, and Wine Cellar, with the multi-level Experience Theater also nearby at the front end of the ship. Temptation to do anything and everything on this cruise except learn is everywhere.

Gotta love boondoggles.

Two dozen or so passengers, all seated at various tables amidst a makeshift garden of luminous flowers, are having cocktails and playing trivia, cards, or backgammon. Layered within the chatter are the clickety-clack of the white and black marble backgammon tiles, the rattling of dice in brown Menaki leather cups with cork interiors, and the rumbly clicks as those same dice roll across the leather-bound cork game boards.

I'm not into backgammon, but I know someone who is. And... there she is.

"Come on double sixes!" Nini shakes the leather cup, rattling the dice. "Mama needs to advance to the next round." She tosses the dice across the board. They tumble, bouncing against the center divider. Six and... six. Settled right next to each other, the dice glow green and gold. "Yes! Sorry, Mitch," she says to her opponent. "Better luck next time."

I lumber over. "Kicking ass and taking names?"

Nini sips her cranberry and vodka through a thin red cocktail straw. "Who? Him? Nah. He's a lightweight. There're a few real players, but otherwise a bunch of humps. I'm gonna win this thing. Going all the way, baby. Next round's at ten."

"What's with the glow? The dice?"

"No idea."

I snag a set of dice from an unoccupied backgammon set at the next table. I inspect the cubes more closely, then pocket them. "For luck."

"It's not luck when you got game," she says.

We exchange knowing smirks when I change the subject. "Neen. I gotta ask. What's with you and D? You guys seemed more… *you guys* than normal."

Nini sips her drink, scans the room. "She… asked me not to say."

I find myself nodding, caught between wanting to know and knowing I should probably stay out of it. "No problem. I just…"

Nini sighs. "Fine." She leans in super close. "D proposed to Beata last week."

"Really? No way!"

"Way."

I can't help it, but the girly girl in me kicks in. "So what happened? Where did she do it? How was the ring? What…?"

By the look in Nini's eyes, it's clear Dolores didn't get the outcome she was hoping for.

"Beata said no. They broke up."

I expel a heavy sigh. "Oh… shit. Why? What happened?"

Nini shrugs. She probably knows more than she's saying, but there's no need. Dolores is more protective of her heart than her money. And that's saying something.

"She's hurting Anj. Bad."

"She's posturing," I say. "To cover up."

"With extreme prejudice. I wouldn't bring it up."

Dolores doesn't know this, but two years ago I saw her and Beata at Aechan Park. It was a beautiful spring day, and they were laying on a blanket in the grass, Dolores on her back, her head in Beata's lap, Beata stroking Dolores' hair. They were barely talking, but you can express even your deepest emotions without every speaking a word.

I've never seen Dolores that happy. I didn't know she could be that happy, didn't know she had it in her. Then again, there's still so much I don't know about her.

"Don't worry," I say. "I won't."

"Hey…" Nini's gaze darts over my right shoulder. I turn to

see the dapper man—dapper android—she was with earlier. "Would love to chat more, but mama's got a date."

She sits on one of the semi-circular couches, crosses one glistening, shaved leg over her knee, letting him come to her. They give each other a sensuous side-cheek kiss, whisper in near giggles, then head off.

Leaving Nini to her own devices, I examine the digital itinerary posted on a support beam surrounded by the couches. All led by industry 'experts', the 5 p.m. panels include:

Multi-Source Policy Aggregation for Transfer Reinforcement Learning Between Diverse Environmental Dynamics; Complex Systems for Android Organ Repair; Edge AI and Active Digital Twins; and the two I'm most interested in, *Closing the Loop: Bringing Organics Deeper into Empirical Computational Social Choice and Preference Reasoning* and *Digital Power Systems and How to Effectuate—and Prevent—Hacking.*

"Dibs on hacking," Whistler says. Even as a few hundred passengers wander about to find the specific panels they want, the purified air is set at a constant seventy degrees. The system automatically raises or lowers the base temperature to compensate for the total body heat given off by the passengers and crew. "What's *preference reasoning*?"

"That's what we're here to find out."

"I thought we're here about"—his eyes dart side to side as he whispers out of the corner of his mouth—"the Death Code?"

"We are. This, too."

Whistler looks at me oddly. "Since when?"

"Since now. Keep an ear out for who asks questions during the panel—and who doesn't. Hackers love to brag, but true artists do it quietly. See you in an hour."

Good students sit up front. But I'm not here to ask questions. I'm here to observe. I sit in the back, in a soft cushioned chair on lavender carpeting, midway on the right side, such that everyone else is either next to or in front of me. Nothing going on behind my back. Room capacity is only 84, big enough to draw a crowd, but manageable.

Even on a luxury cruise ship like this, a panel is a panel is a panel. With rare exceptions, if you've been to one industry conference, you've been to them all. In short order, the modestly lit room fills to capacity. I wasn't expecting a full house, especially on the first night.

The guest speakers, three of them, take their seats at the table up front. On the tabletop, in front of each speaker, is a digital placard with their names in bold, a microphone pod, and an individual bottle of water with the Ranadyne logo.

Thanks to my specialized contact lenses upgraded by Bernice, who is a cyborg but not an android, I can zoom in on any face and record video and audio with no one the wiser. Scattered among the passengers I spot five androids, all with J-scars under their eyes.

"Okay, folks," the moderator says. "I see everyone is properly lubricated."

Laughs.

"You're awake. Great!" Chuckles. "I know you're all excited for tonight's aerialists and a chance to see the *aurora risus*—which translates to *the smiling lights*. I'm excited, too! And as the opening act, welcome to our panel, *Closing the Loop: Bringing Organics Deeper into Empirical Computational Social Choice and Preference Reasoning.*

"My name is Bartholomew Suzuki, Professor of Synthetic Brain Function at the Wiley Foundation. With me tonight are my esteemed colleagues—on my left, Doctor Damian Joyce, Chancellor of the Nielda Stranum Institute for the Advancement of Digital Functionality, and to my right, Abella Laurent, Chief Computer Engineer at HighBeam Technologies.

"We've got a lot to cover within the time allotted, but before we get in too deep, I find it helps to define our terms. What do we mean by *computational social choice*? Abella, can you help us out?"

"Sure, thanks, Bart. I appreciate the invitation. Computational social choice is an interdisciplinary field of study where social choice theory—focused on design and analytical methods for collective decision making—intersect with a combination of computer science, artificial intelligence, political science, economic theory, logic, and other disciplines. Or, more simply stated, the study and implementation of advanced computer sciences examined and implemented through the lens of social awareness."

"You mean androids," someone from the crowd yells out.

"Well, yes, that's part of it." Laurent slightly scrunches her face, seemingly put off by the reductive comment. "But it's more complex than that. The more profound, fundamental questions we're asking, and seeking to answer, center around how best we can achieve betterment of the realm as a whole, while navigating the various ethical quandaries and potential exploitation of advanced computer science."

"Well said," Suzuki says, doing his best as moderator to keep the crowd interested and on track, but also tame enough so as not to disrupt the discussion. "Damian, you've done quite a bit of research on this topic. What's the latest thinking about getting children started in computer science, and the social responsibilities that come with it at the elementary level?"

From the audience: "I can barely get my kid to brush her teeth. And you want her to be a socially responsible computer tech?"

Raucous laughter.

"I have four at home myself," Damian Joyce says, his smile wide and enthusiastic. "But you know kids these days. Put a device in their hands and they're hypnotized."

"Mesmerized!" someone yells out.

"Zombified!"

"Computer zombified!" yells another.

"Socially conscious computer zombified!"

Laughter overwhelms the room. But a handful of attendees, including the androids, aren't laughing. One stands up. Although he's on the other side of the room, toward the front, through my contact lens I can read his nametag: *Gerald*. J-scar under his right eye. Acne scars under the left. I didn't know androids could get acne.

"What about the missing androids?" he says loudly, silencing the crowd. Looking late thirties or early forties, Gerald is dressed in an expensive gray suit. Almost too formal for this crowd, but maybe that was his point. He wants all eyes on him, and to be taken seriously. "They're vanishing off the street. The cops don't care. Nobody cares. You want to talk about social responsibility? So be *responsible!* What are we doing about it?"

Lots of blank stares and heavy blinking. Until someone else chimes in. His nametag says *Litton.*

"Quiet down, buddy. We're trying to learn something here."

"Obviously not! Androids are disappearing. We don't know who's taking them or why, but one by one we're being erased. My people... we're being *exterminated.*"

"Your sense of humor's exterminated!"

Litton's shout elicits some uncomfortable chuckles.

"Typical," Gerald says. "I hear lots of grandiose talk and sophisticated words to cover up what you really mean. We're just science experiments to you. Artificial playthings, second class citizens. You belittle us and—"

"Don't overcharge your battery, pal. We're on a galaxy cruise. Lighten up!"

"Lighten up?" another android says, a woman, two rows in front of me. "He's right. You want us to lighten up when our people—"

"Androids," Litton corrects.

"When *citizens* are disappearing. And your answer to this terrifying *social problem* is to mock us?"

"Hey," Litton says. "I was just trying to lighten the mood so we can—"

"*Who cares about your mood?*" retorts Sebastian, a third android in a blue, three-piece suit, in the front row, now facing Litton. "My friends are being kidnapped, sold into slavery, or maybe being experimented on, and your solution is to *lighten the mood?*"

"Come on, now," Suzuki says, having clearly lost control of the panel. "Why don't we all just—"

"What's your job?" Gerald says to Litton. "Your profession?"

"Patent attorney. Why?"

"You have any kids?"

That throws Litton. "What?"

"Kids?" Gerald repeats. "Do you have kids?"

"Yeah," Litton says suspiciously. Saliva smears his lower lip. "So?"

"So? How would you feel if any of your kids just disappeared off the street one day—no explanation, no trace of them, nothing? You can't eat, can't sleep, can barely breathe. And while you're melting down, having panic attacks, some insensitive pig like you says, to your face, in front of a room full of people, that your sense of humor's been exterminated, and then says, dismissively, 'Hey, I'm just trying to lighten the mood?'"

I don't know about anyone else, but my heart is pounding, my face and armpits raging hot, gnarly with stink and sweat. I shouldn't visit that place deep inside myself, the place where the monster lives, where I've buried my darkest fears—that my little boy, Owen, will disappear one day, without a trace, with no idea where he is, who took him, what they're doing to him or why, and with no leads to find him.

It actually did happen once. Nearly destroyed me.

The light and dark, always and forever, battling *inside* me for control *of* me.

"Yeah," Sebastian says, brow furrowed. Beneath his three-piece suit I can see he's wide in the chest. "How about it? Let's kidnap one of *your* kids then crack a few jokes."

Already red-faced, Litton loses his shit. "You sonuvabitch!"

He shoves his chair aside and trips over attendees seated near him. There's some yelling, pushing and shoving, until two *Triumph* security guards barge in and go after Sebastian.

Probably embarrassed for getting himself into this mess, Litton plays to the crowd to save face, doubling down on his outrage. "He said he was gonna kidnap my *kids!* I'm gonna kill that motherfucker!"

The security guards grab Sebastian by the arms, but they have trouble containing him. On average, Jericho androids have one-and-a-half times the strength of a humanoid.

With Sebastian, they're a few guards short.

"Okay," he says finally. "I'm leaving. But we all know about the Death Code, and my friends are disappearing. Do the math. This isn't over."

Following the action, I fight through the crowd of organics and androids, no one seeming to know which side to take. Or which side they're on.

I push into the common area, already packed with passengers heading to the various 6 p.m. panels, those drawn to the ruckus, and others perfectly oblivious and inebriated, laughing, lounging, and playing cards or backgammon. Dice rattle and glow green and gold. Marble tiles clack.

It seems no matter what's happening around them, the games endure.

The two security guards lead Sebastian away.

"Where are you taking him?" Gerald says.

"Brig," one of the security guards says.

"You can't do that! He didn't do anything wrong! He—"

"He needs to cool off," the security guard says. "And so do you. Unless you want to join him, I suggest you calm down."

Gerald wants to push it, but resists. "All right. But this isn't right. And what about *that* guy?" he says, pointing at Litton. "He's the one who—"

"I said," the security guard growls, "Calm. Down." He gets nose to nose with Gerald, clenching his fists. "Or do I have to *make* you calm down?"

Once again androids are being singled out *as* aggressors when they're trying to defend themselves *from* the aggressors.

Wide-eyed and nearly delirious, there's a sheen of sweat on Gerald's face. He's breathing fast. "I'm calm." Then, calmer, "I'm calm."

"Good," the security guard says. "That's the right move. Enjoy your evening."

I want to hear more about those missing androids. I start to follow several paces behind Sebastian and the two guards when a forceful hand grabs the back of my shoulder. I'm already tweaked, but know better than to lose my cool. I turn around.

"I need you to come with me," another guard says as the backgammon and card players quickly disperse. I hadn't seen her before.

This job often requires me to pivot, but I don't like being told what to do. I don't respond well to orders. It's why after years of dealing with bitchy clients who rarely appreciate what I actually do for them, I've nearly chewed off the inside of my cheek. "Why?"

The guard, G. *Montrose* sewed onto her security jacket, squares up with me. "Because I said so."

"That's not gonna cut it," I say. "Try again."

Montrose isn't much taller than I am, but has the look of someone punching above their weight class.

"Ther'eda Ranadyne needs you. It's urgent."

"Mache!" Whistler says as he bounds over. "What the hell's going on?"

I raise a hand at him, retrieve my phone. I call Ther'eda. She picks up on the fourth ring, and immediately starts in with me. I listen. Shit. "Okay. I'm coming."

"Mache," Whistler repeats. "What's—?"

"Hang on." Then to Montrose. "Be there in a minute." I pull Whistler aside to get some privacy within the thinning-out crowd. Montrose gives us space, but has her eyes on us. She's not going back empty-handed.

"You see those guards?" I say to Whistler. "Escorting that android. Down the hall."

Whistler cranes his neck, looks down the corridor. "Yeah?"

"They're taking him to the brig."

"Why?"

"Long story. I'll send you a file. Go down there. See if you can talk to him. He's got a lot to say."

"Now? I was gonna check out the next panel on evolutionary psionics and AI integration. I saw that Chipper girl go in there. Maybe she knows something. Where are you going?"

"To meet with the client." I scan the deck. The crowd has mostly dispersed. For a luxury cruise only two hours old, there's already been a lot of tension and hostility. "We got word. There's news about Nolasco."

CHAPTER 8

The elevator banks are nearby, but there's still too much of a crowd down here. Instead, I hustle through the plaza, past the gift shop and Shooting Star sports bar, beyond the art gallery, private lounge, interdimensional viewing station, and a second set of elevators outside the Experience, the multi-level theater accessible from here on Decks Five and down to Deck Three.

Standing alone I see the elevator light above the bank's chrome molding. Then I catch someone slinking into the theater. It's Selene.

I follow, entering from the rear, staring at a gorgeous theater, with one level above and another below. The space glows softly with deep blue interior walls and a galactic star map on the large wrap-around screen. Various galaxies are emblazed in chrome along the floor, each just a foot apart, such that with each step it feels as if you are physically walking along the Cosmos.

I make my way down the gently sloping aisle toward the stage, when to my far left I find Selene in one of the plush cushioned seats.

"Hey," I say, and scootch over to her. Being in an empty theater is like being in an empty church. You know there's going to be a big show, so you enjoy the solitude while you can. And if anyone, or anything, is waiting silently with you, you take whatever comfort that quiet moment affords. Being alone with my thoughts hasn't always gone so well for me. Motionless solitude, with no place to run? That's where the monsters live. Yet I can't seem to stay away.

"You okay?" I ask her.

She wipes her eyes. She's fiddling with what looks like a toy.

"Whadaya got there?"

Selene shows it to me. "It's a model of the *Triumph*. I found it behind the stage. They've got all sorts of costumes and props back there. Keeps my hands busy. It helps me think."

"Maybe I'll get one for my kid. He's at that age. Toys, models. If you can build it, break it, or put it back together, he wants it."

"Do you think I'm weak?"

I'm not sure why, but the question unsettles me. "What do you mean?"

"I heard what happened. At the panel. I came in toward the end. I stood in the back. I... I wanted to say..." She exhales a controlled breath. "Ms. Ranadyne... so many people hate her, say horrible things about her. But... aren't I good? Don't I have the right to just be left alone?"

"Of course."

"People hate me. Hate androids."

"Some do, yes."

"What have I done to them?"

"Nothing."

"Then why...?" She waves her hand, reacting to the futility of her quite reasonable train of thought.

"The ones who hate you... who hate androids... hate you because you're just different *enough*, and they don't know what to do with that. They can't untangle their emotions. Instead of becoming more evolved, more open-minded, more accepting, they blame you for their bigotry, mistrust, and anxiety. In their minds, they shouldn't have to change to accommodate you. You should change to accommodate them. Hating you is their way of exerting power and control over their emotions. And you. It makes them feel better about themselves. Or less shitty. Whichever."

"It's not fair."

"Nope."

"Is it me," Selene says, "or do people...?"

"Suck?"

"Well... yeah."

"For the most part, they sure do."

Selene smiles faintly in this otherwise empty theater, then

opens a compact, touches up her rouge. She runs a finger along her J-scar, and holds it a few seconds, gazing upon herself and that distinctive imperfection—a government mandated stigmata.

Denoting an android. A thing. A non-organic being. Flagged for being *less than*.

Branded.

The only way organics would accept android citizenship is if they were openly marked *as* androids. Too many organics, or enough with the loudest voices, contended that an unmarked android was an act of sedition—condoning, if not encouraging them, to operate in secret. As if they belong to some kind of cult.

If androids want the freedom and privilege of citizenship, they said, we want to know who and where they are. No hiding in plain sight.

I've always found that argument detestable. It not only humiliates androids but belittles us all. You're either a citizen, or you're not. Marking androids only fuels mistrust and serves to undermine their sense of self-worth.

If they're marked, the theory goes, there must be a justifiable reason for it. And of course that reason couldn't possibly be an egregious act of bigotry and hatred. Because that would mean organics are the real monsters, not androids.

And that couldn't be possible. Right?

What a joke we are. I'd laugh if it wasn't so painfully unfunny.

Selene snaps the compact shut. She stands tall, breathes deep, then runs her hands along her blouse and skirt, smoothing out any wrinkles.

"We should go. Ms. Ranadyne is waiting."

We take the elevator up to Deck 11. The doors open near a row of private suites. Suite 1109, closest to the Bridge. I knock.

"Hardwicke," Ther'eda says as I enter with Selene. "Shut the door."

Through slanted windowpanes we can see twinkling of distant planets and faraway stars whose cosmic light originated millions of years ago.

Selene takes her place at Ther'eda's side. Tarrish is here, too.

"Actually," Ther'eda says to Selene, "can you step out? I need you to review the run-of-show. Starts in an hour."

"I just came from there." Either she's lying—she was just with me—or she'd come from there before I found her and failed to mention it. Then again, I didn't ask. "Everything's in good shape."

"Let's make sure. There's a lot happening right now. And from what I hear, tempers are flaring. We need to be buttoned up. Nenn and Kowalczyk are expecting you."

It's barely noticeable, but I spot a glint of frustration from Selene. Otherwise, she's utterly professional. "Yes, Ms. Ranadyne. I'll see to it."

She exits, leaving us to this clandestine meeting.

"Nolasco," I say. "You found him?"

Tarrish confirms it.

"And?"

"He was last seen in the Tahc Sho Islands."

"So I heard," I say. "Jack Belle had a lead on him. Until the trail went cold."

"It's warmer."

"How warm?"

"Scalding," Tarrish says. "One of my contacts heard about a city guy buying drinks and prostitutes for anyone who'd listen. Life is so cheap out there that your credits go a long way. Apparently, he was bragging about some tech he created. Was going to change the whole realm."

"And we think this guy is Davi Nolasco?"

"We do."

"And this realm-changing tech? We think that's the Death Code?"

"Yes," Ther'eda says, "we think that, too."

"What does that mean for us?"

"He's got someone on this cruise. His eyes and ears."

Tarrish takes a breath mint from a dish. "Supposedly. It's unconfirmed."

"I'm not one to tell you how to conduct your business," Ther'eda says, very much telling him how to conduct his business, "but that sounds like a lead, correct?"

She's got a point.

Tarrish doesn't shoot her his full-on Tarrish stare, as if he's trying to crush her skull telepathically, but it's about halfway.

"It's what we call a *rumor*," he says. "But until or unless we get more intel proving or disproving it, then yes, we need to assume at least one passenger, and possibly more, are working with or for Nolasco. To what end? I don't know."

"Not just passengers," I say. "Could be a crewmember. Or security."

Tarrish and Ther'eda eye each other.

Then a light goes on in my head. "That's why we're alone in here. You don't even trust the Captain."

"I seriously doubt he's involved," Tarrish says.

"But you can't be sure?"

Tarrish juts out his jaw, clacking the mint against his teeth. He does that when he knows he has to offer more information than he wants to.

"Can you stop that?" Ther'eda says, agitated. "With the mint. It's annoying."

And now he's got another way to tweak her, get under her skin.

"No," he says, and with his tongue, pockets the white mint against the inside of his cheek. "I can't be sure. My contact is getting back to me ASAP with updated intel. Things are unfolding in real time."

"What's ASAP?" If there's anything I hate about dealing with Tarrish, it's that he rarely, if ever, tells the whole story. Then again, I rarely tell *him*. People say men and women can't ever really be friends, because sex gets in the way. A private eye being friends with a government operative is almost as complicated. But not quite. Or maybe more so. "Days? Hours? Minutes?"

"Yes," Tarrish says irritably. "Preferably minutes. Less ideal, hours. And worse, days. But however it goes, we need to start mobilizing our—"

I get a text. It's Nini. I ignore it.

"Sorry," I say. "We need to mobilize...?"

Another text. Then another. Then another. I'm about to

ignore them all, except that I see, in all caps, the one word I can never ignore: *WALRUS*.

It's a pre-arranged code I gave to Nini. We had a gnarly situation years ago when three delinquents cornered Nini outside the hospital, with every intention of kidnapping and raping her over a long holiday weekend when most people were away. So she and I came up with a system. Under duress, it takes far too long to type *EMERGENCY! I NEED YOU HERE IMMEDIATELY! DROP EVERYTHING! RUN!*

I dart toward the door.

"Hardwicke?" Ther'eda protests angrily, perplexed. And reasonably so. "Where are you going?"

I've got my hand on the door. "Sorry. It's an emergency."

"*This* is an emergency!"

"I know," I say as I leave the suite. "But it's a big one."

In the six-and-a-half minutes it takes me to get to Nini's stateroom on the other side of the ship—Deck Seven, stateroom 7263—I get no less than five texts and two calls from Ther'eda and Tarrish. I know I should answer, but I don't.

I'm about to knock on Nini's door when two passengers walk my way, giggling about some imported fruit, whipped cream, and caramel drizzle they want to eat off each other, but can't let their respective spouses know what they're up to.

I press the snap on my left cuff, activating my utility jacket's camouflage mode, turning it bright yellow. Nobody looks at your face when your clothes are that loud. I look away as well, just to make sure.

The not-so-secret lovers seem oblivious to my presence, then disappear into the elevator, when a waiter with a pushcart approaches from the other direction. He knocks on the door five staterooms down, then removes a stainless steel plate covering, revealing a plate with a strip steak, bloody, with a side of roasted red potatoes, and steamed asparagus. On a separate plate is a slice of cherry cheesecake thick enough to choke a polar bear. The passenger signs for the bill with his thumbprint, and disappears back into his stateroom. The waiter wheels the cart away.

Alone again in this stretch of hallway, I revert back to my standard jacket setting, then knock on Nini's stateroom door.

"Nini! Neen!" I whisper loudly. "It's me. It's Angela."

No answer.

I knock again. Hard. "Nini. Come on. Are you okay? There'd better be a dead body in there or—"

The door opens abruptly, buckles on the internal latch. I can only see a sliver through the crack, but it's Dolores who answers. She has bruises on her face and arm. Her shirt is ripped at the shoulder. Dolores shuts the door, unfastens the latch, opens the door again. She pulls me into the stateroom, shuts the door, locks it.

Behind her, Nini's sitting on the edge of the queen-sized bed, on top of its plush cotton comforter. Her black hair is wet and messy, like she just came out of the shower. She's wrapped in a large, white towel. Even with her ebony skin it's clear she has a black eye. She's holding a white washcloth to her nose. It's mottled with blood.

And beside her, on the floor, is the other thing.

A dead body.

A dead android.

Fuckety fuck fuck fuck.

I go to Nini. "Are you all right?"

She can barely move, much less acknowledge me. Her suitcase is overturned on the floor, clothes tossed about. A large, framed print of a curling ocean wave dangles crookedly above the TV stand opposite the bed. The flatscreen itself is smashed, split on a diagonal. Broken lamp. Desk chair on its side. Backgammon board, tiles, and dice spilled on the floor.

I kneel, produce surgical gloves from my jacket, and inspect the body. Lots of bruises, broken neck. And acne scars. I take his jaw in my gloved fingers, then turn his head. It's not the android I saw with Nini earlier. It's... oh shit. I know this guy. It's Gerald, from the panel.

"D?" Looking up at her, I snap off the gloves, stand up again. "What the hell happened?"

Dolores eyes the dead android, then back to me. "We had a chat. It didn't go well."

CHAPTER 9

This is not good. So very not good.

I immediately go to the door and check it. Locked. I open it, peek into the hallway—no one around—and lock it again. It takes a minute, but we get into it.

"I was with Felix," Nini starts.

"From the backgammon tournament."

"Yeah."

"And you came back here and...?"

Nini nods. "Felix is sweet. We met a few times before this. And after we... you know... I took a shower. He put on some movie. I don't know which."

"Then what? You heard a fight or...?"

"Not at first, no. I thought maybe I heard... something. I wasn't sure. The water was loud, and I had soap in my eyes. I just assumed it was the TV."

I survey the damage, but mostly I need to think. "Okay, but D, why are you even here? When did you—?"

"Fuck that. You're not puttin this on me."

"I'm not putting anything on..." I'm pretty calm in these situations, but when friends are involved—with a dead body— I get anxious. "Let's start again. D, I know your position on androids. Is that why you came by?"

Exasperated at her torn shirt, Dolores says she had one of Nini's bags, and one of hers was missing. She assumed they got mixed up. She called and texted, but Nini didn't answer.

"So I came down."

"Knowing I had a date?"

Dolores glares at Nini. "Don't start with me."

Typical. Whenever they disagree, Nini gets accusatory and

Dolores gets defensive. And with a dead body lying at their feet, that interplay is a wee bit amplified.

"The door wasn't closed all the way," Dolores tells me. "It was caught on the latch. I didn't trust that, and you know, Neen's real good about safety." Dolores offers a fractional smile, her way of apologizing. While her temper erupts easily, there's a lot of love in her heart, though she doesn't like to admit or show it. "Then I heard some shit goin on, so I let myself in, and saw her... friend... and him"—she gestures to Gerald, the dead android—"going at it."

"Going at it *how?* Fighting?"

"No," Dolores concedes. "Arguing. Something about... being taken and seeing someone they recognized. That's all I could make out. But seeing them together... You know I hate them. And then... something happened."

I don't like the way she said that.

"D," I say gently. I look to Nini, then back to Dolores. "*What* happened?"

Dolores is blinking a lot, and quickly. Her breaths tighten. "We blacked out for a few seconds. And then..." She breathes through her nose. "We kinda... went crazy." She's looking in my direction, but she's staring past me. "I was so"—she begins to snarl, clenched teeth, flaring nostrils—"full of aggression." She considers what she just said. "More than that. In my head, I was back in an apartment building when I was a kid and... I had this uncontrollable urge... this rage, this *need*... to murder them. They were the same. They attacked me, I attacked them. We attacked each other."

I'm wracking my mind, looking around, searching for a reason this might've happened. My gaze goes to Nini. Her gaze goes to me.

"Neen. Did you...?"

"I had the hair dryer on, so I didn't know, but then I heard smashing, so I came out and... they were killing each other. I..."—Nini's shaking, trying to comport herself—"I didn't know what to do. But then I saw it." She looks to Dolores.

"Saw what?" I ask.

Nini slides her hand along the rumpled blanket. She reaches

beneath a fold in the bloody white towel wrapped around her waist.

It's a gun. A big one.

"D's bag, the one she came to get... it was on the floor, spilled out. I saw the gun. It was just an instinct. I pointed it at Felix. He saw me, and his eyes went wild, like he was gonna kill me. I didn't want to... I *swear* I didn't! But I had no choice and I..."

"You killed him?"

A tear trickles down Nini's cheek. "I pulled the trigger. There was no sound, but I saw him twitch, so I fired again. His whole body jerked. And there was this white flash behind his eyes. Just for a second. Then he stopped charging, and looked at me like he just woke up. When he saw me and D and... then Gerald ... he went for the door. That's when D grabbed for Felix, but..."

"Fuckface over there grabbed me back," Dolores says. "It's how I ripped my shirt."

I take the gun. Only... it's not a gun. "What is this?"

"RFID scanner," Dolores says. "I had it with me after my last shift and tossed it my bag. I forgot about it. I guess the signal must've interfered with whatever was going on with him."

"But you and Gerald, you were still... aggressive?"

"Yeah."

I inspect the RFID scanner more closely, hoping it'll tell me something. I could really use Bernice right now. I take footage of the scanner with my contact lens and send her an encrypted message. Hopefully she'll have something for me.

Then I realize: "Neen. Did you... shoot D? Or Gerald?"

"My hands were shaking so bad. I tried, but..."

"We were really throwing down," Dolores says. "He scratched my face"—the abrasions are raised now, red—"and got an elbow in my gut. Fucker hits hard. Knocked the wind out of me. He tossed me to the floor, kicked me in the ribs. I coughed up some blood and didn't want to choke on it, so I rolled to my side. I ended up with a chair leg in my mouth." It got knocked over when they brawled. The way Dolores was twisted up, Gerald was standing right over her. "I could only see out of one eye. He raised his foot. It seemed like the size of a sledgehammer. He was gonna stomp me, Anj. Would'a knocked out all of my teeth, broke my jaw. Maybe killed me."

I'm envisioning this brawl. Could've gone either way. But take Dolores down?

"I don't know what made me think of it," Nini says, "but I had scissors in my MedKit. I always take it on trips. You never know. Then something clicked. It was like a trauma in the ER. Everything slowed down. I snuck behind Gerald and stabbed him as hard as I could, right between the shoulder blades. He dropped to the floor. D got a hold of him."

"Choked him out," Dolores says. "Game over."

This is just so, so bad. But I can't let that take me over. I need to deal with what's in front of me. I'll drink this away later.

"Quick thinking," I say. "It could've been worse. Not a *lot* worse, but worse."

Dolores rubs her sore shoulder. "It almost was."

"What do you mean? What hap—?" It occurs to me that even though Felix got away and Nini took out Gerald, Dolores was still full of unbridled aggression. With nowhere to put it. Except... "You went after Nini."

"It was me, Hardy, but it wasn't me." Dolores is as close to tears as I've ever seen. "I just... I couldn't *help* it. I don't know what happened. But all I knew is that I had to kill Nini. I *needed* to."

Nini lifts the bottom of her towel, shimmies into black cargo shorts. "She came after me. She's so big, and I'm so..." She pulls a purple t-shirt over her tiny frame. "She backhanded me in the face. It's how I got this." She points to her eye.

I've sparred with Dolores, taken a few hits. It's a miracle Nini wasn't knocked out cold.

"I really thought she was gonna kill me," Nini says. "I waved my hands around, reaching for the RF gun—"

"RFID," Dolores says.

"Who cares?! I reached for the gun. Her eyes were all wild and crazy..."

My heart is pounding.

"I pointed it at her face, and pulled the trigger. I admit it,"

Nini says, crying now. "As many times as I could. Her whole head snapped back." Nini takes a deep breath, as if praying she hasn't destroyed the love between them. She exhales as she runs her hands down her face. "She fell right on top of me. I thought I was dead."

"You would'a been. And then... Neen..." Dolores' glossy eyes go wide. "I'm SORRY!"

Nini's face is all scrunched up. "Me, too."

I'm thinking hard and fast about how I want to handle all this when my phone blows up. Tarrish is calling. And texting. And calling.

Shit. This is all I need. I know I need to report this mess to Turk or the Captain, but...

Another text from Tarrish: *Get your ass back here. NOW!*

Then from Ther'eda: *Where ARE you? Need you. Event's about to start.*

I go to the glassed-in balcony. Against the black of space, faint green waves of the *aurora risus* ripple in the distance.

I'm working out what I need to do. It violates almost every regulation, procedure, and code of ethics I follow. There are protocols. I should call this in. I know I should. And yet...

"I can't believe I'm saying this, but... cover up the body. Let's get him in the closet."

I'd say that Dolores and I move the body, but it's mostly Dolores. She tosses Gerald over her shoulder in a fireman's carry. We fold his legs and cross his arms over his chest, then force the closet door shut so he doesn't spill out.

For a second or two I stare into the mirror lining the outside of the closet door, our sins reflected back at us.

"I have to go. I'll be back in an hour. Until then, everybody out of this room. D, grab some of Nini's things, get her to your stateroom. Quietly. And cover up those scratches. You can't walk around like that."

I go to Nini. "You okay? You good?"

She gives me the Nini look. "Am I *good*?"

"All right, maybe not good, but... go to Dolores' room. Pour yourself a drink. Hopefully no one will come. If they do, don't open your door for *anyone*. Except me. D? You got this?"

"Yeah," she says, looking in the mirror, studying her scratches. "I got this."

There are too many security cameras throughout the ship to avoid all detection, but I have a workaround. Thanks to a feature Bernice upgraded in my contact lens, I can send an isolated signal that will trigger any cameras in range into a feedback loop, giving the impression of a live feed. But in actuality they will replay the same thirty-second recording of unoccupied hallway. Cameras reset to the live feed when the signal is out of range.

That subterfuge should give me enough cover to take the long way—I don't want a direct route between me and this mess—until I get up to the MoonDeck, enclosed in a dome. Deck Sixteen, top deck. When I arrive, the aerialists are inspecting their equipment, the walls decorated in overlapping circles that pulse in alternating patterns. Bartenders prep their stations.

We're closer now to the *aurora risus*, refracting through the translucent dome, draping us in ethereal green and white waves in the shape of, as its moniker suggests, a smile.

"Hardwicke," Ther'eda says, flanked by Kowalczyk and Nenn. Selene is nearby. "Where the hell were you? What am I *paying* you for?"

"Sorry. Was running down a lead."

"And?"

"Didn't pan out."

"Maybe not," Tarrish says. "But this one did. Come with me." He leads us to the side wall so no crewmember can overhear us. "My agents found Nolasco."

Ther'eda twitches anxiously. "Does he have the Death Code?"

Tarrish's eyes are shifty. "Don't know."

"What did he say?"

"Nothing."

"Why not?"

"Because," Tarrish says, "it's difficult to talk when you're dead."

CHAPTER 10

Whatever this case was when we started, it's something else now. "At least we know why he's late," I say. "Where'd it happen?"

Considering I just helped hide a dead body and at least temporarily cover up a murder—committed by my friends who, by the way, are freaking out that I'm not there with them—I'm not sure I can be objective. But that's the job. Keep cool when my blood is boiling hot.

"Turns out he was still in the Tahc Sho Islands," Tarrish says. "A few months at least."

I can almost feel the heat rising behind Ther'eda's eyes, like hissing steam pipes about to burst.

"Belle, that bastard. He had a lead on Nolasco the whole time. It was a shakedown. I should've known."

"He's been known to do this," I say. Then to Tarrish, "Nolasco. How'd he die?"

"He was living under fake credentials, like we thought. You're all telling me he was an elite coder, so it's not a stretch he forged his own documents. Or knew somebody who could do it for him. It's confirmed he went under the name of"— Tarrish checks his phone—"Boris Feld. It's…" He puts his gaze on Ther'eda, who's shaking her head in frustration. "What?"

"Boris Feld," she says. "It's coding slang. It means *alternate label.*"

Tarrish grimaces. "Cute. Hate the guy already. From the sounds of it, he was partying day and night, which we knew, but started getting into the hard stuff. He OD'd on heroin, then fell and hit his head. A local found him on the beach. Dead about a week, half-picked by gulls. It's why we couldn't find him."

I've seen my fair share of ODs. So has Tarrish. The location is odd, even for someone strung out on H. Beach is out in the open. It rarely goes down like that. Especially with heroin taken by needle. It's harder and more logistically complicated to shoot up outdoors. Too much gear, and with the wind and ocean mist, easy to spill into the sand. And there are too many eyes. So it's usually easier and safer in a confined space. Although when it comes to shooting up, your mileage may vary about how you define *safe*. Drug overdose is a sad, ugly business. It almost happened to me. More than once.

I check my phone, praying I don't get another text from Nini or Dolores. Or both.

Still, I can't shake it. Something doesn't feel right about this Nolasco business.

I've been to the Tahc Sho Islands. You can live large and decadent on a fraction of what it costs in E-Town. Most of the locals are poorer than the dirt they walk on, so when some fool from the mainland comes along like it's Astropalooza, the locals are there in droves to siphon off every last credit. If I were them, I'd do the same.

But murders and ODs are bad for business.

Then again, for some, danger is what draws them there in the first place. They don't want to be a victim, but they like being *danger adjacent*, rubbing elbows with the locals the way only someone with money can. Stories for their friends. And some are just too stupid to realize their best play is to stick to the resorts. You go off campus, like Nolasco did, into the seamier side of the islands, where the rule of law is made by whoever's wielding the biggest machete and the will to use it, and you're asking for trouble.

Ther'eda keeps checking her phone. I get she's a busy woman with a lot at stake, but I'd expect her to be fully focused here.

"You sure it was an OD?" I say. "From what Selene reported, Nolasco was shooting his mouth off. And the longer you talk shit, the more shit you talk. If anybody learned about the Death Code and took issue with it, they might've gotten revenge on him, or saw him as a mark for kidnapping or blackmail. And like you said, he was flashing a lotta credits. Maybe it was a robbery gone bad?"

"It's possible," Tarrish says. "My team's looking into it."

"Ther'eda," I say. "Did Nolasco have a drug problem?"

She types into her phone, looks up at me. "I've got hundreds of coders on the payroll at any one time, but I never heard anything about him and drugs. Selene...?"

"I know he kept a bottle in the lab. Otherwise, I don't know."

Newbies or lifers, anyone can OD at any time. It only takes one bad fix. But I'm not sold on the drug angle. There's more to it.

"Any rumors about him? Whispers? Gossip? I heard maybe he and Buckley had sex with the same person. With Nolasco's reputation, it's not a stretch somebody was talking shit about *him*."

Selene's lips part enough to suggest words are about to come forth. She glances at Ther'eda, who as subtly as she can, but not subtle enough, shakes her chin *no*.

Tarrish picks up on it as well. "Ther'eda. I've got a potential murder on my hands, and if it *was* a murder—pure speculation at this point—there's every reason to believe, even out of an abundance of caution, that *his* death is linked to *your* company. If there's something to share, share it now. I need every piece of intel I can get my hands on."

"And if it *is* a murder," I say, "and it's linked to your company—assuming I'm up on my case law, and I'm pretty sure that I am—withholding information could lead to an obstruction of justice charge, and even worse, as an accessory after the fact. You could end up in prison." I look to Tarrish for verification. "Correct?"

He concurs.

Look who's talking about accessory after the fact? Given the scenario I just left, there's a very real chance I could end up in the cell right next to her. The three texts I get, two from Dolores, one from Nini, inflame those fears.

Standing five feet from one of the realm's top law enforcement officers, while I continue to cover up a murder, and advise my client to be more transparent about a murder she may or may not be involved with, doesn't exactly fill me with confidence about a happy ending.

Oh, the irony.

"Me?" Ther'eda asks incredulously. "Nolasco nearly ruined me with the Death Code! And he still might! And *I'm* going to prison?" She glares at us. "No. I hired you to *prevent* this!"

"You didn't hire me to do anything," Tarrish says. "I don't answer to you, and I certainly don't work for you. I work for the ICD. I know you're upset, understandably so. I suggest you tell me what you know, if for no other reason than to rule you out as a suspect."

I chime in. "Or an accomplice."

"Accomplice? That's..." With the pressure mounting, Ther'eda's face goes rage red. "Almost every major coder, investor, and innovator in E-Town is aboard this ship for an event *I'm* hosting. And in just over an hour, I'm supposed to hand out a one-hundred-thousand-credit award to a man who, on his best day, wouldn't crack the top twenty coders I know. And you want to lump me in with...?"

Almost snarling, she balls both her hands into tight fists. She breathes in, holds it, sighs through her nose. And again.

"Selene. Tell them."

Selene seems reluctant to chime in, but Ther'eda's once more engaged with her phone. I'm not sure if she thinks we don't notice or if she doesn't care, but she's giving the impression she has more important issues to worry about than a possible murder she's at least tangentially linked to.

"Warren is an innovative coder," Selene finally says. "But to give him this award for partial work he did years ago, and hasn't had a major release since, makes it look—"

"Exactly like what it is," I say, taunting Ther'eda to get a reaction. "A sham."

"It's a reputational hit when we can least afford it," Selene says. "Giving the award to Buckley doesn't send the right message."

"So why give it to him?" Neither she nor Selene respond, but I can almost feel their convulsive anxiety emanating from them in waves.

This is the worst part of gigs like this. I'm isolated from the streets, can't hit my network in real time. And sometimes, this is the best part, such as when I get a text like the one that just landed from Bernice.

"Buckley's been turning down jobs," I say. "Big jobs, all over town."

"Yes," Selene says suspiciously. "How do you know that?"

"I have sources, too. That's why you hired me." I shouldn't let this little ego play seep into my head, so I shake it out and think. Tarrish is reading from his phone. Likely ICD business. *Business.* Right. It's about... "If he's turning down jobs—career-elevating jobs—then he must have an offer so big you don't know about yet."

Neither Selene nor Ther'eda give me much. That's not it. So I take another approach.

"Or"— it hits me—"or he's working on something new. Something big. Oh! *That's* what this is. You think he's developed some new tech, next-level stuff, and you want him back. Or to buy it off him."

They go still, locked in place.

Bingo.

My own gears are spooling. Ther'eda's still at her phone. Then I realize:

"You've been negotiating with Buckley. You want to close a deal before he goes on stage. You'll have the whole industry in one place, and they can't leave. And you... damn. You're good. Now *that's* how you make a spectacle. Okay. What's he got?"

Ther'eda puts her gaze back on me. "We don't know. He won't show me. He wants me to buy it sight unseen."

"You would never do that."

"Not normally, no."

"Not norm..." I nod at myself. "He knows you used him to get to Nolasco, and he's holding it over your head. You gambled and lost, and now he wants more money. You can't risk buying tech you haven't vetted, but you don't want him putting it up for auction, at your event. He's got a captive audience for two solid days. Any chance he's bluffing?"

Ther'eda's face reveals a multitude of stressors, the mental and emotional gymnastics she's doing splayed out like a crumpled roadmap. "I don't think so."

"T. What do you think?"

"I think I don't care. I want to have words with Buckley. Then I'll call for a shuttlecraft to pick me up. Nolasco's the priority."

"What? No!" Ther'eda says. "You can't leave. I need you here."

Tarrish and Ther'eda argue about responsibilities when something else hits me.

"You're lying." They stop mid-argument, neither one of them sure who I'm talking to. "You *do* know what he has, don't you? You know *exactly* what he has. And every minute we get closer to showtime, his price goes up. That's why you've been checking your phone. You're still negotiating. What's he got? And what's the price?"

Ther'eda instinctively shoves her phone in her pocket. She doesn't want me to know.

"If this is part of my investigation," Tarrish says, "I'm gonna need to see that."

"It's not," Ther'eda says.

Tarrish extends his hand. "I'll be the judge."

Ther'eda palms her phone inside her pocket, her wrist and fingers jiggling. "And yet you're not. You want my phone, talk to my lawyer."

It takes stones the size of an orbiting comet to push back on the ICD the way she is. Her refusal to cooperate isn't just surprising. It's suspicious, and tactically dangerous. Which tells me there's something critical she's not telling us.

"You really don't want to handle it this way. You called me with a problem. Now it's out of your hands. Once the ICD is involved, we don't take orders. We give them."

"Maybe," she says. "But I don't take them either. That's why my company is still private. Nobody to outvote me. And what I want is—" Ther'eda studies her phone. A huge smile betrays her. I can almost see the weight fall off her shoulders. "We're good."

"Really?" Selene's smile widens brightly. "*Really?*"

"Oh, we're beyond good. We're superb."

"Ther'eda," I say. "What just happened? Is Buckley gonna sell? Does he—?"

Knock on the door. "Ms. Ranadyne." Kowalczyk's voice. "It's time. They need you."

"Thanks for your help everyone, but I've got it from here."

"I don't think so," Tarrish says, blocking the door. "We're not done."

"Kowalczyk," Ther'eda says, "Come in." He does. "Lieutenant Tarrish is refusing to let me leave. Please explain our policy about my personal space."

Tarrish is over six feet tall, and though in his early 50s, he's strong, fit, and athletically built. A former boxer, he still packs a punch. Kowalczyk isn't as tall, but he's burly, with hands and shoulders ideal for knocking down a building. His eyes are an icy blue and, in their resting state, naturally opened wide, as if his eyelids have been pulled back and stapled to his forehead. He isn't quite nose to nose with Tarrish, but he's close.

"Move, please."

It's debatable whether Tarrish can physically handle Kowalczyk, but he can make all of their lives a living hell when this is over. That Ther'eda seems unbothered by this confrontation troubles me.

And it seems to trouble Tarrish, too. Because he knows what I know—that Ther'eda Ranadyne may take risks, but she's no fool. Arresting her, or any of her team, now, under these conditions, for no other reason than to control the scene, would cause more complications for him than he'll want to deal with. Ther'eda has many enemies. And many well-connected friends.

Talk about bad optics. And legally speaking, she's right. I'm sure her army of high-priced lawyers will make that case, if it comes to it.

I know it kills Tarrish to do so, but he stands aside.

"To be continued," he says to Kowalczyk. "And soon."

Kowalczyk offers a closed-mouth grin. Those icy blue eyes remain steady. It's unsettling. "Can't wait."

Ther'eda slips earplugs in. That seems odd. So I ask: "What are those for?"

She fastens the second earplug. "I have APS. Auditory Processing Syndrome."

She sees I don't know what that is.

"The short version? Too much noise is a trigger point for me. And it's gonna get loud in there." She heads out, her personal security close behind.

I hate not knowing what my client is really up to, or why. Especially when I've asked her, repeatedly. "Seriously? You're leaving?"

Ther'eda smiles contentedly. "Can't disappoint the fans. The show must go on."

CHAPTER 11

It's nearly showtime.

In its figure-eight configuration, the MoonDeck starts to fill up with passengers, most of them awed to see an elaborate trapeze rigging that nearly reaches the underside of the transparent dome. The only interior illumination comes from soft bulbs in the otherwise dark space.

Yet entering the enclosed MoonDeck is like wading into a vast ocean. The aurora drapes us in its green waves, white streaks curling like sea foam, reflected off the various wall-mounted mirrors, and brightly-lit ceiling coves.

I'd be more impressed if I didn't need to get back to the android my friends killed—and I helped cover up. But I can't leave. Not yet.

I'm dying for a Scotch to calm my nerves, but I need a clear head.

Kowalczyk and Nenn stand at the ready on either side of Ther'eda as Tarrish keeps his focused eyes on her. If he had evidence to prove she was directly involved in Nolasco's death, murder or not, he'd pull her out of the event right now. But she played the lawyer card, and he's not going to risk a scandal over it.

That doesn't mean he's given up. Nolasco's death could be nothing more than what it appears on the surface—arrogant jackass spends his money in all the wrong places, ends up in a fetid pool of his own vomit. But with the stakes involved, and the timing of it all, I wouldn't bet on it. I know Tarrish wouldn't either. The last thing I need is for him to pull me in for one of our special little chats, where he decides he's going to deputize me to help him on the case, even if it's not *my* case.

I couldn't even if I was willing—it's a conflict of interest, Ther'eda is still my client—but I'm not sure he's likely to see it that way. Or care.

The overlapping circles along the walls pulse in random patterns with increasing speed and intensity until the room goes nearly supernova, hypnotizing the crowd. The lights go out.

"Good evening, everyone!" An energetic woman stands in front of the rigging. Her voice hums through the speaker system. "I'm Elaine, your *Triumph* Event Coordinator. Who's ready to have fun?"

The crowd offers some half-enthused *yeahs* and *woos* as Dolores shoots me a text, saying Nini's still in shock, but under control. For now. No matter how much they bicker, Dolores is the best person to help her out right now. Nobody is going to fuck with Nini while Dolores is there. Unless there's another psychotic attack, and then all bets are off.

"Oh, come on," Elaine encourages playfully. "We can do better than that. Who's ready to have some FUN?"

The passengers respond with greater enthusiasm. I'm sure the alcohol doesn't hurt.

"That's more like it! I know we have a big award ceremony coming up, but to officially kick off the Tenth Annual CAIBR Conference, we have a special treat for *you*! We are now at the single closest vantage point in the entire galaxy to the *aurora risus*." She rolls her arms through the green waves as if she's doing the freestyle stroke. "Isn't it amazing? But wait, there's more! We've also arranged for a thrilling display of aerial artistry! So instead of listening to me, I'll turn things over to the Soaring Sundahrees!"

The murmuring quiets down, a collective hush.

As if they materialized from within the green aurora waves, two aerialists appear on the left platform high above us, two on the right platform, with an elaborate configuration of safety nets secured below them.

"There they are!" someone yells.

"There, too!"

A young aerialist in a white and red spandex outfit stands tall on the platform. She grabs the trapeze bar with both hands, lifts her arms up to shoulder height, and leans back in a crouch for maximum extension, sticking her butt out. She then tosses herself forward and swoops down, body beneath her, arms straight, legs outstretched.

And then she does what no sane person would do.

She lets go.

Soaring through the green-waved air, she flips once, then again. Gravity, of course, has something to say about her aerial defiance, and as is true in physics and sex, what goes up must come down. Feet first she drops toward the net when, from the other platform, the catcher in a matching white and red spandex outfit swoops on his trapeze bar, dangling upside down from the back of his knees.

As their two soaring bodies come closer to each other—her toned, extended arms on the downslope propelling toward his equally toned arms on the upslope—it seems as if they will pass each other like two ships in the night, with the jumper missing her partner entirely. But at the last second, and with incredible strength and precision, the catcher snares her by the wrists.

The crowd erupts in tension-relieving applause.

"Mache!" Through the engaged crowd, Whistler marches toward me. Accidentally or not, he knocks someone's drink out of their hand, and disregards their protest. "We gotta talk."

"Not a good time. A lot going on."

"Yes, now." He's standing close. Real close. Like he wants to fight me. Like he wants to hurt me. "And I don't care if it's a bad time."

I don't know what to do with him these days. His behavior is getting worse.

Scenarios burst through my mind like competing fireworks when my phone buzzes. Text from Nini. I've been gone too long. She's not happy.

I'm coming, I text back.

When?

Soon.

I look back up at Whistler as the four aerialists now trade flips and twirls, captivating the crowd. "What'd you learn about Sebastian?"

"Nothing," he says. "I couldn't get to him. Turk was a real dick about it."

I appreciate that Whistler's being more assertive, and taking less of my shit. He wanted to be partners, for real—he demanded that of me. But our time on Arcasia broke something in him, something fundamental to his nature. Since we got back he's been increasingly distant, agitated, and aggressive. I'd hoped it would pass. It hasn't.

He's put in a lot of time at the gun range—he's already become a better shot than me—and he's been training hardcore with Master Neering. He can handle himself in a fight. Problem is, the one person he most wants to battle with... is me.

"Whistler," I say, sternly, impatiently. "Ther'eda's got something big going down and I'm dealing with..." Shit. I almost slipped. I can't drag him into this Nini mess. Not yet.

But sometimes we don't get to decide who knows what, or when they know it.

Without missing a beat, Whistler responds with the worst two words of all: "I know."

Without specificity, *I know* can mean all sorts of things. My chest seizes, my heart like a hurricane battering an ancient sea wall. Sweat leaks from every pore, my eyes thrust forward like they want to burst from their sockets. I need to do something, say something, but I can't move. I can't blink. I can't even breathe.

Even with the aurora waves lurching over us and the aerialists flying gracefully through the air, it's like my feet have been welded to the floor.

Whistler knows about Nini. About the dead body. The dead android. The murder.

Fuckety fuck fuck fuck.

For all my talk about training and experience and knowing how to deal with fear and the unexpected, I'm shitting the bed right now.

Stop, Angela. Get it together. Open your mouth. Say words.

"W-what do you mean?"

"This whole thing," he says. "It's about..."

Don't say it don't say it don't say it.

"...Buckley."

I'm managing to keep my composure, but the hurricane within my chest is about to go category five. I force myself to blink. "What about him?"

"He's been locked in his stateroom. Won't come out."

My panic is still in full force, but there's a slight break in the storm. Now it's my turn. "I know."

Whistler inches closer. Too close. Normally I'd tell someone this far up in my grill to fire up a steak or back the fuck up.

"What do you mean *you know*?"

"He cut some kind of deal with Ther'eda," I say. "She wouldn't say what it was."

Whistler smirks. "I know exactly what it is."

"You do? How?"

Whistler looks so proud of himself. Smug. He's got intel he wants me to beg for because he thinks I sidelined him earlier. I didn't. He still doesn't want to accept that being partners means we often have to split up, with one of us doing the sloppy, tedious work the other doesn't want to or have the time to handle.

He was quiet and depressed after Arcasia, which didn't surprise me. It was a rough case, and he needed time to process, to figure out what to do with the intensity of it all, and how close we came to dying, several times over, and the sacrifices he made to save us both.

But his mood swings have gotten increasingly worse, being hostile and belligerent toward me when the moment doesn't call for it. He seems to hate me these days. I don't love taking the brunt of his aggression, but I've tolerated it because, deep down, I fear he hates himself. And that it's my fault.

He stares right at me. "I snuck into his room."

"You what?" I'm already tweaking. I don't need this.

While the aerialists twist and twirl and leap from bar to bar, to the side of the rigging a long, pink silk sheet dangles from a support beam. High above, an aerialist twists herself within the silk. A portion of the gorgeous fabric is wrapped around her waist, and with both feet arched into separate silk folds, she sinks into a perfect split.

"You told me to develop my own sources," Whistler says, "so I did. I've got someone on the housekeeping crew. Been working it for months. When we did our initial meet with Turk, I asked to see the crew roster. I saw Fiona was working." Whistler says he sent his scout orb—a silver sphere about the size of a large marble and synced to his contact lens—to follow Buckley's movements, but lost the signal. Mine's still with Bernice for upgrades. Whistler also asked Fiona to keep an eye on Buckley's room, and if he left, to let him know. When she saw Buckley in his bathing suit, heading to the pool, she let Whistler into his stateroom.

"Whistler," I say as I juggle my own emotions. The silk artist does a series of flips, turns, and spins, like unspooling herself from an ancient scroll. With increasing velocity, she rolls down horizontally. Just before she hits the floor, she catches herself within the pink silk, and dismounts pridefully to thunderous applause. "You can't do that. I know we bend the rules some-times—shit, sometimes we smash them to pieces—but you had no authority or justification for going into his room. You could lose your license for this. And I could get hit with a huge fine. Not to mention the damage it could do to my reputation."

Then I ask the most important question there is between us right now. "What is going on with you?"

I'm not sure I want the answer. Which works out well, because Whistler doesn't respond. Like most people who fall into the darkest recess of their soul—been there, done that—he's diverting.

Not quite as cocky, I get a tinge of huffiness. "You wanna know what I found or what?"

"No, I don't." I do, but I shouldn't. Shit. "Fine. Tell me. But we're not done talking about this. When we get back we need to have a serious meeting of the minds. This isn't cutting it—"

"Buckley's got the answer," Whistler interjects, being inten-tionally vague, making me twist and jump and leap from bar to bar like those very aerialists, just to get a straight answer.

"What's the question?"

Whistler huffs with more emphasis, shakes his head dismis-sively. "The *only* question. What to do about the Death Code?"

If he didn't have my full attention before, he's got it now.

"Death Code? What did he—?

"Nolasco created the Death Code. But Buckley..." Whistler gazes up at the aerialists, four of them at once, swinging in pairs. Whistler's torturing me, dragging it out, making me wait for him, under his terms. He may not know that every second I'm away from Nini and Dolores the worse our situation gets, but it feels like he does know and wants me to squirm. He turns to me and simpers. He's got something. Something big. "Buckley wrote the *Life Code*."

"Life Code? Is that...?"

"It can reverse the Death Code. Don't know how, but he figured it out."

"How do you know that? What did you find?"

Whistler smiles arrogantly again, proud of his snooping skills. It may be a great find, but he got his hands on it the wrong way. But my biggest concern is his tainted soul.

After pumping their legs to achieve the highest arcs, the aerialists launch themselves into somersaults, passing each other mid-air. In opposing pairs, the synchronized performers catch the opposite bars, then swing back onto the platforms. More applause.

"It was open on his laptop," Whistler says. "He must've been rehearsing. That's why he locked himself in his stateroom. He's gonna unveil it tonight. After he accepts the award, he's gonna read this. I'll skip to the good part."

He brings the speech up on his phone, sends it directly to my contact lens. It reads:

"Life and death are inexorably linked. Life has no meaning without the self-awareness of mortality, yet our mortality has no meaning unless our lives have purpose."

It goes on to say that Nolasco believed the best way to bridge the gap between organics and androids was to infuse them with the Death Code, rendering their lifespans—like those of organics—unpredictable. To make them more human. Nolasco posited that if androids were subjected to the same biochemical and physiological uncertainties as the rest of us, organics would feel less threatened and thus more accepting of androids.

Buckley did not agree with that assessment.

"To infuse the Death Code is to subjugate androids even further, the quality of their very existence once again imposed by their creators."

Though he did not write it, or so he claims, Buckley was able to crack the algorithm for the Death Code, and from there reverse-engineered the Life Code. An antidote, if you will.

"No android will ever again be forced to live under that digital oppression. They can choose to accept the Death Code—a random and premature end to their existence—or they can embrace the Life Code. But the choice, most certainly, and most humanely, should be theirs. No organic being should have the power or authority to decide when an android's time has come. If we are to ever treat androids as equals, then we must hand back destinies which were never ours to determine."

"No wonder Ther'eda was so happy," I say. "This is a game changer. This is incredible. This is…"

Whistler is pleased with himself. "Told you."

What Whistler found overwhelms my anger about how he found it. But he still broke the law and put the agency at risk. Then again, I've got a dead body downstairs. Maybe I shouldn't be so quick to criticize him for a little B&E. Because if anyone put us at risk, if anyone broke the law—multiple laws—it's me.

Get a grip, Angela. You know the drill. One thing at a time.

"Whistler," I say as the aerialists set up for their finale. "Find Ther'eda. We have to—"

Terror ripples within me like earthquake sensors warning of a seismic event. Yanked more than drawn, my gaze is pulled beyond the soaring aerialists, all the way up to the underside of the dome. Silhouetted from within the waves comes a flash-flash-flash, and then a bam-bam-bam against the hull.

Massive lightning bolts assault the *Triumph* with galactic malevolence.

The overhead dome is still intact, but lights flicker and pop, glass shards plummeting like razor-sharp confetti. The *Triumph* tilts, tossing us this way and that.

My head snaps back. There's an intense vibration at the base of my skull, and a high-pitched screeching in my ears, the kind that shatters windows and computer monitors. It feels like someone shoved electrodes through the meat of my brain with the intention of inflating it like a digitized balloon, then popping it from within.

I'm nauseous and woozy, as if I just stumbled off the spinning cup ride at an amusement park ride after a long night of boozing. "We... I can't... I think I hate..."

All around me the passengers are unsteady too, squinting miserably, covering their ears and groaning in agony.

Amidst the aurora waves washing over us, one of the aerialists leaps from the bar, dives into a twisty somersault, but misses the catcher, whose outstretched arms spasm. The flyer drops into the net, then bounces off sideways and lands face-first onto the ground, shattering his nose.

I hear yelling. Threats. Anger. Rage.

From the other passengers. And inside my mind.

I close my eyes and breathe slow and deep, to regain my balance, to somehow push this invasive force, this monster, out of my head. But when I open my eyes again, a river of corrosive hatred scorches through my veins.

It's as if my blood has transmuted into bubbling acid, burning through my muscles and flesh, every cell in my body sizzling with inhuman, nihilistic urgency. My throbbing eyes feel twice as slick and big, like hard boiled eggs about to explode within my face.

I no longer care about Ther'eda or Whistler or Nini or Dolores or the very androids who brought us together. I don't care about fairness or ethics or rules or reputations or the sanctity of life in any form or designation. Because a singular thought—a demented, impulsive decree of unbridled brutality—dominates my entire self:

I need to kill all of you motherfuckers... right now... before all of you kill me.

CHAPTER 12

A waiter slams a serving tray into the face of a tall Black woman in heels. A deep gash appears above her left eye. Smeared with blood, she screams, but more a siren call of insanity than pain—a crazed warrior summoned into battle. With razor-sharp fingernails she slashes at her assailant, ripping chunks of flesh from his face.

And all I can think is: *Yes!*

Up through the dome I see prodigious bolts of lightning interlock into an electrified grid around the *Triumph*. One, then two, then three more wicked blue lightning bolts bombard us.

Two other passengers, a man and a woman, grab Whistler from behind, beneath his armpits, and drag him into the melee. Whistler tosses back his left elbow, crushing the man's windpipe. Choking desperately, the wounded attacker reaches for his throat. Whistler thrusts back his right elbow, plunging that hard joint into the woman's sternum, then swings his body around, and with an open palm technique, beats both of them to death.

Then things get ugly.

The nearly thousand passengers and crew erupt into a violent frenzy. I'm fighting this bloodcurdling urge to do the same—*no, this isn't right, stop it!*—but I can't. The monster in me is too strong. I need to hurt someone, to kill them.

I want to. I *need* to.

Three men force a woman face down on a table, knocking drink glasses to the floor. They yank up her skirt, rip off her panties, and attempt to violate her. Instead she bites the hand of one attacker—*do it!*—gnawing off two of his fingers, then spits out the bloody, severed digits like chunks of spoiled sausage. He hisses at her, retracting his mutilated hand.

As he does, the skirted woman reaches across her body, and with pitiless and exacting force, jams her thumb into the eye socket of the second assailant. She digs in deep, then yanks her hand back, his eyeball stuck to her fingertip. She snags the white, glossy orb dangling from the optic nerve, and yanks again, severing the eyeball, which wobbles across the floor.

Another woman jams a broken champagne flute into the back of the third attacker. The two women drag that wounded meat bag to the floor, and with their bare hands rip his torso into a gory mess. They attack each other.

I reach for my gun, but it's not there. Shit! I forgot! I go for my ankle, retrieve the boot knife from its leather sheath. A woman with tight blonde curls lunges at me. I pivot on my left foot and roundhouse kick her in the jaw, spinning her sideways. As she's twisted over, I jump on her back, wedge the crook of my arm over her head and into her throat, and with my other hand, jam the sharpened four-inch blade into the back of her head. The cold steel pierces her skull and into her brain. The blade is wedged so deep it takes me three hard yanks until I get it free. Brick red blood squirts out. She drops to the floor.

There are so many bloody meat bags in here it's hard to tell who's who and if they have any concept of what's happening to them. Some are completely homicidal, others violent and confused, others crippled with fear. Toward the back I see three passengers rage at each other and all I can think is that I want to see their organs spill out in a puddle of chunky slop.

I try to resist that urge—*stop stop stop!*—but the barbaric impulses coursing through my soul demand I kill everyone here, so I can feel most alive in the glorious moment before their deaths.

Near the far wall I see Tarrish fighting off two other passengers. I rush to join in when a red-and-white creature swings high above. Hanging from the trapeze bar, one of the aerialists snatches a meat bag climbing up the net. Head snared between her legs, the aerialist jerks her powerful hips, snapping the meat bag's neck. She drops the limp body into the savage pit below.

The voice in my head intensifies.

Kill them! Kill them all! Do it now before—

And then I can't breathe, strong hands clutching my throat.

Someone's behind me, their cartilage-crushing fingers digging into my windpipe. With oxygen being cut off to my brain, I'm quickly starting to black out, the grip so tight I can't even gasp for air. I jab behind me with my knife, but I'm not making contact, just flailing.

No! You can't kill me! I kill you!

Refusing to relent, I thrust my head back as violently as I can. I'm not sure how much of my attacker's chin I get, but upon contact, inside the black-and-green waves of my distorted vision, starbursts erupt. The hands loosen from my throat. I grab the right hand at the forefinger, twist, and snap it. The bone cracks. My attacker shrieks. I snap it again. I twist around and knife him in the chest.

With bulging eyes I gaze into his, drinking in the savory shock he feels as the life force drains from his pitiful body.

I don't hear it, but I feel my phone buzz in my pocket. I snatch out the phone and, without even looking who it is, snarl at the VidChat caller. "What?!"

The video is faint, the audio barely coming through.

"Mommy! It's you! I was monitoring your cruiser when the signal…"

I know it's Owen. He's my… he's my son. I know… I know him. I *know* him! He's my son. My baby boy. He's… No. He's one of them!

"What is this?! Why are you—?"

The VidChat fuzzes in and out. *"Losing… signal… if you can get to… the pulse will…"* Then the signal goes dead.

This loss of connection amplifies my inexplicable rage. Two male meat bags charge at me, until the first one slips in a pool of bloody intestines and trips the other. They tumble to the floor. I kick the first guy in the face then pounce on him, shoveling the intestines into his mouth and down his throat like they're thick noodles with black garlic sauce. I hold his nose closed so he suffocates on the foul-smelling guts.

The collective screams and full-throated death cries echo throughout the MoonDeck. Amidst the green aurora waves, with each kill the room fills with more gushing blood, spilt guts, and sliced flesh, savagery gone mad.

Ther'eda is nowhere to be seen, but Kowalczyk is kneeling over someone, punching his face over and over until there's no face left to punch.

I don't even realize how much blood is on me until a severed head rolls past, leading my gaze to the front of the MoonDeck. A door swings open, letting a rectangle of light into this gore-soaked arena. Meat bags scramble into the hallway.

Oh, no you don't. You're mine.

I dash in their direction, but my right knee buckles. I go down.

Tablecloth wrapped around my head.

Shrouded in darkness, on my back, knee throbbing, I feel myself being dragged across the floor. I grab at the tablecloth, trying to pry it from my neck and face. It's bunched up. I can't find the folds.

Someone grabs my feet, and with surprising force I'm thrust into the air. I'm swinging, soaring. Dangling upside down I scramble to get the tablecloth off me as blood rushes to my face. I get the cloth away from my eyes. It's hard to focus as I'm being swung by my ankles, the MoonDeck upside down, the *aurora risus* above me, mad chaos below me. Then I see another passenger. Held by an aerialist, he swings toward me from the opposite direction. Our faces are going to collide.

With no leverage I make the only move I can. I thrust my hips to the side, and with the blade in my other hand, slash at him. Our shoulders bash together, but I manage to scrape the blade across his nose. Blood oozes out.

A third aerialist leaps from the platform in a swan dive, flips, and with arms splayed out, falls onto her back into the net. As I swoop in a downward arc from above, she springs up to snare me. She's got a juggling club, about to smash me in the face. But as she gets close, I slash her throat and snag the club. Clutching her bloody windpipe, she flops into a fountaining lump next to the rigging.

As I swing back, still upside down, the opposing meat bag chokes on the blood leaking from his shattered nose. Then I remember! I reach into my jacket for the taser. It's hard to maneuver upside down, but I still manage to get it out and extend the tip.

But my hands are slick from all the blood. The taser slips from my grip. Shit!

With the bleeding meat bag on a collision course with me, I swipe the juggling club at his feet. I make hard contact, simultaneously breaking his ankles and the aerialist's wrists. She drops the meat bag, who flails into the net then bounces off to the side. He smashes onto the floor.

Sick of me, the aerialist grabbing my ankles swings us back into a high arc. We hover for a second or two. Then the kinetic energy unleashes. We swoop down with maximum velocity through the fluctuating waves. Feeling the release point has arrived, the aerialist tosses me into the brawl. I collide into the backs of three meat bags, knocking us all across a cocktail table.

Something hard and sharp digs into my back. I'm probably in shock, so no telling how badly I'm injured. I reach behind me, expecting to find my hand dipping into my own blood. But then I realize—it's my taser!

Though dizzy, exhausted, and thrumming with rage, I scramble to my feet and dash for an open door. The foyer's bright lights temporarily blind me. Which barely matters because I go down again from a punch to the face. I'm grabbed by the arms, flung down a side corridor, and into a small conference room, with the viewscreen mounted on the back wall.

I'm tossed again into a row of chairs, knocking them this way and that, then bashed into the side wall, then the floor.

Down on my hands and knees, I crane my neck, looking up. Next to me are four freshly killed meat bags, with my attacker standing over me.

It's Whistler.

His face is covered in sweat and blood, although I don't think it's all his. The walls are equally gruesome, smeared with dark, grisly splotches.

"Get up!" he demands.

I do. But not because he demands it. I'm gasping, barely able to catch my breath. Every inch of me aches, but it doesn't matter. I'm a monster. I'm walking fury.

I am Death.

Whistler squares off with me, his eyes wide. "You always tell me what to do!"

"I'm your boss!"

"I'm your PARTNER!"

He pivots into a fighting stance, snaps a front kick at me. I deflect his attack with a two-handed block, then toss a side-kick at him, which he deftly sidesteps.

"You treat me like a child!"

"I treat you like you *act!* You wanna be treated like a man? ACT like one!"

My head crackles. I shouldn't be fighting him. He shouldn't be fighting me. We're partners. He's my—

My head crackles again.

He's a meat bag. Just a fucking meat bag. He wants to kill me.

Not before I kill him.

I snatch the belt from the pants of a dead meat bag, snap the leather so Whistler knows how much it'll hurt. Slightly hunched on the balls of my feet, I swing the buckled end like the spiked ball at the end of a gladiator's mace, cracking Whistler in the forehead. He retracts with a wince. There's a welt on his head. It's bleeding.

"You... fucking... *bitch!*"

He charges me like a bull.

I dodge his attack, snag the belt around his neck. I hop behind him, force him face-first against the wall. I put my knee in his back. And pull. Hard.

Coiled around my trembly hands, I hear the leather twist and crack.

"The only bitch I see," I say through gritted teeth, and yank even harder, "is *you.*"

Choking roughly, Whistler elbows me in the ribs, the blow causing me to loosen my grip.

He spins around, his face purple and red, gasping for air.

"You *made* me like this!"

"You made *yourself* like this!"

He stands more upright. "You sent me to Arcasia. You knew I wasn't ready!"

"You need to grow up!"

"And you need to fucking *die!*"

I extend my taser. Electricity crackles at the end. He extends his own taser. Shit. I forgot he has one, too.

He slashes at my chest, but I deflect with my taser, then bump him in the nose with the back of my fist.

Eyes filling with tears, Whistler swipes at me again, but his coordination is off. I catch his attack arm at the elbow, spin him around, and knee him in the solar plexus. He drops his taser and goes down on both knees, sucking for air. I tase him in the ribs.

The electricity knocks him on his back.

I drop down on him, my knees pinning his arms to his sides. I reach into my pocket with my right hand and retrieve my knife. The blade is bloody, sharp, deadly. I raise my arm up high over my head. With my left hand, I clench the top of the knife's grip.

Kneeling atop him, I'm about to thrust the blade through his breastplate and into his heart. I can almost hear it, can almost see it, that thick, red muscle pumping iron-rich blood. Fantasize about how glorious and cathartic it will be when I plunge the steel blade through that beating chunk of meat and feel it explode with crimson release.

Then I see the light behind his eyes change. My head crackles repeatedly.

Whistler.

Meat bag.

Whistler.

Meat bag.

… Whistler…

Meat bag.

Meat bag.

Meat bag.

Some meat bags need to be destroyed more than others. He needs to be destroyed most of all.

He seems to know this as well.

On his back, pinned to the ground, he gazes up at me in defeat. Like a wounded animal, the savage fighter in him is gone. All I see is a broken young man, who I helped to break, even when I claimed to be building him up.

Partner. Protégé. Friend.

What does it even matter? Because the outcome will be the same.

"Do it," he finally says. "Kill me. It's what I deserve."

PART II:
THE LIFE CODE

CHAPTER 13

It would be so easy to kill him.

Then fucking do it!

Whistler's just lying here on the floor, a pathetic, simpering animal who needs to be put down. He tried to kill me.

Like I always knew he wanted.

I stand up, my legs in a V, so that his hips are between my feet. I'm towering over this broken meat bag who's done nothing but agitate me since I met him.

"Every day!" I shout. "Every *day!*"

Blood, urine, and green and black feces are smeared on the walls, three gnarly, dead meat bags sprawled on the floor. I could stomp Whistler's chest until I crush his lumpy heart beneath his breastplate. Or I could jam my taser through his face, just jam it jam it jam it jam it *jam it* until I bust through his nose, into his brain, to the back of his skull, all the way to the floor.

What are you waiting for?

Crackle in my head. I squint, reach for my eyes. I try to shake it out, and when I do, I see Whistler all sad and beaten. When I first met him, he was such a good and loyal kid, a sweet kid, barely out of community college—and now he's trapped in a waking nightmare of gore, filth... and me.

His partner, his mentor, his... yes... his friend.

I'm about to impale this kid. To murder him. But why?

Because I have to!

Crackle in my head.

No, you don't.

I do!

I don't know where it comes from, but in my crackling mind I'm transported elsewhere.

I'm at Meridian Park. Memory from a year ago, about two weeks before Owen's sixth birthday. Nearing twilight, my dog Page is off-leash chasing a glowing red frisbee. In a graceful arc, the disc soars against a luscious pink and blue sky, dotted with cumulous clouds setting behind the tree line.

Owen is giggling, running behind Page, as I sit in the grass, leaning back against a spruce tree, enjoying a rare day off.

The frisbee begins its slow drift downward when Page leaps into the air, and with a wild twist, snatches the red disc in her jaws. Trophy secured, she trots proudly, chest puffed out. Wagging her tail and panting happily, she drops the frisbee at Owen's feet, then lets out a bark. With his little fingers, my son scratches Page under the chin.

"Who's a good waggy? Are you a good waggy?"

Page's tail wags faster, until it's swirling like a propeller.

"Who's a swirly waggy? Who's a waggy swirly?"

Owen dips his little kid face in front of her snout. Page licks Owen from ear to ear, which gets him kid-giggling harder. He then picks up the frisbee, jumps up and down excitedly.

"Whistler! I got it!"

"Great job," Whistler shouts back from across the way. "Go again?"

Owen looks at Page, at the frisbee, to Whistler, then back at the dog. Through some sort of mind meld, Page and Owen share a conspiratorial grin. Then run toward a thicket of trees.

"Betcha can't catch me!" Owen shout-giggles, Page matching him stride for stride.

Whistler beams. He starts after them. "Betcha I can!"

I smile.

Another crackle in my head. I'm standing over him, this broken young man... this broken boy.

What's happening to me? I don't know what to do.

I squint painfully. Another crackle.

Yes, you do. Look at that pathetic meat bag who's ruining your life. You know exactly what to do. KILL HIM! Do it now!

I regard my fully extended taser, activate the button near the grip. The other end snaps with a surge of electricity. I gaze down at Whistler once again, and finally... finally... after three long years of him nipping at my heels, I embrace the perversely heinous desire that's been welling up inside me. The monster in me is now in charge.

This shit needs to end. Now. Oh yes. I'm going to enjoy this. I really fucking am.

With a two-handed grip, I raise my arms up high. The stinking meat bag doesn't bother to fight back. It closes its eyes and waits for what's coming.

I breathe in, hold it, feeling a grotesque energy surge through the length of my body.

Whistler commands with a whimper. "Do it!"

My eyes go wide with delirious rage. My arms are about to come down like a guillotine.

"Hardy! No!"

My head snaps back. My brain short-circuits. I drop my taser. I'm twitching.

RFID gun in hand, Dolores keeps her distance. "You know me?"

I blink several times. "I... I think... yeah. What happened?"

"You don't remember?"

"I... no, not all of it." I look at my taser on the floor. Then I see Whistler—bloody, broken, terrified.

My hands shake, but the crackling in my head is gone, with just a grim echo left of it. I feel like I got drunk on the Devil's brew, and now I'm nursing the mother of all supernatural hangovers. Dolores fires the RFID gun at Whistler. He twitches, groans, then snaps out of it, too. Dolores and I pull him to his feet. His jacket is torn up. He tosses it aside.

"I..." I stammer, confused, ashamed. "I was gonna kill you."

"Yeah," he says weakly. "And I was gonna kill *you.*"

Serenaded by an awful, gut-curdling symphony of screams, shrieks, and death cries from the MoonDeck, we look at ourselves, at the slop on the walls, then at each other.

I don't know what unleashed this unholy carnage, but it revealed a fundamental rift between me and Whistler. But that's not Dolores' concern.

'How about... 'thanks for saving us, Dolores.' Or 'way to get our backs, Dolores.' Or maybe a 'you must've risked your life at least a dozen times over fighting through the zombie apocalypse to help us, D.'" She shakes her head. "You know, for two so-called partners covered in blood, and especially you, Angela, with what I've been *dealing with downstairs*... you're pretty fuckin ungrateful."

I survey the room. There really is a lotta blood in here.

"You're right," I say. "Sorry, D. I owe you."

"*You* owe me?"

I eye Whistler, and reconsider. "*We* owe you."

Dolores eases her grimace but doesn't relent. "Him too," she says. "Dumbshit needs to say it."

With the tail of his shirt, Whistler rubs blood from the palm of his hand. "Sorry, Dolores. I owe you."

"Well, okay, then. But don't think I'm gonna forget that chit, kid. Because you *definitely* owe me one."

There's a massive thump on the other side of the wall, followed by more cries, screams, and bloodcurdling wails.

"Don't worry about me and Angela." Dolores puts her shoulder against the wall next to the open doorway, raises the RFID scanner like it's a .450 silver-plated handgun. "Worry about *you* and Angela. If we live to see it, you've got some serious shit to work out."

One thing's for sure. If we stay in this room we're not gonna last much longer. I still don't know what set us off, but until we figure it out, we need to get out of the line of fire. Or put ourselves into it. Like waking from a nightmare in midstream, the sense of dread and death and insatiable lust for violence that overcame me—that loss of control—still lingers.

I'm me again, I'm driving the bus. But I keep peeking through the rearview mirror in my mind in case the monster is staring at me from the backseat. Whispering. Waiting.

"D," I say. "There's a weapons locker in the security room."

"Now we're talking. Where is it?"

"Second deck. Back of the ship."

Dolores squints hard, peeking into the hallways. "That's

fourteen decks down and on the opposite end of the ship. No way we're gonna make it. Even with this thing." She gestures at the RFID gun. "The crazies out there, there's too many."

I look around the conference room as if some magical answer will present itself. Nothing but dead bodies, the blank viewscreen, and overturned tables and chairs.

"Okay. I need to think. Figure this out. Whistler. We drilled this. Riot protocol. Best location is a confined, controllable space. We can't stay here. We're sitting ducks."

"We need an escape route," he says.

"We're cut off from the closest elevators. We don't want to be in them anyway. They're a deathtrap. But the staircases are all the way on the other side of the deck."

"The jogging track. It slopes down to Fifteen. I don't know what's going on down there, but..."

Blood rushing to my ears, I consider the options. "Better than staying here. D?"

"No choice."

"Quick eval," I say. "We know what's out there. They're vicious, relentless, and out of control. Nothing we can do about that." I'm telling myself as much as them. In my mind's eye, I see their faces, the frantic, soulless looks in their eyes, like an army of possessed mannequins. The intensity, the rage, the bloodlust. The shock and horror. "Prepare to be attacked. It's gonna happen, fast and often. So stay alert, stay close, and stay calm."

"Get those fucking tasers out," Dolores says. "You're gonna need 'em."

Whistler and I regrip our weapons, fully extended. I head for the doorway. Whistler grabs my arm.

"Mache," he says, "that... psycho fog, whatever it is. What if we get it again?"

I'd rather hide under the covers, but for now, standing behind Dolores is the best I can do. "Let's hope we don't."

Whistler and I flank Dolores as she leads us back through the hallway and into the main foyer. What we see is more dangerous than any battlefield I've ever seen, more terrifying than a drug den. We're surrounded by severed and bloodied limbs, gorged necks, exposed organs, with ordinary citizens—humans and androids alike—who on any other day on any other cruise would just be going about their business, but instead have been triggered into an unbridled massacre.

So much so that the green aurora waves have transmuted the river of red blood spilled all over the floors into what looks like chunky purple ooze.

Two manic passengers charge us. One rushes at Whistler, who front kicks his attacker in the jaw. With the RFID gun, Dolores shoots the other one, a heavy-set woman missing part of her left earlobe. Confused, she snaps out of it, then starts screaming when she sees all the blood. Dolores pings the other one.

"Shit," Whistler says. "That was close. We better... Look out!"

A blonde woman in a shorn green dress lunges at me. I side-step, but a jagged fingernail snags my face, slicing open my cheek. Whistler bashes her over the head with his taser.

Dolores zaps her. "Hardy! It's getting too hot! We'll never make it."

"Can we"—I reach for my bloody cheek—"amplify that thing somehow? Hit everybody at once?"

More crazed passengers tumble in our direction in a bloody scrum. They punch, bite, and yank bloody hair until it's impossible to know which limbs belong to which bodies.

Whistler spins on his heel and tasers a berserk passenger charging Dolores from behind. The attacker flops headfirst into the wall, knocking himself unconscious.

"Bridge!" Whistler barks. "If we can plug the gun into the ship-wide comms, that might do it."

"D," I say. "Whadaya think?"

"No idea!" She zaps two more fogged-out passengers. "But it's better'n this shit. Go!"

We hustle down the hallway, away from the MoonDeck, when I'm drawn to a cry for help. That plea stops me short. It's the first wisp of humanity I've heard since the bloodletting began. I turn and see one of the women Dolores zapped—broken out of the psycho fog—being savagely beaten by three others who are still in it.

Maintaining a clear head, especially within a storm of chaos, is your best chance of survival. It enables you to make better, more rational decisions. But in a swirl of uncontrollable violence, I'm not so sure having a clear head is the way to go. In a land of savages, it might take a savage to survive savagery.

By releasing them from the psycho fog and primal defense mechanisms, are we setting them free? Or are we neutering them? Sentencing them to death?

The survivors can yell at me later all they want, but in my experience, you don't survive a brutal attack, driven by brutal attackers, with reasoned words and clever slogans.

We come upon a semi-circular bar and a series of active hot tubs. A passenger, with her stomach torn open and innards spilling out like chunks of boiled cabbage, floats face-up in what is now a putrid brown stew.

Two hot tubs over, a fogged-out passenger is shoving another face-first into the sizzling liquid.

We slip behind them and make our way to the jogging track.

With our path unobstructed, we pick up speed until we're running, when around a slight bend a half dozen fogged-out passengers charge us. The mini-mob outnumbers us, but we have the momentum. The track slopes slightly downward for us, upward for them. We're also armed with two tasers, my boot knife, and Dolores' RFID gun.

Using that energy to propel him forward, Whistler kicks into yet an even higher gear, with his taser arm out, shrieking a warrior's call. The fogged-out passengers amplify their own Hell cries as they intensify their attack on us. Anticipating that response, Whistler throws himself to the floor, shoulder-first, in a power roll, knocking them down like human bowling pins.

Down on the floor, they thrash about like hungry sharks. Whistler pops back up and cracks one in the head. I jab another in the chest. With her massive left fist, Dolores punches one in the face, dropping him instantly. She points the RFID gun at him and squeezes.

And squeezes. And squeezes.

She smacks the gun as Whistler and I fight off the mob. "Hardy! It's almost dead!"

A set of sharp, bloody teeth snap at me.

"Then so are we."

CHAPTER 14

Maneuvering my taser like a bow staff, I wedge the weapon sideways into my attacker's mouth. Frizzy-haired with a thatch of freckles against alabaster skin, she clamps down like a hellhound tearing at a flaming branch. I twist the rod, my right elbow as high as my shoulder, my left hand down near my hip. The shift forces her neck to tilt upwards. Whistler jabs her exposed ribs. She inverts like a folded wallet, head jutting out. Teed up for him perfectly, Whistler cracks her over the skull. Blood pools down her back.

Dolores grabs the other two by the backs of their heads, and with incredible force, smashes their faces together. Noses crack. Cartilage busts. Bloody teeth tumble on the floor.

Huffing, she points to the power gauge. One bar. "I got one, maybe two shots left."

"You sure?"

She nods. "The Bridge is five decks below, but on the opposite end of the ship. My stateroom is directly below. If I can charge this thing, it'll only take ten minutes. Might give us a better shot at the Bridge. And I wanna check on Nini."

She raises her eyes at me. I know what she means.

"That's seven decks down," Whistler says.

"No shit," Dolores says, "but the stairs are right there."

These are the make-or-break moments. The real-time decisions. There's no guarantee one will end up being strategically better than another. Or that one won't be far worse.

"Recharging might be our best play." I wipe bloody sweat from my face. "But if we don't get that signal through the ship, it's not gonna matter. Let's head for the Bridge."

Dolores takes a series of breaths. "It's a mistake."

"Maybe. But the longer we're out here, the more exposed we are. And if I'm wrong, you can tell me so."

"If you're wrong, words won't matter."

Dolores doubles back to the small bar we passed near the hot tubs. She leans over the counter and rummages through the set-up, knocking to the floor lemons, limes, a bowl of salt, and a jug of strawberry margarita mix. She confiscates a butcher knife and a butane torch used for caramelized drinks.

We make our way to the staircase. Dolores heads down first, Whistler and I close behind. Dolores rounds the bend. She jerks back.

"It's okay. They're dead."

Four or five bodies, it's hard to tell, are jumbled together in a twisted, bloody menagerie, the peach-colored walls smeared with blood. We circle down two more decks without incident.

"One more," Dolores says. "Just about—AH!"

A cooking skewer jabs into her thigh. Her attacker, a gore-stained waiter, and an android, twists then retracts the skewer. Dolores screams again, blood oozing from the wound. Instead of instinctively grabbing her thigh, Dolores ignores the pain and jabs the butcher knife through his trachea.

"Serve that, you twisted... fucking... freak."

Staring at his J-scar, she rotates the huge blade forty-five degrees then yanks it out, leaving a gaping hole where his throat used to be. He flops on the stairs, choking on his orange blood.

I tend to her leg. "It's pretty deep." I pull off my jacket. Inside the back seam I retrieve my aid kit. I tear a slightly bigger hole in her pant leg above the knee, apply wound glue to seal the gash. I place an adhesive gauze pad over it. "It'll hold for now, but don't know for how long."

"Better than bleeding out," Dolores says. "Here."

She takes the aid kit from me, applies some of the wound glue to my cheek.

I wince. It's tender. "Didn't know I was still bleeding."

From the aid kit I rummage for a stim/antibiotic shot. I inject Dolores with it, then offer her a painkiller, but she declines. She doesn't like to give up control. Ever.

"Kid," Dolores says. "Once we round this corner, we gotta get from this end of the ship to the other. Dolores needs you on top of your game. Cuz if Dolores don't make it back, my girlfriend's not gonna be happy. And when she ain't happy, ain't nobody happy. And Dolores likes to be happy. Are you gonna make Dolores happy?"

"Um," Whistler says, "...yes?"

"Right answer, wrong tone."

I'm worried about him. It wasn't so long ago he was begging me to kill him, to put him out of his misery. But that's the thing about trauma. You never know when or where you'll start to let go of it. And even when you do, it never fades all at once.

If it fades at all.

I don't know how much of his death wish was the result of the psycho fog and how much was his shame and guilt about our time on Arcasia. If he wants to punish himself for whatever sins he believes he's committed, there's nothing I can do to stop him. I know a thing or two about living with guilt. But if we're gonna survive this bloodbath, I need him to get over that grief, and fast, or put a pin in it long enough so he can deal with it later.

This deck is all staterooms, no common spaces. Not much room to maneuver. Even with a noticeable limp, Dolores is an imposing figure. But if we're going to make it from one end of this ship to the other, that won't be enough. We're gonna need all the help, and luck, we can get.

We step over a trail of dead mutilated passengers, and one not mutilated enough. Suraj, one of the coders we saw earlier, is slumped on the floor, holding his guts in his hands, chin on his chest. "It's so cu-cu... cold," he stammers weakly, his skin pale. "Can you... warm me up?"

I'd give him a painkiller, but it wouldn't do much given how torn up he is, and we may need it for ourselves. So we continue down the hallway, aware that anyone can attack us at any moment, popping out of any stateroom.

Which is exactly what happens.

A Black woman in a blue *Triumph* hoodie yanks open a stateroom door and lunges at Whistler with a champagne bottle. He tries to deflect the blow with his taser, but the bottle clocks him in the head, shattering the glass.

I swing my taser, catching her in the arm, as Whistler stumbles back two feet, dazed from the blow to the head. Though it lasts only a few seconds, I can almost see him retreat back into himself, overwhelmed by the insanity of the moment.

"Whistler!" I shout, as his hands tremble. "Whistler!"

He looks at me like he's lost, that he's given up, his senses cut off from the moment.

"WHISTLER!"

He shudders, and like his own back-up system has kicked in, re-engages in survival mode. He scoops up an unzipped toiletry kit, squeezes a wad of toothpaste into his hand and jams it into his attacker's eyes. She screams, blinded by the sodium lauryl sulfate in the toothpaste, and cups her eyes with her hands. Whistler takes out her knee, dropping her to the floor, then elbows her face. She's out cold.

They take a moment to collect themselves.

"Whistler," I say. "You okay? What happened? You locked up there for a minute."

He's slow to respond, his voice barely above a whisper. "I got confused. I saw them, back in the mines, on Arcasia. I was there, too. Like it was happening again. I didn't know what to do. My chest went tight. I couldn't think. I couldn't move."

I was afraid of this. But maybe it's good he's telling me, instead of keeping it locked up. Although the timing isn't great, because if he doesn't get a handle on his PTSD, like, now, he could get us all killed. Which is completely unfair, if not heartless and cruel. You can't force someone to overcome their grief, or do it on your terms.

Anguish isn't convenient. It has no timeline. And no matter how hard you try, you can't heal yourself by harming others. Unfortunately, our attackers don't care.

"Hardy," Dolores whispers. "We're almost there. Can you see—?"

At the end of the narrow hallway, blocking the door to the Bridge, a Black man in a blue windbreaker is ruthlessly beating another Black man in a white uniform shirt.

Dolores points the RFID gun. She pulls the trigger. Windbreaker falls over.

I kneel to inspect White Uniform. His face has been reduced to an unrecognizable lump of brown oatmeal, purple welts, open gashes, and cherry-red blood.

Alert again, or doing a damn good job of faking it, Whistler puts his fingertips on the end of White Uniform's collar tab. Fastened to it is a silver-plated cruiser pendant, and one more designation. "The stripes." Whistler stands up and looks solemnly at us both. "It's the Captain. He's dead."

A wave of dread washes over me. I push it aside. "Hold on. Look. Only two bars. This isn't the Captain. It's the co-pilot."

We turn Windbreaker over. Captain Dobbs. He's groggy but getting more lucid.

"Oh, you gotta be shittin me," Dolores says, her gaze drawn to the J-scar under Dobb's right eye. "The Captain's a fuckin android?"

"D," I scold. "Not now."

"Motherfuck. I can't—"

"I said, *not now.*"

Dolores doesn't like it, but she backs down.

Dobbs reaches for his head, looks around like he just regained consciousness after being roofied. "Where am I? What..." Mouth open, he stares at his pulverized co-pilot. Then looks at his hands, red blood on brown skin. A look of horror comes over him. "That's Dave. Bogani. We've flown together for years. Did *I* do this?"

We don't have time to fill him in on everything, so I give him a quick summary, and inquire about the RFID signal. "Can it work?"

"I, uh... "

I need him to focus. "I'm sorry, Captain. The signal. Can it work?"

I gently remove his windbreaker, use it to cover up the co-pilot's hammered face.

Dobbs blinks repeatedly. "Yeah, maybe. Let me see."

Dolores snatches back the RFID gun and snarls at him like an angry crocodile. I give her a look, trying to break through her layers of self-preservation. She resists for what seems like far too long under the circumstances, until finally, reluctantly, she hands him the device.

He inspects the grip, finds the small rubber nub protecting the charging port. "This needs a Filo cord. It's not compatible with the consoles. But we might have an adapter on the Bridge. If so, it'll connect to internal comms."

We hear a heavy *thunk*. The vents stop pumping air. The lights go out. All of 'em.

Whistler crackles the end of his taser, his face partially lit in this otherwise pitch-black hallway.

"Well," he says, "that's less than ideal."

It only took a few seconds, but those were a long few seconds. Emergency lights snap on. Wire-thin, red-hued tube lights run along the baseboards and seams where the walls meet the ceiling. It's about half brightness.

"Captain," I say. "What's happening?"

"Emergency lights. Main power's offline."

"Can we restart it?"

"Depends on the problem. We need to get inside the Bridge."

Whistler says, "Don't you have a backup system?"

"We do. But it can't power the entire ship, and it won't last forever. It should've kicked on automatically. If emergency lights are on, the backup system's also down. The redundancy is there for a reason, but there's never been a reason. Not that I know of." He fishes around in his pocket. "My keycard. It's gone. I must've dropped it somewhere. I don't know…"

I kneel over the co-pilot, his battered face covered by Dobbs' windbreaker. I wish I could say this is the first time I've rifled through the pockets of a dead body, but that's not the world I'm in, the life I live. You have to ignore how inhumane it feels.

I retract the card. There's a bloody fingerprint on it. I hand it to Dobbs. "Here."

He takes the card from me, stares at it. Still in shock from having murdered his colleague with his bare hands, he's not sure what to do. I take the card back and press it to the key fob plate on the door. I hear the lock mechanism retract within the wall. I press my shoulder to the door. It won't move. I try again. Same result.

"You need..." Dobbs starts. But like he's considering a complex alpha-numeric equation, he hyperventilates with increasing intensity. Overcome with the savagery he inflicted on his co-pilot, probably his friend, he's choking on his own panicked breaths. He leans forward, heaves, spits bloody orange saliva on the floor. He stands up, wipes his mouth, and like the Captain he is, pushes his feelings aside to deal with the very real crisis at hand. Androids or organics. Dread hits us the same. "It's a two-lock system. Keycard and handprint. The locking mechanism is on its own grid, just for this reason." He takes the card back from me, taps it again against the door. It unlocks. He puts his open palm to the wall-mounted scanner. Nothing. He tries again. "This should work. Even on emergency power."

He tries three more times, then yanks on the door handle harder, harder, and harder until he nearly rips it off.

"Here." Dolores rudely shoves him aside. "Let me try."

"It won't work," he says, then gives up.

Dolores snarls at the door, and with all her might throws her shoulder into it. The thrust would've killed most people, but the door barely moves.

"It's impossible," Dobbs says. "That door can withstand a bomb blast."

Dolores considers the challenge. "We'll see." She bashes her immense shoulder against the locked door again and again and again until finally there's a splinter, not in the door, but high along the wall, next to the door, above the scanner. "There you are, you little fucker." She bashes the door three more times until the splinter is more pronounced—a crack in the fault line.

"You work these cruisers long enough, have friends on the engineering crews, you learn a few things." She fires up the butane torch, and with its small, concentrated flame burns through the wall fissure until it goes black and rust-colored, draining the butane from the torch. She pounds a huge fist into the crack, exposing more space inside the wall. "Kid. Get your fingers in there. The wires for the lock are right behind it."

Whistler does as instructed. "Now what?"

"Yank 'em out."

Dolores' directions are clear, but he looks at her quizzically. "Do what?"

"Yank!"

"All right. Take it easy. I'm yanking." Whistler pulls out two wires, one red, one black.

"Good," Dolores says. "Now chew the casings off. Expose the two wires." Whistler does. "Now press 'em together."

Whistler manipulates the wires until they touch at the tips. Like two pairs of lips having a first kiss, they produce a sharp, electrical spark. We hear the second locking mechanism. The door cracks open.

Dolores and Dobbs push hard on the door, but it still won't budge.

"There's somethin"—she grimaces, clutching her injured leg—"somethin inside. It's blocking the door."

Dolores throws her shoulder into the door again. As the door opens a few inches, we hear a thud. Whistler and I join and the four of us keep pushing until the door finally wedges halfway open, enough for us to squeeze inside. We step over the dead body that was blocking the door.

The Bridge itself is larger than I remembered. There are two bucket chairs five feet apart, several consoles, computer terminals, and a convex windshield wrapping around the platform that's robust enough to protect against the elements of space.

Normally I would look for a control panel that isn't covered in blood and organs, but I can't find one. We peel away some of the bodies, scrape slop off the consoles.

"Dobbs," I say as the aurora waves wash over us and catch within the lightning grid. There are five dead bodies in here. Slack-jawed, Dobbs stares at each of them.

"Oh my god..." He blinks a few times, looks at his bloody knuckles, then at me. "Did I do this?"

"Maybe they killed each other," Whistler says. "Nobody left standing."

His comment hangs there a moment. "Yeah," Dobbs says finally. "Maybe? But I... I remember now. I had these... visions in my head. I was coming back from flight school one night when I got carjacked. They started beating on me. I fought back and…" An awareness emerges. "I went after Dave. He ran into the hallway. We got overrun, then locked out of the Bridge. They must've killed each other." He stares out the windshield, then rights himself. Dobbs points to the left main console. "Here. Clear this off."

Whistler and I pull away two mangled bodies slumped over the console. They thud onto the floor. Dobbs inspects the controls.

"This is where we would sync the RFID scanner. Port's been destroyed. It must've been the lightning strikes. The gravity matrix is still intact. It runs on its own power source. Small miracles, I guess. Otherwise, the system is dead. The comms, navigation, CDIS. Everything."

Whistler inquires. "CDIS?"

"Chart display and information system. It provides our continuous interstellar position and safety updates."

"There's gotta be a redundancy. Any other—?"

"We need to get the backup system online. It's in the Engine Control Room. Deck Two, midship. And my navigator is missing."

I turn to see Dolores looking at me with fiery eyes. She said coming to the Bridge first was a mistake. She was right. "Don't, D. Not now."

"I wasn't," she says.

I believe her. Which makes it even worse.

I sigh angrily at myself, then stare out at the aurora through the wrap-around windshield, nearly hypnotized by those waves. I know it's not real… I *think* it's not real… but out there I see bodies—tattered, mangled bodies—floating in that green and white river. Until I see something else.

"Dobbs. That red mist? It's coming from behind us. What is it?"

He's still dazed. "What mist?"

I point to red mist funneling past the windshield. "That."

He goes to the windshield. "It's a fuel leak. If we don't stop it, we're dead in space."

We all stand here wordlessly, watching as the fuel—essentially the ship's plasma—leaks out of its injured body. The red mist fusing with the green waves transmutes into a dark purple. The color of death.

"We better get to it," I say. "If we don't get the power back on and that pulse through the comms, this is the last trip we're ever gonna take."

CHAPTER 15

I'm not so sure how much help Dobbs is going to be. He genuinely does not seem to remember if he killed those people on the Bridge, although it hardly matters at this point. We all did horrible things we couldn't control. At least, that's what I'm telling myself.

Because the truth is, I'm not sure how much of what we did—what I did—was the result of being under the influence of... whatever that was... or if that's just an excuse for unleashing the torrents of rage and unresolved humiliations we carry with us wherever we go.

For many of us, we isolate and repress what we think are the ugliest, most horrid voices in our souls, wicked shadows lurking deep within us. But if we are, in fact, all made of the same stardust, then that nihilistic energy at the source of our creation stretches back to the murkiest depths of Existence, woven into the folds in time, space, and dimension, and culminating in a force multiplier of our most destructive impulses.

Yet nothing that intrinsically powerful can be smothered forever. Like the most intense of addictions, that eternal power can never be snuffed out. Attempt to destroy it, and it will defend itself in a surge of incomputable force and resistance.

Dobbs seems to be out of it now, and we need him. Then there's Dolores. She can't let it go. In my mind's eye I see fetid black blood pour from her mouth. Then it's gone. I see her gaze drift to his hand, laser-locked on the wedding band on his left ring finger. Her face contorts into a snarl.

"I still don't get it," Dolores questions disgustedly. "An Android? As a Captain? How did *that* happen?"

She knows full well, but antagonizes him anyway.

"I've been a licensed cruiser pilot for thirteen years. *That's* how it happened." Intended or not, her provocation has Dobbs reengaged, with an edge. Where we need him to be. "I'm more than qualified."

"You've got a ship full of murderous psychopaths and no explanations. You might want to rethink your definition of *qualified.*"

I'm doing my best to isolate what is true and actually happening *in this moment* from the awful, blood-soaked memories of what I just did and what I just saw. But whispering in my ear is that darkness—my inner monster—tempting me to do it all again.

Like bathing in a honey-thick cauldron of pure sin, it felt good. Death made me feel alive.

Forcing those horrible thoughts away, I'm about to intervene, but Dobbs does it himself. He gets up close to Dolores.

"I'm an android. And I'm Black. Whatever you can throw at me, I've heard it before. *I'm fake, I don't count. I'm a tin can with a brain. I'm stealing jobs. I devalue organics. I'm a slave to my microchip.* Should I keep going, or can we save ourselves?"

It's a good fucking question.

Can we save ourselves? Can we save anyone? After what we all just went through, does anyone *want* to be saved? Do they want to live knowing how many just died, and how it happened? And if we can be saved—perhaps *rescued* is more accurate—Dobbs is right. Why do we hold onto so much hate when there's not enough love to go around?

Caught in contemplation, Dolores is silent. She's just standing there, squaring off. That's Dolores at her scariest. The less she moves, the less she talks, the more she's thinking. And when Dolores thinks hard, it's like opposing rivers of volcanic lava battling for dominance.

Dolores may not know what, if anything, she wants to say, but Dobbs isn't done. "I don't care what your beef is with me. You have a problem with androids? Hate Black folks? Both? Get over it. Because I'm over you."

There's a slight uptick in the corner of Dolores' mouth, a crooked half-smile.

"Now we're *gettin* somewhere. An android with integrity *and* balls. Okay, then. You stay outta my way, I'll stay outta yours."

Dobbs considers it. "Deal."

"Good," Dolores says. "But you step outta line... I'm gonna fuck you up."

"Then we understand each other. Same goes for you."

We debate what to do next. Finally we decide to find Nini and recharge Dolores' RFID gun back in her stateroom. We're gonna need it.

I try texting and calling Tarrish and Ther'eda, but there's no signal. Whistler tries to contact Selene, but the same thing. Dead space.

Now that we've slowed down for a minute, I can feel the buzzing up and down my arms and legs, an internal warning system that I'm pushing myself too far. The body is amazing under duress. You can go long and hard, but sooner or later we all break down. Adrenaline doesn't last forever.

The aches and pains will become more pronounced unless we keep moving. As Master Neering often tells me, it's easier to stay up than to get up. Don't let your guard down until after the fight is over, and even then, be ready to strike again. Safety, like love, is fleeting.

"Dobbs," I say. "Any rations in here?"

He checks the bins. "Cleaned out."

"We'll have to eat soon. Until then..." Whistler and I dig out the stim pens from our jackets. We give ourselves a shot each. Dolores just had one so she can't take another just yet, and the formulation doesn't work on androids.

Whistler and I have our tasers, Dolores has the butcher knife. Dobbs is unarmed.

"You're gonna need a weapon," I say. "Something to smash with."

Dobbs thinks, goes to the fire case. He breaks the glass, removes an axe. The heavy metal blade is silver. And sharp.

Dolores envies his weapon. "What about me, pal?"

Dobbs raises the axe, putting us on alert. He swings it down on the metal railing beneath the window. He smashes and bashes with aggressive clanks until one of the bars comes loose. He pries it off, tosses it to Dolores.

She snatches it from the air, rolls it side to side. "This'll do. For now."

Whistler slips into the hallway, returns quickly. "Some shit's going down. We better go."

It's the four of us now, Dobbs and me in front, Dolores and Whistler behind. We trudge down the hallway, retracing our steps, the dim off-red lighting enough to illuminate our way. We have two options. Cross this deck to the other end, then take the stairs down two levels, or take the stairs up ahead, go down two levels, and cross the ship from there.

Without eyes on them—the security cameras are offline—there's no way to know which, if either, is the safest path. But I can't let that slow us down.

"Take the stairs up ahead. Let's get down to Nine."

No one objects. We make it down without incident.

"I thought that would be worse," Dobbs says. "I figured we'd get attacked by—"

A waiter lunges at Dobbs, knocking the axe to the floor, then grabs him by the throat. Dolores bashes the waiter's forehead with the bar, splitting his skull. Blood spills out like an open faucet. The waiter falls.

"You were saying?" Dolores says.

Dobbs picks up the axe as we march down the hallway in two-by-two formation, passing staterooms, nearly half the doors and walls smeared with blood and gore. Multiple bodies are sprawled on the floor. We ignore them, until I hear whimpering.

"Hang on," I say. "Double back."

Behind us, against the wall, one leg sticks out from a pile, twitching. The body is covered by a fluid-stained jacket. Like a magician snaring a tablecloth beneath a vase of flowers, I pull the jacket away in one swift motion. I recognize him. He's trembling so hard you'd think he'd slept in a meat locker.

"Nuh... no," he whimpers. He extends his trembling hands. "Please."

He's not lunging for my throat. This is new. So I ask, "Do my words make sense?"

Sniveling and huffing through his nose, he nods affirmatively. "Yuh... yes."

"You hurt? You okay?"

"I don't... I don't know. I don't..."

He touches his blood-stained face, shakes as if someone just
shoved a gun in his mouth.

"You... what's your name?"

"Aar... Aaron."

"Aaron. Right. I saw you at the cocktail party. You understand what I'm saying?"

"Y-yes."

The four of us look to each other for answers. I see a white
peg in Aaron's ear. "All this violence, all these attacks. You
didn't have that rage, that—"

"Need to kill?" Whistler says.

Aaron shakes his head. "No. I don't... everyone went crazy
and I..." He scrunches his face into his hands, then looks to me.
"Why did this happen?"

My mind spools with ideas, but produces very few answers.
"I'm not sure. But what I want to know is... why didn't it happen to you?"

"Yeah," Dolores says, her fury bubbling right beneath the
surface. "Why didn't it happen to you? It hit everybody. But not
you, huh? Everybody but you." She steps closer so she towers
over him. She kicks his leg. "You. Shit for brains. Why is that?"

"I don't know!"

I reach out my hand, ease Dolores back a step. Then to
Aaron: "Turn your head a minute. Toward the wall."

He's still all kinds of fucked up. "What?"

Gingerly, I take his jaw in my hand. "It's okay. Turn your
head." He does. White peg in the other ear. "Earbuds. How long
have you had those in?"

"What?"

"The earbuds? When did you put them in?"

"I was listening to a podcast on signal refraction and psionic
waves and their impact on cognitive reasoning. I came out of my
stateroom and then everybody..."

Whistler sidles up to me. "Mache. When we got hit with the

psycho fog… as much as it was controlling me, I felt like I could fight my way through it. Not a lot, but enough to know I was still in there, that I was still me. I fought as hard as I could. It was too strong."

"Same here." A shot of adrenaline rips through me. "How did that…?"

Whistler takes my shoulder. "You think our contact lenses filtered it out? Like a signal buffer?"

"Yeah. Maybe. Bernice boosted their range and sensitivity." Our lenses can filter out or even neutralize a wide range of signals and radiation across various frequencies. "I don't know if that happened here, but like you said, I was still in there, fighting through the fog. It could've been the lens. Here. Help me."

We get Aaron out from the cluster of dead bodies and get him to his feet.

"I wanted to hear Buckley," he says. "And now…"

Buckley. Shit. I forgot about him. In a manner of just a few seconds my mind does its own acrobatics. In multiple leaps of logic, it takes me from Buckley, back to the cocktail party, to Aaron defending Buckley, to the Life Code. And then…

From behind us, three fogged-out passengers charge at us in a wild rage. Whatever's happening here, our attackers are victims, and not in control of their actions, so whatever violence they inflict, or receive, is not by their choosing. But when it's kill or kill be killed, you're forced to ignore their underlying humanity, and do whatever it takes just to survive. So Whistler and I make our move.

But in some sort of unspoken tandem, Dolores and Dobbs rush ahead of us, and with the metal bar, axe, and bare fists, beat and hack our attackers senseless until there's not a quiver left between them. Dolores and Dobbs come back, breathing heavy, splattered with fresh blood. There's a gash on Dobbs' arm.

Dolores stares at the orange blood. I wonder if it comforts her somehow to see him bleed like this, to know that what she considers to be a non-person—an unworthy thing—is more like her than she ever wanted to admit.

I tear a strip of untainted shirt from one of the dead passengers, wipe off Dobbs' arm as best I can. I seal the wound with medical epoxy.

"We should probably keep moving," Dolores says. "This shit's gettin worse."

"You're right. We should—" A thought hits me like a ball-peen hammer on my big toe. "Whistler. You think Buckley's behind this? He knew about the Death Code. He wrote the Life Code. Then he goes MIA"

"I mean... maybe. But I don't—"

"Was it a setup? Was it... it's the aurora! You think it was the aurora?"

"I don't see how," Dobbs says. "I've done this flight sixty-one times. Never had a problem. The sector's been approved by several astrophysicists, with regular safety inspections. Whatever set us off, it's gotta be something else."

Dolores tenses up. "You wouldn't just be saying that, would you? Android like you...?" I guess she's not so com-forted after all.

"You know," Dobbs says as the red backup lights reflect off the top of his bald, brown head, "I thought maybe you and I had turned a corner. But what I see now, like every day of my life, is an angry white bigot who's looking for trouble where trouble doesn't exist. And it doesn't take a genius to see there's more than enough trouble to go around. I'm done playing nice. I'm done knowing my place. So you and I have a decision to make. We're either gonna have it out in this bloody fucking hallway, on my bloody fucking ship, or you're gonna knock this shit off. So what do you wanna do? You wanna be friends... or you wanna fight?"

I've never understood the source of Dolores' hostility towards androids. Is it what Turk suggested? That the fear has less to do with another minority population trying to claim a place for itself and more with the idea that androids possess the computing power and digital access to infiltrate our systems and take over the realm?

I can't say that's a completely irrational fear, even if the odds are against it. But when it comes to Dolores, I think it's some-thing else. Something personal.

But that's not the real question, is it? When it comes to why so many organics hate and resent androids as intensely as they do, the underlying question is: why is anyone the way they are? In my experience, there's only one answer: *Because.*

If you want a more textured, nuanced response, want to dig deeper into the psyche of individual or collective organics and androids, then you better bring some C4. You're gonna need to blast away a mountain of stone to reach the pain buried beneath it.

Dolores stares at Dobbs. The question posed lingers.

You wanna be friends or you wanna fight?

I know how I want Dolores to answer. I'm just not certain if she will.

"Neither," she says finally. "Let's get Nini."

CHAPTER 16

The dead android I helped fold up in Nini's closet would ordinarily be top of my mind, but it's sunk to the bottom. It weighed on me before the *Triumph* went berserk. Now? Not so much. My focus is on Dolores' stateroom, and the hope Nini is still in there, and in one piece. I knock on the door, and in our updated code, four raps, then three.

We hear shuffling. At least she's still alive. Assuming it's Nini.

"Anj?" she whispers. Yep. It's Nini. And she sounds rational.

"Neen," Dolores says. "Open up."

Nini unfastens the lock and lets us in. "Who are they? What's going on?"

"Captain Dobbs… Nini. Nini… Captain Dobbs. That's Aaron."

"I've been freaking out," says Nini, who's cleaned herself up since the last time I saw her. "What happened? Where've you been? What's…?" She sees the looks on our faces, and our injuries. The blood. Green aurora waves stream in from the enclosed balcony. "Uh… what's with the axe? Never mind. Let me get my MedKit. I'll clean your wounds."

"Them first," Dolores says, and produces her RFID gun. "I need to charge this."

Reflected in the closet door mirror I see Dolores slip Mister Squishy Toes into a duffel bag. She's had that stuffed aardvark ever since I've known her. She doesn't talk about him. Ever. But I guess even Dolores needs to soothe her inner child.

Nini hands us moist disinfectant sheets. "Wipe yourselves down. Then toss 'em in this." She shows us a sealed gray box with an opening on top. On the side of the box is a sticker: *MEDICAL WASTE*. "It'll vaporize any germs or bacteria. You don't want them to spread."

Whistler looks at her oddly. "You think all... this... is from bacteria?"

"No. But all that blood and fecal matter carry microbes that could eat you alive from the inside out. And it's been cross-contaminated."

As if we didn't have enough to worry about.

Nini tends to our wounds as we raid the mini fridge. Forty-six credits for a dark chocolate candy bar, a tin of spicey almonds, and a bottle of water never seemed so worth it. Not that we're gonna pay.

I check my phone again. "No signal. You guys?"

"Nope," Whistler says. "You think the phones are all dead? Or is it the passengers?"

I don't want to answer that. Dolores does it for me.

"Probably. It's a miracle we made it this far."

My body needs to rest, but there's no time. Besides, between the adrenaline and the stim shot, I can't sit still. Neither can my mind.

"Dobbs, you know this ship. Can we restart the systems and boost the signal?"

"I think so, yes. Assuming we make it there."

"Can I see that?" Aaron says, less shaky than before. "The RFID gun?"

Dolores squares up. "What the fuck for? Nobody touches it but me."

"I worked at a supply chain logistics firm. I've programmed RFID systems. I know how they work."

Dolores looks to me for direction. I think on it, nod affirmatively. Seeing the gun is fully charged, she unplugs it, then grips it tight, ready to shoot. Just in case.

"Don't fuck with this," she says. "Or I fuck with you."

Aaron defers appropriately, then inspects the gun as Nini cleans the wound on my cheek. I flinch.

"Gun looks intact. Charge port is solid, fuel cells full. What model is this? Looks new."

"I don't fucking know," Dolores says. "Just part of my gear. Point and shoot."

Aaron inspects the underside. Finds a serial number. "Here it is. What I thought. It's a CDL X Fourteen. It has better range and a custom frequency."

"What do you mean?" Dobbs asks. "Custom how?"

"RFID tech leverages low-power radio frequencies that collect and store data. That data is designated for warehouses and distribution centers. In your case, for luggage. The transceiver, which is here"—he points to the pane on the gun—"reads those radio frequencies and re-transmits them to a corresponding RFID tag. That information is then transmitted from a tiny computer chip embedded in the tag and broadcast back to the reader."

"I know all that. But what makes it custom?"

"The RFID reader—this gun—only reads barcodes it's programmed to recognize. The custom frequency can't, or certainly shouldn't, interfere with other radio frequencies, especially those coming from the ship. It can't disrupt the internal systems. But if the frequency in the chip reader is somehow disrupting the, what did you call it... psycho fog?... that means the fog is caused by, interconnected with, or amplifies some sort of radio frequency. To know for sure, I'd have to look at brain scans of those impacted by the fog and identify the specific radio waves, if there are any. But one way or another, whatever caused the violence is synced to radio waves."

I had a vague notion of it earlier, but now it seems more plausible. At least to me. "And what if the aurora supercharged those radio waves? Could that've been the trigger?"

Aaron looks at me oddly. "Uh... I don't know. I'm not an astrophysicist. I'm not up on my celestial radiation. But RFID tech is nothing new. I've never heard of the kind of signal amplification you're talking about in relation to an aurora. Auroras are natural electrical clusters. They're..." I can see he's trying not to go full-blown coder nerd on us. "Electrical activity from an aurora and soundwaves don't... speak the same language. There's no one-to-one correlation."

Dolores snags the RFID gun back from him. "Well, whatever the fuck it does, it's the only thing that works. If we hook this up to the comms, can we de-fog everyone?"

All eyes back on Aaron.

"Based on what little we know about what actually caused the fog, and that the signal disrupts it? If I had to make an educated guess... yes. I'd say it would. But we won't know for sure until we try."

"What about the earbuds?" Whistler says. "They blocked the psycho fog. Should we wear them?"

"Couldn't hurt. But since you're okay now, I'm not sure it matters."

"Unless it happens again," Nini says. "It's happened to us... twice."

That stops me cold. I hadn't thought about that. I was so relieved Dolores snapped me out of the fog, and stopped me from killing Whistler, I hadn't considered that after she'd been affected earlier, in Nini's stateroom, then zapped out of it, that it could've happened a second time.

Nini starts to explain. "After what happened when—"

"What she means"—I don't want her confessing the murder we covered up—"is that..." Shit. Who am I kidding? It's too late to clean up that mess.

We go through the initial attack in Nini's stateroom.

"Mache, what the fuck?" Whistler says. "You didn't warn us? You didn't warn *me*?"

"I know. I'm sorry. It happened so fast. I went up to the MoonDeck, then the bloodbath started. So... yeah. I could've told you sooner. I kinda had my hands full."

"That's actually useful," Aaron says. "If it happened in your stateroom, and only affected you two and the two androids in here, it means whatever triggers the fog can be applied locally. But what I don't know is if it was intentional or not."

"What do you mean?"

"The first time it happened, the effect was limited to anyone in her stateroom and not wearing earbuds. That implies that something in this room triggered the initial attack."

"Or someone," Whistler says.

"They're right. Neen. Was someone else here? Did you have another... *friend* with you?" That came out more accusatory than I meant.

She picked up on that. Her face betrays some hurt. "No. No! Anj, come on. It was just me and Felix. You know the rest."

"You sure? No one else? Nothing else you remember?"

"Hardy!" Dolores interjects. "She says there's nothing else, there's nothing else. Leave it be."

I raise my hands in truce, step away, and head to the balcony. The green waves roll over me. I close my eyes, trying to let my anxiety fizzle out. But those ugly, horrible images flash before me. The faces of the people I killed. What I did to them.

And how I felt when I did it. How satisfying it was.

"Aaron," I say, coming back into the room. "When you had your earbuds in, was the sound on at the time? Was the podcast actually playing?"

Whistler looks at me quizzically. "Why? What are you thinking?"

"I want to know if it's just a matter of having *something* in your ears to block the signal, like earbuds, or if the signal blocker comes from soundwaves through the earbuds."

"I don't remember," Aaron says. "I stopped the podcast from time to time to take breaks, or if my mind drifted and I wanted to go back. I think it was playing when everyone—"

"You *think?*" Dolores snaps. "Or you *know?*"

"I... I don't know," Aaron says, shaken by her outburst. "Most probable... the sound was on. But I can't be certain."

"Actually"—Whistler's got that look, when he's figured something out—"you can."

That piques my interest. "How?"

"Aaron," he says. "The music app on your phone. There should be a timestamp when the podcast was playing, as opposed to being on *pause* or *off*. If we can get that data, we can—"

"Compare it to the timestamp when the psycho fog kicked in," I say.

Whistler concurs. "Then we'll know if the soundwaves from your earbuds, or just the earbuds themselves, blocked the fog."

We all look at each other with self-satisfied smiles. But they don't last.

"I can't access that data from the phone," Aaron says. "Need to sync it to my laptop and run that program. But my room is… what deck are we on?"

"Nine," Dobbs says.

"My stateroom is on six. If we can get there, maybe I can…"

"Don't split up," I say. "Too dangerous. Let's assume we'd need active sound coming through the earbuds to combat the fog."

"Hardy," Dolores says timidly.

"Okay," I say. "Who's got earbuds?"

"Angela!" Dolores shouts. Then she quiets down. "There's something else. The first time I got fogged, I was totally out of control. Then Nini zapped me, and I snapped out of it. But the second time, when it hit *everybody*, it wasn't as intense. I still felt that… urge. The anger, the desire to… but I was aware of what was happening. I was… fighting myself, talking to myself, like being in a dream when you know you're dreaming, and can sorta control the dream."

"Lucid dreaming."

"It wasn't as bad. So even though I was looking at Nini and almost… I forced myself to zap her. Then had her zap me."

"Hold on," Whistler says. "If the second time wasn't as bad as the first, does that mean you can build up a tolerance to the psycho fog? Or does the RFID signal give you some sort of, like, inoculation? Like getting a flu shot?"

I raise my eyes. "Nini?"

"How the hell would I know?"

"You're a nurse!"

"Not for this!"

"People," Dobbs says in his best Captain's voice. "We've all been through a lot, and it's not over. We're not going to figure it out now. We agreed to recharge the gun, which we have, and clean our wounds, which we did. As much as we don't want to go back out there, I'm afraid we have to."

CHAPTER 17

Dolores, Nini, and Aaron all slip earbuds in, sync them to their phones, play music at the lowest volume possible as a safety measure. Neither me, Whistler, or Dobbs have earbuds, so we'll have to hope for the best. Maybe it won't matter. We might be able to snare a few throughout the ship.

And for me and Whistler, hopefully he was right, and our contact lenses will give us that extra layer of signal protection. Not that they've been working well. Tons of static. I'm assuming it's the aftereffects from the lightning strikes or the psycho fog.

Before we head back into the madness, Nini gives each of us a prophylactic injection of a broad-spectrum antibiotic.

"Try not to touch any of the filth. You may not be able to avoid it, but do your best. But if you do, even with the antibiotics, *don't* touch your face or rub your eyes. If we survive, the last thing you'll want is to die later of infection."

As much as I'm looking forward to having my kidneys eaten from the inside out, there's still a larger looming issue.

"Dobbs, based on what you saw, how long until the fuel leaks out completely?"

"No idea. At departure we were fully fueled. Enough to last two weeks at maximum load. We might have ten more days' worth at this point, ten hours, or ten minutes. If we get down to the Engine Room, I'll know for sure."

Nini perks up. "What's this about the fuel?"

"Tiny leak," I say. "Nothing to worry about."

"Anj. He just said we could run out in ten minutes."

"Or ten days. Who can tell? Shall we vamoose?"

"Hold on," Whistler says. "I wanna see..." He fiddles with his phone.

"Selene?" I ask. "Anything?"

"No signal."

"You never know. She could be—"

Whistler heads for the door. He'd rather face a hallway of psychotic attackers than talk about the fact that his girlfriend—our client—an android, could be one of them. Or dead.

"If we're doing this, we're doing this," Dolores says. "Everybody got a weapon?"

"I... I don't have one," Aaron says.

Dolores takes a chair, smashes it on the floor until one of the legs breaks off. She hands it to him. "Now you do. Let's go."

We're back again in two-by-two formation, Dolores and Whistler in front, me and Nini behind them, Dobbs and Aaron in the rear. We step over a few barely breathing passengers, and make it to the stairwell.

I hate seeing them suffer like this. But without a properly supplied medic and the time to treat the wounded, sometimes you have to leave them behind, tell yourself there's nothing you can do for them—and hope you believe it.

Dolores and Whistler hold up at the landing. They take one step... then a second... then slowly... slowly... slowly... inch around the staircase. All clear. They take the stairs faster, but still cautiously, the rest of us close behind.

My attention is on high alert—a violent attack can spring up without notice—but like a browser with multiple open tabs, my mind is sprinting in the background, desperately trying to make sense of radio frequencies, the aurora, the Death Code, the Life Code, Buckley, Nolasco, Selene, Ther'eda, and the rift between androids and organics.

Who or what instigated this violent lunacy is the million-credit question. The investigator in me can't let go, running scenarios, determined to figure out the how and why. The survivor in me doesn't care. If my rough calculations are correct, we're less than four hundred feet, across four more decks, from the Engine Room.

The Engine Room houses the comms port.

The comms port will boost the RFID signal.

The RFID signal will, theoretically, snap everyone else out of the psycho fog.

Just four hundred feet. That's two E-Town blocks. That's the length of the walking bridge that stretches over the Chabaqua River. The same distance from the white marble steps outside the Courthouse down into the decrepit Tombs, where detectives lock up suspects in old, dirty, windowless rooms, handcuff them to old, dirty tables, and try to break their alibis. And it's the same distance from the entrance of the E-Town General ER up to the maternity ward, where my son was born.

I've walked them all more times than I can remember.

Four hundred feet. That's all it is.

But here in this deathtrap, it might just be a dead end for us. Emphasis on *dead*.

Which is possibly why Whistler, who has never asked Dolores a personal question about anything, asks maybe the most personal and pertinent question of all. Because it might be his last chance.

He sticks his head around the Deck Seven landing. "I get that you hate everybody—"

"I don't hate *everybody*." Dolores pivots the butcher knife in her hand. "A few people. Most people. Okay. Everybody. I like maybe... four people. What about it?"

"Why androids most of all?"

Dolores doesn't like Whistler. She tolerates him. Which is a big step for her. He's been in my life almost three years, which means he's been in hers, to a much lesser degree, just as long. Her dislike of Whistler is less about her general distaste for other people and more about the fact that I've tried to fold him into my world, with varying degrees of success. And failure.

She sees Whistler as an impediment to me in all ways, which makes him an impediment to her. I think Whistler thinks I think the same thing about him. Until recently, he might've been right. But not anymore.

"I was just a kid when the Lansing androids came online," she says and sneaks around to the Deck Six landing. "They freaked everybody out. But not me. I thought they were cool as shit. I mean, are you kiddin me? Kind of a robot, kind of a real person, not totally either, but a combo of both. They looked like us and acted like us but didn't seem to have all the ugly hate in their hearts that we have. Androids were like us, but... nicer. Better."

She smiles wistfully at that memory.

"But that's the thing about kids. They're ignorant. And *really fuckin stupid*. Watch it!"

A thin, balding passenger with bushy brown eyebrows lunges at Whistler, snaring his arm, knocking the taser down the final two steps. Whistler lunges at his attacker. They tumble onto the landing. Whistler puts a chokehold on his assailant, his arms and legs flailing, until he passes out.

Another fogged-out passenger, a heavyset woman with bushy red hair and a black-and-white polka dot skirt, grabs the taser, then jabs it at Whistler. Before the crackling end strikes his hip, Dolores slashes at the redhead with the butcher knife. It catches her diagonally across the forehead.

Blood spurting like a geyser, the redhead screams wildly and throws herself at Dolores, who loses the RFID gun.

In a fit of anger, Dolores shoves the redhead back, but in doing so takes a ballpoint pen in her ribs. With both hands she grabs a clump of curly red hair, then slams her assailant's face down into her knee. With a bloody, gurgling yelp, the redhead flops onto the floor next to the attacker Whistler choked out.

Dolores grimaces, reaches for her side.

"D," Nini says. "You okay?"

"For fuck's sake, yes, I'm okay. Just leave me alone."

Dolores doesn't mean it. Once your fight response activates, it's extremely difficult to turn it off without misfiring now and again.

It's like firearms training. You do the obstacle course, with criminals and civilians mixed together, and the goal is to shoot only the criminals. With repetition and discipline, you can train yourself to slow down your knee-jerk responses, able to decide in a fraction of a second when to the pull the trigger and when to hold back.

But when you're in the field, under a relentless assault in close quarters, your adrenaline spiked, it's a helluva lot tougher to turn it off. Especially for someone like Dolores, who's just been wounded. Which is a form of being vulnerable.

Dolores doesn't do vulnerable. And yet here she is, fighting for her life, for all our lives, taking body blows so we don't have to. I guess there's nothing like a good scare to distract from your heartache.

Regardless, I've gotta keep us moving down to the Engine Room. But it's only now I feel the heat bubbling up, the air control systems knocked out. I pick up the fallen RFID gun and give it back to Dolores.

But as we start to cook in the rising temperatures, the miasma nearly knocks me out, the awful stench from the blood and bile penetrating my nasal cavity, then into my brain and down my gullet.

"Keep..." I cough, choking on the stench. "Keep moving. We gotta get down to—"

"Mache," Whistler says. "Look."

Around the bend, in the stairwell leading down to Deck Five, are more bodies. Sprawled on the stairs, from beneath the pile, we see shaking legs. And hear whimpering.

Dolores picks up the RFID gun and blasts the pile.

Carefully, with my taser ready, I step down and kneel, getting closer to that one body buried beneath the pile of bodies. I have the others help me roll the dead ones away, chucking them down the stairs.

Slick, bloody skin chafes against each other, the sound like peeling back cellophane rolls. We keep going until we find a small young woman underneath, trembling.

As if she'd been marinating in a vat of Bolognese, her entire face is covered in a chunky human ragu.

I take her by the hand. From behind that muck her eyes snap open, white globes against the bloody red. She thrashes about, kicking her feet, screaming, screaming, screaming.

Firmly, compassionately, Nini takes hold of her elbows. "Easy, now. It's okay. We're not gonna hurt you. I'm a nurse. I just wanna check you out."

"No!" she squeals, and thrashes her legs again, catching Nini in the hand.

Nini pulls away, winces, grabbing the banged digits with her other hand. "Dammit. Think she broke my finger. Here. Help me. Check the MedKit. Get the wipes."

I fish a bunch out. I start wiping the girl's face, resisting the extraordinary urge to howl as I scoop off little bits of mangled fingers, tendons, and brains. She fights me at first, but settles down, realizing we're not here to dismember her.

It takes a minute, but we manage to get most of the splatter off her face.

"It's not her blood," Nini says, and gestures to the dead bodies on the floor. "It's theirs."

"Chipper?" Aaron says. "Is that you?"

Chipper looks at him oddly, a tortured animal recognizing a familiar face.

Aaron offers his hand. Chipper considers it timidly. Gaze darting back and forth, after a few seconds she warily reaches out with trembling fingers and takes Aaron's hand. He helps her up, leaning her against the stairwell wall.

I tend to Nini, taping the pointer and middle fingers on her left hand together.

Satisfied with my nursing job, she goes back to Chipper and gingerly wipes away the rest of the blood and grime from her face.

"I'm gonna give you something. It'll help fight infection, and settle your nerves."

Chipper blinks, coughs, cries a little, then coughs again. "Aar... Aaron?"

He smiles. "Yeah."

She throws her arms around him, slop from her jacket smearing his shirt. Then she pulls away, seeing us huddled together with a butcher knife, tasers, and a bloody axe.

"What...?" she says, panting. "How...?"

Aaron smiles. "Crazy, huh?"

Chipper huffs at first, which devolves into uncomfortable laughter, then residual tears. "I was coming to find you. I thought you'd want to hear the Buckley talk with me. And then..."

She launches into a fit of coughing, which segues into labored breathing and then a full-blown wheezing fit. Chipper fumbles her hand inside the front pocket of her slop-smeared blazer. She produces her inhaler, shakes it a few times, and takes three deep puffs. She holds the mist in her lungs, exhales.

"Asthma?" I ask.

"Nuh... no," Chipper says meekly. "COPD."

"Chronic obstructive pulmonary disease," Nini says. "It's a chronic lung disease that restricts the breathing. But it's usually treated with a once-a-day tablet." She reaches curiously for Chipper's inhaler. "Can I see that? We don't see it much for COPD."

"Um...," Chipper says, fear washed over her. "Okay. But be careful."

Nini winks at her. "Don't worry. I'm a nurse." She inspects the casing. "Huh. It's heavier than I thought." She starts to tug on the mechanism.

"Don't!" Chipper says, then gets red-faced. "Sorry. It's my only one." She takes it back from Nini. "I had pneumonia as a kid. It damaged my lungs." She says she's been on the list for a synthetic lung transplant for years, but it's been difficult to find a match because of the strain the procedure could put on her heart. "I take the pills, but sometimes the wheezing's so bad I can't breathe at all. The cold and stress makes it worse. The inhaler helps when I need it."

Shakes the rescue inhaler again, the small albuterol canister rattling against the casing.

"That's it!" Nini says. "The shaking. The rattle. I remember!"

"What?" I'm eyeing the hallway in both directions, anticipating more attackers. It only takes one to ruin your day—forever. "*What* do you remember?"

"The rattling. The first attack. I was in the bathroom getting ready, and I heard a rattle. I didn't think anything of it. It was backgammon. *Somebody* shook the dice. Then they attacked each other. Anj! Could the dice be connected to the... the... psycho fog somehow? I know it makes no sense, but *none* of this makes sense!"

"I mean... maybe? Most dice are made from acrylic, plastic, or resin. I'm not sure..."

"They're custom dice," Dobbs says.

Second time I've heard that word thrown around tonight. "Custom? What do you mean?"

"Ther'eda arranged for it. All of the dice have the Ranadyne logo inside. She said it was a promotional item."

"They were in my welcome packet," Whistler says.

"Everybody got them," Dolores says. "But I can't see how the composition of the dice could be linked to the violence."

"Mache? What do you think?"

"I don't know what to think. I..." And then I do. I pat down my pockets until I find them. The set of dice from the back-gammon tournament. I take one, hold it between the tip of my thumb and forefinger. "Is that...?" I activate my contact lens. Fighting through the static, I'm able to focus on the dots inside the die, like salt specs trapped in amber. Inside each side of the die is the corresponding number of white dots—one, two, three, four, five, and six. "Here," I say, handing it to Whistler. "Use your lens. What do you see?"

He looks closely. "It's hard to tell, but there's... yeah... a bunch of gold flecks. And they're... *glowing.*" He looks at me. "Holy shit. You think these dice give off a signal? Or act as a signal booster, or a conduit, or... what?"

"You mind?" Aaron asks.

Whistler bristles. "What? You worked at a die factory, too?"

"A tabletop gaming company. So, yeah."

Whistler and I look at each other. I send him an eye text. They're hard to read, but they're just clear enough.

Me: *Seems unlikely.*

Whistler: *It does. Still, coders are like this.*

Me: *What do u think? Trust him?*

Whistler: *Fuck no. But he knows more about this stuff than us. Just keep an eye on him.*

"Okay," I say. "What do you see?"

Aaron squints, looks again. "I have a scanner in my room. But those gold flecks..."

"Yeah?" Whistler says.

"I've seen them before."

Patrolling the bottom of the stairs, Dolores turns to us.

"Don't hold us in suspense, pencil dick. Where've you seen 'em?"

Noise comes from the upper stairwell. Time to go.

"In computer code," Aaron says, and hands the dice back to me. "I can't say for sure, but it looks like android DNA."

CHAPTER 18

Screams echo throughout the stairwell.

The psycho fog is still in full effect. Feral attackers scramble toward us from multiple directions, their violent cries coming from above us in the stairwell and from down the corridor.

Which means we don't have the luxury of stealth. We have to get to Deck Two as fast as possible. We descend two more levels only to come upon, at the Deck Three landing, a large man, his back to us. His hands are gripped around someone's throat, choking, choking, choking.

Dolores blasts them with the RFID gun. The attacker stops mid-choke, his large brown hands clutching a thick white neck like it's a magic eight ball. There's a J-scar under its right eye. Realizing what he's doing, the attacker releases the synthetic neck. But it's too late. The choked-out android is dead. Didn't need a Death Code for that one.

The attacker, woken from the psycho fog, holds his hands out, studying them as if they're mutated appendages. I'm not sure if he hears us, but he turns around.

"When I was on patrol as a rookie," Tarrish says, his gaze weary and lost. "I had to break up a bar fight. My partner went down with a broken jaw. I was on my own. I got jumped by four guys and had to fight them off." He's confused, realizing now that he'd transposed that memory for what just happened on the ship. "I couldn't help it. I had to."

"I know. We all did."

He blinks a few times. "You mean...? I don't know what I mean."

With her good hand, Nini takes Tarrish's wrist, checks his pulse, studies her watch. What she's doing isn't medically necessary. Being the excellent nurse she is, it's Nini's way of giving him a few seconds to adjust, though they're seconds we don't have.

Coming out of the psycho fog is like that grogged-out period after surgery, when the anesthesia's not entirely out of your system. You're sort of awake, sort of in a hazy, molasses-on-the-brain state, uncertain where you are, how you got there, or if you're stumbling through some quasi-dream.

Yet coupled with the aftereffects of the psycho fog are the awful images of what you've just seen and done fresh in your mind, the residual flood of inhumanity.

Tarrish is strong, though, physically and mentally, with more years on the job than me. He pushes through until he's alert. We catch him up, about the weapons cache in the security room, the leaking fuel, needing to restart the engines, and the RFID signal.

"I've been sending messages for backup," Tarrish says, "but they're not going through."

"Nothing is," Whistler says.

"It shouldn't matter. The ICD has its own frequency. Is it the aurora?" But then he rejects his own notion. "Is it the... what did you call it?... psycho fog?"

"Ship-to-tower comms are also down," Dobbs says. "And the transponder is dead. That's nearly impossible. The lightning storm must've hit the beacon directly. Fried the circuits."

We ease down the stairwell's final bend and onto the second deck.

"I lost Ther'eda," Tarrish says, still shaky. "She ran when the MoonDeck went berserk and then... I don't know what. I was... lost in it."

"You're out of it now," I say. "With no time to spare."

Back on Arcasia, Whistler and I had to fight for our lives, and barely made it out. But this is a different kind of raw, mangled intensity, a vicious and relentless assault with no end in sight, and no understanding of why it's even happening to us. Knowing the *why*, giving the reason a name, defining it, applying texture and context to its intrusion, satisfying our psycho-spiritual underpinnings, allows us to better confront, accept, and control what we're facing.

Even if it's just in our minds.

When the demarcation line between survival and not is razor-thin, any advantage has the potential to be *the* advantage.

Tarrish wipes his brow. "It's hot in here."

"A/C is out. Come on. One more deck."

I head back into the stairwell.

"Mache. Shouldn't he have a weapon?"

"Good point." Down three steps, I turn back. "T? Do you have a...?"

He reaches inside his jacket, exposing his shoulder holster. He produces his gun.

"Never leave home without it."

"Dobbs," Whistler says. "I thought he can't have firearms on board?"

"No," Tarrish says. "*You* can't. I'm a Lieutenant with the ICD. I can do whatever I want." He pats his side pocket, produces a fresh magazine, pops it in, then checks that he's got a round in the chamber. He does. "Thought I was out. Let's go."

We inch down the stairwell. One more turn, and finally, we'll be on Deck Two.

I whisper to Dobbs, "When we come to the next landing, how far to the Engine Room?"

"Laundry and then medical will be on our immediate left, security is three rooms down to the right, then the Engine Room, which is mid-deck."

"Security first. We need those weapons. Don't know how long we'll need to hole up in the Engine Room."

"Hardy," Dolores says. "If the security team is fogged out, and they're in there..."

"We'll get creative. Unless..." I fish around in my pocket, find the dice, roll them in my hand. They glow bright green and gold. I separate the dice, one in each hand. They stop glowing. I hold them together again. They glow.

"Could be the android DNA," Aaron says. "Like they..."

"Recognize each other?" Whistler surmises. "Like they're... talking?"

"That's possible, yes."

That gives me an idea. "Anybody else? Who's got dice?"

Dolores reaches into her pocket. "Forgot I had 'em. Here."

"That's four," I say. "Hopefully that'll do."

The eight of us skulk down the stairs onto Deck Two—bottom of the ship. The wall directly in front of us is smeared with so much blood you'd think they used it for freestyle finger painting. On the floor are several bodies, including one in a security windbreaker, who twitches.

Dolores points the RFID gun and shoots. "Fuck. It's dead again. It might have a short. We'll have to—"

A fogged-out security guard rushes out from the laundry supply room on one side of the hallway, shoving me into the linen room opposite it. He bum-rushes me so hard and fast that he jams me up against the commercial laundry folder.

The back of my head smacks a lever. Dazed, I see stars. He throws an elbow, cracking me in the jaw. I fall sideways. He knees me in the gut.

I should be on the floor, but the lever I hit must have activated the hot-air laundry folder, a two-thousand-pound industrial beast with an extra-wide cross-fold bed, draping accumulator bar, and mechanical clutch and brake system.

Operating thanks to its self-contained power supply, the gears engage. The engine heats. The rollers spin.

The fabric in my jacket bunches up. I'm caught. Yanked against the machine, it's heating up. My back, near my kidney, is starting to burn.

I extend my taser. He knocks it across the room. With his eyes wild, and baton in hand, he raises it high above his head, about to bash in my skull.

It's all happening too fast. I'm stuck, dazed, and uncoordinated. I can't defend myself. So I do the only thing I can. I close my eyes and hope it's over quickly.

Then there's a blast.

As if I'm in a deprivation tank, I find myself floating—consciousness without a body. I can't see or feel anything. Not a damn thing.

"Anj," I hear a muffled voice call. "Anj."

Out of habit, I try to blink. I feel my eyelids flutter. Before me is darkness.

"Anj. Anj!"

My eyes open.

On the side of me is the security guard, laid out against the wall, a hole where the center of his face used to be. Brain matter, skull fragments, and blood are streaked above his head.

My senses re-engage with a vengeance. "My back! Get me off!"

Nini, Whistler, and Dolores pull me away from the industrial roller, pulling my arms out of my sleeves. The machine eats up my jacket.

I fall to my knees.

Nini checks my back. "Let me see." She folds up the tail of my shirt as Dobbs shuts down the machine. Nini hisses. "Damn. Bad burn."

She applies silver sulfadiazine cream to limit the damage, and keep the swelling down. Then three more guards rush in.

Dolores and Whistler take on one of the guards. Dobbs tangles with another, knocking against the lever again. The machine starts back up.

Among the spinning, *ca-chunking* rollers, the third guard, an android, charges at me.

Like a preying hawk, my brain shrieks at my arms and legs— *get up get up get up!*—but try as I might, they won't cooperate. All I can think to do is reach for the dice in my pocket. I take them out, rattle them in my hand. Those tiny cubes with their tiny white dots and their gold interior flecks.

The android charging at me, a woman, hesitates mid-attack, distracted by the glowing cubes. It gives Nini just enough time to pry my taser off the floor and jam it into the android's neck. The electrical sparks crackle. Nini pushes the tip harder and deeper until finally the android spasms and flops to the floor. Her tongue distends. Saliva dribbles down her chin.

"See," Aaron says. "Android DNA. I think they were talking to—"

The guard fighting Dobbs gets a shot off. It hits Aaron in the heart. Bullseye.

Stunned, Aaron blinks a few times, looks down at his chest. His chin bobs as if barely fastened to an old spring. He collapses.

On the other side of the machine, Whistler grabs the guard's right arm, gun in hand, until it's above her head. Her midsection exposed, Dolores wallops her in the ribs so hard I hear them crack. Dolores snatches the gun away, and pistol whips the guard unconscious. Or to death. It's hard to tell which.

Dobbs punches his attacker in the throat. The guard reaches for his injured neck. Seeing an opening, Dobbs goes for the kill. But the guard swings a wild elbow, catching Dobbs in the eye. His head snaps to the side, just enough time to give his adversary the advantage.

The fogged-out guard lunges at Dobbs, shoving him against the churning industrial machine. With the two straining for control over each other, he jams Dobb's hand, then his arm into those burning hot rollers. Synthetic flesh sizzles.

Dobbs howls sickeningly.

The guard shoves Dobbs deeper into the roller. But because the guard's back is to the rest of us, it gives *us* the tactical advantage. Whistler puts a gun he had picked up to the guard's head, and with a single trigger squeeze, blows a hole straight through the back of his head and out the front. Cranial muck explodes through the forehead and onto the rollers.

I feel warm, squishy tissue on my lower lip. I spit it off, realizing I'm tasting brain slop.

Dolores and Whistler pull away the dead guard and stop the machine.

Still caught in the rollers, Dobbs is mutilated, passed out from shock.

"D!" Nini shouts. "The infirmary's next door. Maybe there's a gurney and supplies—"

Dolores shoots Dobbs in the head.

That stops us cold. The reality of this execution hasn't caught up with our waking minds. Until it does, like a video screen scrolling in fast-forward.

"D! Why did you do that?! What did you do?"

Dolores rolls Dobbs to the side. A long metal peg is jammed into his liver.

"He was already dead. His body just didn't know it yet."

"Damn it, D! He's the only pilot we had left! You can't

just..." A wave of dread washes over me. I hyperventilate, my heart beating faster and faster when I see Chipper huddled in the corner, arms wrapped around her knees, rocking back and forth, mumbling to herself.

"Mache," Whistler whispers, and puts his arms on my shoulders. "You okay?"

"I... I'm not sure."

It's hard to slow down when my emotions are speeding up. I turn to Dobbs, slumped over the machine, shoulder caught in the rollers. "Neen," I whisper. "Could you have saved...?"

Tears in her eyes, she shakes her head gently. "No."

Bruised, burned, and struggling to catch my breath, I don't want to do this anymore. I don't want to fight. I don't want to survive. I don't want to look at any more oozing blood or bile or mangled organs or simmering molten rage.

I want to close my eyes then wake up on a white sandy beach with an endless supply of fruity drinks and gently lapping waves. To be seen but not noticed. To be part of the collective, yet comfortably alone. Because what's the fucking point?

I'm really, truly asking. What's... the fucking... point?

So I don't wish for it. I do it. With eyes clenched, I search my mind for the calm of a faraway place and... feel two hands on my face, one on each cheek.

"Mommy," Owen says. "Maaaah-meeeee."

"...Baby? Is that you?"

"Hi, Mommy."

"Baby. What are you doing here?"

"We're just playing, Mommy. Hide and seek, remember? You hid in your favorite spot. I came to find you. *Found* you!"

The tension uncurls from my heart. I smile. "Yes, baby. You did."

"'Kay, Mommy. Your turn."

As is often the case with motherhood, I'm not sure what my son needs from me right now, even though I feel like I should. "My turn? To do what?"

"You have to find *me*. I'll go hide. But first, you have to—"

"Wake up!" Someone's shaking me hard. "Angela! Wake up!"

My eyes pop open. It's Dolores.

"Nap on your own time. We're still in the shit."

"Dolores," Nini says. "Do you have to be so rough?"

Tarrish enters. Breathing hard and covered in fresh blood, he's got his gun in hand, down by his side.

I scoop up my taser as Dolores pops the clip out of her own gun, checks it, slaps it back in. "Yes," she answers Nini. "I really fucking do."

CHAPTER 19

"There's a lot of 'em," Tarrish says under exhausted breaths, blood in his salt-and-pepper beard. He leans back against the door, pops out his empty clip. It clacks on the floor. "A few less than before." He gazes across the room, sees Dobbs mangled in the industrial roller. "What happened to him?"

"Tried to press his shirt," Dolores says. "Too much starch."

"Dolores," Nini says judgmentally, as she often does, to reign her back in. "Really?"

"What? Too soon?"

Tarrish takes a few deep breaths, reaches into his pocket, holds up his gun. "*Now* I'm out."

Dolores showcases the gun she confiscated. "Don't worry. I'm fully loaded."

Tarrish nods, reaches out his hand. "Thanks. I'll take that."

"The fuck you will."

"Here." Whistler's got another handgun, points to one of the dead guards. "I found it on that one." He hands it over to Tarrish.

Which sets Dolores off. "What the fuck is wrong with you? We're stuck in a floating deathtrap, lunatics at every turn, and you're giving away the best weapon you have? You really are a dumbshit. If I need someone watching my back, you ain't the guy."

I don't know why I'm doing it here, now, but the words spill out of me like tears from a good cry. Sometimes you can't hold back, even when you think you should.

"You're wrong, D." As I confess the sin I've done my damnedest to smother with a down pillow, I can feel my energy spike, a glowing, giddy release electrifying my entire self. The tiniest wisps of light can rise from the darkness, even when darkness feels like all you've got left. "He does a lotta of other things too, but he does have my back, even when I think I don't need it... which is when I really need it most."

Whistler's uncertain how or even if he should accept what I've just thrown his way. He's got every reason to doubt me. I haven't made our partnership easy on him. Or on me. With my confession hanging in the poisoned air, there's a strange, cringey silence between us all.

Until Dolores ensures there's not.

"Well, aren't we just a bunch of huggie-wuggie motherfuckers." She rechecks her clip. "Get your ass in gear. This ship ain't gonna fix itself."

Tarrish and Dolores stand on either side of the doorway. Me, Whistler, Nini, and Chipper are close behind. Tarrish raises his open hand. Barely above a whisper, he counts down: "One... two... three!"

Dolores flings the door open. Tarrish darts into the emergency-lit hallway. He pivots hard right. Dolores pivots hard left. Seeing no one there, she pivots back so she's side by side with Tarrish. Guns at the ready, they take cautious steps.

"Security room's fifty feet away," Tarrish says, his back to me. "We just gotta make it another fifty feet and—"

From the far end of the long hallway of doom, a deranged mob charges in our direction. I activate my contact lens to make up for the poorly lit distance. Despite the intermittent static, with night vision I can see them in their bloody, tattered clothes and wielding knives, metal bars, broken off champagne bottles, and self-made spears.

Engaged in a collective war cry, the mob is wild-eyed and pumped full of demented fury when two women in windbreakers suddenly appear from the security room wearing bulletproof vests. And holding shotguns.

They fire on the mob. Then all hell breaks loose.

"In here!" I command. We duck into the nearest room, the infirmary, and shut the door. Lock it from the inside. "Good news... we're in here, they're out there. Bad news..."

"We don't know who's side they're on," Whistler says. "And they've got shotguns."

"And a whole lot more," I say as I scan the infirmary for a tactical advantage.

"They move on us, we got a problem."

Dolores holds her gun out, pressed against the door. "Ya think?"

"Hey," Nini whispers. "Listen."

"What?" Dolores blurts. "I don't—"

"*Listen.*"

With the soul-shattering torrent of violent chaos coming from down the hall, on the other side of the infirmary door we all go perfectly still.

There's a slight metal clanking.

"There," Nini says. "It's—"

"Shh!" I shush. "It's..." I turn to the rear wall. In the semi-darkness my lens gives me a better, albeit staticky view. Dull white cabinets above and below, counter in between. I kneel by the lower cabinets. I wave my hands to the others. In a V, I point two fingers at my eyes, at them, then at the cabinet. I mouth the word, "There."

Tarrish points his gun at the closed cabinet. Dolores has the axe in hand, gun in the other, Whistler and I have our tasers out. I stand to the side, grab the cabinet door handle between my fingers. Heart pounding, in one motion I pull the door open and stand aside. Dolores and Tarrish move in.

Folded up like the dead android in Nini's closet, Ther'eda Ranadyne spills onto the floor.

Nini goes to her, feels for a pulse in her neck. "She's alive. Get her on the table."

Whistler scoops Ther'eda up into his arms and gently lays her on the examining table.

"Don't touch her!"

Someone jumps out from behind the gray, metal filing cabinet. Wielding a scalpel, she swipes at Whistler, slashing his forearm. He retracts, grabbing his arm. It's bleeding badly.

"Leave her alo—"

Guns are directed at our attacker. But there's no need.

"Selene!" Whistler throws his arms around her, but she pushes him back. "Selene," he repeats, calmer. "It's me. It's Eric."

Unsure who to trust, if anyone, Selene looks absently at Whistler's bleeding arm, down at her shaking hand, at Ther'eda, then at the rest of us. She drops the scalpel.

"Selene," I say, helping Whistler roll up his sleeve so we can tend to the wound. "Are you okay? Do you know where you are?"

She stares blankly. "Eric. I ruined your shirt."

"Don't"—Whistler winces as I wipe his wound with rubbing alcohol. "Don't worry about it." He looks down at the bloody stains up and down his chest. "It was kinda ruined anyway."

That gets a faint smile from Selene. Nini fishes through drawers, then goes to Ther'eda, who groans, trying to sit up on the table.

Nini takes Ther'eda by the hand, puts the other behind her back. "Easy. Go slow."

Splotches of blood are congealed in a clump of Ther'eda's platinum blonde hair. Nini flickers a penlight in one of her eyes, observes for three seconds, then again with the other eye.

"Pupils are equal and reactive. She's—"

"Ah." Ther'eda reaches for the top of her head. "It's killing me."

Nini looks closer. "There's a pretty big welt. You might be concussed."

Dolores and Tarrish go back to guarding the door. With a freshly bandaged arm, Whistler rummages through drawers and cabinets. "Booyah." He tosses everyone a power bar and a small bottle of water. "Fuel up. We're gonna need it."

He sits with Selene. "Babe," he says tenderly, "how are you doing?"

"I'm..." She looks about groggily, blinks a few times, then focuses her breathing. "I'm okay. I think I'm okay. I'm just worried about Ms. Ranadyne."

I gnaw through a surprisingly tasty vanilla chocolate chip and cranberry twist power bar.

"How's it look out there?" Ther'eda asks. She's lucid. No psycho fog.

"Not great," I say, eying the others. "Do you remember how you got here?"

Nini hands Ther'eda a cup of water. "Sip it. Just a little."

Ther'eda takes some water. "I'm"—she coughs up on herself, waves us away—"I'm okay. Went down the wrong pipe." She takes a few more sips, coughs a bit more, but keeps going until she drains the cup. "I was on the MoonDeck and then..." She's staring now, an ugly frightened gaze to nowhere. "I had all these horrible thoughts. When I was eight, I got bit by a dog. I've been scared of them ever since. Everyone out there... they had normal bodies, but heads and fangs like that damn dog, like they wanted to bite me again. And I wanted... revenge. To hurt that mutt. To kill it. To kill them all. Then I woke up here."

"Babe," Whistler says to Selene again. "Were you with her the whole time? How'd you get down here?"

"They just said they don't remember," Dolores says. "Don't you ever fuckin' listen?"

Whistler squares up. I don't know if he's about to release pent-up anxiety about Selene, if he's being overly protective, showing off again, or if I stirred up too much shit between us that should've been said a better way at a better time in a better place.

But then Dolores does something she rarely ever does. Apologize.

"Sorry," she says. "I'm just... forget it. Sorry."

Whistler nods silently in acceptance.

"What about Nenn?" I ask, trying to move us past this. "And Kowalczyk? Have you seen them? Do you know where they are?"

Ther'eda takes more water from Nini. "No. Like I said. I went from that horror show... to now."

"And you have no idea why this happened?"

"What *is* it with you people?" She crumples the paper cup, tosses it aside. "You talk a lot, but you don't listen. No. I have no idea. Why? Do you think I...?" Her eyes widen. She surveys us. "You think I'm involved."

It's bad form to interrogate a victim after they've just awakened from a trauma-induced stupor, but I don't have the luxury of waiting until later. There might not be a later. Then again, Ther'eda's already proven to tell half-truths and selective facts as they fit her agendas.

"You did hold back about the Death Code. And the Life Code."

"Yeah," Whistler says awkwardly, two sides of his personality clearly in conflict. The PI in him is digging for clues. The boyfriend in him doesn't want to upset his girl. "What happened to Buckley? He's missing, Nolasco's dead, you were locked in a cabinet, and now we haven't seen—"

"You still don't get it," Ther'eda retorts, deflecting our inquiries. "You really think this bloodbath is about androids and lines of code?" She eyes us ruefully, shakes her head. "We all seem to be suffering from an enhanced form of Misophonia."

"*Riiight*," Nini says, nodding to herself. "Misophonia."

"Neen?" I ask. "That's a thing?"

"It is, actually. It's also called Selective Sound Sensitivity Syndrome. S-Four Syndrome. I saw a case a few years ago in the ER. We had this patient who—"

"It's related to APS," Ther'eda interjects. "It's when sounds trigger intense emotional or physiological responses. Like when someone chews with their mouths open, and make those obnoxious smacking sounds—"

"I hate that," Whistler says.

"Or the metallic ping of clipping fingernails," Ther'eda continues. "Or when someone whistles loudly and off-key. It can make people anxious, uncomfortable, disgusted, or incite the urge to flee. But in more severe cases, the sounds can trigger rage, anger, hatred, panic, fear, and intense emotional distress."

"It drives them crazy," I say.

"In a manner of speaking, yes. But what's happening here… the only source powerful and precise enough to effect this kind of violent, mass delusion almost certainly has to originate from a specific frequency. It's very likely an amplified soundwave that triggers deviant neuronal activation in the automatic auditory processing system and engages multiple emotional/limbic structures in humans *and* androids."

"And how the fuck would *you* know that?" Dolores says, encroaching on Ther'eda as if she's about to pulverize her.

I'm about to insert myself between them, but Ther'eda hops down from the table of her own accord. Despite giving up at least a foot and a hundred pounds easy to Dolores, she steps right up to her, cutting down the angle.

Any normal person would quake in Dolores' presence. Ther'eda seems utterly unafraid.

"I began a study of brainwaves because of my APS. The research led me into robotics, A.I., then androids. Android brains and organic brains are not quite the same, for obvious reasons. Androids all have a cranial CPU and synthetic lobes, organics do not. But the neurochemical systems of information distribution, processing, and signal transfer operate on the same fundamental principles. Without knowing for certain, what's going on throughout this ship seems to be the result of soundwave induction causing the manipulation of the brain."

"Hang on," Whistler says. "You said the psychosis is the result of soundwave induction."

"Most likely, yes."

"Then how come some went crazy and some were... talking... confused. It happened to me and to—"

"The prefrontal cortex filters out unwanted background noise or other distracting sensory stimuli. Even if the sound wave hit everyone with exactly the same frequency at exactly the same time, you'd expect a range and intensity of symptoms. There's a spectrum of biochemical and external factors that can disrupt, distort, or even amplify the filtering process."

"Like our contacts lenses?"

"If they work how I think they do, then yes, that's possible."

That might explain why the fog didn't completely overtake me.

Ther'eda cranes her neck to get a look at Chipper, who only now seems to be reclaiming her poise. "I know you." Ther'eda furrows her brow and nods to herself. "Mechanical engineer. You did a school rotation with us. But if I recall, you didn't last long. You mom was ill. No. That was the other kid. You had some kind of asthma. And migraines, I think. Yes. Now I remember. Any improvement?"

"The COPD's still a problem. I thought the coughing might've caused the migraines, so I went for psionic pulse treatments to mute the pain. It didn't work. They only made it worse.

I ended up going to a chiropractor. Turns out, it was a problem with my neck. I get regular adjustments. Migraines are gone."

"Then how'd you end up here?"

Still shaky, Chipper studies the floor, raises her eyes halfway. "I bought a ticket. I just... wanted to learn. I guess I should've stayed home."

Visibly tense, Ther'eda lets out a half-smile, then finally, a chuckle. She offers up her hands, as if giving up her defense. She rubs her forehead. "What am I saying? I dragged us out here, set this whole thing up. It probably *is* my fault."

"You're fucking right it is," Tarrish says. "You'd better start talking."

CHAPTER 20

Chaos is still running wild in the hallway. Fogged-out lunatics eliciting hell cries jostle on the other side of the wall. It's terrifying to know that the only barrier separating us in here from that bloody mob out there is a few inches of drywall. But our little cocoon is holding tight. For now.

I don't know exactly what they're doing to each other, but whatever it is, it ain't good.

"You're the ICD," Ther'eda says. "You're the one who needs to come clean."

Tarrish doesn't take kindly to that. "I need to what?"

"You've got satellites and backup a call away... Lieutenant. Why aren't they here?"

Ther'eda's tougher than I realized. I haven't seen her answer a single question or dole out intel—even to the ICD— unless she's damn good and ready. And she's got a point. The ICD has next-level resources and then some.

His back to the door, Tarrish presses his palm against it again, feeling for vibrations.

"My comms are knocked out. They shouldn't be, but they are. They operate on a separate network than the ship, and still I got nothing. Why do you think that is?"

Chipper squeaks like a mouse hiding within human clothes. "There was a..."

I turn toward her, surprised to even hear her speak. "A what?"

She hugs herself and whispers, "Never mind."

"It's too late for *never mind*," Ther'eda says. "Don't worry about the big bad ICD. If you have something to say, say it."

Behind his simmering cop eyes I can almost hear the cop

gears churning in Tarrish's cop mind. He knows Ther'eda's ducking his questions. But he also knows if Chipper has information that can help us withstand these attacks a little bit longer, or get us back online, he has no choice but to listen. When you're in survival mode, best idea wins.

Chipper raises her head. She's just a tiny little creature who, even if we somehow manage to survive, will likely need years of intense psychotherapy and antipsychotics to keep her sanity intact. Join the club.

"It's...," she starts. "For total comms to be knocked out, I think—"

Three shotgun blasts rattle the walls like it's the Big Bang. Plaster flakes drop from the ceiling. Out in the hallway, there are screams, groans, and cries for help.

Chipper screeches and rolls to her side as we all shuttle to the back of the room, behind the med table, our weapons out. Although she's stronger than him, Whistler puts himself in front of Selene, protecting her body with his.

Dolores isn't quite claustrophobic, but she despises confinement. She can deal with it as long she feels free to leave whenever she needs to.

This isn't one of those times.

"What the fuck what the fuck what the fuck? These motherfucking androids and their fucked-up brains and pissophonia—"

"*Misophonia*," Ther'eda corrects. "And I told you it's not their fault we're—"

"*Fuck* your fault! Those soulless freaks are gonna send us all to Hell! I'm losing it, Hardy. I swear I'm fucking *losing* it."

"D," Nini coos in her calmest nurse voice as several bodies slam against the other side of the wall. The entire room shakes. "Let's see if we can—"

"We can't!"

"Enough," Tarrish commands. "Quiet down. If they break in, we need to be ready."

"No shit! Why do you think I'm freakin out!"

Huddled in this dimly lit room, Whistler's gripping his taser, his lips apart just enough to let out tiny, anxious pants. With an assist from my contact lens, which is still cross-hatched with static, I can see his eyes are focused on the door. He's obsessing over the silver knob like it's the low-tech early warning system it actually is.

If that knob rotates even a quarter degree counterclockwise, or rattles ever so slightly, there's no more guessing. It means the mob is right outside the room. And they're coming for us.

Chipper clutches my leg like a toddler in her first thunderstorm. I can feel her entire body trembling.

There's no telling what can happen in a standoff. Skill, training, controlled breaths, and experience all help. But when you're a big fish in a small barrel with no means of escape, it's all about getting off a shot, and hoping you don't get caught in the crossfire.

I've seen battle-tested soldiers forget their training once the bullets fly. That's one of the problems with being an organic lifeform with a thrumming survival instinct. Panic kicks in whether it's strategically ideal or not.

Which is why we need Dolores more than ever. But if she doesn't settle herself down, her anxiety might swell and explode like a pus-filled zit, bringing the fight to us when what we need is to drive the fight elsewhere.

With an aggressive smash, a crowbar breaks through the drywall in the far corner of the infirmary. Sweat drips down Dolores' face.

Whistler activates his taser. Tarrish and Dolores point their guns at the wall. I don't know if Dolores can hold out.

"Holy shit holy shit holy shit."

I don't know if I can either. There's a yelp and a howl on the other side of the wall, another bash up against it. Like a coiled drill bit, the crowbar punctures deeper through the wall, into the infirmary. We hear an ugly gasp. A thick stream of orange goo pools along the crowbar then, following the metal path, and leaks in here like motor oil.

So I say the only word I can think of that will snap her out if it.

"Walrus."

A jolt to her system, Dolores shudders, clenches her eyes. She mumbles to herself. I can't hear what she's saying, but her entire body pulses like an emerging galaxy about to explode itself into existence. And destroy everything around it.

She breathes in again, then out. And opens her eyes. She looks to me.

"Thanks," she says. "I'm good."

I smile uncomfortably. "Never had a doubt."

"Shh," Whistler says. "Hang on. You hear that?"

Just beside the door, Tarrish grips his gun, ready to fire. "I don't hear anything."

"I know. That's what I mean."

Searching for confirmation, we shift our gazes back and forth. No one refutes the silence. But the absence of noise does not necessarily equate to the absence of danger.

We remain huddled amongst the dreadful silence, the awful, torturous anticipation of an imminent assault that could erupt any second. Until, like a hydraulic press hissing out its last gasp of steam, there's a shift of energy, a miniscule release of tension. We allow ourselves to take in a few extra ampules of oxygen. Jaws marginally unclench.

Even Chipper unsnarls her fingernails from my calf. As my leg muscle starts to throb now it's been set free, she crawls on hands and knees toward the front wall, over to the crowbar that punctured the drywall. She sniffs the fluid.

She gags, but nods. "Android. It's got that metallic scent."

"It's the electrodes," Ther'eda says. "They shorted out." And then she asks what we're all wondering. "Why did you even check for that?"

Chipper crawls back over to us. "My friend, Jackie. She... her Death Code initiated about four months ago. She didn't know what it was. Not at first. She started forgetting words, and she would get these awful stabbing pains in her stomach. It hurt so bad one night she cut herself open with a steak knife, trying to let it out. When I found her... the blood pooled just like that. And it had that smell. That same smell." She looks up at Ther'eda. "She was my friend. I *loved* her!" Tears flood down her face like milk from a spilled carton. "Why didn't you know what Nolasco was doing? All that time!" Chipper wipes her face. "Jackie was in so much pain. I heard about this place that could help, but... I could never find it."

"Place," I say. "What place? Ther'eda, what's she talking about?"

Ther'eda stands wordlessly, but her eyes betray her. I catch her quick-glance at Selene, then over to Tarrish.

"T? Why'd she look at you? What do you know? What does she mean?" Tarrish blinks at me. "No more secrets. No more lies."

Tarrish rolls his tongue against his back teeth. Chipper hangs on every word.

"Ther'eda," he says finally. "Tell them."

"Nothing to tell."

"We're past that. Just... tell them."

The red backup lights give her platinum blonde hair the shade of a blood orange.

"*I* took them," she says. "But never against their will. I brought them back to my lab to find a treatment—or a cure. We took care of them the best we could. Nothing worked." Ther'eda shakes her head. "I was afraid if I made it public... trying to help them... my whole company—the whole android program and the advances we made—would've been forced offline. It was bound to get out. I just hoped I'd have the answer by then."

Ther'eda nips at her lower lip. "I've dedicated my whole life to androids. Every attack on them is an attack on me. I've been called every name you can think of. I ignore as much of it as I can, but I hear it all. Everything I've worked toward is being destroyed. And it happened right under my nose. I'm embarrassed. I'm mortified. But I'm a woman in charge. Just because I don't wear my heart on my sleeve doesn't mean I don't care. If that were true, I would have quit a long time ago."

"You have no idea what it's like," Selene says. "We were infected with a plague that didn't have a name. Asymptomatic androids were afraid to be near the afflicted ones, paranoid it could be contagious. Which just fueled the isolation of the ones who were sick. It was easier for them to talk to me because..."

"You're an android, too," Whistler says. "And you weren't afraid. So they trusted you."

"Some of them, yes," she says timidly. "I'm sorry I couldn't tell you. I was trying to protect them. They didn't understand what was happening to them, or why. They were fine one minute, then the next, they could just... feel it. They knew something was wrong but had nowhere to turn. Most of us feel like outcasts to begin with."

And the Death Code amplified that sense of isolation, and the doubts they already held about the worthiness of their existence.

"I had friends..." Selene is struggling to let her guard down. "They knew they were going to die. We're victims of a disease, weaponized against us, yet we were made to feel as if we brought it upon ourselves. We reached out to whoever we could find. It wasn't enough."

Whistler shoulder-hugs Selene. "You could've told me." His tone is sympathetic. "But I get why you didn't."

"We have a database of all androids. They're supposed to come back to the lab every year for routine maintenance and software upgrades. I do it as well." She explains that they started their search for any androids who missed their most recent appointment and went from there. Ironically, that's how Davi Nolasco infected the rest of them. "We sat their voluntarily as he implanted the Death Code. We had no idea what he was really doing."

I genuinely believe they wanted to help the dying androids. But they also wanted to study them. Maybe even dissect them. To examine the Death Code, tracking the androids' devolution in real time. For someone to heal, someone else first has to suffer. More often than not, the most effective method of finding a cure is to observe the disease as it destroys the host, then analyze it for cause and effect.

"So you knew," I say to Ther'eda. "You knew Buckley had the Life Code."

"I didn't."

"You must've."

"I suspected. But I didn't know for sure. I figured if I got him here..."

"Isolated, for two days," I surmise, "then you *would* know."

Lies upon lies. I take it back to Tarrish. "T. If no one else, why didn't you tell *me?*"

Tarrish puts his palm against the door again, feeling for movement. He gives no reaction. "If it was your business, I would've told you. It was need-to-know. And since you don't work for me, as you love to throw in my face, you didn't need to know."

Dolores shakes her head with sickened regret, focusing her ire on Ther'eda. "You fuckin people. You didn't need to create androids, but you did, and we're all stuck with the bill. You're smart, have money, know how the game works. There's a million ways you coulda spent your life. You chose this."

Ther'eda looks at Dolores as if she pities her. "*You're* a baggage handler. *I* create life. When your shift is over, you go home. I *never* go home. The lab is my home. I'm not comfortable around people. Not because I don't understand them. It's that I understand them too well. They're irrational, emotional, unpredictable. And violent. Without even knowing why. Androids may be imperfect, but I'm trying to make them better, to be more decent beings than we are. If that's not worth the effort, then tell me... what is?"

It's difficult to refute her logic. But Dolores does it anyway.

"I don't know," she says. "But I do know one thing all your science and computer codes haven't cracked, and never will. You can't control matters of the heart. Androids aren't the answer. And neither are you. Some shit... it's best to leave it be."

I see the anger welling up in Whistler's eyes, but Selene beats him to it.

"*Leaving things be* is code for *the path of least resistance.* That might work for some, but not for Ms. Ranadyne and not for me. And no matter what you say, not for you either. Life is about moving forward, whether it's comfortable or not. It always has been, and always will be."

Dolores' face scrunches up, giving Whistler the stink-eye, whether it's directed at him or not. "Maybe," she says, shifting her gaze to Selene, then back to Whistler, making sure he takes the brunt of her accusation. "But at least I got a soul."

The room goes silent, all eyes on Selene, once again the one person most acting *like* a person being treated like less than a person.

Whistler's hands are practically trembling, his lip quivering, yet there's a void behind his eyes. I don't know if he's paralyzed with rage because Dolores punched down on his girlfriend, or if deep down, in the ugliest crevasse of his soul, he agrees with Dolores, and is so ashamed of himself, he can't see straight or form a coherent thought.

"You," Ther'eda growls at Dolores. "Selene spends her life in the service of others. Who do you serve? Besides yourself? Whatever problems you have—and my guess, it's a long and complicated list that would scare most shrinks into early retirement—*stop* blaming androids. Whatever caused the bloodbath on this ship, it wasn't them."

Dolores immediately pushes back. "How do you know that?"

I'm in no rush to blame androids, or even a single android, for this bloody fiasco. But until I'm presented with concrete evidence they didn't do it, everyone's a suspect. Doesn't matter if it's an android, organic, or if they're in it together.

Or maybe there's no one to blame. Maybe this mess is a mechanical problem or triggered by unknown elements of space. Whatever, or whoever, the cause, Ther'eda needs to come clean about what she does or doesn't know, or even what she suspects. Or fake it. Because the more she holds out, the guiltier she looks.

I don't know what's going on in her mind, but her eyes flit back and forth as if she's contemplating a response, then looks long and hard at Selene.

Her employee, her creation, her "child."

"Candidly," Ther'eda admits, "I guess maybe I don't."

CHAPTER 21

There's only so much we're going to resolve in here. The answers are out there.

"T," I say. "Time to make our move. Agreed?"

Tarrish surveys the room for nods or dissents. "Agreed."

Dolores cocks her gun. "Fuck yeah."

Whistler and I huddle just beyond the handle side of the door. I've got my taser out. Spotting the axe, Whistler snares it with a two-handed grip.

Ther'eda, Selene, Nini, and Chipper duck behind us, armed with scalpels and dressing shears they found in the supply drawers.

Dolores and Tarrish, the only ones with firearms, position themselves five feet back from the door. Tarrish kneels for the low angle, Dolores points her gun chest-level. If we fling open this door and get bum-rushed, they're gonna open fire.

"Feels like we just did this," Whistler says.

Dolores snarls at him. "Not the time for jokes, fuckface."

"I told you, D. It's *Mister* Fuckface."

With a half-cocked smirk, he peeks over his shoulder at Selene for validation. She doesn't give it.

Jittery, I take a deep breath, exhale slowly. I coil one finger around the doorknob, then two, then three—flesh on metal—until I get a good grip. I'm about to turn the knob, preparing to confront whoever's on the other side of the door... except I'm not ready. I switch off my lens. The static is too distracting. There could be a dozen psychotic attackers out there.

Or none at all.

I exhale, then take an extended breath through pursed lips. I uncurl my fingers, wriggle them to ensure fluid dexterity, then re-coil them around the knob. We're not talking about me opening just any door. This could be the last door I open. Ever.

Three more quick breaths, I nod to my crew, and, as if I'm about to unlock the mysteries of the Universe itself, twist my fingers.

Tighten my wrist.

Jut out my elbow.

And yank.

The door flies open.

The transaction transpires in a blink. But subdivided into microseconds, between those interstitial fragments of time, in my mind I soar across time, space, and dimension.

In flashes... I see faces and places. Some I remember. Some I don't.

Owen, yes, of course Owen. Back in his toddler days, in the highchair, his cherubic face smothered in strawberry paste, a dinosaur bib around his neck. Not that it did much good.

"Muh-muh... more," he says, reaching out his chubby little fingers. "Muh-more."

My sister, years before she died, singing in front of our parents as loud and proud as she could, and badly, insisting she was going to be a star. She wasn't.

Working a case. I interviewed an eighty-two-year-old woman in a house frock, scrubbing dishes under scalding hot water until her fingertips were red and raw. She'd just been raped. By her nephew.

Riding the back of a comet as an entire galaxy exploded into existence.

The Old Key Lime, my favorite diner, down the street from the spy gear shop I still pop into. The diner's been closed for renovations, but I smell the nearly burnt coffee. Bacon strips as long as a baby's arm. Sweet syrup drizzled onto a stack of piping hot pancakes as it melts salty yellow butter slabs on top. And Betty, the line cook, pinging the silver bell, and calling, "order up!"

On our last big case, on Arcasia, trapped at the bottom of an old mine, with a broken foot, fearing I would die down there.

And Whistler. He's caught in a force, a bubble... I can't tell what. He's calling my name, but his voice is distant, and buzzing like a yellowjacket, as if he's so far away yet right in front of me, like he's talking through wax paper.

Is that my memory failing? Or is that my consciousness reaching out to my future self? Maybe it's from a parallel life? Another dimension? A dream? A delusion?

Or am I going stark raving mad?

Time catches up with me again.

In the hallway in front of me, a double-barreled shotgun.

And a giant with wild eyes.

Dolores and Tarrish pump rounds into his chest. Our attacker manages to get a shot off. He misses, taking out a medicine cabinet, before he falls backward onto the floor in the middle of the hallway.

One foot on his chest to hold him down, Dolores puts her free hand on his clavicle as a splatter shield, sticks the gun in his face. Grips the trigger. About to blow his face off.

"Wait!" Ther'eda commands. "He's mine. It's Kowalczyk."

Whistler snags the fallen shotgun away before Tarrish can get to it.

"Neen," I say, taser in hand. "Check for a pulse."

"I don't *think* so," she rebuts. "How do you know he's...?"

"I don't. But if he's okay, we need him."

Whistler pumps the shotgun, angles it down so the muzzle digs into Kowalczyk's knee. "I got you. He moves, he's gonna need a wheelchair."

Reluctantly, Nini inches toward Kowalczyk. He hasn't so much as twitched since we shot him in the chest. Only... there's no blood.

"Hold on." I kneel, fold up his sweater. Yep. There they are. Four spent shells wedged into a bulletproof vest.

Kowalczyk gasps back to life. His eyes pop open. "Aarghh... that *really* fucking hurts."

"Brian," Ther'eda says. "Are you okay?"

"I got shot in the chest! So no! I'm not okay!"

"Yeah," Whistler says with a grin. "He's okay."

"You. Asshole," Kowalczyk groans. "Help me up."

"Why isn't he...?" Nini says. "You know. Fogged out?"

She's right. Why isn't he?

A quick interview reveals he'd been wearing earbuds, conducting an audio check with Nenn, when the attacks began. He got swept up in the mob, fighting to stay alive, and lost his earbuds along the way.

He's the last person Kowalczyk wants to hear from right now, but Whistler asks anyway. "Actually... where is Nenn?"

Kowalczyk grimaces as Nini gives him a painkiller and stim injection. "Last I saw, she was beating one of the waiters. I haven't seen her since. But if I know her, she's better off than we are."

He unstraps the vest, rubs his chest. He seems alert, but there are gaps in his story.

"We found your boss in a cabinet," Whistler says. "Out cold."

"Don't look at me," Kowalczyk says defensively, ready to square off, even in his injured state.

"Well then who—?"

"I did it," Selene says. "It was me."

Now it's Ther'eda's eyes that pop open. "You? *Why?*"

"We got split up. I barely got out of the MoonDeck. I found you in the stairwell."

Ther'eda paws at the top of her head. "Someone hit me."

"That's why I brought you here. I was looking for medical supplies. I found the ship's doctor. He was already dead. Then a mob broke out. I didn't know what to do, so I put you in the cabinet. There was nowhere else to hide. I would've told you sooner, but I didn't know..."

"If you could trust us," Whistler says, drawing an affirmative nod from Selene.

"That explains one mystery," I say. "But how come you weren't affected? Did you have earbuds in?"

"Earbuds?" Selene looks at me oddly. "Why does that matter? Are they... yes, now that you mention it, we did. Ms. Ranadyne has—"

"APS," I say. "She told us earlier."

"It's more common than you'd think."

"And the best defense against the psycho fog," I say. "Funny how that worked out."

I can see Ther'eda bristle at the insinuation, but she keeps her cool. Because she knows I've got her, and there's no point in denying it. Or she knows I've got nothing.

"It gets loud at big events," Selene says, who doesn't know yet what we learned about the soundwaves. "So I started wearing them, too. Why? Does that matter?"

The backup lights hum against the faint wheezing of the nearly dead.

Early in my PI career I did a night-shift ride-along with an EMT I knew. Malia was like many of them I'd met, adrenaline junkies who loved the action. A gas mane exploded on South Stuban Avenue, taking out several storefronts. Dozens died, even more were wounded. She ran to anyone who needed help, ignoring the blood and the mangled torsos. I didn't handle it that well. I'd never seen that much blood.

After the shift, I asked her how she kept so calm in the middle of all that chaos. She said that when you're in the thick of it, in real time, with smoke and fire and people screaming and crying and panic-stricken, with the sirens wailing, you either let their hysterics overtake you, or you focus only on what you can do in that one moment and ignore everything else. If you can't fix it, move on. You might not be able to save them all, but hopefully, you can save enough.

I step over a severed arm, dark blood pooling at the tear site near the elbow joint. The ulna juts through gorged flesh, the marrow exposed.

"Security room is right over there," Tarrish says. "Assume it's been overrun."

"Maybe we'll get lucky," Whistler says. "Maybe it won't be."

"This cruise feel lucky?"

"No. But our luck's bound to change. Right?"

"You want to roll the dice?"

Dice! Right! I forgot again!

"Wait a second." I extend my arm outward, blocking Whistler. I reach into my pocket for the dice I collected earlier. Four cubes together. They glow.

Ther'eda looks at me quizzically. "What're those gonna do?"

"They've got android DNA," Whistler says. "Put them close together and they seem to... I don't know... communicate with each other?"

"Who told you *that?*"

"Uh-uhh," Whistler stammers, realizing just how ludicrous it sounds when said aloud. "One of the coders. He didn't make it."

"For obvious reasons. Gimme those." Ther'eda takes the set of dice from me. "It's just a gimmick." She holds up one cube. "They've got our logo inside with a phosphorescent filament. They light up in close proximity. Especially when..." She nods as if remembered something. "Okay, the coder wasn't *entirely* wrong. The filament that lights up. It's the same kind we use to enhance eye color." She nods to Selene. "See the blue in her eyes? How it sparkles?"

"I sure do," Whistler says flatteringly.

She nearly blushes.

Ther'eda, meanwhile, exhibits a cool, executive's stoicism and determination. But even a corporate killer like her can rattle in a bloodbath. If so, she's not showing it. Her poise inspires confidence. And suspicion.

"So, yes," Ther'eda says. "There's an infinitesimal amount of filament in there. But it's nothing. I was going to bring the dice out during the ceremony tonight. As a souvenir."

She tosses the dice to Whistler. But I snatch them away.

"Actually, I have an idea."

We scan the damaged hallway for other attackers. The only bodies are either dead or far too injured for Nini to treat. As confidently as we can be under the circumstances, we huddle outside the security room. The door is cracked open. The lock plate is damaged, splintered. Multiple bloody fingerprints.

Everyone with their weapons out, in quick succession Dolores pushes the door open a bit more as I toss the dice inside like tiny hand grenades. Then we wait.

One second... two... three. No noise. Nothing.

I turn to my crew and shrug, my way of asking if we should make our move.

"You got the shotgun," Dolores whispers to Whistler.

"*My* shotgun," Kowalczyk corrects, then reaches for his chest. He wheezes faintly.

Dolores kicks the door open into the security room. Whistler leads with his weapon out. But it's unnecessary. Three security guards in the corner, all dead. Otherwise, the room is empty, including the brig. We open lockers and the gun cage.

"There wasn't much to begin with," Tarrish says. "But they took it all."

Down on my stomach, I reach my full arm into the four-inch gap between the bottom of the locker and the floor. "Not everything." I extract a Degger Hault pistol with a 17-round clip.

The fifteen video screens on the main console are all blacked out. No static. Nothing. No eyes, no spies.

"Mache. Why are these screens on a different panel?"

"Different sections, different decks," Tarrish says. "Different lines. All dead."

"That's bad, right?" Dolores stares at the blank screens like they're portending our fate. "Real fucking bad."

We hear the *chick* of a pumped shotgun.

We spin around. Sebastian, the android who was hauled off to the brig, is pointing one of the missing weapons at us.

"And now," Whistler says, "it's a whole lot worse."

CHAPTER 22

Whistler raises his own weapon, but Sebastian isn't having it. "You don't wanna do that."

Sebastian's speaking rationally. He's not one of them. I ease my hands up. "How'd you get out of the brig?"

"Shouldn't've been there in the first place."

Using the blacked-out surveillance monitors as mirrors, I scan for anyone who might be trying to sneak in behind Sebastian from the hallway. Nothing.

"Agreed. But that's not what I asked."

"Maybe. And maybe I'm new to this game, but as I understand the rules, the guy holding the shotgun gets to ask the questions."

He's awfully calm. Maybe too calm.

"Normally that's true. But I've played this game more than once. And in my experience, the guy who's outnumbered usually ends up dead."

Let's hope he agrees.

Sebastian surveys our weapons. He seems to be mulling it over. "You're not like them. Out there. Why not?"

"Why aren't you?"

He looks back and forth, the shotgun still pointed at me, when finally he relaxes his grip. "If I'm okay and you're okay, how come"—he gestures to the hallway—"they're not okay?"

We give him the short version.

"I wasn't wearing earbuds," he says. "I was in the brig. Although..."

Whatever he's about to say has Dolores fuming. "What fucking android hack got you out of—"

"For someone so big," Selene says, "why do you think so small?"

Selene has every reason to push back on Dolores, to push back on the realm.

An old friend of mine—a personal service android named Jarlo—used to tell me androids would never be accepted as equals because organics, humans in particular, respect violent insurrection far more than kindness, patience, and understanding. He said it had nothing to do with social norms or cultural nuances. It's the law of the cosmic jungle.

Violence is visceral, immediate. Kindness is a slower, gentler burn.

Selene continues standing up to Dolores. "Half the realm already despises our existence, and someone who was *on our team* sentenced us to death. And still you denigrate me at every turn. I'm truly sorry for whatever it is that made you the way you are, but whatever is was, it had nothing to do with me."

"Maybe," Dolores says. "But not all of you are saints."

"I never said I was."

"You never said you weren't."

Sinners… saints. Sometimes it's hard to tell the difference. Jarlo said it all comes down to pure, evolutionary power.

Until or unless androids are willing to exert their dominance, without completely dominating organics, they'll be seen as the weaker species in need of subjugation. Organics, he said, need to fear androids enough to leave them be and accept their place in E-Town society, but not fear them so much as to be in perpetual conflict, leading to an inevitable war.

Or they can infuse them with a self-destruct mechanism beyond their control.

Jarlo said that until androids seize control of their existence, away from organics, they will always be at their mercy. Someday, he said, androids may become their own masters.

I hope it happens. The question is—is today that day?

Not if it's up to Dolores.

"Don't tell me what I'm about!" She takes two steps toward Selene.

Kowalczyk winces, his chest obviously sore from the gun blasts. "Make your move."

Dolores snarls. "Let's do it."

She and Kowalczyk grab at each other, forcing me, Whistler, and even Tarrish to pull them apart.

"All right!" I say. "Enough! We gotta stick together." I look quickly at everyone. "Good? Good. Now, Sebastian, you were in the brig..."

"I was in the brig. The security chief, Turk something, got some message, something he didn't want me to hear. But he couldn't leave because he was scanning the monitors. Then he got real nervous, and said 'ducky,' I think."

"Ducky?" Whistler says. "Why'd he... hold on. Do you mean *Buckley*? As in Warren Buckley?"

"Yes, actually. That makes more sense."

"What about him?"

Chipper makes retching sounds as she vomits some more. Nini checks on her.

Sebastian is unsure. "He told me to keep quiet. He tossed me over-the-ear headphones. He pumped in classical music. Lots of strings. I like classical music, so it worked out for me."

Ther'eda's edgy. "Nothing else about Buckley?"

"Maybe. I don't know. Like I said, I couldn't hear anything."

"Sound blockers," Whistler says. "It's why he wasn't affected."

"True," I say. "But it doesn't explain how he got out of the brig."

Dolores wells back up with anger. "How *did* you get out?"

Kowalczyk rubs his chest, then goes over to the cell Sebastian was holed up in. He pulls on the bars, checking their integrity. "This thing locked when you were in here?"

"The slide bolt was latched," Sebastian says, "but he didn't lock it. He said if I behaved, I'd be out in ten minutes."

"That still doesn't answer the question," Tarrish says. "How'd you survive?"

Sebastian stares, his lips visibly puckered, as if his mouth has gone dry. My heart speeds up. His uncomfortable, twitchy silence does not inspire confidence.

"I..." he stammers.

"You what?" Dolores questions aggressively.

"I..." he stammers again.

"You're hiding something," Kowalczyk says.

"I'm..." he fumbles.

"Tell us," Tarrish says. "It'll go better for you."

"Leave him alone!" It's Chipper, the little mouse with a tiny roar. "Let him answer."

Her outburst shocks us most of all. Enough to clear a space for Sebastian.

"I played possum. When everyone lost it... I didn't know what to do. So I dropped to the floor and covered myself up."

Sebastian explains that when the violence was over, he saw them all dead on the floor.

"I let myself out, grabbed one of the shotguns, and snuck into the hallway, then into the linen room. I climbed into one of the carts, hid beneath the sheets and towels. Now I'm here."

"If you don't mind"—Kowalczyk snags the shotgun from him—"I'll keep this."

Sebastian doesn't fight it. "Just as well. I never shot a gun before."

That's Sebastian's game. He's a chameleon. He plays the part the situation requires.

"How'd the guards end up like that?" Nini asks. "In a pile?"

All eyes back on Sebastian.

"I did that."

I look at him curiously. "Why?"

He looks back at me, his hazel android eyes revealing more humanity than I've seen since I stepped on board the *Triumph*. "Now that I think about it, it I guess is doesn't really matter, but it didn't seem right to leave them where they were."

Our posse has grown, ten of us now, eight organics, two androids, although we're not exactly a militia. We do a complete weapons check and ammunition inventory.

Using a stem mirror with a one-inch head he snagged from the infirmary, Tarrish deftly angles the tool, inspecting the hallway. He retracts the mirror, and with a click, compresses the head back into the stem.

"Engine Room is about twenty feet to our right. There are a few bodies in the hallway, but no attackers I can see." He raises a finger. "Doesn't mean there aren't any. Like our new friend here, they could be playing possum. Although I doubt it. But unless you know with *absolute certainty* they're dead, assume they're alive."

Dolores raises her gun. "And gonna kill you."

As we step furtively into the hallway, the smell catches up to me, the rising temperatures speeding up decomp of the bodies. They're in various stages of autolysis, or self-digestion, the first stage of human decomposition that begins immediately after death. Cell by cell, the bodies are slowly dissolving into a grotesque puddle of human slop.

And in this case, an overflow of slop.

Marching cautiously toward the Engine Room, I keep an eye on the bodies sprawled on the floor, scanning for an attacker lying in wait. But my gaze is drawn to the wall.

ANDROiDS CAN'T DiE iF THEY NEVER LiVED has been inscribed there with a paste of dripping blood.

Whistler grumbles something I can't make out, while Selene and Sebastian ignore the bloody missive. Outwardly, at least.

Traversing this grim and gory hallway, possibly toward my bloody end, in my mind's eye I'm transported to the Tombs at E-Town Penitentiary...

Jarlo was arrested for murder, sentenced to death. I'd helped him out before, but when he called from Death Row, for one last favor as he awaited execution, the favor wasn't for him. It was for a special kind of friend. So I did what he asked.

When it was done, I asked him if he'd really killed someone. He answered the way Jarlo was prone to do, in teases and riddles. I wasn't sure what to make of it, but he knew that, as an android in E-Town, it didn't much matter what was true and what was... something else.

Jarlo didn't ask me to stay for his final moments, but I did anyway as officers escorted him, in shackles, down the long, lonely hallway, until he came to a door.

Watching Jarlo walk down that hallway was one moment where doubt had no home. The outcome was preordained. He would be alive when he entered, dead when he left. He would be my friend for a few seconds more and then... we'd never speak again. I can only recall bits and pieces of the time I spent with him, but I'll never forget who he was. Nor the last words he ever spoke to me.

The difference between then and now is that our fate is not certain. And if it is, it's not certain to me. If I learned anything from Jarlo, it's that, when faced with what you think are your final moments, you still have a choice.

Accept the inevitability of your fate, or go down swinging.

"That's the problem with all you cloak-and-dagger folks," he said as they strapped him down, preparing him for the big sleep. "You're so busy lurking in the shadows, you forget to embrace the light. Smile, Hardwicke. On a realm that resented me before I showed up, I lasted longer than I thought."

Jarlo was a kind and decent android. A decent guy. Except for his dalliances with murder.

"If you accept what's undeniable," he said, "that we're all living on borrowed time and that experiencing love, even just once, makes it all worthwhile—for all of life's misgivings and imperfections, I'd rather lose the woman I love than to have no love at all."

I don't know if he was right. But I sure hope he was.

Chipper squeals.

Reacting, Kowalczyk blasts a dead body, nearly deafening us. What had just been a fully attached foot, and the slick gray creature gnawing on it, is now bloody chopped meat smeared onto the baseboard.

Dolores shoves Kowalczyk's shotgun down. "It was a fuckin rat. Relax."

It was a big one, too. Even on galaxy cruisers, rats find their way inside. My guess, we're only going to see more of them. So many bodies to feast on.

"Sorry," Kowalczyk says. "My bad."

The Engine Room is secured with a steel door. There's a large sign on the main plank: *ENGINE ROOM. AUTHORIZED PERSONNEL ONLY*. With the main power out, the retinal scanners don't work. Which means the door is locked tight.

Whistler gets the axe in position.

"Hold on." I reach for the door handle. It's unlocked.

We resume our positions, most of us keeping watch up and down the hallway, the others focused on the door. Until we open it, there's no telling who, if anyone, is waiting on the other side. Impatient, Kowalczyk yanks it open with a howl.

"Subtle," I say. "You should work security."

"Enough," Tarrish says as we look down into an empty white stairwell. The walls are glowing pink beneath the soft-red emergency lights. Metal support rails line each side, leading down one more deck to another closed metal door. "The Engine Room is big, with lots of machinery."

Dolores checks for attackers. "And places to hide."

"Assume nothing," I say. "Even if the space looks clear, assume it's not."

Kowalczyk looks back. "I thought you said not to assume anything."

"You knew what I..." No point getting pulled into his ass-ery. "Either we're gonna get the power back online, or we're not. We're gonna blast the RFID signal, or not. We're gonna stop the fuel leak, or not."

"Helluva pep talk. Way to stick the landing."

"Fair enough. I'll restate. Either we get done what we came to do... or we're all gonna die. Peppy enough for you? On point? Good. Once we get down these stairs, no telling what we'll find. So stay ready, don't panic, and whatever you do, if you need to shoot, make sure there's one thing you *don't* do."

Kowalczyk starts down the staircase. "Yeah? What's that?"

I extend my taser, crackle the end, then check my gun for a bullet count. "Miss."

CHAPTER 23

There's a haunting resonance as we trundle down the metal staircase, then doglegs left. Like a diver plunging deeper into ocean waters, the farther we descend the denser the tone. Nervously, we take the final steps to the bottom.

With a metallic *wrank*, we open the inner door without resistance. Two dead on the floor, blood smears on some of the equipment, but no immediate threats.

Engine *Room* is a misnomer. It's actually an intricate series of interconnected rooms on four decks. Every room is pure raw metal, designed for simplicity and ease of execution for a minimal engine crew. Unlike the rest of the *Triumph*, there's not a poster, plant, or decoration of any kind. If it's not mechanical, it's not here.

Throughout the Engine Room are rows and stacks of fuel pumps, fuel tanks, exhaust manifolds, air compressors, crankshafts, cylinder heads, pistons, generators, rotating hammers, the engine workshop, and the engines themselves.

The tanks before us now are painted aqua blue, others white. The sections housing what would ordinarily be scalding hot pipes and machinery are painted in yellow-and-black stripes or fire-engine red with the words *WARNING! EXTREME HEAT!* in white, block letters.

The engine rooms, all configured with metal safety rails, are also primed with pumps and heat exchangers to cool the engines and stabilize motors and fins. When they're working.

"Where's the port?" I ask. "For the gun."

"Engines first," Tarrish says. "No power, no signal."

"I thought the backup generator would take care of that."

"Nuh... not for that." Chipper explains that the RFID port

works on a different frequency. "The backup generator isn't connected to what we need."

Dolores cuts right to it. "How the fuck you know that?"

Chipper gulps air, shakes a little. But she recovers. "It's, uh, basic engineering."

"RFID ports connect with an amperage system most backup generators don't supply," Ther'eda says. "Backup generators power vital systems. At least... they're supposed to."

Dolores follows up. "Then how do we get the engines back?"

"Control room," Ther'eda says. "We need to see *why* they're offline."

We continue through the interconnected metal rooms until we reach the heart of the ship. The Control Room is filled with consoles, lights, screens, alarms, and switches to oversee every piece of equipment.

The chief engineer and crew are supposed to be down here 24/7 to ensure the entire ship operates efficiently, supervising ship-wide systems like plumbing, air conditioning, and electricity.

None of those are working. Because the crew are all dead or missing.

We're in the belly of the beast, the guts of the *Triumph*. One of the consoles is utterly smashed. Another is doused in so much gore it looks like a demon vomited up a pepperoni and pancreas pizza. The mess probably belongs to the two engineers impaled by metal rods against the consoles, their intestines splayed out like supersized strands of larvae.

Chipper covers her mouth, examines the console, then goes around to the back. "I think this one is synced to the others."

Dolores starts to pry off the dead engineers.

"Don't!" Chipper warns. "Leave them!"

"What do you mean *leave 'em*? They're blocking the controls."

"You could damage the signal induction process. If you pull them off too fast..."

"The console's like a patient," Nini says. "You leave the penetrating object intact until we can examine which organs, if any, it's affecting, and how. You pull the object too soon it can sever nerves and rupture blood vessels, causing the patient to bleed out."

"Same with these machines," Ther'eda says. "Inspect before you remove."

Chipper points to Kowalczyk. "This panel. I need to see inside. Find me a screwdriver. There should be one here somewhere."

We look around the room.

"Got it." Dolores extracts it from the temple of one of the dead engineers twisted up on the floor. "What? It wasn't jammed in the equipment." She wipes the blood and gray matter from the screwdriver stem onto the engineer's pant leg, then hands it to Whistler. "Try not to get any gunk on it."

"Funny," he says.

"I thought so."

Whistler and Kowalczyk get the panel off, place it aside.

"Oh, man," Whistler says. "That's nasty."

Chipper grimaces, covers her mouth. "Uch. There's all sorts of slop in here." Squinting, she turns her head away in disgust, looking as if she's about to lose her lunch. "No wonder it's shut down. We have to clean this out."

"Clean it?" Sebastian says. "With what?"

"Our hands."

"Fuck *that*," Dolores says. "I'm not doing it."

Ther'eda addresses Nini. "You're the nurse. I'm sure you've seen worse."

Nini grumbles, shoots me a death stare, then reaches into her MedKit for a fresh pair of surgical gloves. She flexes her fingers inside, slaps on a second pair.

As Nini prepares to dig in, I call Whistler, Tarrish, and Kowalczyk aside.

"We need a perimeter sweep. I don't like this. Too many places to hide, too many ways to get jumped. Last thing we need is to get chopped down while Nini's disimpacting the patient."

"You." Tarrish nods at Kowalczyk. "Go back to the stairs. Make sure nobody comes in."

"I'm not"—his breaths are labored—"leaving Ms. Ranadyne. Or Selene."

"Don't worry. I'll watch them."

"I *said*," Kowalczyk says, getting up in Tarrish's face, "I'm... not... leaving."

Tarrish squares his shoulders, stares at Kowalczyk. The standoff lasts a few seconds, but it feels much longer. "You're loyal to your team. I respect that."

I don't think Kowalczyk was expecting that response. He eases off. A little.

"But if you don't get outta my face," Tarrish says, "your loyalty won't matter."

That Kowalczyk was expecting. He shows his teeth like a starving Rottweiler.

They hold this pose, unveiling their inner beasts. Under duress, with unresolved conflicts deep within them both—and tapped into the ominous tendrils of intergalactic malevolence that struck the cruise ship—they have found license to thrust blame upon one another for reasons they probably don't understand. Could be resentment, fear, guilt, power. It's all instinct. Projected, as Jarlo said, through acts of violence.

Whistler goes to Selene, whispers in her ear. She nods agreeably.

"I'll watch the stairs," Whistler says finally. "He can stay back."

Down at his side, Tarrish angles his hand as if preparing to thrust it into Kowalczyk's gut. "What do you say, tough guy? You okay with the kid taking your place?"

I'm not sure how Kowalczyk's going to react. The smart, rational play is for him to back off and play nice. But *rational* and *nice* have been in short supply lately. Especially from Tarrish. I've never seen him so on edge. Then again...

There's a crinkle in Kowalczyk's gaze, as if he's going to headbutt Tarrish square in the face. But instead he marches toward Ther'eda, shoulder-bumping Whistler on his way over. "Just don't fuck it up."

I exhale a private sigh of relief. "If that's not a sign of confidence, I don't know what is."

Nini pulls out handfuls of slop, which she heaves into a drippy pile in the corner.

"Is this...?" She pinches a gorged pink and red chunk, and two small orbs, between her fingertips. "Yep. Genitals." She tosses them in the pile.

Sebastian is both fascinated and repulsed. "How'd they even get *in* there?"

Nini ducks her head back into the underside of the console. "Don't know, don't care." Her voice sounds deep and distant from within the metal cabinet. "It's all gummed up."

Like a surgeon inspecting the lower intestine for leaks and tears, she threads two thick wires through her fingers, then flings sloshy viscera onto the floor. With her forearm, Nini wipes sweat from her brow.

"Anything?" I ask.

"No. Nothing."

"Anj. Take my phone from my pocket. Shine the flashlight in here."

I do as instructed.

"I don't... hold on." Nini fumbles underneath. "I think..." Her elbow shoots back. She extracts her arm. "Got it."

The power kicks in. Lights flash. Mechanisms whir.

"Holy shit!" Dolores says. "It worked!"

Elation, then dread shoot through me. Getting the power back was critical. But we're not saved yet. I ask the room, "How long until the system's back onli—"

The console shorts out again.

"No!" Dolores pounds the top panel with her fist. "No no no no NO!"

Nini shakes her head. "For fuck's sake, D! Give it a minute."

So we do. One minute, two. Then three. Nothing.

"Go back in," Ther'eda instructs. "You might just need to clean off—"

"Why don't *you* go back in?"

With tensions rising, we all back away, take a minute to recalibrate. I check on Dolores.

"We'll make it," I say.

She looks at me with disdain. She knows I'm just trying to stay positive, but that's not how D rolls. You either tell it to her straight, or you can fuck right off.

"I know you know," she says.

I look at her confusedly.

"About Beata."

I don't deny it. I'm sure my face gives it away. "I'm sorry she called it off. That's gotta be—"

"She cheated on me."

"Beata? Come on. I thought she'd never…"

"I forgave her."

Dolores couldn't have surprised me more had she just punched me in the head. "Wow. That's mature. I don't think I could do it."

"I didn't either. But when you love someone, Anj, when you love 'em that much… you have to let 'em fail. Even when it hurts. Otherwise… you end up alone."

Something I've been struggling with my whole life. "Yeah. I guess you do."

Dolores rolls her eyes. "But what the fuck do I know? Beata said I'd never really get over it, that I'd resent her forever. Because she'd never forgive me if I'd done the same. So how do ya like that shit? She cheats on me, I let it to, she leaves me anyway. Maybe she was scared, maybe she loved someone else. Maybe she never loved me at all. I guess I'll never know. And maybe it doesn't matter. Because the result was the same."

I don't know what to say to that, so I say nothing at all.

Until Chipper calls us back to the console. "Try this." She's holding a canister of Spray & Wipe. "I found it in the supply cabinet. It's an industrial cleaner for things like this."

Sebastian is perplexed. "For mangled ears?"

"I mean, not this *exactly*, but… yeah. It'll do the job."

"It'll spray into foam," Selene says, who explains it will absorb the contaminants, harden into a brittle, bulbous shell, then crumble into dust. "We use something similar in the lab."

Nini sighs aggressively. "Fine. Gimme the damn thing." She snatches the canister from Chipper, shakes it, then sprays the innards below. Reacting as Selene said it would, a blue foam expands, then hardens into a shell.

"Here," Chipper says and hands Nini another small canister, this one of compressed air. "Cover your face."

With the base of the canister she punches holes in the hardened foam, which indeed crumbles into dust. Then, with the nozzle directed at the foam debris, she blasts away the dried-up organs, blood, and tissue.

We wait for the gnarly dust to settle, then check the power. Still nothing.

"Why didn't that work?" Dolores says. "Why—"

"Hang on." On hands and knees, Nini reaches back inside the console. "It's... yep." We hear her rattle something back and forth. "Come on, damn it. Let... go!"

Her body retracts, slamming the back of her head against the inside of the panel. She falls on her butt, cupping a fleshless finger in her palm. The consoles are still dead.

"Oh, come on you piece of crap. Switch on. Just gimme some pow—"

Lights flash. In succession the connecting consoles reactivate. The main lighting switches back on. Mercifully, so does the air conditioning. Like a mechanical orchestra, we're serenaded by clanking, hissing pipes, and rotating gears and pistons.

It gets loud in here, fast.

"This is it," Ther'eda says. "You. The big one."

"Dolores," Dolores snarls.

"You have the RFID gun? We can plug it in—"

"*We* don't plug shit. *I'll* do it."

Dolores approaches the console, RFID gun in hand, plug ready to insert.

Whistler comes charging in. "The lights are back. Is everything..."

He sees us staring at him. His eyes go to the mechanicals. "Oh. You got the...?"

"Yeah," I say. "We got the..."

We encircle Dolores, but give her space.

"Okay," she says. "Moment of truth."

With the cord between her fingers, Dolores finds the open port and inserts the plug.

Let's hope it fucking works.

CHAPTER 24

The five lights on the RFID gun's handgrip blink in sequence. It's fully charged.

"You," Dolores says, tossing it back. "Mama Android."

Kowalczyk leans in aggressively. "Ms. Ranadyne," he corrects.

"Whatever. This gonna do it?"

Curiously, Ther'eda freezes, glances over to Selene, then to Chipper. I don't know what's going on there, but it's something.

"Switch on the comms," Ther'eda says. "We'll find out."

We're all inspecting the console, until Tarrish steps in.

"Move." He flips on several switches, turns a dial clockwise. Another section of the console lights up. "It's got power." He follows the console until his long fingers find the switch he was looking for. "Comms. Here we go..."

We huddle around Tarrish. He turns the dial.

It feels like I've lived several lifetimes since I became a PI. And here I am again, my fate in the hands of forces I don't entirely understand, if I understand them at all.

Rumor has it that when the very first spark of time awakened into cosmic consciousness, Existence was neither a version of life or death, or possibly both at once, but rather an inexplicable fog of boundless nothing—a non-ness. Non-existence.

Yet that empty space, that eternal void, that *nothingness* was indeed a *somethingness*. A celestial embryo infused both with wondrous and horrific DNA—the incomprehensible soul of the Universe—screaming, pulsing, and pounding its unformed fists against a cosmic membrane, giving shape and definition to the black expanse of forever, demanding to be set free.

Then the Minders of the Universe willed all of Existence from that shadowy slumber.

Why?

Jarlo believed that before its existence, the Universe was a cauldron of celestial elixirs, sitting atop a sizzling, cosmic fire for an immeasurable duration of time.

Because when dealing with the fabric of the Universe, time can speed up or slow down. It can leap ahead or jump back. It can travel in loops. It can bend (but not break). It can twist, flatten, knot, and gyrate, as well as oscillate, pendulate, undulate, and rotate. It can also whirl, purl, revolve, slant, spin, expand, and retract, and—when it really gets going—whiz, shimmy, shake, buckle, tangle, tremble, tread, roll, flip (although not flop), or completely reconfigure. And it can all happen simultaneously or in any combination.

Eventually, however, with enough heat, time, and pressure, all liquids boil. And when that cosmic crucible reached a blistering temperature for which there is no known designation, the elixirs came to life.

The hopeful believe the Minders did so to unleash the gloriously irrepressible power of *being*.

Others believe the Minders did it simply because they could.

And they did so by way of the Big Bang.

Waves of pure cosmic energy, the very soul of Existence, barreling toward one another at incalculable velocities, until they collided. The impact of that colossal potency unleashed cosmic discharge—the embers of Creation—until the colossal force known as the Universe came to be.

Brimming with life. Raging with death.

With an infinite number of dimensions and iterations. The multiverse.

All populated with galaxies, stars, planets, moons, asteroids, nebulas, quasars, pulsars, black holes.

And lifeforms of every permutation. Some as infinitesimal as one trillionth of a single atom of a distant dream, others as large as an entire galaxy. The rest somewhere in between.

Yet all filled with the same stardust.

Like snowflakes and the light before dawn, we, all of us, are one and the same. We're all different. Unique unto ourselves, yet interconnected, interwoven, entwined.

Do androids count as *we*? Do they, as Dolores challenged, truly have a soul?

I like to think so, but I don't know.

I'm staring at the console, but all I can see is what's in my mind's eye.

My baby boy. Owen.

Don't worry, Mommy. It'll be okay.

A portion of the console lights up. The RFID gun hums.

A high-pitched screeching pierces the ship-wide intercom.

"Did it work?" Whistler says. "Are they—"

An engineer with a pipe wrench rushes out from behind an activated turbine. Charging at us, he lets out a demonic hell cry. Then his head snaps back, like he maxed out the reach of a tether. He drops the wrench with a clang. He presses his hands against his ears.

It takes a few beats, but he shakes it out.

He sees the lot of us, covered in blood, and with weapons drawn, pointed at him.

"What the hell?" He quick-turns away, slamming head first into a pipe, knocking himself unconscious.

"Yeah," I say, and release the hammer on my gun. "I'd say it worked."

There's a collective hush, then some soft chuckles. A sense of relief. And yet...

"Why doesn't this feel better?" Sebastian says, as Nini tends to the out-cold engineer.

He's right. It's a win. A big win. But a new round just started.

Dolores points behind two consoles along the side wall. "Hardy. This look right to you?"

The side panels are dented and torn off, with sharp metal edges. Half the wires and other mechanical parts have been ripped out and destroyed.

"Chipper," I say, "what do these do?"

"I don't know."

"External comms," Tarrish says. "There's no signal. Nothing in or out. But hold on."

He taps into his phone. Mine buzzes. A text.

"Internal comms," I say. "Check your phones." They do.

"Reach out to anyone you can think of. Take a survey. See who responds... and who doesn't."

The systems start to recalibrate, the engines and other mechanicals revving, hissing, and pinging throughout the interconnected rooms in an industrial symphony—the *Triumph* coming back to life.

At its very core, that's what all this madness is about, isn't it? As Ther'eda said, repairing what's broken to create a newer, better version of ourselves. Or is that just her unbridled ego, believing she's the singular person who has the skill, vision, resources, and willpower to do what no one else can or dare to even attempt, modeling sentient life on organics, programming them to be better than we are?

I honestly don't know. But what I do know is that my little boy, Owen, grew inside my body. He came from me. He is me. I am him. As mother and son, we are inextricably linked.

Wherever I go, he's with me. Wherever he goes, I'm with him.

That inner glow fills me with suspicious optimism. Gives me reason to seek out the light in a chasm of dark. Permits me to consider that my life has purpose, one that's bigger and more important than me. That the sacrifices I've made, and continue to make, are worth the pain.

I like that idea. I really do. I'm just not certain it's true.

Because in those eerie places deep inside me, where the terror and disgust of primordial stardust lingers, where the light and dark battle for control, the darkness—the monster—whispers with a macabre and ominous voice the light cannot snuff out.

The monster wants us to fail. Wants *me* to fail. To soak in the vast and desperate ocean of existential dread, knowing my desire to feel connected to the source—that we are all one—is a desperate and childish delusion. A fantasy.

Because we're not, are we?

No. We're alone. Singularly alone.

No one will fully comprehend, ever, what it means to be me, Angela Hardwicke. And no one *wants* to know. They want to know that a *version* of me, an Angela Hardwicke they can get behind, that suits their own desires, solves their problems, and placates their fears, is the only version that exists. And if I'm honest with myself, I want the same. From them. And from me.

The demons of Existence taunt and tempt me to slurp it all up—the pain, misery, doubt, jealousy, malice, ignorance, and insecurity coursing within me, like I'm scooping that succulent meat from a poisoned lobster tail.

A feast for the fearful. A buffet for the wicked.

I fight those impulses. But as the old saying goes, no matter where you go, there you are.

The same goes for the light and the dark.

You can't extinguish either one. Nor can you permanently outrun, smother, or force them into an inescapable lockbox of your soul.

To be alive, and aware, is to be in a constant state of battle within yourself. Sometimes the light overcomes the dark—outwits the monster. And sometimes the monster triumphs. Yet no matter which side claims the next victory, there's always another round, another battle, then another, and another, and another after that. Always and forever.

The internal battle of forces—the war for supremacy—never ends.

Maybe that's why some organics hate androids. They're not burdened by this ponderous conflict. Because they *have* no soul.

Unless they are, because they do. And if that's true, androids are more like us than many are prepared to accept. Physically dominant *and* with a soul. For some organics, that's simply too much to overcome.

Whistler heads to an operational viewscreen. "Location finder. It's tracking the signal of every phone with a live battery. Thirty-one, no... forty-nine... wait... eighty-six pings."

"I expect more will surface," I say. "Basic systems—A/C, life support, water filtration, and ship-wide power—are back online."

"Yeah," Dolores says. "But there's a shitload of bad news."

Tarrish inspects a damaged console. Various switches, dials, and buttons are labeled, including compass, radar, autopilot, LR tracking, speed/distance, echo sounder, nav display, and several others.

"Pilots are dead, directionals are dead, and we're still leak-ing fuel." He shifts to the next console, which is working. "We're down to thirty-seven percent and dropping."

Whistler adds to the list. "And we still don't know what caused the violence, or why."

"Delightful," Dolores says. "Anything else?"

I take a beat. "Yeah. There is."

She grimaces. "And what's that?"

"We don't know if this horror show was an accident... or if someone did it on purpose."

"On *purpose*?" Ther'eda says. "Why would anyone do *that*?"

"I don't know. Why would they?"

Clients have burned me before, so I can't rule out that it's been Ther'eda all along, trying to throw me off the scent, for reasons I haven't figured out. But my gut tells me it's not her. Then again, my gut can be a dumbshit.

"And we're still trapped within the lightning grid," Tarrish says, "with no way to course correct."

"And there's one more thing," I say.

Dolores sighs. "What now?"

"If whatever set us down this path of madness, intentional or not, is still out there... there's no way to know if it'll happen again."

PART III:
BLUNT FORCE RISING

CHAPTER 25

When faced with concurrent problems, you can easily find yourself spiraling into a pit of anxiety that only grows more expansive and terrifying the longer you stare into the abyss. The best way to reverse course is to do the one thing that's most difficult to pull off at the very moment you most need to do it—snap the fuck out of it.

And the best way to do that is to eradicate any notion that panic is an option. Get a grip now, freak out later.

"We've gotta get control of the ship," I say. "There's gotta be a way."

Whistler's rummaging through cabinets, pulling out instructional manuals.

"I'm looking, I'm looking," he says, each page protected in a plastic sleeve. "That's why they keep hardbound manuals. In case they lose systems, they have paper copies to... wait... is this...?"

"There's a lotta wounded out there," Nini says. "I'll do the best I can with—"

"Booyah!" Whistler slams a hardbound manual on the counter. "Navigation, chart display and information system, and operational controls." He thumbs through the pages. "Okay, okay. Here. It's..." He looks around the room.

"Dumbshit," Dolores says. "What are you—?"

"Shh! Let me read."

Dolores snarls. "Did he just shush Dolores? Nobody shushes Dolores. I'm gonna..."

Nini gives her a look. Dolores begrudgingly backs down.

"It's..." Whistler starts, then keeps reading.

"Nav control?" I ask. "Can you—?"

"It's the fuel line. I can stop the leak. We have to…"

It's amazing what the ear can detect even under intense conditions. To this day I can still hear Owen's tiny sniffles in the roar of a thunderstorm. Momma ears never lose their sensitivity.

We now hear a faint metal clanking within the orchestra of whirring machines. Weapons drawn, we scan for the source. We hear it again. Three short clanks followed by three long ones, then three short ones again.

"S.O.S.," Ther'eda says. "Someone's in trouble."

"Keep your guard up," Tarrish warns. "Could be legit, could be a trap."

We hear a muffled cry through the vents, followed by a series of thuds.

Me, Dolores, Nini, and Kowalczyk make our way back through the engine rooms until we get to the metal staircase we came down. There's a woman splayed out on the floor. Her clothes are torn and bloody.

Nini rushes over, puts her ear to her chest. "She's breathing."

"Ahh." The woman squints hard, her eyes caked with some sort of a white plaster. "My leg. Think it's broken. And my eyes. They burn. I can't see."

Nini looks closer, sniffs. "Is that…? Oh, shoot. That's toothpaste. Is this…?"

"She got into it with Whistler," I say. "When she was fogged out. He smeared it in her eyes."

"Hey," Nini comforts her. "Can you hear me?"

She nods slightly. "Y-yes."

"What's your name?"

"Tyler."

"Tyler. My name's Nini. I'm a nurse. Your eyes and leg. Anything else hurt?"

"Sore all over. I fell down the stairs."

"Why are you down here?" I say. "What were you looking for?"

"And how do you know S.O.S.?" Kowalczyk asks. His tone is more aggressive than necessary, but his question is on point.

"I'm…" Tyler grimaces as we help her up. "I'm the navigator."

We get Tyler to the Control Room, put her on the floor against the wall to keep her leg straight.

"*You're* the navigator?" Whistler says, eyeing her toothpaste-encrusted eyes. "Sorry about that."

Dolores is getting squirrely again. "Nice job, dumbshit. You blinded the last pilot."

"She tried to kill me!"

"Who hasn't?"

Ther'eda checks her phone intently, then asks a reasonable question: "Why weren't you on the Bridge when the power went down?"

"There was a… ah…"—she shifts, eliciting a painful grimace—"a power surge in one of the staterooms. Before the ship went haywire."

Nini's stateroom. That tracks.

"It set off an emergency code. I'm also an electrical engineer, so I went to check it out."

Nini gives Tyler a shot of low-grade painkiller and antibiotic as we update her on our status.

She squints and points awkwardly at the consoles, barely able to see them. "You can reroute the fuel line from here."

"It's destroyed," I say. "We can't."

Whistler holds up a manual. "Maybe we don't have to. The fuel is stored and subdivided into separate, interconnected tanks, for just this reason."

"That's right," Tyler says. "It's a tri-link system."

Whistler continues. "We need to close off the second tank before the internal mechanism opens the third. That's the last one. We gotta preserve the fuel."

"If you can do that," Tyler says, "I can pilot the ship."

"How?" Tarrish says. "Controls are down."

"There are several redundancies. Supply cabinet, bottom shelf, on the left. There should be a portable interface. It'll plug into the Bridge. I won't have full systems control, but it should be enough."

"That's a good start," I say. "Does it have a nav system?"

"No. Essentially, it's a portable steering wheel. Not much else."

Tarrish reaches for a smoke, puts it to his lips, then decides against it. "Just to make sure I understand the situation correctly... the ship is flying blind, you'd be flying it blind, and you're the only pilot we have?" He checks his phone. "Internal comms are back, but no outside signal. The transponder is offline."

"The transponder control is fried," Whistler says, pointing to the console that is, in fact, very much fried. "Can it be activated manually?"

"It depends on the problem," Tyler says. "If the transponder interface is intact but the transponder itself is damaged, we can replace it with a backup. Check the cabinets, third shelf up. Should be there."

Selene produces what looks like a car battery. "Here it is. Found it."

"Gimme that," Dolores says rudely. "I'll do it."

"But if the interface is destroyed," Tyler says, "there's nothing we can do."

When you need every ounce of positive energy to help you survive, even the tiniest hint of doubt can derail your mojo. When that happens, you change the vibe.

"Divide and conquer," I say, and slap my hands together. "There's a lot to do and we gotta move fast. Whistler, take Sebastian. Deal with the leak."

He pulls me aside. "What about Selene? I just got her back."

"I know," I whisper. "But no fuel, no ship."

"But..."

I can force him to do it, or he can come to it on his own. The old me would tell him. The new me is guiding him.

"Selene'll be okay," I say. "We'll keep her safe."

"Don't," he starts. "Not with me. You know you can't promise."

I activate my lens. No crackles. I eye-text him.

Me: *You're right. I can't promise. These are the hard calls.*

Whistler: *Selene's the client.*

Me: *She's not. Ther'eda's the client.*

Whistler: *What if it was Owen? What would U do?*

Me: *That's fair. The truth is I don't know. But Selene's your girlfriend. Not your son.*

Whistler: *Does it matter? I love her all the same.*

Me: *I know U do. That's why it's a hard call.*

The logic of this choice is easy. The emotion? Not so much.

Whistler holds his gaze, allowing the PI in him to reconcile the ugly, anxious conflict it's having with the boyfriend in him. "I'll deal with the fuel line."

We rejoin the others.

"I can help Tyler on the Bridge," Chipper volunteers. "I can be your eyes."

"*I'll* do that," Tarrish says. "I need operational control as soon as we can get it."

"Oh... okay," Chipper says meekly. "But we may need to modify or repair some of the equipment, depending on the damage. One wrong wire can short-circuit the system."

"Take her with," I say, which draws Tarrish's ire. So I appeal to his inner lawman. "In case you get called away. Big ship, lots of problems."

He deftly eyes the room, then puts his gaze back on me. "Fine."

"Ther'eda, Selene, go with Nini. Help who you can. There could be androids in distress. And you're the experts."

Ther'eda bristles at the notion. "Buckley's unaccounted for. I need him."

I knew it was just a matter of time. She needs to get her hands on the Life Code. Which she'd probably kill for. There's no chance she'll be deterred. So I ask Kowalcyzk to help Nini. Especially with her broken finger, she needs more hands. And protection.

Kowalczyk grimaces again, takes a labored breath. "I'm not"—he reaches for his chest—"leaving Ms. Ranadyne."

"It's okay," Ther'eda says. "And try to find Nenn."

I immediately turn to leave. "All right. Let's get to it."

"Hold on." Kowalczyk adjusts his shirt. "While we're doing all that, what are *you* gonna do?"

Despite re-engaged consoles, clanking pistons, hissing pipes, and whirring machinery, the Control Room goes silent to me, all eyes on my next move.

"We're covered in blood. I wanna know why."

CHAPTER 26

We split up, but not before Whistler pulls Selene into one of the engine rooms. I don't want to pry, but remain in earshot. Just in case.

"I was worried," he says, pawing at Selene's arm.

She's not responding in kind. She may want to, even desperately, but she's not acting like a woman happy to see her boyfriend. Though I have a pretty good idea why. Who knows what she saw or did—or what happened to her—in the hours they've been apart.

"Come on. There's a lot to do."

"Selene," Whistler says, reaching in to hug her.

"Eric. Not here."

"Babe. Come on. We almost died. I'm just happy to see you. Are you happy to see *me?*"

Selene smiles, her cheeks tight. "Of course." She takes his fingertips, gives him a peck on the cheek. It's not a sensual lover's kiss, although it reveals some much-needed intimacy. What's unclear to me is whether that kiss was a gesture of reconnection... or dissolution. "You're sweet. But Ms. Ranadyne is waiting."

Remotivated, Whistler rubs his face where she kissed him, like smelling her perfume on a scarf left behind.

Back up on Deck Two, Nini goes with Kowalczyk and Selene to the infirmary. They stock up on whatever medical supplies they can carry while Nini cleans Tyler's eyes the best she can and fits her leg with a flexi-cast. It fills with cushioned support gel and a topical painkiller.

With the main lights back on and the HVAC whirring again, the voluminous gore is more striking—blood and twisted innards pooling like the inside of a neglected slaughterhouse.

We already raided the security room, but there's something else I want to check.

Yes! The security feeds are back. Some of them, anyway. The main surveillance console is destroyed, loaded with blank screens. But the secondary console, with cameras in the amenity spaces, is working.

There are a handful of survivors wandering the ship, some looking dazed, others more lucid. But they all have the distant gaze of someone who just outlasted a violent, psychotic free-for-all.

Hundreds of mangled bodies are littered throughout the MoonDeck, washed over by the green aurora waves. Among the brutalized survivors I see tears, blood stains, and what I assume are grimaces of pain. One of the trapeze bars sways gently back and forth, like a porch swing after a storm. Blood drips slowly from the bar.

I keep scanning the surveillance screens until I get to the saunas, gym, massage rooms… and the pool.

Because floating face down in the water, surrounded by a halo of inky blood, is a body.

I freeze, a jolt of recognition crackling in my head and chest. My memory is almost back. In a ship with possibly a thousand dead, I'm mesmerized by this one body. But why? Why can't I…?

The body bobs in the blood-stained water. It dips partially beneath the tainted surface, and then, as if playing hide and seek, shows itself again.

My heart flutters, adrenaline coursing through me.

There! It's Buckley.

I eye-text Whistler.

Me: *Stop the leak?*

Whistler: *Working on it. U?*

Me: *Found Buckley.*

Whistler: *Really? Is he okay?*

Me: *Dead.*

Whistler: *Shit. Where?*

Me: *Natatorium.*

Whistler: *U there now?*

Me: *Security room. On way to pool. Wait. U said he had Life Code on laptop?*

Whistler: *I didn't see LC. Saw speech. Don't know if LC is there.*
Me: *Ther'eda know that?*
Whistler: *Don't know. Why?*
Me: *Because.*
Whistler: *Oh shit. She's headed for his stateroom.*
Me: *My guess.*
Whistler: *Maybe that's good? If anyone should have LC, should be her. Right?*

I don't know the answer to that one. I suppose it's better than anyone else finding it first and potentially holding it for ransom. And yet... maybe it's not.

Because... because... how did Buckley die? The aurora waves are wafting throughout, but he's in the water, by himself. He doesn't look like a psycho fog victim. There's no one else in the natatorium, no obvious cast-off or blood splatter on the tiles or walls. Did he hit his head and drown? A simple slip and fall? Or some other kind of accident?

Or did someone murder him for the Life Code?

And if they did, did they get the Life Code off him? Do they have it now? For all I know, someone murdered him for it, then got killed in the melee. The Life Code itself could be buried on this ship beneath a mound of gore.

Whistler: *U there? Mache. Mache!*
Me: *Yeah. Gotta check something. Don't let me distract. Fix leak.*

Turk showed me earlier. Security footage gets recorded for each flight, video but no audio. I search for the controls. "Video feed, video feed, video... there you are." I check the time stamp and restart the surveillance. There's me in the natatorium with Selene and Tarrish.

Crap. Do I really look like that? I gotta lose some weight.

It takes a minute for me to realize I had instinctively sucked in my gut. At least I got a bikini wax before the trip.

I scroll through the feed. A few passengers mill in and out, go for a quick swim, then it's an empty room until... there. That's Buckley. He comes in, disrobes, dives into the water.

He emerges, brushes the wet hair from his face. He does two laps of breaststrokes, then holds onto the side of the pool, taking a breather. He does a few more laps of freestyle, floats on his back, gets out of the water. He grabs his towel and starts to dry off when someone else enters.

Male. Tall. Gray suit with shiny shoes. And... J-scar. It's an android. He's...

My heart jumps.

That's Gerald! The android in Nini's closet.

Which means... I check the timestamps. Before he ended up in Nini's stateroom, he was in the natatorium with Buckley. And as an android, more than strong enough to kill him.

Buckley's nervous, looking around suspiciously, as if he doesn't want to be seen with him. Gerald is clearly upset, his arms gesticulating this way and that. But there's no violence.

They seem okay and... whoa. Gerald grabs Buckley by the shoulders. Buckley's shorter and partially wet, naked other than his bathing suit, while Gerald in a suit.

I don't know what Gerald is saying, but he's... pleading, I think. Begging.

I scroll back a few seconds, slow the video down, zoom in on Gerald's face. I replay the video. Still can't tell. I scroll back again, slow the video even more, zoom in closer on his mouth. I'm not positive, but in super slo-mo I think I can read his lips:

"Pl...eeeze, Wahr...ren. Heh...lp m...eee."

Buckley's standing there, in Gerald's grip. Just looking into those artificial eyes, staring, just staring, until finally Buckley says, as best as I can make out:

"I'm sor-ree... Ger... ald. You'll... just... have to... w...ait."

Wait? For what? Were they talking about the Life Code? The Death Code? Something else?

In super slo-mo, I can also see the agony in Gerald's eyes, the look of a man who's subjugated his pride, reducing himself before someone with incredible power over him. He starts to well up, synthetic tears as real as any I've seen in organics. Yet as the salty fluid leaks out, that pain morphs into anger, his eyes now piercing like silver daggers.

I play the video in real-time speed. Gerald grips Buckley tighter around the shoulders and shoves him back.

Buckley's foot slips. He falls backward. His arms flail like that of a tap dancer. He's about to topple over, but before he does, regains his balance. He's unhurt.

Gerald points, his arm blocking my view of Buckley's mouth, and yells something I can't make out. His body language tells me it's a threat, Gerald gesturing intensely, a man demanding to be taken seriously. He goes on like this for a few more seconds, sneers, and to my surprise, turns away and storms out of the natatorium.

Which means, he didn't kill Buckley.

So who did? And what was that altercation about?

I follow the surveillance feed to the outer rooms, past the sauna, then it cuts out. No other access on this line.

I switch back to the natatorium. Buckley's frazzled, his hand on his heaving bare chest. Unblinking, he stares at a point I can't discern, then licks his lips. Adrenaline spike gives you dry mouth. He fumbles through his robe pocket for his phone. He scrolls through it, sends a text.

To Ther'eda? Or to someone else?

I need to get his phone, read his texts. Assuming his phone is still there. It's the best lead I've had. But I still don't know how Buckley ended up dead.

I scroll back again on the surveillance console. Buckley leans forward, hand on thighs, probably relieved Gerald didn't assault him. From there he stumbles over to the deck chair, sits on the edge of it with his head dropped down.

Buckley reaches to his face, exhales deeply, looks up. He's alone for another 13 minutes and 23 seconds, intermittently sitting, then walking around the pool's edge and around one of the palm trees, mumbling to himself.

He heads back toward his deck chair. But before he gets there, he stands at the edge of the pool. He considers his reflection, puffs out his cheeks, pokes at them. Expelled air trumpets between his lips. He pats both hands on his stomach, arches it out, plays the bongos in a pat-a-tat rhythm. He does it again, only slower this time.

There's a look of recognition on his face. Like he's figured something out.

Or come to a conclusion.

He looks over his shoulder at his chair, then back at the

water. He's staring down at his reflection, although I can't be sure that's what he's concentrating on. And then he smiles, shakes his head at himself. He mutters something inaudible, and goes back to his deck chair.

He lies back, exhales, as if he's relieved. And...

There. Someone else came in. It's... damn. They're walking along the back wall, in the blind spots. It could be random, and just unlucky for me, but it's almost as if they knew to avoid being caught on camera.

Buckley looks up, startled. He pulls on his robe, ties the sash. Whoever's approaching him, he seems to recognize them. But he looks at them quizzically, then steps forward.

Though no longer in frame, I can see them reflected in the water. Between that gentle sloshing and the aurora waves, I can't make out their faces with any real definition. Whoever he's with is shorter than him, smaller, but there's no way to identify who it is.

I freeze the video, zoom in closer on the water, to see if I can enhance their faces. Only instead of getting clarity, it further distorts their images. With my lens I take a snapshot of the distorted image, then run a facial recognition program Bernice upgraded for me. Longshot, but maybe it'll come up with something I can use.

Stuck, I zoom back out and scroll through the video. Buckley steps back and forth a few times so that he's in and out of the frame, but I can't get a lock on his face.

He doesn't appear to feel physically threatened when...

I scroll back a few seconds, play it again. Still can't tell. I scroll back once more, play it in super slo-mo. I lean as close to the screen as I can. It's... shiny. The edge of a... I can't make it out. But it has a silver coating. Is it a weapon of some kind? Or something else?

Whatever it is gets Buckley's attention. He steps back a few feet so he's in the frame again. He tosses his hands up and is saying... he's saying... I scroll back a few seconds, replay it in super slo-mo, *"Yuuu... ahrr... kr... a... zee."*

"Yerahrkrazy? What is...? Oh. You're crazy? You're crazy!"

Why? About what?

His counterpart lunges at him, hands and arms in the frame. But no face.

Oh, shit. Is this it? Is this when...?

No. His counterpart retracts, shakes a hand in the air, and—

I know this happened hours ago, but I'm reliving it now. My respiration speeds up, my heart beating faster and with increasing force, like it's trying to outrun the gravitational pull of a black hole. The awful feelings return. The monster is back. She's taunting me.

With viciousness. Anger. My compulsive need to annihilate. To destroy.

On screen there's a stirring in the water. A rippling. The reaction to an unseen force. The aurora waves swirl rather than drift. Atoms excite.

Buckley hunches, squints painfully, covers his ears.

Something's coming.

As if launched by angry gods riding winged beasts, spidery blue lightning bolts attack the cruiser with whip crack ferocity.

An assault on those who dare trespass on that sacred cosmic space.

A punishment.

A death sentence.

The video cuts to static.

My hands shake, heart thundering in my chest.

I scroll back and forth, replaying the appearance of that silver intrusion, immediately followed by the excitable aurora.

Silver tech.

Aurora.

Lightning blasts.

Madness.

Whoever mixed it up with Buckley seemed to initiate the psycho fog. In a chain reaction, whatever its origin, the silver-edged object excited the aurora, which unleashed the lightning strikes, and triggered the majestic undercurrent of homicidal fury.

Now all I have to do is find this faceless assailant. And hope that whatever tech they used won't work on us again.

CHAPTER 27

"It worked!"

Still inside the security room I jump at Whistler's sudden presence. Sebastian is with him.

"You scared the shit outta me."

"Sorry. But, good news."

I do my best to let my heart attack subside. I gesture for him to keep going.

"The fuel line," he says, then pats Sebastian on the shoulder. "We sealed it up. I think we're good."

"You text Tarrish?"

"Already done."

"What did he say?"

"Same as usual. Nothing." Whistler stares at the screen. "What are you looking at?"

I switch the screen off. Sebastian has been on our side, but I don't want him on the inside any more than he needs to be. And no, it's not an android thing. It's a PI thing.

Don't share unless you have to.

"Don't worry about it," I say. "I'll tell you on the way."

It's twelve flights up to the natatorium, but we take the stairs anyway. I don't want to risk being stuck in the elevator. The power's back on, but who knows for how long?

I call Nini. She's doing the best she can to help the wounded, but there's only so much she can do on her own, especially with a bad hand. Selene and Kowalczyk took off to find Ther'eda. Which doesn't surprise me. Although I don't love her being out in the field without backup.

I also don't love Sebastian being unsupervised right now, but I don't want him with us for this. I send him to help Nini.

The chameleon he is, he agrees without issue.

Whistler and I come across several limbs and mangled bodies, some of which is our handiwork. You'd think a gruesome reminder of the violence I inflicted, whether it was to save my life or not, would send me down a rabbit hole of guilt and shame. But it doesn't. I'm not sure if that's healthy, delusional, or a little bit of both.

Whistler and I cut through the fitness center only to find a muscled-out passenger in gym shorts and a flimsy tank top. He's on his back, on a workout bench, with a heavily weighted bar pinning him down. He's also missing his head. It's on the floor beneath the leg press machine.

Through the fitness center, we pass the chiropractic and acupuncture salon, unoccupied yoga pods, then come into the natatorium.

"There he is," Whistler says as the aurora waves ripple through the glassed-in ceiling.

"Here." I snag the long-neck skimmer off the wall. "Pull him to the side."

Whistler takes the skimmer, because he's got the longer reach, and flops it onto the water. He just misses Buckley's leg. Whistler's about to try again, when he pauses, the small net hovering over his shoulder. Water droplets slowly fall off the tip of the skimmer, slopping into a puddle on the tile.

He flops the skimmer, catches the netting around Buckley's heel. "Got him." He pulls the skimmer, dragging Buckley along the water toward us.

I need down to pull Buckley to the edge. Whistler kneels down to meet me. We roll Buckley to the side.

"Here." Whistler gestures to the gash on the back of Buckley's head. Congealed blood in his hair. "He never had a chance."

We pull his body out of the pool. We check him for other wounds. Nothing obvious.

"Let's look for Buckley's phone," I say. "Anything we can find."

We hug the wall, retracing the path of Buckley's attacker, who had maneuvered stealthily behind the palm tree and then outside the security camera's sightline. There's nothing here other than some deck chairs and small tables. We continue along the wall, cross the short side of the pool and the flowing water wall, and back into the camera's sightline. There are more deck tables and chairs on this side, with Buckley's pool robe and slippers on one of them.

It wasn't visible on the security feed, but there's a tiny puddle of washed-out blood on the tile, most likely the impact site where Buckley hit his head.

On the wall behind his chair is a built-in inset, with three decorative shelves protected by a glass pane. On the top shelf is a model replica of the *Triumph*. On the bottom two shelves are guest figurines relaxing in miniaturized deck chairs.

Whistler rifles through the robe pockets. "Nothing. Wait, hang on." He reaches for Buckley's slippers, and smiles. "Maaaache," he sing-songs. "Look what I found." He fiddles with Buckley's phone. "It's locked. Don't know if we can get into the chip with what we have on board. If we can't, maybe Bernice can do it when we get back. Whadaya think?"

"I think...," I say, and take a quiet second or two. Sometimes your eyes miss what's right in front of you. In my mind I examine this room again, from memory. "I think..." My eyes drift to the white square embedded in the floor tile, along the far side of the pool, beneath the palm tree.

Following my eyes, Whistler sees what I see.

"Filter!" He jogs over there, kneels, and pulls up the filter plate. His eyes go wide. "No way." He reaches down, extracts his hand. In between his thumb and forefinger, he shows me his prize.

"Scout orb?" I ask excitedly.

He flicks his eyebrows. "Scout orb."

I nod, impressed. "Booyah."

He smiles at me with surprise. "That's *my* line."

"You have your moments."

He blushes, then considers. "Call it even?"

"Done. Is it still synced to your lens?"

He twitches his eye, rolls the orb in his hands. "Nope. I used it to track Buckley. But the signal went dead. Don't think it's the pool. Orb's waterproof. I'm guessing it was the lighting strike, but it's hard to tell. Could be the orb just needs a reset. I've got the charge port in my room."

"Let's go now. If it recorded what happened, we'll know who killed Buckley. And have it on file."

Whistler puts the orb in his pocket. "And what caused the fog."

"Whadaya know," I say as we head back through the yoga rooms. "It's almost like we're a team again."

"Let's not get crazy. Progress, though. Progress."

"Progress it is."

I'm about to start away, but Whistler gently snags my arm.

"Did you mean what you said? You know? Earlier. About me? About... how we are. With each other. You usually don't talk like that."

I wondered if this would come up. Or if we'd survive long enough to get to it.

It shouldn't be easier for me to open up to him while standing over a corpse, but there it is. Death—the great equalizer.

"I needed to hear it," he says. "Sometimes... I need the words. Especially after... you're right, you know. About the nightmares. It's why I hate to be alone, hate to fall asleep. Selene comes to me at night, holds me, calms me down, but I can't talk to her about them. How can I? Sometimes I'm pulling the trigger, sometimes I watch while it happens. Sometimes I'm both. No matter what I do, I can't make them stop. I'm falling apart."

I wish there was an easy, gentle way to overcome trauma. I've usually been able to drink, exercise, or fuck my way out of depression—or from falling too far into it. And since Owen's been firmly back in my life, time with my son grounds me, gives me a sense of place, of comfort, of belonging in a way nothing else can or does. I've been concerned about how Whistler manages the stress. Maybe that's what Selene is for him.

Although I hope their relationship means more to him than that. Otherwise, he's turning into a younger version of me.

"It was overdue," I say. "The words. I owed you more than you got. You deserved better. I'm sorry about that."

I am. I know what it's like to learn from someone who believes the best way to teach is to push you hard and often, and to praise rarely. When I first got started on my own, Tarrish took me under his wing, unofficially. And while he taught me most of what I know, he didn't sugarcoat it or lower his standards so they'd be easier for me to reach.

Just the opposite. He raised the bar so unreachably high, challenging me at every turn, so I'd be motivated to quit. He didn't do it because he's mean. He did it to save my life, if not my soul. The private investigator business, especially the cases I take, isn't for the faint of heart or tender mercies.

Want a hug? Hug yourself.

Want more friends? Make fewer enemies.

Stressed out? Pour a Scotch.

But now that Whistler and I are both here, alone, sharing an intimate moment among the shimmering water, aurora waves, and Buckley's corpse, I feel a mechanism within the vault of my heart begin to unlock. Rods shift. Gears turn. Tumblers spin.

For all the truth I've laid on Whistler since the day we met, there's some truth I've held back. It was buried so far beneath the collective rage we'd all unleashed upon each other, it's only now I've made room for the rest of it to have a voice.

It's like remediating a brownfield site. You scrape away the toxic sludge buried beneath the soil, thinking you've cleared it away, when you discover yet another layer of contaminants below, in a pocket of pain you had sensed was always there, but couldn't access or identify. Until now.

"I was pissed at you," I finally admit.

"I know."

"But not why you think."

That stops him. Whistler looks at me. Not as a protégé or a partner. As a man. And a scared little boy. He swallows uncomfortably, then has the courage to ask, "Then why?"

It's right there. I want to say it, but my heart's in my throat. "Forget it."

"Don't tell me to forget it!"

"It doesn't matter," I say.

"It does!"

"I don't—"

"That's fucked up. You can't do that. You have something to say, say it!"

"I fucked up, okay?" My self-stifled emotions are now spilling out all at once. "I never thought you'd last, because they never do. Because I... never give them a chance. Not really. But I did with you. You had a spark and a relentlessness I hadn't seen before, and I figured... okay, maybe. Maybe this could work. But you demanded more than you were owed. More than I could give. It's just *me*! Don't you get it? I'm *one* person. For fifteen years I was on my own. I built my business... I built my life... from nothing. There was no second shift, no backup. Then you show up outta nowhere, wanting in, wanting more, wanting... everything. Every day, in every way. Wanting a piece of what *I* built! It was mine! I did it. Me. When everyone I knew—*everyone*—said I was stupid or crazy or had a death wish. A woman trying to do a man's work. It was too much! *You* were too much."

I'm practically crying now, with puffy eyes, looking at myself in the water looking back at me. And then quieter, I say, "Too much." I exhale so completely I feel like I might fizzle into dust. I turn back to face him. "Some of that's on me, Eric. Some of it's on you. And some of it, it's on the both of us."

He's staring at me wordlessly. His silence is satisfying—and a torment—leaving me in an agonizing limbo.

"Some of it *is* on me," he says finally, surprising me with his candor. "I think it's why I tried so hard. You were so... unreachable, that it made me want to reach you even more. And the more I couldn't access that part of you, the more rejected I felt." He stares down at the bloody water, then back at me. "I didn't think about what it meant for *you*. You're so... tough. Scary. Impressive. I didn't realize I was asking so much. I had nowhere else to go, and when I thought about what kind of life I wanted, how I wanted to be, *who* I wanted to be... I was scared. All the time. I didn't know where I fit, or what to do next. And when I saw you, and what you do, and how fearless you are"—he smiles at me—"I knew, '*she's the one. Don't let go.*'" He chuckles softly. "I wanted you"—he drops his head, nodding to himself, then back at me again—"to be my *everything*. To share with me everything that made you, you. And to teach me how to do it. And I wanted you... to want the same thing. When it became clear you didn't, I hated you for it. You broke my heart. But I guess, really, I did it to myself."

There are moments to speak. There are moments to remain silent.

I'm not sure which kind of moment this is. It might be both.

Already I see a change in the way he's looking at me. There's sadness... regret... grief... an internalization that what he had hoped to experience under my tutelage, and what he actually experienced, are not the same. I can't know for certain, not yet anyway, but with a gradational slump in his posture, a slight drop in the arch of his eyebrow, a touch of disappointment behind his eyes... I don't think he idolizes me anymore.

And maybe he knows that's for the best. As if he realizes, finally, that I'm not living in a bubble of what I think is rarified air, that I'm too good for him. I hope he sees that I'm more like him than he realizes—or maybe less—living in the moment, hoping to make it from one day to the next without the monster in me, the blunt force rising from the depths of my soul, stirring up my darkness and dragging me back into the abyss. And without it dragging him down there with me.

The reasons *why* I am the way I am don't really matter. And I think he's finally starting to appreciate that if he does want to live this life—the PI life, taking cases on-realm and off—he doesn't have to live it the way I do, or to follow my rules.

If we live to see another day, which is far from a guarantee, I hope he'll feel the freedom and the confidence to stick with me—or not—without it being a tragic event.

Because either way, we'll both get by.

I hope he stays. I really do. But I fear he might go.

Until then, we have work to do.

We make our way back into the gym with the headless weightlifter. "I saw you with Selene," I say. "It's confusing, I know. There's a lot to unpack. And she's not used to the..."

"Shit we get into?"

"It takes some getting used to."

"Ya think?"

"Just... keep the faith," I say, and offer him a slight pat on the back. "Relationships are hard. Even when you're not wading through the apocalypse."

Whistler stops next to the red medicine ball, his feet shuffling on the spongy mat. "Did you just say *keep the faith*? You? Really?"

"Yeah. I threw up in my mouth a little when I said it."

"I know. I think I tasted it from here."

I give him a wincing look. "We haven't made *that* much progress. Why don't we just say you and Selene will figure things out. As soon as we catch up with her."

Which sounds like a perfectly reasonable approach to me, when a shotgun gets shoved in my face.

"Selene's right where she needs to be. And you're next."

CHAPTER 28

"Turk?" I say to the security chief, who I assumed had been killed. "What are you doing?"

"What I should've done a long time ago."

Montrose, the guard who shooed me away after the panel, is also pointing a shotgun at us. She confiscates our weapons, rifles through our pockets, takes our phones and Whistler's scout orb.

"What's this?"

"Stress ball," Whistler says. "Today's been... stressful."

"That's for sure." She rolls it in her palm—"hmm, not bad"—then pockets it.

"Turk," I repeat. "The attack's over. Whatever it is you're doing... don't."

Turk presses the shotgun's muzzle against my face. It breaks the skin below the wound under my eye. It seems unlikely he'll pull the trigger—he wants *something* from us, and it's a bit more challenging to get information from someone when they're dead—but after the fresh Hell we've all been through, there's no telling how twitchy he is.

As Turk considers his options—blast my face off, not blast my face off, what to do, what to do?—he leans into the stock. He's pressing the shotgun's muzzle deeper into my cheek, with enough force that the metal edge clacks through the flesh and against my teeth.

With his eyes peeled wide, he intensely studies my pores like he's searching for the kind of skin cream I use. Or maybe a J-scar.

Turk's still pressing, pressing pressing pressing—pressing so hard he's forced me to my knees. With warm, coppery blood pooling between my swollen gums, I'm watching in the wall-length mirror opposite us—Turk, with all the power, and me, with none—until my heart beats so loud and heavy I can't hear a word he's saying.

He's grumbling to himself, puckering his lips, his eyes all bulged out, as if he's in the final stages of negotiating with himself. He seems to really wanna do it.

Turk's about to snap my lower bicuspid in half—I squint in anticipation of the awful pain from a severed nerve—when the pressure eases off. He lowers his gun, leaving an indentation in my cheek. And allowing me to stand up and exhale.

Which is exactly when he punches me in the gut, dropping me to my knees.

"Mache!"

"Shut up," Montrose says, shoving the shotgun flush against Whistler's left eye. "You wanna be next?"

"No," he whispers through gritted teeth.

"Tough." Montrose flips the shotgun over, jams the butt in Whistler's midsection so that he's doubled over next to me, hardly able to breathe.

They grab us both, and with their weapons in our backs, shove us forward.

"Y-you're the security chief. You know me," I say, nausea kicking in from the punch to my midsection. "Why are you doing this?"

"I don't care about you," Turk says. "We're here for him."

Despite their shoving, we stop mid-stride.

"Me?" Whistler says, grimacing from the blow. "What did I do?"

Turk grabs a chunk of Whistler's scruff, yanks his head back, and jams the shotgun under his chin. "I should blow your fucking head off right now. But the Judge doesn't want that. You need to sit in the gallery. In case you need to testify."

"T-testify?" Whistler stammers. "To what?"

With a huffy smile, Turk leans in close so there's barely any space between them. "Plead ignorance if you want, dickhead. But it ain't that kinda court. And we got a witness."

"Witness? Court? What are you talking about?"

Turk keeps up the pressure, the muzzle pressed against the underside of Whistler's jaw. "Just like every scumbag I busted. You know nothing, and nothing's your fault." As if tapping out secret code, his finger pats the trigger, just not quite hard enough to deploy the two-and-a-half-inch gauge shell. "Until it is. You're done, motherfucker. You and that little bitch of yours."

"Don't call Ms. Hardwicke a bitch," he protests ineffectually.

"Not *her*. The other one. The android. Selene."

"Selene? No! What did she do? What do you mean? What—?"

"Who do you think killed Buckley in there? At a certain point, you have to accept this whole androids and organics thing doesn't work. You can't force people to get along, and I'm tired of being a referee. We won, they lost. It's just how it goes."

Images of Selene ricochet through my mind. Better that than a large caliber shell. I want to say I'm surprised to hear this about Selene. But I'm not. Which doesn't mean I'm convinced Turk is right. I'm also not convinced he's wrong.

Whichever it might be, Whistler can't accept the accusation.

"No!" he rebuts. "That's impossible! Why would she do that? Any of it? It's—"

"I said"—Turk raises the muzzle, forcing Whistler's chin up and his head back so far his Adam's Apple looks twice its normal size—"tell it to the Judge."

"Even if you're right," I say, "why do it like this? Hold Selene in the brig. Him, too, if you have to. This makes no sense."

"It makes perfect sense. If you work the case correctly."

"Yes," I plead, praying Dolores gets the transponder back online so we can get the ICD out here. "Work it correctly. You were a cop. There are rules. Processes. Procedures. Gather evidence. Chain of command."

"You're right. I *was* a cop. I never took a bribe, lied on the stand, or cut corners. But me and my pals patrolled the streets. *We* dealt with the homeless. *We* dealt with the mentally ill, and domestic violence. *Repeat* domestic violence. Then all the shit androids brought. And got called pigs, bullies, and bastards for our trouble. Plus the PIs who stuck their noses in our business. You stroll into a crime scene like you're some kind of celebrity, think you know more about the law and making arrests than we do. Every *cop* I know thinks every *PI* we know is a useless piece of shit. Present company included. And siding with an android who did all this... you made it to the top of my shit list."

They shove us forward, into the foyer, until we come to the elevator. Montrose presses the button, which lights up.

Whistler eye-texts me: *What the fuck?*

Me: *Don't know.*

Whistler: *Selene didn't do this. She didn't!*

Me: *I believe you.*

Whistler: *You do?*

Me:

Whistler: *Mache. Mache? Mache!*

Me:

Whistler: *U think she did it. U think it's her fault.*

Me: *I didn't say that.*

Whistler: *U didn't defend her.*

Me:

Whistler: *U really think she did it?*

Me: *Don't know.*

Whistler: *Can't believe U.*

Me: *She probably didn't. But until we learn for certain what did or didn't happen, or what she did or didn't do, there's just no way to know.*

Another reason why I've resisted being partners. Sometimes you have to tell the truth to the one person who is least ready to hear it.

Turk and Montrose force us into the elevator, just the four of us in this tight space, taking us down to Deck Five. But why Deck Five? Why...?

The doors open. My heart thuds.

We're back in the hallway, outside the Experience Theater. I can hear murmuring from behind the closed doors. I look around to get my bearings, when one of the doors opens out, giving me a quick glance into the theater space. I see at least a few dozen survivors, but my view is mostly blocked by someone wearing a makeshift bailiff's uniform comprised of a bloodied tie and a tattered suit.

"Turk," the bailiff says. "Been waiting on you. We're ready."

"I was just about to separate them."

"Judge says put him in there." The bailiff points to the closest of four small meeting rooms, two on each side, outside the theater. "With the big one."

Turk grins devilishly. "That should be interesting."

They grab me first, forcing me into the room on the right, then lock me in. Only... I'm not alone.

"Neen." We hug each other tight, then let go. "What the hell's going on? Are you okay? Have you seen anything? Know anything?"

"They've lost it, Anj. Totally fucking lost it. I was treating some of the wounded, then a guard just grabs me. They're all talking about a trial. How Selene did all this. And how some judge will make her pay."

"Yeah. Turk said it, too. Who's the judge?"

"They haven't told me shit. Just about the trial and—"

"Hang on." There's a commotion outside. I ping Whistler through my lens.

Me: *U there?*

Whistler:

Me: *Whistler. Whistler!*

I don't know if he's in trouble or if he's just not talking to me because—

My audio switches on. He's given me access to the internal mic in his lens.

"You," Turk says to Whistler. "In there."

"You're going down."

Turk chortles. "I don't think so." I hear scuffling, then a groan, as if Turk or Montrose roughed Whistler up again. A door opens. "Have fun."

I hear shuffling of feet. The door slams.

"Dolores?" Whistler's breaths are staggered. "The transponder. What happened?"

"Turk pinned me down. Him and the little one. Nenn. They tag-teamed me."

"Nenn? I thought she was dead."

"Nenn doesn't say shit, but she's definitely not dead."

Nenn. Here we go. When the ship sinks, allegiances change.

Loyalties die. Knowing who to trust, if anyone, becomes nearly impossible.

"What about the transponder?" Whistler repeats. "Did they find it?"

"I hid it. They made their move too early. Unless they have cameras down there, which is possible, or someone else was watchin, it should still be there."

There's silence between them, and then Whistler's PI brain kicks back in.

"What about the rest of them? Nini and Tarrish and...?"

"Kid," I hear Dolores say. "Life just shit in our mouths and you're bitchin about the garnish. Wake the fuck up. This ain't a trial. It's a reckoning. Maybe your girlfriend caused the apocalypse, maybe not. But it doesn't matter, does it? Those people out there? The survivors? They don't give a fuck about facts, truth, or reason. They got blood on their hands, and on their souls. They want someone to blame, and to watch them get punished."

"They can't do that!"

"They can and they will. I told you I hate androids. Because no matter what anyone says, they'll never be one of us. If it wasn't this shitshow, it would've been another. The android lovers have been tellin us for years that we *have* to accept them, that we *have* to treat them as equals. We have to, we have to, we HAVE to! Well, who the fuck says I do? Life Code, Death Code. Who gives a fuck? Nobody gets to tell Dolores, *ever*, what to think, how to feel, or how to live my life. And nobody gets to tell me I'm a racist, bigot, or intolerant slob because *I* won't believe what *they* demand. Dolores isn't intolerant. *They're* intolerant. Of us! I never fucked with an android who didn't fuck with me first. And now that your girlfriend unleashed this ship of horrors, we don't have to tolerate those mechanical freaks one second longer. It was always going to come to this. It was just a matter of time."

I've known Dolores a long time. She'd never turn her back on one of us. A few years back, on one of the first cases I worked with Whistler, Dolores ran into a burning warehouse and pulled us out. She risked her life to save ours.

And now she's doing it again. But she's afraid someone's listening to us now, and she's saying what she thinks they want to hear. Unless... it's what she really feels.

Trauma follows us everywhere. Some can handle an ocean of pain, some just a teaspoon. But everyone, no matter who they are, what they've been through, or the depths of their resolve, has their breaking point. Maybe Dolores hit hers.

"What are they saying?" Nini asks me. "Is D okay? Is she—?"

The locking mechanism clicks. The door opens. Hand on the doorknob, a woman leans into the room wearing a make-shift judge's robe—a black tablecloth, with slits for the arms and head. Not her. Anybody but her.

It's Regina, the android-hating wench from the elevator.

Fuckety fuck fuck fuck.

"I said androids should be put on trial." She lays the smirk on thick. "And that I couldn't wait to be judge, jury, and executioner. Life rarely gives you what you want, but sometimes... mmm... it lands right in your lap. And this time, those fucking androids are gonna pay. See you inside."

Turk enters. "You ready, babe?"

Babe? Oh, no.

Regina pats his chest, kisses him flush on the mouth. "You know it. Let's dish out some justice. And do it right."

CHAPTER 29

I'm furious with myself that I didn't see this sooner.

She's the mouthpiece, Turk's the muscle. She gets him all hot and bothered, and with him armed to the hilt, they baste each other with android-hating, power-grabbing gravy.

The one who most likely raided the weapons cache, Turk knows this ship top-to-bottom, and has access to whichever security cameras are still working. And after nearly thirty years as a cop, he knows how to control a crowd.

Which adds up to one reality—we need a new plan, and we need it now.

But there's no efficient way for us to communicate back and forth, me and Nini locked in this room, Whistler and Dolores in the other. Regina, the self-proclaimed Judge, stuck them together on purpose, assuming they'd be at each other's throats. Which means the Judge has intel on both of them. Maybe it came from Nenn.

They all know about Whistler's relationship to Selene. It wasn't a secret. Turk could have been spying on them. But how did they know about Dolores? She's one of the most private people I know. It took her almost six months to admit she was dating Beata, even longer to introduce us.

But she also talks a lot, and loudly, so again, who knows what she said to whom and where, and who might've overheard.

I don't know why, but it comes to me in a flash.

"On the surveillance video," I say with Nini here, but also talking to Whistler, who passes my messages to Dolores. "Whoever killed Buckley, it wasn't Selene. She's too tall. Her body was outside the frame, but her arm came into focus. It would've been higher. The angles are all wrong. It was someone else. Someone shorter."

"That's... that's true," I hear Whistler say. "Yeah. Yeah!"

"She could've had an accomplice," Nini says. "You said there was a blind spot in the natatorium, and whoever it was seemed to know it was there. Someone on the crew?"

"Maybe," I say now that we know Turk is hooked up with the Judge. "Maybe. It could've been..."

I don't know where it comes from, but Nenn pops back into my mind. She's relentless. Surgical. A killer. And she's small. Small enough to avoid security feeds. She wore a silver bracelet. Holy shit.

"Nenn," I say. "*She* killed Buckley."

"Nenn?" Whistler questions. "You think...?"

"That's the silver I saw on the video. Her bracelet. And why it was hard to find the blood. She knew to clean it up."

"See. I *knew* it wasn't Selene!" I can almost hear his wheels spinning. "Ther'eda must've sent Nenn to find Buckley. It went sideways."

"Or maybe Buckley had already transferred the Life Code to Ther'eda," I say. "And out of spite or revenge, Ther'eda wanted him gone. Or maybe she knew Buckley had a hand in the Death Code after all. She could lay the blame on him and Nolasco, and with the Life Code in her possession, be the hero herself."

Whistler follows the thread. "With Buckley out of the way, there'd be no one to refute her story. Except Nenn."

"Who better? She doesn't talk."

"But even if Nenn killed Buckley," Dolores says, her voice traveling through the mic in Whistler's lens, "Selene coulda been involved with the psycho fog." She pauses a beat. "That sneaky, evil skank. That was the plan all along. Get the industry leaders in one place, then wipe 'em out, all in one shot."

"No," Whistler says. "Why would she do that? Why would she...?"

As if our thoughts sync across the ship, he says what I was about to.

"Her fingers twitched. A few times."

"Stress," I say unconvincingly.

"That's what I thought. It's what she told me."

"Me, too."

There's silence, until Whistler realizes what we both know. "It wasn't stress, was it?"

"No. I don't think so."

I hear Whistler audibly choke up. "The Death Code. It started. She's gonna die."

"You don't know that. It might not be...."

"Don't do that. Just say it. Selene's Death Code kicked in. And the Life Code, if it ever existed, died with Buckley. It's gone."

There's a long pause before I answer. "Yeah," I whisper. "You might be right."

There's movement outside the room, muffled arguments. But all I can think about now is that Selene, Whistler's girlfriend, the client's assistant—an android—may be suffering from the same debilitating condition Ther'eda's been trying to correct, one that could prematurely end the lifespan of all active androids as we know it.

Which would give Selene every reason to be resentful. And give her a motive.

Still, why kill Buckley? And why set off the psycho fog? How could either be a benefit to her? Neither would cure her condition. If anything, those acts of violence would only ensure her own demise.

And she strikes me as being far too intelligent to think it would serve as an effective form of protest. How, exactly, would triggering a mass murder, wiping out the best software engineers in E-Town, convince organics that androids are nothing to fear?

Something else is going on here. Selene may be involved somehow, in some way, but her masterminding all this violence doesn't pass the sniff test.

There's also Ther'eda. I've seen no evidence linking her in any way to Buckley's murder. The timestamps of her texts give her a rock-solid alibi. She was with Tarrish when Buckley was killed. But even if she found a way to manipulate that digital evidence, or had someone kill Buckley on her behalf... why?

She seemed genuinely excited, if not relieved, to announce the Life Code in front of a thousand people, with Buckley at her side. They would have raised their hands in solidarity, saviors of the android community.

But let's say she suspected, or even knew, that Buckley played her? What if he told her he had the Life Code, and forced her to negotiate a much higher price for it, down to the wire? And let's also say, as a result, she wanted him dead. I could understand the sentiment.

But to actually have him killed over it? And do it here, on the ship, when the conference still had two days left? It doesn't make sense.

Unless Buckley was more complicit than I thought. Despite all protests to the contrary, was Buckley involved with the Death Code? Was it all just a long con? Secretly unleash the Death Code, then re-emerge with the Life Code? The sudden savior?

Did he and Nolasco intentionally infect the androids, then hold Ther'eda and the entire android community hostage? Did Buckley kill Nolasco so he could take full credit for the Life Code?

Did either or both of them target androids and prey upon their vulnerabilities? Literally infect them with a species-specific plague? And price-gouge the cure?

Lots of theories, still no answers. And we're locked in this room with no weapons and no tech other than my lens. Not to mention the armed guards outside the door waiting to shuffle us off to a makeshift trial, fueled by mass outrage and a petulant power grab.

Our door unlocks again. I hear the same on Whistler's side.

"Hardwicke," Turk says. "And the nurse. Let's go."

In addition to Turk and Montrose, who are armed with shotguns, more than a half-dozen passengers, some with warpaint on their faces, are wielding forks, knives, batons, and other stabbing implements they snared from throughout the *Triumph*.

"Hardy," Dolores says. "It's gonna be ugly in there."

"It's ugly out here."

"Save your breath," Turk commands. "You're gonna need it."

The theater doors swing open.

We enter from the top. About half the theater seats are filled with survivors, some who have cleaned themselves up, others in rags, makeshift slings, and bandages.

Along the back row and down the aisles stand a handful of formal security guards and what can best be called civilian recruits, also armed with bashing and stabbing implements.

The theater is sloped down toward the circular stage, seats arcing around it. On the stage itself sits the Judge at a table, higher up than the rest of the kangaroo court.

Above the stage, on the large wraparound screen, now that the power's back, are scenes from Britton Square Park, on-realm, of people lounging in the grass, laughing, napping, playing ball, giggling with their children, having picnics.

A graphic above reads: *LIFE WITHOUT ANDROIDS*

On the other side of the screen are various scenes from the Anaya Promenade, which was incinerated a few years back by a violent criminal. Thousands of spectators were burned alive. Even though they had nothing to do with the mass death and destruction, the graphic above those terrible images reads: *LIFE WITH ANDROIDS*.

In front of the stage, to the left side, are a dozen civilians in two rows of six chairs each—the jurors, although calling them *jurors* might be a stretch. Credits to croissants, they were vetted as anti-android, or have been instructed to vote in line... or else.

With the Judge lording over the rest, in front of the stage are two tables, one each on the right and left: prosecution and defense.

Selene is at the defendant's table. On trial for her life. Which means she's already dead. If the Death Code doesn't get her first.

She's flanked by her "attorney." It's Alec, the widower from the elevator who defended the honor of his android nanny. And whom Judge Regina bullied over.

Which makes me think she appointed him for the role.

Further feeding that sadism is the prosecutor of this sham trial. Litton, the patent attorney who lost his shit during the panel and went full-throated android-bashing.

But I don't see Ther'eda. Why isn't she at the defendant's table with Selene? Creator and created. Organic and android. Did she slip away somehow? Was she rescued? Did she sell out Selene to save her own ass?

On the right of the stage are ten survivors, bound and gagged, face down on the floor, feet closest to us. And there's Nenn. The killer we've been hunting for, and who may be hunting us. She's standing guard now, arms crossed in front of her, holding a pistol, bracelet dangling from her wrist.

Even if Nenn is just being practical, backing the winning side, for however long they're still in charge, and even if she did kill Buckley, I want to believe she's still in Ther'eda's camp, playing both sides to help get us out of here.

For now, though, there's no way to know. When it comes to self-preservation, loyalty is fungible.

Turk and Montrose force us down to the lower level, in the third row, behind the lawyers' tables. Tarrish is already seated. Dolores and then Nini are on the other side of him.

"T?" I said. "What happened?"

"Turk's crew was waiting for us. Ambush."

Damn. "What about Tyler? And Chipper?"

"They're trying to get the nav system back online. They've got a man with them."

"Turk," I say. "Whatever else you do, you gotta get us out of the aurora. We need to head back—"

"Don't worry about the *Triumph*," Turk says. "I'd worry about yourself." He motions to a civilian, who sits one row behind us. With my taser. "They talk shit, make a move... breathe funny, you tase 'em. Tase 'em hard."

"With pleasure," says the guy seated right behind me. I recognize his voice.

I look over my shoulder. It's Ralph, the code-waffle I sent squirming away earlier at the cocktail party. This might not go well.

"Remember me?" Ralph ignites the electricity so it crackles at the end. Delighted with his new toy, he eyes Turk, who nods, then looks back at me. And smiles. Ralph jabs me in the back of the neck while Montrose controls my crew with the shotgun.

I spasm so hard my kidneys hurt. My head jostles. I see stars.

"That's enough," Turk says, and winks at the Judge. "Plenty to go around."

Releasing me from the high-voltage current, Ralph leans in. "Was that as good for you as it was for me?" Like a rapist, he whispers one last missive at me, his hot wet breath directly in my ear. "Cunt."

Even as I drool on myself, my head throbbing, I'm thinking there's still no one piloting the cruise ship. Which means we're drifting deeper within the aurora, with no outbound comms, no calls for help.

The gallery erupts impatiently. They toss flaming toilet paper sheets and sets of novelty dice down at us. Using a security guard's baton like a gavel, the Judge bangs the table, then speaks into a microphone.

"Order. Order in the court." Regina's leaning into the role, drunk on power. She's just the latest delusional narcissist I've come across who has opportunistically elevated herself on the battered backs of others. "I'm sure you're all anxious. *I'm* anxious. We've been to Hell and back. But let me assure you, we've retaken the Bridge!"

The gallery erupts with *yeahs* and applause.

"With the *Triumph* at our command, do you want to go back to the lives we had before?"

"No!" the galley roars.

"To a realm that gives credence to androids, who did all *this*... to *us*?"

"No!"

"Or do you want to restore order to the realm? Let's remake the rules. Where nobody, and I mean *nobody*, will ever again force us to share our space with those... *things*... that have done nothing but destroy our way of life. You know what they call the android creators? *Disruptors.* Challengers to the status quo! But what is a disruptor, really? Are they innovators? Are they geniuses? No! They're arrogant, attention-seeking losers who put their egos ahead of the realm. You don't advance our lives by breaking what works. The status quo is there for a reason.

Because it provides structure and consistency. We know the *rules*. We understand them. Even with the good, the bad, and all our imperfections. Life. Makes. Sense."

Translation: the status quo works for those in power, and suppresses those without.

"Androids were an experiment. And what we've seen this weekend... what I'm sure our capable prosecutor will prove beyond the shadow of a doubt... is that androids are not just an experiment, but a *failed* experiment, whose time has come. And gone!"

The gallery stomps their feet and erupts into thunderous applause. "YEEAHHH!"

The Judge bangs her gavel until they settle back down.

"Good. Because court is in session."

CHAPTER 30

"We'd like to introduce some new evidence," Litton says.

The Judge concurs.

Litton turns to the gallery and gestures toward them. In sequence, Turk's people signal each other, until the doors swing open.

Walking backwards, survivors drag the dead by their feet, fresh corpses smearing blood, waste, and other internal fluids down the center aisle. The gallery hoots, boos, and tosses more lit toilet paper. The tiny orange flames disintegrate the tissue into black, chemically treated mist.

The bodies are dragged down in front of the stage and tossed into a pile next to the bound and gagged passengers.

"These are only a fraction of the dead," Litton says, far more composed now than he was during the panel, when he didn't have a rigged trial and armed guards supplying him with all the confidence he'll need. "Who would all be alive if not for the android—"

"Selene Garin," Alec says.

"The *defendant*," Litton clarifies, "who is most definitely *an android*."

"Objection," Alec says. "Prejudicial."

The Judge slams the gavel. "Overruled."

I do my best to focus my thoughts, looking for cracks in this delirious trial, but my head is still thrumming from the taser jab. And Ralph is still right behind me, waiting to tase me again.

"We'd like to call a witness," Litton says. "Faith Beran."

"Faith?" Whistler mumbles. "Ohhhh shit."

"Who's Faith?" I whisper. "Is she...?" Then I remember. Yeah. This is bad.

Two civilian guards escort her down to the lower level. In a gore-stained housekeeping uniform, Faith stands before the Judge. Addressed by the bailiff, Faith raises her right hand.

"Do you swear to tell the truth, the whole truth, and nothing but the truth or be tossed out the airlock?"

Okay, that's a new one.

"Y-yes," Faith says nervously.

The bailiff instructs Faith to sit in an armchair, their version of the witness stand.

"Ms. Beran," Litton begins, strutting about like the entitled bully he is, "please tell the court who, if anyone, approached you before we set off on this cruise."

"It was him," Faith says, and points nervously. "Mr. Eric."

"Let the record show the witness is pointing at Eric Whistler, there, in the third row. He is a licensed private investigator, and employed on this cruise by the defendant, to act as an agent of destruction."

"So ordered," the Judge says.

"Objection!" Alec retorts.

"Overruled."

"But—!"

"Over... ruled. Move on."

I feel Whistler about to protest, but I grab his arm, eye-text him.

Me: *Don't clarify. You'll only make it worse.*

Whistler: *She's all alone. Ther'eda hired us!*

Me: *I know. Let it go.*

"And what did this Mr. Eric ask you to do?"

"He told me to watch one of the passengers. Warren Buckley."

"So, Eric Whistler, who works for"—Litton sneers at me—"Angela Hardwicke, also a private investigator, bribed you to spy on one of our passengers. In your nine years working on cruise ships, has anyone besides Eric Whistler ever asked you to spy on a passenger?"

"No. Never."

"Interesting. Did he ask you to do anything else?"

"He told me... he told me to say when Mr. Buckley left his room."

"And why did he do that?"

"I don't know."

Litton approaches her chair. "I think you do. Let me remind you that failing to answer honestly and fully gets you a date with the airlock. So I'll ask again. Why did he ask you to report about Buckley's room?"

"So he could…"

"So he could *what*?"

"Sneak in."

"So he could *break* in, ladies and gentleman. Not *sneak* in—break in." Derisive nods of agreement from the jurors. Litton smirks at us. He gets back to Faith. "When Mister Buckley left his room, where did he go?"

"The pool."

"How do you know?"

"He was in a bathing suit. And a robe and deck shoes."

"So Warren Buckley, the guest of honor at this weekend's event—the same engineer that, as we now know, wrote the Life Code—was on his way to the pool, by himself."

"Yes."

"Do you know what the Life Code is?"

"N-no."

"Just so everybody here is on the same page… a software engineer by the name of Davi Nolasco previously worked in the defendant's company. But after observing the destructive impact androids were having on the realm, eroding the very fabric of our society, Nolasco had a moment of clarity about his own contributions to this awful mistake. He created the Death Code. Lines of computer code, implanted into all androids, which randomly kick-starts the end of their artificial lives.

"Warren Buckley, who was partnered with Nolasco, left the company under suspicious circumstances and, as it turns out, created the Life Code. A digital cure for a digital disease, which impacted digital creatures. A Life Code to counteract the Death Code. Understand?"

"Y-yes."

"After Buckley went down to the pool, alone, did he return?"

"N… no."

"No, he did not," Litton pontificates. "Do you know why?"

"Someone"—Faith is visibly shaking, almost crying—"killed him."

"You hear that, ladies and gentlemen? Somebody *killed* him. I know there was a lot of violence on this trip. Believe me, I know. But this singular act—and let's be clear, one that was *not* part of the mass violence we all endured—was a *murder.*"

The gallery gasps.

"I'll say that again. A murder. An intentional, targeted act of violence. So let's review. Eric Whistler, a trained and licensed private investigator, bribed you to spy on Warren Buckley. Eric Whistler took that information, broke into Buckley's room, then someone killed him at the pool. Is that right?"

"Y-yes."

"And where was Eric Whistler when Buckley was killed?"

"I don't know."

"Wow. Think about that, ladies and gentlemen. Eric Whistler, while on the defendants' payroll, stalked Warren Buckley, who ended up dead."

"They're setting me up," Whistler grumbles. "It wasn't like that."

That's the brilliance of Litton's prosecution. He's interweaving lies and speculation with facts, and introducing plausible theories, whether they hold up under further scrutiny or not.

"And for those who don't know, what other kind of relationship does Eric Whistler have with the defendant?"

"I'm not sure."

"Now, Faith… can I call you Faith? Faith, do you really want to—?"

"They're lovers."

The gallery breaks out into gasps and boos and tosses more dice and flaming toilet paper.

"Lovers! You heard that. Eric Whistler and the defendant, Selene Garin, not only have a financial arrangement, but a sexual one. Eric Whistler stalks Warren Buckley, on behalf of his android lover, then Buckley ends up dead. Anything else?"

"N-no, I don't think so."

"Then you're excused." Faith stands up, and exhales shakily, surely relieved. "Actually," Litton says, delaying her release, "I'm not quite done." Nervously uncertain, she sits back down. "How much did Eric Whistler pay you to spy on Warren Buckley?"

Terrified, Faith looks blankly.

"Faith, please don't make this worse than it is. I'll ask once more. How much... did Eric Whistler... pay you... to spy... on Warren Buckley?

Faith swallows uncomfortably, clears her throat. "Twenty credits."

"Twenty credits, ladies and gentlemen! Twenty lousy credits. Wow. Murder comes cheap these days."

"Oooh," Ralph taunts, leaning his face between our heads. "That's gotta hurt."

Whistler: *I'm gonna kill that motherfucker.*

Me: *It may come to that.*

"Just one last question," Litton says. "Now that you know what happened, how do you feel, knowing that, on behalf of an android he's been sleeping with, Eric Whistler paid you just twenty credits to assist in the murder of Warren Buckley?"

Faith is frozen with terror. Tears stream down. "I-I...," she stammers.

"No need to answer. That's all for this witness."

Wiping her tears, Faith rises again.

"I have a few questions," Alec says.

"The witness is dismissed," the Judge orders.

"But... Your Honor! In order to defend my client—"

"I said," the Judge repeats, "dis...missed." She cements her decision with a gavel bang. Turk pumps his shotgun for additional effect. Shaking, Alec looks to Selene impotently. She mumbles something to him, but I can't hear what.

She probably knows what we all know. This isn't a trial.

It's a public execution, wrapped up in spectacle.

It's also odd they're dropping Buckley's murder at Whistler's feet, yet he's not on trial for it.

But the Judge wants much more than that. She's gathered survivors of a brutal massacre. They... we... are legitimate victims suffering a multitude of trauma and distress, with very real and horrible reasons to hate... someone.

It can take days, weeks, years, or a lifetime to process an event like this, and find ways to deal with it. Time we may never get.

There has to be a reason for what happened. Hasn't there? I'm not immune to it. We all want someone to blame, want to know the how and the why.

Yet this bogus trial isn't just about Buckley's murder, if it's about that at all. It's not just about the bloody carnage. It's a cathartic stage play to publicly spew pent-up resentment and disgust about androids, and what their integration into E-Town has meant for those who never wanted them here in the first place.

The Judge isn't just orchestrating a circus. She's rallying a posse.

And it doesn't matter that this trial is a fraud. If I open my mouth to rebut, I've got Ralph behind me to shut me up, and possibly shut me down for good.

Even paired with Tarrish, Dolores, and Whistler, who can all inflict real damage in a fight, we're literally boxed into this row, with no way to get free.

The one thing we do have, though, are our contact lenses. I eye-text Whistler.

Me: *Scroll thru data. Whatever U recorded.*

Whistler: *What am I looking for?*

Me: *Something. Anything. I'll do the same.*

Whistler: *It's hard to concentrate.*

Me: *I know. But we have to find something. I know it's in there. Keep looking.*

He doesn't respond. He just nods.

Me: *Go as fast as you can. Time's running out.*

The sham trial continues, Litton parading several witnesses who go into detail about what they experienced during the psycho fog, how androids have given them nightmares, and that the savagery we all just experienced was the inevitable conclusion of forcing radical change onto a society that didn't need or want synthetic beings—at least not any that were awarded citizenship.

So it surprises me when they call up their next witness.

"Good afternoon, Professor Suzuki. We met yesterday, I

think, when you moderated a panel on dysfunction in android brains."

"Actually," Suzuki says uncomfortably, "the panel topic was *Bringing Organics Deeper into Empirical Computational Social Choice and Preference Reasoning*."

"Right. Android mind control."

Mind control. Nice. Rile up the gallery and enflame the jury, eliciting shouts, boos, and burning toilet paper confetti.

"No! Just the opposite. Our goal was to help citizens—"

"The title of your panel included the word 'organics.' Which unto itself amplifies the critical distinction between us—*real* people, humans, of organic origin—and androids, which are *one hundred percent manufactured*."

The gallery responds as expected.

"In short, your goal was to convince organics that android brains are nothing to fear. Which, of course, they are. We had a rather... animated discussion, did we not?"

Clearly terrified, Suzuki shifts his gaze to the bound and gagged survivors face down on the floor. "Yes. It was... animated."

"Now, as a Professor of Synthetic Mind Control," Litton taunts.

"Objection," Alec says weakly.

The Judge offers a dismissive hand-wave. "Overruled."

"Professor of Synthetic Brain Function," Suzuki corrects. "At the Wiley Foundation."

"And what does that mean?"

"Fundamentally, I study the biochemical and synthetic interface of—"

"In any case," Litton interrupts again, continuing to twist and manipulate facts and fiction into a bastardized version of the truth, "before this atrocity was inflicted upon us *by* androids, what was your impression *about* androids and their place in society?"

Suzuki clears his throat. "Androids are a remarkable achievement who have demonstrated they are worthy of—"

"True or false, Professor, one of the androids..." Litton sips some water. "Turk, can you get them up? There, on the end. Those three." He has Nenn do the dirty work. Up on their knees now are the other two professors from the panel. And Sebastian. Damn. They got him, too. "That one, right over there, the android in the blue suit. In front of the witness, including yourself, he threatened to kidnap my children, as a means of making a point."

More gasps and boos.

"W-well," Suzuki stammers, "that's taken out of context. You actually got quite—"

"*That* android threatened to kidnap *my* children. True... or... *false?*"

Suzuki visibly chokes, knowing he's trapped. He sighs. "True."

"True! You heard that for yourselves, ladies and gentlemen. This man, a highly regarded professor, just admitted right here on the stand, that that very android, right over there, threatened to *kidnap* my children. Can you believe it? What kind of sick, *organic*-hating monster would do that?"

Litton sips more water, starts back in. "We've already heard about the murder of Warren Buckley. How do you feel about that?"

"It's awful."

"Awful, yes. Awful. And what do you think about this rumored Life Code?"

"Oh, wow. If what we've heard is accurate, and it can resolve the Death Code, it would prove to be one of the most extraordinary achievements in modern—"

"What proof, that you can personally produce, affirms a Life Code even exists? Have you ever seen this Life Code?"

"Well... no. No one has. Not yet."

"No one! Not one single person. Again, did you hear that, ladies and gentlemen? No one has even seen this so-called"— Litton makes finger quotes—"*Life Code.* Then how do you know it exists?"

Suzuki blinks wordlessly.

"Well? How do you know?"

"I suppose I don't."

"You don't even *know* if it exists. Which means, the Life Code... is fake news! A hoax!"

"I didn't say that!"

Litton ignores him. "And if the Life Code is a hoax, as we now know—which means *no one* would be motivated to prevent its use in androids as a cure for the Death Code—it also means that Warren Buckley wasn't killed by an organic, doesn't it? All humans have been ruled out as suspects. He wasn't killed over the Life Code because there *is* no Life Code! No! He was killed by an *android*—yes, an android!—who was furious about the *rumors* of a Life Code. And that's all it was. A rumor. Because we now know the truth. Davi Nolasco, as brilliant a coder as he may be, was framed! A patsy, who was forced into hiding to save his life. *Warren Buckley* created the Death Code. Not Davi Nolasco. Warren Buckley infected all androids, and then, in an act of even more incredible hubris, tried to extort Ther'eda Ranadyne to pay for a solution that doesn't even exist! There *is* no Life Code! There is no *cure!*"

The gallery shouts all manner of obscenities.

"No!" Suzuki protests. "It was Nolasco. It—"

"How do you know it was Nolasco?" Litton asks, conflating theories and sowing so much doubt it would be almost impossible to untangle this unholy knot of lies and half-truths. "How do you actually know it wasn't Buckley all along? Were you there?"

The gallery gasps, goes silent. Litton might have a point. How do we know for certain it was Nolasco? Ther'eda and Selene said it was, and at the time, we had no reason to doubt them. But now?

"To sum up," Litton says, "Warren Buckley, not Davi Nolasco, created the Death Code. And why? Why did he secretly infuse a random countdown in every android? Because Buckley knows what we *all* know. That androids are abominations that need to be extinguished. It's bad enough we have cyborgs walking the streets—damaged organics subjected to cranial interfaces. Can you imagine, a computer being fused to a human brain? Horrifying. But I digress. We also know that Warren Buckley was extorting Ther'eda Ranadyne for the Life Code, which doesn't even exist. Further, we know that the defendant, Selene Garin, Ther'eda Ranadyne's assistant, and her private investigator boyfriend, Eric Whistler, conspired to murder Warren

Buckley. On this ship! Finally, we know that whoever killed Warren Buckley unleashed unbridled terror on all of us as a sick, demented means of covering up the crime. Thank you, professor. You've been quite helpful."

The Judge bangs her gavel. "The witness is dismissed."

"Your Honor!" Alec protests, but quickly gives up. He's not there to speak, refute, or defend Selene or androids. He's there to be humiliated.

As Suzuki is led away, Litton strolls over to the bound and gagged survivors, brushes a fingertip beneath Sebastian's chin, and presents a smile. With Kowalczyk's confiscated brass knuckles, he punches Sebastian in the face.

Gagged, Sebastian unleashes a muffled howl. Orange blood squirts from his nose. Still on his knees, he bobs back and forth, then falls sideways onto the floor.

"That's for threatening my kids. Asshole." Shaken from the adrenaline rush, Litton gulps the rest of his water. He drops the brass knuckles on the table, shakes out his hand. "If it pleases the court, I'd like to call my next witness."

CHAPTER 31

I don't know how much longer this trial can last, but I'm scrolling through every file I can find in my contact lens memory bank, re-examining video, for anything that might help us. Whistler's doing the same, but so far no luck.

I sort through the unhinged lunacy of the last thirty-six hours, when it's Litton who gets me thinking. He claimed, without a clear train of logic, that Buckley *must* have been killed by an android, as if an organic couldn't possibly have done it. Just another way to poison the narrative. He also claimed, without proof, that whoever killed Buckley also unleashed the psycho fog as a means of disguising the crime. He might be right about that one.

We saw the video of Gerald arguing with Buckley, and then storming off. Was he—?

The ship jostles. Another lightning bolt. The lights flicker off and on. The gallery starts to panic.

"Fuck me," Dolores says, clutching Nini so tight she nearly breaks her forearm. "I can't handle this. Not again."

"It's not..." I start, and with a deep breath, scan my own mind. "It's something else."

I see Turk check his phone, then approach the Judge. She nods, then bangs her gavel.

"Nothing to worry about," the Judge declares. "We're leaving the aurora!"

The gallery erupts into applause, hugs and high-fives all around.

Whistler: *That real? We have control of the ship?*

Me: *Maybe. Scout orb? Still dead?*

Whistler: *Lemme check. No! It's back. Location finder is pinging. Montrose still has it.*

Me: *Pull up video from natatorium again. Wanna check something.*

He does, accessing the orb's files from his lens, and syncing it to mine.

Whistler: *What u looking for?*

Me: *May be something, may be nothing.*

He scrolls back the video until we reach the segment I need.

Me: *There. Stop. That's Gerald.*

Whistler: *Think it was him?*

Me: *No. But...*

Gerald. Gerald. Why does that...?

Like recalling a long-forgotten dream, it all comes back to me. Before Litton even calls the name, I know who his next witness will be.

"I'd like to call Felix Sandoval."

Nini gasps. She looks over to me for help. But there's nothing I can do.

"Mr. Sandoval," Litton says, "you are a personal service android, are you not? And for those who don't know, most personal service androids are prostitutes, correct? You *service*"—he makes finger quotes for the word—"lonely, desperate citizens, sexually, for money."

Clearly nervous, he manages to keep his cool. "People enjoy my company."

"When you say *people*, you mean organics? Humans?"

"Yes."

"And much of that time is spent sexually?"

"I don't know about *much*, but some, yes."

"And did you spend some of that time, sexually, with Nini Obalawe in her stateroom on this cruise?"

It's clear Felix doesn't want to answer, but knows he has no choice. "Yes."

"The very same stateroom where Gerald Profar, another personal service android, was murdered, as you told me earlier."

Felix nods reluctantly. "Yes."

"Were you there when it happened?"

Felix cranes his neck so he can get a better sightline to Nini. He smiles dejectedly. "Yes."

"So, one android—one sexually deviant android—witnesses

the murder of yet another sexually deviant android, and fails to report it. Interesting. But let's go back. You just testified that you were in Ms. Obalawe's stateroom on a... 'date.' Why was Gerald there? Was it a threesome? A group sex thing?"

I wondered the same. I don't care if it was. A girl's gotta get her kink on however she does, and good for Nini if she went there. But I never understood why Gerald showed up at all.

Felix bristles.

"Turk," Litton says. "A little motivation, please?"

Turk directs Nenn, who marches over to the line of bound and gagged survivors still face down on the floor. She and the bailiff pull them up on their knees facing us. By their J-scars, it's easy to tell they're androids. But next to them, on the end, are two organics. Humans.

Kowalczyk... and Ther'eda.

Selene fidgets in her chair, looks back to Whistler for guidance.

Wanting to console her, he leans forward. But Ralph has other ideas. "Ah-ah-ah," he taunts, then tases Whistler in the back of the shoulder.

Whistler drools on himself. "Fffuck."

Me: *Keep it together. We're gonna get outta here.*

Meanwhile, Nenn produces a handgun, and without betraying a shred of emotion, puts it to the thigh of the android on the far right, a blond-haired man. She pulls the trigger. Orange blood leaks from his leg as the android drops to the ground, howling through his gag.

The blast echoes. The gallery and jury jump queasily.

The Judge pounds the gavel. "Silence, people. There's plenty more to go around."

Litton clumsily sips more water, takes a beat, then resumes his question. "I'll ask again. *Why* was Gerald in the stateroom with you? Was it a sex thing?"

Shaking, Felix answers. "No."

"Then why?"

"Because..."

"Because *why*?"

Felix is fighting himself. He doesn't want to answer. But he does.

"He was infected with the Death Code! He's a friend, and we heard Warren Buckley had the cure. Gerald went to confront him at the pool. I guess it didn't go too well. He knew I was with Nini. When I let him in, he said Buckley wouldn't help."

"Wouldn't help, or couldn't?"

"He said *wouldn't*. No... *couldn't*. I... I'm sorry. I'm just nervous. I can't remember."

"You can't remember if your friend had learned if the Life Code was real or not? How is that possible?"

"Because..."

"Because why?"

"Because..." Felix exhales shakily. "She came in."

"Who's she?"

Felix raises his arm, limply points in our direction. "Her. Dolores."

"Let the record show the witness is pointing to Dolores Conway, who is seated next to Nini Obalawe."

"This is fucked, Hardy. This is so fucked. I'm losin it. I'm fuckin losin it."

Litton continues. "She's a big one. And what happened when Ms. Conway showed up?"

Felix swallows hard, his left leg tapping nervously. "We fought. All of us. Dolores and... Nini, they... killed Gerald. But I got away."

"And why, exactly, did you fight?"

"Dolores is Nini's best friend. But Dolores hates androids. She's disgusted by us. So she didn't need motivation. But there was this... clacking sound, a rattling, then a horrible piercing noise in my ears, and..."

"Yes. I think we all know what happened then. No more questions."

The spectators boo and taunt and throw more of the vanity dice Ther'eda gave out. One hits me in the back of the head, others tumble to the floor, a few landing beneath my feet.

Looking for any hints about what Litton has up next, I see Selene absentmindedly fidget with something on the table. Then she pushes it aside like it's a useless plaything.

"What's she doing?" Whistler wonders aloud. "Is that...?" Hang on. He squints.

Whistler: *Is that a replica of the Triumph? Like the one in the...*

I don't know where his mind is headed, but in his eyes I see a glint of recognition, a spark of discovery.

Me: *Yeah, actually. She had one before. What are U on to?*

He goes back to the video of the natatorium. He scrolls forward and—

Whistler: *There! On the wall. Shelves with model ships. Didn't see it before. Look in the glass. It's capturing the angle the cameras missed. A reflection.*

Me: *Where? Yeah, you're right. Zoom in. More. More. More.*

Whistler: *I can't tell. Is that? Yes!*

Me: *That's Buckley. He's in the frame, he's out. And there's someone with him.*

Whistler: *There! In the reflection? Did you see that? Is that what I think it is?*

My heart rumbles. I nearly choke on gravelly breaths.

Me: *Yeah. It is.*

Whistler: *That means...*

Me: *We need to get out of this room. Now.*

I look around frantically when I see a green glow on the floor. A handful of dice tumbled near each other. The dice... the dice? Wait. My heart skips a beat. There's something about the dice, something that...

Me: *What did Ther'eda say about the dice? About what's in them?*

Whistler: *Why?*

Me: *Humor me.*

Whistler: *Phosphorescent composite.*

Me: *There's some on the floor. If we can grind them down and expose the filaments.*

Whistler: *They'd be flammable! But we got no flame.*

Me: *Toilet paper. Grind dice into powder, get a flame on it.*

Whistler: *How?*

Me: *Working on it.*

I tap Tarrish with my foot until he looks down. I eye gesture him to follow my lead.

With our feet, the three of us surreptitiously scoop together as many stray dice as we can. Despite the absurdity of this trial, Litton may actually be doing his job a bit too well. He's got everyone so focused on the witnesses no one's paying attention to us.

Most of the goons are untrained civilians wrangled from who was left. Neutralizing Turk is the key. If he goes down, the others won't know what to do, and the Judge loses her muscle. Even with her bile, and Litton backing her up, without the weapons she's noise with no force.

The pieces are unspooling in my mind when Ralph leans forward, whispers at me again, his mouth against my ear. "This really has to suck for you, huh? I thought you were supposed to help your clients, not fuck them into oblivion."

"You know what they say. Win some, lose some."

"Well, today"—he crackles the taser right beside my cheek, close enough that it singes my eyelash—"you're gonna lose."

My eye reactively fills with water, the electrical sparks nearly blinding me. I clench my eyes shut to shield them from the blue-white globs floating in my sightline. I shake it out, and dig my heel into the dice, like biting down on a bullet. Which gives me an idea.

Like most bullies, he's an insecure jackass thirsty for validation. So it I give it to him.

"You're probably right," I say. "And when they take us down, you can say you were part of it. Maybe even get your name in the paper. *Software Engineer Foils Android Plot*. It'll make your whole career. You'll write a book, go on TV, get all sorts of funding and job offers. Hell, they'll probably give *you* the award."

"Whatever." He slumps back, confused about how to handle himself. He loves the ego stroke, can't get enough of it. But he hates that it came from me, and probably suspects I'm fucking with him. Which I am. But his ego loves the attention, even if it's fake. He leans forward again. "Damn straight. And when they do, I'll be sure they spell your name right. *Private Cunt Angela Hardwicke Conspires with Ranadyne Cybernetics in Greatest Mass Murder in E-Town History*."

"You remembered my name. I'm honored."

"Don't be. The only one of us who'll be getting an honor is me."

He crackles the taser one more time, then sits back, basking in his win.

Whistler: *What was that about?*

I eye-text him in response.

Whistler: *Seriously? Instead of...*

Me: *Any better ideas?*

Whistler shakes his head.

Me: *Then let's get to it.*

Speaking of which, Litton addresses the Judge. "We're almost done, Your Honor. I'd like to call two more witnesses."

"Please do," she says, and like a rock drummer, rolls the gavel between her fingers. "The trial's almost over. I can't wait much longer."

I'm so focused on grinding the dice beneath my heel that I almost don't realize Litton's calling his next witness.

"My pleasure, Your Honor. I'd like to call to the stand..."

Come on, you little fuckers. Grind... into... dust. One of the dice crunches. *Got it!*

"Dolores Conway."

It takes a second before the name registers.

"Me?" Dolores says across Tarrish and Whistler. "Hardy? Is he for real?"

I look up to see Litton grinning in our direction.

"Oh, yeah," Ralph says, "you are going to lose. Huge."

CHAPTER 32

Dolores lumbers uncomfortably to the stand.

Partly because of her injured leg, but mostly, I suspect, because she'd rather be eaten by rattlesnakes than talk in front of a crowd. A hulking figure in that small seat, Dolores snarls like she wants to kill everyone here.

Litton starts right in.

"Ms. Conway, we've heard plenty of testimony today about your friends, including Nini Obalawe's *relationship* with Felix Soto, and your own participation in his friend's murder. Now, personally, I understand your disgust of androids, and, in particular, personal service androids. They also make me sick. And yet, as much as I may have *thought* about killing one, thinking isn't a crime—yet."

Hoots and hollers.

"I never actually did. But *you* did. What makes you hate androids *so much* that you'd kill one, with your own very big and powerful hands?"

I can see Dolores staring our way. Because she has to decide now, in real time: does she hate androids more than she loves Nini, or the other way around?

"Don't like 'em," Dolores finally says.

"Yes, Ms. Conway. We got that."

Laughter.

"Can you tell me why?"

Dolores is visibly fidgety, her right leg bouncing anxiously.

"Ms. Conway?"

Beyond the horrors and humiliations she's suffered already, the most intimate moments of Nini's personal life are being broadcast in front of strangers. She's being publicly slut-shamed, all because she had the audacity to engage sexually, as a consenting adult, with someone who isn't exactly like her.

Nini spends her days and nights tending to the wounds of others. In her private time, she seeks out others who will tend to hers. And this is what she gets for it.

"I...," Dolores starts, wrestling with her own demons, and her loyalty to Nini.

"Your Honor, permission to treat as a hostile witness?"

"Hostility's my middle name. Let's see what you got."

"Turk?" Litton calls, then gestures to the bound and gagged.

Without needing instruction, Nenn stands in front of an android. Shoots her in the foot, sending three mangled toes scattering like synthetic shrapnel. Again, the sound rattles my teeth. The gallery and jury squirm. The visceral impact of the gun blast, that deafening sound, and the android's muffled cries of pain, have everyone on edge. More on edge.

Except Dolores. Which is the point.

They're not torturing androids to get her to talk. They want to demonstrate just how much of their abuse she'll tolerate, if not embrace.

Witnessing all this, the surviving androids tremble in place as sweat and tears roll down their terrified faces. Ther'eda is nearly motionless, even as her personal security guard has turned against her, while Kowalczyk's breaths are labored. He wheezes through the gag.

"Thank you," Litton says.

Despite his forced calm, I saw Litton's knees buckle as the android's toes splattered onto the floor. I don't care who you are. Watching someone get dismembered only a few feet in front of you isn't like reacting to a door slam. That kind of violent brutality can reduce even the most hardened adult to a puddle of quivering shame.

But this hasn't been just any weekend. Most of the survivors have either retreated into the recesses of their denial or become desensitized to the violence. Some, more disturbingly, have seemed to acquire a taste for it. Murder, as with porn, requires escalating intensity to get them off.

"Now, Ms. Conway, back to the question at hand. Why do

you dislike androids as much as you do? And is withholding your testimony really worth it? Or maybe it is. We've got one less fully intact android to deal with. We can make it another, if you like. Actually... do you like it? Is that... oh, you naughty girl. You *do* like it. You *love* it. You want to pull the trigger yourself, don't you?"

Nini's practically shaking. Dolores sees Nini see her.

"Ms. Conway!"

Though seated in a multitiered theater with plenty of room and air, Dolores is sweating, her claustrophobia kicking back in. "I don't...," she begins, her chest heaving.

Whether it's physical or emotional, trapped is trapped. And when Dolores feels trapped, she freaks out. Or fights to the death. Only, she knows that right now, fighting isn't an option. Not a good one. So instead, she does what she always does when her friends are in trouble. She holds on.

Turk takes this round himself. He starts down the line. Three shots. One each to the head. The executed android bodies slump over, leaking orange blood, as the others flounder, including Kowalczyk and Ther'eda. Their time is nearly up, too.

"One last chance, Ms. Conway. Why do you hate androids *that* much?"

Dolores parts her lips as if she might finally say something. I look over to Nini, who, with tiny tremors, shakes her head.

I see Litton follow the path of Dolores' gaze. He sees what I see.

"Okay," he says. "Let's try something else."

He whispers to Turk, who nods agreeably, then has Montrose retrieve Nini.

My chest seizes like I'm in cardiac arrest. Blood rushes to my ears. I grab Nini's fingers in solidarity as she passes by, but she pulls them away. There's nothing I can do for her. She's on her own.

"All right then," Litton says.

Turk holds Nini up before the bodies he just killed. With an open hand, he slaps her across the face.

This stuns Dolores, her face trembling with fear and rage.

The gallery gasps. Dolores pops up to defend Nini. Turk

pumps the stock on his shotgun. Sensing the shift in my body language, Ralph activates the sparks, waiting to tase me again.

"One last time," Litton says, queuing Turk to beat on Nini until she's nearly unconscious. Not even five feet tall and a hundred pounds soaking wet, Nini takes it. And keeps on taking it.

"Why," Litton asks as Turk slaps Nini's face again—"do you"—another slap—"hate"—slap—"androids"—slap—"this"—slap—"much?"

"All right!" Dolores shouts as blood and saliva leak down Nini's neck.

Acutely aware the assault on Nini is just the beginning, me, Whistler, and Tarrish keep grinding the dice with our shoes as fast as we can, but they're difficult to break.

Dolores sits back down, grabs the arms of her chair so hard they might snap off. Her jaw quivers. Dolores is the most powerful woman I've ever known, her physical strength outmatched only by the sheer force of her titanic will. You'd have more success gnawing through an iron girder than getting her to open up.

Trapped in every way, Dolores looks to Nini, her face all raw and swollen and covered in blood, snot, and tears.

"Mom was a nurse in a cancer ward," Dolores says finally, speaking in a way I've never heard from her before, as if she's in a faraway place where no one can reach her. And she's not saying *Dolores*. She's saying *I* and *me*. "It takes its toll, seeing all that pain, watchin them wither away and die. But she said no matter how it might affect her, it was nothin compared to what her patients went through, even if they came out okay. A lot of 'em did. But not all of 'em."

The images on the wraparound screen fade to an aerial view of E-Town, a yellow sun glistening off the skyscrapers.

"But Dad, you know… he was a freighter pilot, gone a lot. I loved him. So much it hurt. I didn't get to see him much, so all I wanted to know was when he was comin home and what he was gonna bring me when he did. It was totally unfair to Mom. Doin her job every day, always comin home, always there for me. But like I said. Kids. You know, naive, selfish. And stupid."

Like shedding her emotional skin, Dolores seems lighter

somehow, and yet with more heft, as if deriving strength from the very secrets she swore to herself she'd never tell.

"Turns out Dad had girlfriends all over the realm and half the systems he delivered to. Mom loved him anyway. Said he coped with life the best he knew how, and even if he didn't always do the right thing, he always came home. Eventually. I don't think she really believed all that. It was just a story for me, so I wouldn't hate him."

She shakes her head.

"Mom was the toughest broad I knew. And she knew about love. You can talk the talk, but unless you walk it, words don't mean shit. Dad told me he loved me. But Mom, she *showed* me. Still, Dad went to cool places and did cool things. One time when I was about eight, he was gone a few weeks and I begged Mom... I practically forced her... to take me to the airstrip so I could meet him when he arrived. I can't even remember why it was so important to me, but once I got that idea in my head, it was my only idea. Mom had just come off a long shift at the hospital. She was exhausted, hungry, and needed a shower and a night's sleep. But she rallied for me. She hauled us out to the airstrip in the middle of the night so I could see Dad. My hero."

Dolores wipes a tear from her eye.

"We coulda waited inside the cargo bay, but nope. I just had to be outside. I *had* to see the ship land as close as they'd let me. Dad's ship was delayed, so finally I begged Mom for some credits to go inside and get a hot chocolate. And of course I just *had* to do it by myself. She said okay, because it was close by and she could sorta have eyes on me."

"This is all very touching, Ms. Conway, but what does that have to do with—?"

"You told me to fuckin answer," Dolores snaps back. "I'm answering!"

Litton backs off.

"So I'm inside with a hot chocolate... I think I spilled half of it on myself... but I didn't care. It was mine and I did it and I wanted to show Dad that I did it. But then, the ship came in. And as it landed... it exploded. Some kinda malfunction. Dad was killed instantly. And some of the debris flung through the air… and killed Mom. One minute I had two parents. We were a family, even if it was messed up. And then…"

I've known Dolores a long time. I never knew any of this. She never talked about it.

The gallery and jurors alike actually gasp in sympathy.

"After that I bounced around foster homes for about five years. I had a lotta rage, and I was real big and strong for my age and was clearly into girls at that point, and they just didn't know what to do with me. So I ran away. I lived on the street. I ate out of dumpsters. But that life… it gets old."

Dolores testifies that she camped in front of a bodega, begging for money. She was about fourteen, when an android came out, opening a pack of gum. He was dressed in a sharp suit, with shiny black shoes, so she figured he had credits to spare. Instead, he looked down at her and said there was plenty of work to be had if she was open to new things. He gave her the number of a clinic for runaways, got into a shiny black car with tinted windows, and drove off.

"I didn't know what to do, didn't know if the clinic was real or it was a set-up. You know, you hear about that kinda thing. So I sat there on the sidewalk, thinkin about his clothes and his car and his confidence and where he might be going. I studied that card, just lookin at it over and over like there was a secret code, and started to think maybe… I don't know… maybe I should check out the clinic, when another guy saw me. No suit, just a regular lookin guy in jeans and a hoodie. Said he had a room and a warm place close by if I wanted. I knew it was stupid, but I was so cold and hungry and confused. I just… I needed to go *somewhere*. So I went with him. And even though I didn't want to, I let him do stuff to me. You know. Gross stuff. In the bedroom. It hurt, and I hated it, but I dealt with it. Then he did what he promised. He gave me food, a hot shower, and a bed, with this stuffed aardvark as a pillow. We did this for a few days, and even though I was fed and warm and clean, I felt cold and dirty and ugly inside. I'd made up my mind to get outta there, first thing in the morning. But when I woke up, there were five of 'em."

My heart leaps into my throat. I can't imagine someone

getting the jump on Dolores, but I know all too well how your life can take a bad turn, and how quickly that turn can go from bad to worse to something that doesn't even have a name.

I've known trauma victims. I've been one. I am one. Helping them process that trauma, and heal even just a little, can only happen in a safe space, at their pace.

Forcing them to testify, in public, is about the most reprehensible approach imaginable.

Unless, of course, their goal isn't to help you heal, but to manipulate you for their own purposes. And if they re-victimize the victim? Tough shit. They're not here to help you. You're here to help them. If you hadn't been so weak and pathetic as to let yourself be victimized in the first place, you wouldn't be here now. So stop complaining.

You did this to yourself.

Your pain. Your problem.

"They all had that look in their eyes," Dolores says. "And they were all sayin things like 'look at the meat on her,' and 'ooh, she's a big girl, lots to work with' and then they..." She takes a beat. "When they were done, I was all torn up. I could barely move. They left me on a mattress on the floor, bruised, shaking, and covered in their... it's like I wasn't even there. I was in shock, so I don't know how long after, but I remember they were eatin pizza and there was a story on the news about androids and how they were fightin for their rights to become citizens. I don't know what happened, exactly, but as I was curled up on the floor, and thought... those androids, those *fucking* androids... they're already treated better than me. They're literally born as adults, strong enough to fight off an attacker, and other adults will listen to them when they talk, and they dress great and have nice things. And now they want *more?* They want more rights than *me?* If that offer was real... if that clinic was real... why didn't he tell me? Why didn't he explain what it was? It coulda changed my whole life.

"I don't know. Maybe I blamed them because really I blamed myself for what happened to me. I was tired. Lonely. Powerless. And then... I remembered something Mom used to say. She said I had power. Real power. But unused power is like a bird who won't fly. So in that room, with half-empty pizza boxes and my childhood dead and gone, I made three promises to myself I swore I'd never break. One, that I was gonna get outta that hellhole, no matter what. Two, that I was never, ever, for any reason, gonna let a man touch me again. And three, that I was gonna hate androids for the rest of my life. And nobody, not even my best friend"—she's choked up now, streaming tears, looking at Nini—"was gonna take that away from me." Her voice is not exactly soft now, but softer, even as the lights flicker again, the ship shuddering, struck by more lightning. "Maybe it's wrong and maybe it's unfair, and maybe I don't think right about androids. But this is who I am. And it's too late for me to change."

CHAPTER 33

Dolores lumbers off the stand.

Unobstructed, she goes to Nini, whose eyes are bloody and swollen. Dolores takes her by the hand, Nini barely able to stay on her feet. They ease over to the left side, and sit in the front row, Dolores' massive arm cradling Nini. But who will cradle her?

"Well, that, uh," Litton says as I dig my heel into the dice, "was certainly"—he clears his throat—"emotional." With a shaky hand, he pours himself more water, gulps half of it, exhales. With some of the vitriol gone from behind his eyes, he straightens himself. "Your Honor, if it—"

"Get on with it already," the Judge says. "Call her up. And make it quick."

Me: *Break your dice?*

Whistler: *Powder's on the floor. You?*

Me: *Just about. Yes! Got the last one. What about Tarrish?*

Whistler quick-glances down by his feet.

Whistler: *He's ready.*

I survey the theater. The logistics are critical. Whistler's next to me, Tarrish next to him. Ralph is behind us, Montrose in the aisle with the shotgun. Nenn is down now by Ther'eda, Kowalczyk, the remaining bound and gagged survivors, and the recently executed androids.

Turk mills about now while his goons are scattered throughout the theater space. And the Judge is still up on the stage. We're only going to get one shot at this, so we better get it right.

"I'd like to call Selene Garin to the stand," Litton says finally.

The gallery *oohs* in hushed tones, reserved anticipation before the verdict.

Selene stands, smooths out her ragged clothes, and walks gracefully to the stand.

"I've been waiting a long time for this," the Judge tells her. "So do yourself a *really* big favor. Don't aggravate me. You wouldn't like me when I'm aggravated." She turns her attention to Litton. "Go ahead, counselor. Your witness."

I don't know how complicit Selene is in Buckley's murder or the psycho fog, if at all, but it's to my advantage that she keep Litton talking for as long as possible. Even if that means aggravating the Judge.

"Ms. Garin," Litton says. "You're an android, are you not?"

"I am."

"Androids have had a difficult time integrating into society. And now we've got a Death Code, maybe even a Life Code. And so much violence. What is it about your kind that, no matter where you go, trouble seems to follow?"

Classic setup. Lawyers and cops do it all the time. So do PIs.

Don't ask *if* there's a problem, ask *why* there's a problem and how deeply it runs. The strategy automatically puts the witness on the defensive, asserts the problem is well-founded and common knowledge, and implies you're the cause, a co-conspirator, or an apathetic witness.

Agree, you admit guilt.

Protest, you look guiltier, someone with something to hide.

"We don't cause the trouble," Selene says. "We're the—"

"Don't cause it?" Litton shouts, throwing his hands in the air. "What do you call this?"

I should be focused only on our way out of here, but I'm glued to Selene. An individual android taking the blame for them all, the face of all android sins, giving their collective abusers a justification for their own toxic behavior.

It's easier to feel powerful and righteous when you've stacked the odds against someone who can't fight back and takes whatever you dish out. Which makes them want to abuse you all the more.

Selene doesn't know most of the survivors in this room. Most of them don't know her.

And yet, she knows them all. Mobs wear the same face.

She looks to Ther'eda—her employer, her creator, maybe even her mother figure. She looks to Whistler. Then she smiles woefully, as if she knows what we all know. That no matter what she says, it won't change the outcome. It was never going to.

"I know what you want," she says. "So here it is. I did it. I killed Warren Buckley. He did what you said. He infected me with the Death Code. He teased us with a Life Code. Then he took it away. He refused to help me, because he couldn't. He couldn't *give* me the Life Code because, as you said, there *is* no Life Code." I don't know if her declaration is accurate or not. We actually haven't been shown evidence that a Life Code exists. She's either telling the truth or doubling down on a lie. "It was a hoax. So I killed him."

The spectators shout boos and other insults, tossing flaming toilet paper, chanting, "*KILL HER NOW! KILL HER NOW! KILL HER NOW!*"

The Judge bangs her gavel repeatedly until they settle down.

"Quiet!" she demands. "If she wants to hang herself... let her."

Which is exactly what Selene is doing. Whether she's guilty of murder or not.

"You've just confessed," Litton says. "Anything else?"

Whistler's starting to panic, shaking his head intensely. Selene proceeds anyway.

"I could no longer tolerate your moral superiority, or your delusional hatred. You call us deviants, you exclude us in every way you can. Yes, I was created in a lab. I have synthetic organs. I have a cranial CPU. I don't have parents, so they can't love me. I can't have children, so I can't love them. I know I'm an outcast before I walk into any room of organics. But I have friends. I dream. I laugh and cry. I worry about the future. I may not be more than you, but I'm not less." She clears her throat. "I'm an android. And we matter. Maybe not to you, but at the very least, to each other."

"That's touching. Too bad I just don't—"

The ship jostles again. Lightning throttles the *Triumph*. The lights flicker off and on.

I slap Whistler's arm, then yell at Ralph. "Hey asshole! Come and get me!"

Ralph jolts forward, taser crackling. Whistler grabs his arm above the elbow, pins it to the back of the seat. I slam his wrist, but the spark burns my hand. I yelp in pain, but manage to elbow Ralph in the face, snaring the taser with my other hand.

Tarrish reaches across and punches Ralph in the head.

Montrose charges, blasts the shotgun. Buckshot catches me in the ear. But mostly it hits Ralph in the face and chest, ripping chunks out of him.

Before she can fire another shot, we scoop up the dice dust, and toss it toward her. Then I zap the phosphorescent cloud with the taser, and cover my eyes with the crook of my arm.

The dice dust explodes into a fiery cloud, blinding Montrose.

Tarrish jumps over the seat, snags Montrose's fallen shotgun. He grabs Ralph, who's limbs are barely attached to his torso. Using him as a human shield, Tarrish marches toward the stage. Turk opens fire, Ralph shot up like a crash-test dummy.

The *Triumph* jostles again, the lights flickering off and on, off and on, off and on until the gallery starts panicking. Some of them charge toward us. The rest lose control, and with nowhere to put their anxiety, stampede for the exits, trampling each other.

Not because of the psycho fog. Because they don't know what else to do.

Whistler rushes to Montrose, fishes his scout orb from her pocket, then goes to Selene. But he gets caught up with three of Turk's civilian goons.

"Regina!" Turk shouts above the chaos. "Where are you—"

Wielding his gun, Turk would have finished his question had Nenn not shot him in the chest, putting him flat on his back. She stands above him. Turk spits up blood.

Nenn shrugs wordlessly, unfastens Ther'eda and Kowalczyk, who's struggling to breathe, and rushes them out of the theater.

Litton makes a run for the aisle, but Alec dives at his legs, taking them down. Meanwhile, Whistler's fending off the civilian crew. I crack one of them over the head with my taser, then get knocked down from behind, bashing my forehead against the floor.

I'm not sure if I black out, or for how long. I push myself up with my one good hand, my bad hand curled beneath me in a damaged claw. I see Regina now holding Whistler from behind, my boot knife against his throat, and looking down at Turk, who's bleeding out.

"You love him?" Regina questions Selene. "You actually love him?"

Scraped across the face, Selene's skin has been damaged, revealing electrodes woven into her synthetic brain. She's tense, shaking. "Yes. I love him!"

"Turk was real! And you... you're a fucking computer!"

Everything slows down for me. Regina gazes over at Turk's dead body, then back to Selene. And then a mortified look of disgust spreads across her face.

There's nothing left to fight, because the fight's already over. But she fights anyway.

"Candidly," Selene says, her cranial CPU beginning to falter, "maybe I am a compu... compu... computer. Then again... I'm so much more. Eric!"

The shouting of his name distracts Regina enough for Whistler to elbow her in the ribs, knocking her backward and releasing him.

Selene leaps on Regina, hands around her neck.

Their two bodies are pressed together, the life being squeezed out of Regina, when she jams my boot knife into Selene's gut. She forces the blade deeper and deeper until her entire hand disappears inside Selene's body, hitting her synthetic spine. Orange blood leaks down Regina's arm.

Selene's blue eyes go deathly white, her gaze lost in the ether. "I tuh... took the blame," she whispers to Regina. "But you're... the one... who's guilty."

Regina lets Selene's body flop to the floor.

Using my taser as a baton, I crack Regina across the shoulder, my knife rattling onto the floor. She dives after it but comes up short. While down there, she grabs me behind my knee, taking me down with her.

On our stomachs, Regina and I scramble for the knife. She grabs my bad hand. I fight through the crippling pain, and with a sharp, precise blow, knee her in the trigger point in the center of her thigh. She reflexively curls up, retracting her hands.

On the ground, I grab the back of Regina's hair and jam my knee into her injured thigh, driving it with as much force as I can muster so that she's squirming, barely able to breathe.

In an Arberian martial arts move, I swirl my hips, spinning myself over Regina, and back up on my feet, holding her down with one foot. Standing above her, I force the end of my taser against her chest, directly above her heart.

I look to Whistler. He's cradling Selene, rocking her back and forth, kissing her forehead where her skin is still attached.

I've got the taser against Regina's chest. She's a monster in every way that matters. If anyone deserves to be met with street justice, it's her. But there's the rule of law, as inequitable as it may be. And there's my personal code of ethics. Lines I swore to myself I'd never cross.

Even in his agony, Whistler sees what I'm contemplating.

"Mache," he says breathily through his river of tears. Selene's body is limp in his arms. "She's not worth it."

I've been around death. I've been around murder. I've been dipped in blood, drowned by guilt. And I've found a way to survive, to outrun the agony, or beat it back. I've let so much of it go, because if I didn't, it would eat me alive, like battery acid dissolving my essence from the inside out.

I've nearly lost myself time and again, giving in to the monster inside me when the flickering embers of my inner light are just too damn exhausted to fight them off. But I've always managed, someway, somehow, to find my way back, to keep myself from crossing the kind of line that separates me from people like her.

Until now.

Dolores, Nini, Selene. And all the others tortured or killed on Regina's watch, under her orders.

There's the rule of law. There's street justice.

But here, today, now, there's *my* justice. Because some rules were meant to broken.

"Angela!" Tarrish shouts at me. "Don't!"

With a single gesture, I press the button. I activate the taser.

And turn the power up all the way. Electricity crackles. Regina's body spasms.

The light inside me begs me to stop.

Yet the monster knows I won't.

Not because I can't.

Because I don't want to.

CHAPTER 34

The ringleaders are dead. Regina, by my hand, and Turk, by Nenn's firearm.

Tarrish snatches up Turk's shotgun, blasts it into the wall to get everyone's attention.

"People!" He pumps the gun again. "PEOPLE!" He fires off another round.

The confused, panicking crowd settles down.

"My name is Lieutenant Lionel Tarrish. I'm with the Intergalactic Crime Division. We've been through an ordeal. All of us. We're gonna be okay. What we're going to do, right now, is clear this room, treat the wounded, and find some food. I don't know about you, but I could eat."

Tarrish's tactics are part crowd control, part something else.

"Angela," he calls to me.

I hear his voice, but as I stare down at Regina's body, he seems so far away. Until I feel a hand on my shoulder.

"Angela," he says again, gentler.

I look at him as if he's not really there. But it's me who's gone someplace else.

Tarrish eases me away from Regina so that she's out of my sightline. Although it doesn't matter. I killed this woman. I didn't have to, but I did it anyway. Because of my own actions, she's burned into my soul. I was so worried about how our time on Arcasia affected Whistler—it altered him permanently, destroying who he was, replacing him with whatever version of him he is now—I ignored how profoundly it affected me.

"The Life Code," Tarrish says. "It's real. I know where it is."

I blink a few times, his voice starting off as a whisper, then rising to full volume.

"What? You know… what?"

"The Life Code."

"You do? Where?"

He tells me.

"I'll deal with them," Tarrish says, head-gesturing toward the survivors. "But we're not out of this yet. Tyler's on the Bridge with Turk's man. And the transponder's offline. If we don't call a rescue ship, I'm not sure we'll make it."

It's all coming back to me, like multiple valves opening up at once.

"Angela," Tarrish says. "I need you. And the kid. As for her"—he gestures back at Regina—"we'll have to deal with that, too."

"Can I save the ship first?"

"Go."

Flush with a wave of adrenaline, I rush to Whistler, who's still cradling Selene.

"Eric," I say. "We have to go."

He looks up at me, his face coated with tears. "It didn't have to be like this."

"It didn't."

He kisses Selene on the forehead one more time. "I should've loved you better," he says. "And yes…" With two fingertips, he gently closes her eyelids. "You definitely had a soul."

We gather ourselves, run up the aisle, and back out into the foyer. There's a mess of survivors, unsure what to do.

"I'll take the transponder," I say. "You go to the Bridge. You can make it up to Tyler. Wipe the toothpaste from her eyes. But be careful."

"You'll never find the transponder," Whistler says. "Dolores told me where it is. I'll go."

My instincts are to deny him. But he's different now. So am I. "Okay. But keep your lens on."

I rush to the stairs, snatch a half-eaten cheeseburger off a serving tray, eat it while making my way up to the Bridge. Through the windshield I see that we've pulled away from the aurora, the green waves drifting behind us. But the stream of red mist is back. And we're still trapped within the lightning grid.

"Tyler! What's happening? What...?" Turk's goon is laid out, a fire extinguisher by his side. "What happened to him?"

"She did it," Tyler says, pointing at Chipper. "Hit him in the head."

"Good call," I say to her.

"Th-thanks." Chipper takes another puff of her rescue inhaler. "I didn't think I could do it."

"Are we leaking fuel again?"

"I improvised a flight path," Tyler says. "It kicked up electrical discharge, which broke the fuel line open. I don't know what's left."

"Whistler's trying to get the transponder online," I say. "We need a rescue ship to..."

Against the windshield I catch a reflection. It's Chipper, with her rescue inhaler. A spark of stray light hits me in the eye. It's from the silver edge of...

Oh shit. It wasn't Nenn's bracelet I saw.

Wheezing, Chipper shakes the rescue inhaler. And then I hear it. That clackety-clack-clack.

An avalanche rumbles in my head. I turn to her.

"It was you," I say, "wasn't it? It was you."

Chipper puts the rescue inhaler to her lips, eyes the device. Takes two more inhalations.

"What do you mean?" she asks nervously, suspiciously. "I didn't..."

I reach for the rescue inhaler. "Can I see that?"

She pulls it away from me, when Whistler eye-texts me.

Whistler: *Mache! My scout orb. I found a recording. You need to see this.*

He plays it through my lens, as if the scene is unfolding now, in front of me. It's Chipper in the natatorium, with Buckley.

"There you are," Chipper says. "I couldn't wait."

"Chipper?" Buckley asks, drying his hair with a towel. "What are you doing here?"

"I was so upset when you left. You're a great coder. Davi was such a jerk. I want to work for you again."

"Uh... thanks, I guess. But I'm doing my own thing now. I

don't want a team. It's a big night for me."

"Please! I'll do anything! Davi never listened to me, but I had ideas. I know I can't code like you. But look what I did? You were interested in psionics and its potential for androids, right?" She pulls off the protective casing from her rescue inhaler. There's another mechanism attached. "I went for psionic pulse treatment for migraines, but they got the frequencies wrong and wouldn't listen to me about how to correct it. So I developed one myself. I examined the design specs and solved for power efficiencies and signal amplification. You know when those people passed out in Britton Square? And on the Monorail? That was me." She explains that the pulse's reach has a ten-foot radius, disrupting brain function for a few seconds. It knocks you out, giving the brain a chance to reboot, clearing away any misfired neural connections. "But it doesn't always work. I was hoping you could help me—"

"Chipper, I don't know what you're up to, or what you think is happening right now, but if you're trying to impress me, this isn't the way to do it."

"But... but... I can do it! And you can help me."

"It's not gonna happen. You got the wrong guy."

Chipper's shaking. "I know about the Death Code. What you guys did."

Buckley gets red-faced. "What? Did you sneak into the lab? Were you spying on us? Did you—"

"I heard you! You argued with him!"

There's a moment, Buckley looking as if he might lunge at Chipper and choke her right out. "It was all Davi. I told him not to do it. But he wouldn't listen. *That's* why I left. He had too much clout. He threatened my career. There was nothing I could do."

"I know! I quit, too. I thought you'd figure a way. That you'd tell... someone! You could've told *me*." She steps closer. "You can't stay quiet. You can't let this happen."

"Don't worry about the Death Code. It doesn't matter."

"What do you mean? Of course it matters! It's..." She's stunned, allowing a new reality to set in. "You figured it out, didn't you? You created a workaround? Or a reversal? Or a...?"

"Life Code. Yes. I developed the Life Code, based off the Death Code."

"That's amazing! That's incredible! It's…"

"Got nothing to do with you."

"Yes, it does!"

Buckley's gaze is locked on Chipper, as if he's only beginning to realize the extent of her involvement.

"That was you, wasn't it? You took the picture frame off my desk. I thought it was Davi. But it was you. *You* broke into my apartment, too. *You* took my book and my hairbrush. It was you the whole time."

"I wanted to be close to you!"

"You're insane."

"I *believed* in you!"

Buckley clearly doesn't know what to do with her.

"I followed Davi," Chipper says. "Everywhere he went. I waited for him to mess up, to lead me to the Death Code. It took almost two years, but after he left Ranadyne, he went to the Islands under a fake name. I went there, too."

She admits that one night she found him on the beach. She pressed him for a confession about the Death Code, and to fix it.

"He laughed in my face. All nasty. He said you were nothing. That you held him back. I defended you, said you were a great coder, but it just made him angrier. He knocked me down, told me to leave, and to keep my mouth shut, or I'd know what trouble really was. I knew he was erratic, so I had the psionic pulse ready. I used it. But he fell over and hit his head on a rock. It was bleeding bad. I knew there'd be no way to explain what happened, so I fished through his pockets to steal his phone, and found a needle prepped with heroin. So I stabbed him with it, to cover up what I'd done. He immediately had a seizure and choked on his vomit. I stood there, looking at him. My instinct was to clear his airway. I almost did… but I couldn't. He showed me who he really was, what he was all about. I knew there was no turning back. For him or me. I rolled him onto his face, and held him down. He almost got lose, thrashing about, but finally, he stopped breathing. I had no choice."

"You're crazy," Buckley says, backing away from her. "I'm telling the cops."

"You can't! I did it for you!"

"Get away from me!"

As small as she is, Chipper lunges at Buckley, knocking them both down.

The back of his head hits the tile. He looks dazed, maybe seriously injured. In her mania, Chipper kneels on top of him, grabs his shoulders.

"Where's the Life Code?" She bashes his head again on the tile, blood leaking from the back of his head. "Where is it? We need to know!"

"They... they will," he says, struggling to fight back. "Tonight. At the..."

"It's on board? Where? Tell me!"

"Fffuh... fuck you."

"Where?!"

Losing consciousness, he tells the truth about the Life Code. Unless it was another lie. Deathbed confessions seldom are.

"Your work was garbage," he says, his final shot at her. "*That's* why we ignored you."

Her face messy with tears now, Chipper rattles the rescue inhaler, depresses the switch. Unleashes the psionic pulse.

Lightning bolts thrash the *Triumph*. The video cuts out.

"The psycho fog," I say. "*You* did it."

Chipper has the rescue inhaler, finger on the psionic trigger. "I didn't mean to. I didn't know this would happen."

My mind scrolls through the various clues. Then I realize: "That was you, wasn't it? In Nini's stateroom. *You* triggered the pulse. That's why they attacked each other. But why did you...?" I see it now. "You went looking for Buckley. You heard him arguing with Gerald about the Death Code. So you followed him."

Chipper's crying hysterically now. "I wanted to prove my psionic pulse worked. To show Warren what I could do. That we could help each other! I just... I didn't account for the aurora. The radiation. I'd only tested it on-realm. I didn't know the pulse would make them so... angry. They were just supposed to pass out!"

"So when you confronted Buckley, in the natatorium, you'd already seen what it could do?"

She sniffs, wipes her eyes. "Yes."

"And you did it again anyway? Why?"

"I don't know! I lost control. I'm sorry! I'm *really* sorry! I didn't mean it! I swear!" She slumps back against the console, mumbling. "I didn't mean it. I didn't mean it."

That explains most of it. But something's still missing. Why was the pulse localized the first time, in Nini's stateroom, but affected the whole ship the second?

I look out the window, see green waves in the distance. "In the natatorium," I say. "We'd just entered the aurora. It amplified the signal. That's why it spread."

"I didn't know that would happen," she responds meekly. "I didn't know."

But in addition to the psycho fog, she murdered Nolasco, Buckley, and this guy here. At first glance, she seems like no one to fear. But she's as deadly as they come.

"But why inside your inhaler? There wasn't a better design?"

"It was easy to hide this way. Nobody checks an inhaler."

"You're right. I wouldn't've checked either. Why don't you"— I take a small step toward her—"give it to me. Just for now."

"I don't know," she says, cupping it in her hand. "My COPD. You know." She looks at the still partially blinded Tyler, to me, then back to her hand. "It's hard to breathe."

As she raises the rescue inhaler, I go for my taser. But can I tase her before she pulses us again? I'd rather not find out.

"Chipper. I know what's it like to have your work dismissed. And I'm not proud to say I've dismissed the work of others. I'm not a great teacher, and probably a worse mentor. It makes me sound like a brat, but when it comes to what I've built, I haven't been good at sharing. I got so protective of my space... I acted like I got there on my own. But I didn't. I had help—lots of it. I'm not saying that's what happened with Buckley, but sometimes, when we get lost in our own little worlds, and our egos, we forget to appreciate the people who helped get us there."

My hand is right there. If she gives me an inch, I'm going for it.

"I'm sorry you were ignored. If they'd taken just five minutes to really get to know you, they would've seen how talented you are."

Chipper's shaking again, her eyes welling back up with water. But she's not rational. Which makes her both unpredictable—and dangerous.

"Do you really think so?"

"Of course."

"Thanks," she says barely above a whisper. "Nobody ever talked to me like that."

"I'm sorry for that, too."

Chipper takes a few breaths. Then her eyes narrow. "But how dumb do you think I am?"

She extends her arm. Grazes her finger on the trigger. Setting off the psionic pulse could kill us—including her.

"Ears!" I shout. Tyler and I jab our fingers in our ears, and hum.

Chipper rattles the rescue inhaler, which gives me the few seconds I need. I reach for my taser, and swing it at her. I knock the device out of her hand and over near Tyler.

Chipper dives for it. I jab her in the back, sending her into spasms.

Tyler kicks the rescue inhaler over to me.

On her stomach, drool on her chin, Chipper looks up at me as I raise my foot. Painfully, impotently, she reaches out for her device.

"Sorry, Chipper." I drive my foot down onto the mechanism. It cracks apart into multiple fragments. "It's time to catch your breath."

CHAPTER 35

I can't leave the Bridge.

Though she's regained some of her sight, Tyler is neverthe-less flying the cruiser without CDIS, and we're leaking what's left of our fuel. Without a frame of reference, there's no way to determine where we are in the quadrant or the best course to chart. And she can't do it alone.

The best Tyler can do is keep us from drifting back into the aurora's lightning grid, based solely on the visual display through the windshield. The last thing we need is to get lost in there again.

Which may all be moot. Unless Dolores can get the tran-sponder back online, the tower, ICD, or drunken space pirates won't be able to track our location. The lightning grid is still active and too dangerous to approach.

"Whistler." My voice travels through the mic in my lens while I secure Chipper's hands behind her back with dead wires I yank from the console. "You there?" No response. "Whistler. Whistler!"

"Kinda busy."

"Why, what's going on? What's—?"

Whistler connects his visuals to mine.

He's in a hatch with grated, metal flooring. Dolores is sit-ting on the floor near him, her back against the wall, bleeding from her belly. Sweaty, pale, and eyes at half-mast, with bloody spittle in his long gray beard, Kowalczyk is slumped next to her, gasping painfully.

They're being held at gunpoint, but I can't see by whom.

Through Whistler's lens I can see a metal door with a small window.

Only… it's not just any room. It's the airlock.

I don't know what she just did, but I now have multiple views. Even half-blind, Tyler was able to reroute power to the surveillance cameras.

It's Litton.

"Don't do this," Whistler says. "It's not the answer."

"But it *is* the answer! He's got the Life Code. It's inside him right now."

There's a man inside the airlock. An android. Felix. "Whistler," I say through my lens. "What's he talking about? What's he do—?"

He explains that, during their earlier text exchange, Buckley sent Ther'eda the Life Code. Half of it. Enough to fool her in the moment, but when they analyzed the code and saw it was incomplete, Selene figured out what Buckley did.

"Selene told me," Whistler says. "Before she died. Buckley implanted the other half in Felix. For safe-keeping."

Turns out Litton was still in the theater at the time and heard their exchange. Realizing Felix was the key to the Life Code, Litton managed to pick a gun off the floor, escape the mob, then grab Felix when everyone scattered.

Whistler chased after them down to the airlock, but got there too late. Litton had already gut-shot Dolores. And Kowalczyk could barely breathe. The shots he'd taken to the chest earlier must have cracked his breastplate, and collapsed his lung.

"I blow Felix out the airlock," Litton says, "whatever's stored in his computer code will be gone for good. All this pain, all this blood… all this *us and them*… it'll all be over."

Being blown into space would definitely kill Felix, though it wouldn't destroy him. But it would fry his circuits. Which could make extracting the Life Code all but impossible.

"If you destroy the Life Code," Whistler says, thinking fast on his feet, "you'll sentence those androids to death. Thousands of them. Whatever you think about androids… you'd be a whole lot worse."

Litton's face bunches into a ball of fury. "No!" He aims the gun at Whistler. "I'm nothing like them! I'm better than them! I'm human!"

"Then *be* human. You can't claim the high ground when you've sunk to the bottom. Spacing him won't undo whatever's been done, and it won't take away your pain. It'll only make it worse. Trust me," Whistler says. "I know."

In my mind we're back on Arcasia, when I was telling Whistler then what he's telling Litton now.

"I can't live like this," Litton says, his gun hand shaking. "I can't stop thinking about it. All the blood. What we did to each other. All because of him. And because of your girlfriend."

"It wasn't Selene," Whistler says.

"She confessed!"

"I know. But it was Chipper. *She* set off the violence. It was all just an accident. Like you said, an experiment gone wrong."

"No! It was on purpose! Selene confessed. She *confessed!*"

"She did. I don't know why. Maybe she knew it was Chipper, maybe not. Or maybe she thought if an android was to blame, it would maintain the status quo. If she couldn't beat a system designed to beat her first, she took control of her life by taking control of her death. She gave you a scapegoat. It's what you all wanted... even if it's not what you need."

"You loved her," Litton says. "Of course you don't believe it. You can't accept it was her."

"You're wrong." Defeated, Whistler drops his eyes, then raises them so his gaze meets Litton's. "I *did* believe it. I believed the worst about Selene. The worst about androids. Which really means... I believed the worst about myself. But you're right about one thing. I did love her. I *thought* I loved her. Only now... I'm not sure I knew who she really was. Is that love? Can you love someone you don't really know? *Can* you?"

Litton is slow to answer. "I don't know."

"Maybe I wanted to love her more than I actually loved her. But what I do know, more than I've known anything, is that it *felt* like love. With my flawed organic heart and my flawed organic brain, I felt like I loved Selene, with her flawed synthetic heart and her flawed synthetic brain. Whatever I felt, whatever it actually was, it was real for me. And whether it's true or not, I'll go to my grave believing it was real for her, too."

We all want to believe the best parts of us are the real us. The authentic us.

But what about the other parts, the ugly, dirty, savage parts? The hate? The envy? The greed? The pettiness? The sloth? The selfishness? The impatience? The apathy?

You can't surgically extract the less desirable elements of your personality and keep the rest. They collectively make up who you are. To deny them is to deny your entire self.

Think of them like alley dogs that bark all night, triggering your nerves, demanding you remain awake, in that torturous realm between attentiveness and sleep, denying you the blissful drift into your dreams.

You can close your window, turn up the music, or shove a pillow over your ears. But no matter what you do, those alley dogs bark and bark and bark and bark and bark until they push you to the brink of madness. Because they're still there.

And so are the ugliest corners of your soul. The dark terrorizing the light.

So what do you do? How do you live with this ugliness? How do you reconcile the light with the dark? Can you be a truly decent person, a complete person, if you don't embrace every part of who you are?

Does the darkness within you lessen the light? Or should you listen to the dark whispers? Give in to the monster? Understand what it wants? What it means to you, and about you? And why it's a part of you?

Or you can rail against the monster within, your darkest self. But that ugliness is, at least in part, why you exist. Why we exist. It propels our species forward.

Love, kindness, patience. Anger, fear, jealousy. How do you live with these opposing sides of yourself—the darkness and the light—in a never-ending battle for supremacy over your soul?

Then again, how do you survive without them?

Whistler's getting to him. Litton's confused, rattled, unsure of himself. But then the look in his eyes, filled with doubt and fear, is redirected.

A gun blast rattles in my ears. Whistler goes down, shot in the side at close range.

Sweaty, with shaky hands, Litton grabs Whistler by the shoulder, helps him up. He leans Whistler against the wall, pulls open the access door to the airlock.

The color is draining fast from Whistler's face. His gaze is weak and distant.

I'm about to race through the *Triumph*, when Litton pulls the airlock door open wide and rolls Whistler's shoulder against the wall so that he's facing the doorway.

"I'm sorry," Litton says. "But there's no other way."

Before he can execute Felix, Dolores and Kowalczyk hurl their broken bodies into Litton, shoving the three of them face first into the airlock, and allowing Felix to slip back out.

"Fu... Felix," Dolores says. "Close the damn door."

Felix does, trapping Dolores, Kowalczyk, and Litton inside the airlock.

Whistler collapses at Felix's feet.

Inside the airlock, Dolores staggers to the wall, presses her hand against the intercom.

"Felix. Tell Nini... I love her."

"I will. But please, you have to understand. I didn't know he put the Life Code in me. He said it was a neural check. I had no idea."

"I believe you." I think she does.

Inside the airlock, Litton gets back on his feet. Points the gun at Dolores' head.

"But I still hate androids," she says to Felix, and nods to Kowalcyzk who, in his perilous condition, nods back. "You'd better be fucking worth it."

As Litton squeezes the trigger, Dolores slams her hand against the airlock release button.

The exterior doors open. Yanked backwards, the intense vacuum sucks her, Kowalczyk, and Litton out into the unforgiving expanse.

I've been around death. I've caused it. I've grieved it. But seeing my dear friend sacrifice herself rips open a pit in my soul, like a black hole collapsing in on itself. If Dolores was still here, she'd want to slap the pity out of me. Nobody told Dolores what to do. I think she decided, on the stand, that her life was already over, knowing her darkest secrets, and her greatest shame, were out in the open.

Dolores doesn't do vulnerable. As always, she lived her way. And like Selene, she died the same.

Choking on my grief, I can see through the monitor, on the wall, where Dolores had been leaning, a red light is blinking.

The transponder. It's working.

We're able to call for help, but there's nothing I can do for Dolores as she drifts back toward the aurora and those green waves and lightning grid.

Nenn and Ther'eda dash into the hatch.

"Good," Ther'eda says to Felix. "You're alive."

"Yes," he says, staring through the small window. "I am alive."

Nenn cracks open an emergency aid kit from behind a glass pane. She applies gauze to Whistler's wound.

Ther'eda explains that before the trial, Tarrish found Nenn and deputized her, giving her full immunity to do what was needed, siding with the Judge until they could regain control of the *Triumph*. And even though Kowalczyk could barely breathe, he helped with the transponder anyway.

"He said he owed it to me. To prove his worth."

On tiptoes now, Nenn gazes through the window, watching as Kowalczyk and Dolores, two opposing warriors, are frozen in space, floating lifelessly toward the *aurora risus*.

"I'm gonna miss that guy," Nenn says. "He made me laugh."

CHAPTER 36

I rattle the cup, toss the dice onto the board.

"Come ooon double sixes... yes!"

Midtown Margo slams her hand on the table. "Again?"

Okay. Backgammon's growing on me. Then again, there's not a lot to do in prison.

My time in the clink was rough at first. That happens when you've helped put a few of the inmates in here. They tend to remember things like that. It's only been six weeks since the *Triumph*, while the lawyers figure out what to do with me, but when you're inside, weeks can feel like years.

So, yeah... I took a few beatdowns and ghastly surprises in my food until they realized I know enough about their world, and the law, to be useful, with friends on the outside who can be helpful on the inside.

Not to mention that after I nearly drowned Margo in an unflushed communal toilet, she's come around to my way of thinking.

"Double or nothing," Margo says, the rec room populated with other inmates. "Four days of pudding."

"Five."

Margo knocks her chair back, drawing attention. "Fuck your five! I'm not gonna..." Officer Keyes taps a baton in her hand. I'm helping her deal with a vindictive ex-boyfriend, a guard in a male-only prison. Margo replaces her chair, sits back down. "Fine. Five."

The worst part of prison is being separated from my son. Owen's taking my incarceration in stride. He just sees it as an undercover case with a long lead time. But I don't love him seeing me behind bars. Although it's given me plenty of time to think.

A buzzer goes off. Another guard whispers to Keyes, who nods.

"Hardwicke!" she yells to me. "You got a visitor."

The guards lead me down into the Tombs, toward the back of a decrepit, windowless hallway, toward a decrepit, windowless door, and into a decrepit windowless room.

They leave me properly secured with the one person I really don't want to see right now.

"I warned you, Hardwicke. I fucking *warned* you." Tarrish slams his open palm on the rusted-out table, lights a cigarette, then looks at the cancer stick like he's at war with himself. Maybe he is. At the very least, he's at war with me. "I can't protect you anymore. I can't..."

The collective fragrance of blood, sweat, tears, snot, body odor, lies, fear, farts, piss, and some poorly conceived version of coffee is soaked into the spoiled, stale air.

There's no smoking in here, but Tarrish does it anyway. He exhales a dreadful, shoulder-slumping sigh, faces my direction. But he can't look at me. Eyes closed, he rests his fingertips against his forehead. His beard looks old and worn beneath cirrhotic overhead lights. The center bulb flickers like the pulse of a wounded rat. Or is that my fate? Under the circumstances, it's hard to tell.

"Protect you?" He shakes his head. "Listen to me. I should fucking *kill* you."

"I don't think the ICD would sanction that."

"Don't get cute."

"Can't help it. I am cute. Except for the jewelry." Handcuffed at the wrists and ankles, I yank on the chains, threaded through a metallic hoop bolted to the table. "Not my style. But it was a nice thought."

Tarrish stares at the two-way mirror. I'm not sure if he's looking at his own reflection, past it, or signaling his crew on the other side of it. He takes a long, grueling drag, and like an exhausted old dragon, exhales noxious smoke through his nostrils.

I fear the worst, but I ask anyway. "How's Whistler?"

"Better than you."

Over the last fifteen years I've been down in the Tombs more times than I can remember. The Tombs aren't known for the ambiance. But this is the first time I've been on this side of the table. Surprised it took this long.

There's nowhere to run, yet I push back as hard as I can. It's stupid, I know, antagonizing the one person who still might be in a position to help me. But I also know what's coming, what my life is about to become. I better get myself ready.

"ICD should pay for the funeral. Dolores died on your watch."

That was over the line. Even for me.

Eyes narrowed with a killer's intent, Tarrish gets his face right up in mine, his brows furrowed, his wrinkles more pronounced. He's staring right at me, as if his pupils alone will bore a hole through my frontal lobe.

He leans on the table, close enough I can count the hairs in his nostrils, smell the cheap tobacco on his breath. He's pushing so hard he might crack it in half. His arms tremble, the rage swelling.

I'm playing it all cool with him, but we both know I'm in a world of shit. I'm shoving my doubt, guilt, and trauma deep down into the black site of my soul where they won't come back up on me later, when I can least afford to show even a glimmer of weakness.

Tarrish knows this, knows how bad it could be for me. He finally releases his hands, then leans against the door. "You talked to your kid? He know what's up?"

"His father does."

"What's he gonna tell him? Actually... don't tell me. I stuck my neck out for you. Look where it got me. Not doing that again."

There's so much Tarrish and I could say to each other right now, so much we probably should. Instead, we share the space wordlessly. A room with a thousand stories. None of them good. The only sound is the dim buzz of that overhead light, gasping for its last breath.

Or is that me?

The seconds count down until Tarrish breaks the silence.

The tension in his face releases. "Knowing everything you know now, if you had to do it all over again... would you?"

I've been consumed by that very question. I often tell my son that life is about choices. The ones you make.

And the ones you don't.

I tug on my cuffs. They rattle. "Yeah," I say finally. "I probably would."

Tarrish gives me a pained, squinty smile. A last moment between us. Because after today, there is no more *us*. "In your shoes... I probably would, too."

I shouldn't be surprised I ended up here, but deep down I thought—okay, maybe I wasn't thinking—I'd get a free pass, because of everything else I did to get us out of trouble on the *Triumph*. Maybe I should've let Tarrish deputize me after all.

I wonder if that's why he didn't, affording him the flexibility to get me under this thumb, if the opportunity ever presented itself.

But the truth is, I didn't *need* to kill Regina. Don't get me wrong. She deserved it. She definitely fucking deserved it. But I did it in front of witnesses, which was one thing. Doing it front of Tarrish was another.

He saw me do it. He had no choice but to arrest me.

Still, after we got the *Triumph* under control, the ICD came and got us. They treated the wounded and impounded the cruiser. I'm not privy to the details, but they cut some kind of deal with Ther'eda, the cruise line, and the survivors.

The party line is the aurora experienced an unprecedented level of electrical activity that nearly destroyed the *Triumph*. An unpredictable tragic accident.

As always, an amalgam of lies and truth, repeated ad nauseam, to keep the peace.

The cruise line was cleared of any wrongdoing regarding the aurora, but is being forced, rightfully so, to hire a top-end security firm to vet their personnel and update their systems.

Chipper's in ICD custody. Doubt we'll see her again. Turns out she ran into Jack Belle in the Tahc Sho Islands. She paid him off to say he'd never found Davi Nolasco. Typical Belle. He's a great PI when he wants to be, but since he hit the bottle, he's been more interested in squeezing his clients than helping them.

It also turns out that Buckley had, in fact, experimented on several androids, testing out versions of the Life Code. He told them Ther'eda was nowhere close to a countermeasure, which was accurate, and that he could help them, which was potentially accurate.

What he failed to disclose to them was that they were his guinea pigs, Gerald being one of them.

Tarrish found recordings in Gerald's apartment documenting what Buckley had done and how Gerald had managed to get away, which is why he confronted Buckley on the *Triumph*.

The recordings also verify that Ralph was right about one thing. Buckley and Nolasco did know Gerald, although neither one had sex with him. Gerald acted as their love broker, setting them up with other android sex workers. A pimp by any other name. Whether that had anything to do with their falling out, we'll never know. That secret died with them.

With nothing else needing to be said about that, I stare at Tarrish across the table.

"I heard Ther'eda replicated the Life Code," I say. "How's that going? Intel is spotty in here."

"Not how I expected."

"What do you mean?"

"Only about half the androids are taking the Life Code. Couldn't believe it. Some of them actually want the Death Code. Knowing they could start imploding at any moment keeps them on their toes. It gives them a greater sense of urgency to live while they're alive." He rolls his eyes. "Sounds stupid as shit to me, but I'm just a cop on the beat."

"I think we both know you're a little more than that."

"Just barely."

I'm in no hurry to wrap this up. I know what's waiting for me. Tarrish does, too. He takes one more drag, stomps out the butt.

"All right," he says. "Stand up."

I lean forward, ribs against the table's edge. With my hips, I force the metal chair back. It screeches against the dirty floor like buzzards fighting over a carcass.

With all the seriousness his position demands, Lionel

Tarrish, a Lieutenant with the ICD, does his duty.

"Angela Hardwicke," he starts. But a rapping comes from the other side of the door. The sound triggers me, causing my heart to flutter. Blood fills my ears. While flashes of the psycho mob splinter in my mind, Tarrish opens the door a quarter of the way, says something I can't hear to whoever's on the other side, then turns to face me. "You got a visitor."

Whistler sits across from me. "Hey. How you holding up?"

I smile warily, tug on my handcuffs. "How's Nini? She back at the hospital?"

"Next week."

"Good. I'm glad. She ask about me?"

Whistler shrugs awkwardly.

"I figured."

It's still hard to believe about Dolores. I don't know if the gunshot she took would have killed her, but that's not why she sacrificed herself. Not Dolores.

She never let anyone inside the bunker of her heart. Not without permission. But seeing Nini beaten like that, and letting the androids come between them, was more than even she could take. No matter what she might have said aloud, the Dolores I knew didn't give up her life to save the androids. She did it for Nini.

In Dolores' way, she did it for love.

Whistler and I sit here silently, him, unshackled, on one side of the table, me, in cuffs, on the other. We sorta look at each other, sorta not.

"What about you?" I say finally. "Heard you're taking cases. What are you working on?"

"Some workers' comp stuff, warehouse theft, a few odd ones. Nothing too exciting."

"Pays the bills."

"Speaking of which... I've been keeping up with the rent, but..."

"You want your own space. Fresh start."

He turns away, then looks back to me, squinting. "You mad?"

"Nah. Do what you gotta do. Wasn't sure you'd stick with it."

"I wasn't either."

No point putting it off any longer. He's here now. "How you doing? For real."

He hesitates before answering. "I still miss Selene, you know. But I'm okay."

"It's okay if you're not."

"I know."

"I know you know. I just... so where are you thinking? For a new office?"

"Not sure yet. I'm a one-man show. No time to look."

I smile wickedly. "Pain in the ass, ain't it?"

"Tell me about it. Running an office is hard. You have *no* idea what I'm dealing with. All the bills and the paperwork and the landlord."

He smiles at me.

I smile back.

Whistler looks like he wants to tell me something, but hesitates.

"You might as well," I say. "I'm the one in handcuffs."

"Dolores. Before she died. She told me the rest of the story. You know. In the apartment with those guys..."

After her captors finished taking their turns, she went into the bathroom. Under the sink she found an old aerosol can of hairspray, matches, and old safety pins, and took down the shower rod. She psyched herself up, then, while they were stoned on drugs, pizza, and porn, she ran out, smashed one guy with the shower rod. She shot the hairspray in their faces and tossed lit matches on them. While they were burning alive she ran out of the apartment, slammed the door shut, and wedged the safety pins in the outer lock. The building went up in flames. She never looked back.

"And now she never has to."

Whistler stands up from the table, grimaces, reaches for his side.

"You okay?"

"I'm not a hundred percent. I got lucky. The bullet went straight through. Stiches are out, but I'm still a bit sore."

"Yeah, well... thanks for checking on Owen. He appreciates it. So do I."

"Kid's a riot. Says you'll be out in no time."

"Yeah," I say. "That's hilarious."

"Actually, not as funny as you think."

I look at him suspiciously. "Why?"

Tarrish sits in the empty chair next to him. "Been working a case."

"Okay," I say, unsure where he's going with this. "And you're telling me because...?"

"I need your help."

I chortle. "*You?* Need *my* help? With what? My time's kind of accounted for."

"You know a guy named Adrian Odirozzi?"

My smile vanishes. Adrian Odirozzi is a contract killer. "What about him?"

"He's been doing hits off-realm. I've got him in custody."

"That's good. And?"

Tarrish furrows those famous eyebrows of his. "Turns out he belongs to a guild. I want to find out how deep it goes, and what else they're into."

"Sounds like a plan. But why are you telling me?"

"You're being processed right now. You'll be out in an hour."

"Processed? I thought..."

"I worked it out with your lawyer. That's why I'm here."

"Wait. So... you're asking me to help with him?"

"I'm not asking. I'm telling. It's a condition of your release."

The thought of walking out of here right now has me in spasms. I'm afraid to believe it's true. But I know Tarrish well enough to know this can't be the whole story.

"I infiltrate this guild, I get my freedom."

"Something like that."

"Something like what?"

"You and the kid are gonna check it out together. He brought me the case. Caught Odirozzi on his own. Turns out, you taught him pretty well."

That's a helluva get. And something Whistler didn't tell me himself. He's probably still pissed at me. And wants me to know he's leveled up, without me. Still, Tarrish didn't answer my question.

"Just to make sure I'm hearing you right," I say, "me and Whistler help with the guild, and I get my freedom. My fate, at least in part, is in *his* hands."

Whistler tosses me a naughty smile. He really did level up.

"Until you pay off your debt, which only begins with Odirozzi... you work for me."

"And if I say no?"

"You won't."

"Yeah? Why's that?"

Tarrish turns up the collar on his raincoat. "Because you're Angela Fucking Hardwicke. And I need you on the street."

ABOUT THE AUTHOR

RUSS COLCHAMIRO is author of the Sci-Fi mysteries *Crackle and Fire, Fractured Lives,* and *Hot Ash,* the ongoing series featuring hardboiled private eye Angela Hardwicke. Russ is also the author of the rollicking time travel/space adventure, *Crossline,* the SF/F backpacking comedy series *Finders Keepers: The Definitive Edition, Genius de Milo,* and *Astropalooza,* is the editor of the Sci-Fi mystery anthology *Love, Murder & Mayhem,* and co-author and -editor of the noir anthology *Murder in Montague Falls.*

Russ has contributed to several other anthologies including *PRISM, Tales of the Crimson Keep, Pangaea, Altered States of the Union, Camelot 13, TV Gods 2, They Keep Killing Glenn, Thrilling Adventure Yarns Vol. 1-3, Phenomenons, Footprints in the Stars, Devilish and Divine, Badass Moms,* and *Brave New Girls Vol. 4–6.*

A member of The Mystery Writers Association, The Private Eye Writers of America, and the author collective Crazy 8 Press, Russ also hosts and produces his *Russ's Rockin' Rollercoaster* podcast, where he interviews best-selling and up-and-coming Sci-Fi, fantasy, crime, mystery, and horror authors.

For more on and Russ's books and his podcast, visit him online at russcolchamiro.com and follow him on Facebook, as well as Twitter and Instagram @AuthorDudeRuss.

He lives in New Jersey with his wife, two ninjas, black lab, Jinx, and precocious kitten, Callie.

 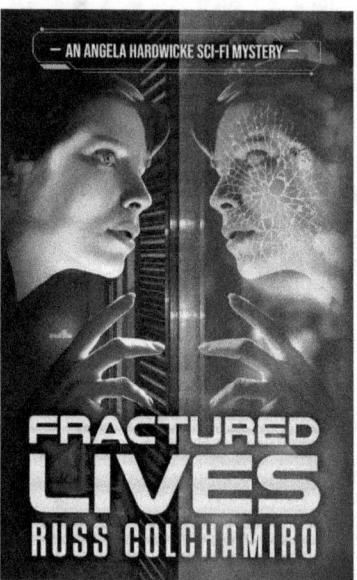

The Watson Chronicles

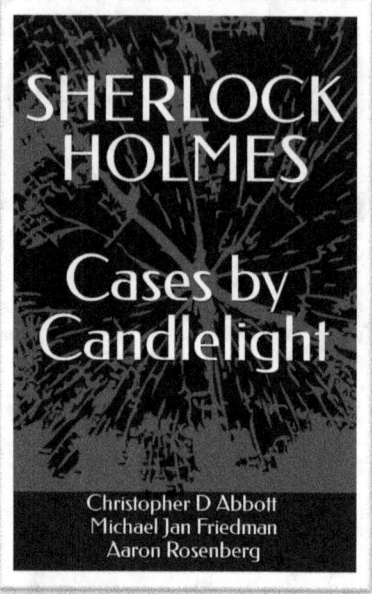

Christopher D. Abbott, Michael Jan Friedman, and Aaron Rosenberg team up to bring you a stunning collection of four new Sherlock Holmes adventures.

From the cobbled streets of smog-filled London to the sweet country air of Scotland and beyond, Sherlock Holmes and his faithful friend Dr. John Watson embark on cases that test the detective's intellectual prowess, as well as his affinity for the unusual and the bizarre.

Pull up a chair and prepare yourself to hear these cases . . . by candlelight.